'No more thank yous.
go,' she whispered, as
disappeared, presumably to answer it.

'And I have to learn to jump to it,' Emily gave Judy a sad little smile. 'Have a good journey back.'

Judy stayed long enough to watch her friend walk up the stairs. Emily looked so small, lost and alone, she couldn't help feeling that she was abandoning her. She recalled Robin Watkin Morgan's good looks, swaggering self-assurance and flirtatious manner. No doubt he had already moved on to the next girl. It was so unfair. If her own experience was anything to go by, all the 'fun' involved in conceiving a child was purely on the men's side and they could walk away any time they chose to, leaving the woman quite literally holding the baby.

Catrin Collier was born and brought up in Pontypridd. She lives in Swansea with her husband, three cats and whichever of her children choose to visit. Her latest novel in Orion paperback is *Sinners & Shadows*, and her latest novel in hardback, *Finders & Keepers*, is also available from Orion.

By Catrin Collier

HISTORICAL

Hearts of Gold
One Blue Moon
A Silver Lining
All That Glitters
Such Sweet Sorrow
Past Remembering
Broken Rainbows
Spoils of War
Swansea Girls
Swansea Summer
Homecoming
Beggars & Choosers
Winners & Losers
Sinners & Shadows
Finders & Keepers

CRIME
(*as Katherine John*)

Without Trace
Six Foot Under
Murder of a Dead Man
By Any Other Name

MODERN FICTION
(*as Caro French*)

The Farcreek Trilogy

Homecoming

Catrin Collier

ORION

An Orion paperback

First published in Great Britain in 2003
by Orion
This paperback edition published in 2003
by Orion Books Ltd,
Orion House, 5 Upper St Martin's Lane,
London WC2H 9EA

Reissued 2005

A CIP catalogue record for this book is
available from the British Library.

Typeset by Deltatype Ltd, Birkenhead, Merseyside
Printed in Great Britain by
Clays Ltd, St Ives plc

www.orionbooks.co.uk

Dedication

To Kathleen Ann Garland Churchill, née Richards, for her loyal and unselfish friendship over so many years, especially during my unhappiest time, my secondary schooldays. (Although in all fairness it was probably even unhappier for my teachers.)

And to Fiona Tromans 1948–1969, who was a friend to us both.

ACKNOWLEDGEMENTS

I would like to express my gratitude to everyone who helped with the research for this book and so generously gave of their time and expertise:

Dr Marguerite Aitcheson for her friendship and sharing with me her experiences of both private and public adoption procedures of forty and fifty years ago; also for giving me an insight into the way unmarried mothers' homes and hostels were organised and run well into the nineteen-sixties where the primary object appeared to have been to humiliate the girls and punish them for their 'sins'.

Jill Forwood for her friendship, inexhaustible knowledge of Swansea, impeccably researched factual articles in her much loved and read 'The Way We Were' features in Swansea's *Evening Post* and her kindness in answering my endless list of queries.

My 'almost' brother-in-law, Edgar Goodwin, and Austin Leend, two of the last batch of conscripts into National Service, for sharing their memories with me.

My husband John and our children Ralph, Ross, Sophie and Nick and my parents Glyn and Gerda for their love, support and the time they gave me to write this book.

Margaret Bloomfield for her unstinting friendship and help in so many ways.

My agent, Ken Griffiths, for his professionalism, friendship and making my life so much more interesting than I ever thought it could be.

Absolutely everyone at Orion, especially my wonderful

editor Yvette Goulden for her encouragement and constructive criticism, Emma Noble, my publicist, for the miracles she performs, Juliet Ewers, Rachel Leyshon, Sophie Wills, Jenny Page, Dean Mitchell and all the editorial, sales and marketing teams.

And all the booksellers and readers who make writing such a privileged occupation.

Thank you.

Catrin Collier, July 2002

Note

Today's world is very different from that of forty to fifty years ago. Growing up in the fifties and the sixties I became gradually aware that some girls suddenly disappeared from everyday life – school and college friends, neighbours and relatives of friends. Sometimes they reappeared after a stay in the country with an aunt, but no matter how hard they tried to conceal what had happened, the gossips inevitably discovered the truth, and not only the girl but her entire family would be shamed because she had given birth to an illegitimate child.

It is difficult for some people to imagine now, but the disgrace tore families apart, and practically everyone of my generation knows of a father – or mother – who threw their daughter out of the house as soon as her pregnancy was discovered. Young girls without money or the support of their families had no option but to enter a 'charitably run' home or hostel, where they were forced to give up their child for adoption after the mandatory six-week nursing and breast-feeding period, a separation that must have been every bit as traumatic for the baby as it was for the mother.

I have talked to many women permanently scarred by the experience and adults who have spent years trying to trace their birth parents without success. While respecting their request for anonymity, I admire their courage and would like to thank them for sharing their heartbreaking stories with me.

Catrin Collier

Chapter One

Helen walked into her bedroom, set a couple of dry-cleaning bags on to the double bed and turned to the bank of pale oak wardrobes. As she opened the doors, she wondered why a gentleman's wardrobe had so many more fitments than a lady's. Deep drawers for socks, glass doors to keep the side shelves dust free, a pull out rack for ties, cravats and belts, a shallow, sliding tray for cuff links and tiepins. Did the manufacturers think a woman wouldn't appreciate the same care and attention, or did they provide a single rail in the expectation that everything other than a woman's costumes and dresses could be stored in a dressing table?

She opened the glass door and smoothed a crease from a vest; closing it she pulled out the sock drawer and looked down on a dozen pairs, all neatly folded and not a darn to be seen because they were new. Would Jack notice that she'd replaced practically all the clothes he'd left behind and would he be annoyed with her for throwing out everything she considered shabby? The only major items she'd kept were two suits he'd bought, one before and one just after they'd married; a grey mohair for their wedding and a black wool for her grandmother's funeral.

She opened one of the dry-cleaner's bags and unbuttoned the jacket and waistcoat of the grey mohair. Lifting them and the trousers from the wire frame, she transferred the suit to a wooden hanger before covering it with a cotton slip. She hooked it on the rail next to two white cotton shirts Jack had bought along with the suits. They were the only ones she'd hung up; half a dozen new ones, fifteen and half – his collar size – lay stacked in boxes on the top shelf. Opening the second bag, she drew out the black suit and tried to imagine Jack in it.

The only photographs he'd sent her during the last two and half years had been snapshots with his fellow National Servicemen. Inexpertly taken groups, often too dark or blurred to decipher individual features and, with every man dressed in khaki shorts and shirts, it had sometimes been difficult to work out which one was him.

She glanced at the silver frame on her bedside table and studied the photograph her father had taken outside Swansea Register Office on their wedding day. Slim, dark, handsome, his hair brushed into a quiff, Jack smiled down at her. Would he have changed? Had she changed?

She rushed to the mirror to compare herself to the girl in the photograph. Was it her imagination or were there wrinkles around her eyes? Had she put on weight? If anything she had lost it – would Jack think her too thin? Twenty-one was so much older than eighteen . . .

'Helen!'

'Coming.' She lifted another hanger from the wardrobe.

'Helen! How long does it take to hang up two suits?'

'Two seconds, Judy, I'm coming.' Folding a cover over the black suit, she hung it next to the mohair and closed the wardrobe door. She checked the room. The bedroom suite gleamed from the polishing she had given it. There was a light, pleasant scent in the air from the lavender bags she had placed in the wardrobe and chest of drawers, and the lavender water she had sprinkled over the sheets when she had ironed them. A bowl of crocuses chosen to match the floral bedspread and curtains was just coming into blue and yellow bloom on the dressing table.

She straightened the curtains that brushed the top of the window seat. Familiarity hadn't lessened the pleasure she took in the view. Darkness had fallen black and gleaming over the sea and in the distance a fairytale sprinkling of red lights outlined a ship's mast. But breathtaking view or not, the bedroom also faced the road and it was time to close the shutters. She folded them over the windows, switched on the electric fire and lamps either side of the bed and turned off the main light.

'Helen!'

'I'm there.'

'You're not.' Judy stood in the doorway, her green eyes shining with amusement.

'Just making sure everything's ready.'

'Aren't you being a bit premature with the electric fire? Jack won't be home for another three hours and presumably he'll want to eat before you go to bed.'

'It's hot in Cyprus,' Helen retorted defensively. 'I don't want him to catch cold.'

'He's been in Germany for the last two weeks and it's supposed to be colder than here.'

'You and Lily ready to leave?' Helen picked up the wire hangers and the bags, and smoothed the bedspread.

'We have been for the last ten minutes but, before we go, I'd like you to check that I'm only taking what you want me to.'

Helen went to the door but she couldn't resist one last look as Judy ran down the stairs. The bedroom looked pretty and inviting; she only hoped Jack would think so.

'I caught Helen switching on the electric fire in the bedroom,' Judy announced to their friends, Katie and Lily, when Helen finally joined them.

'There's nothing wrong with wanting to make everything comfortable for your husband.' Katie gave Helen a conspiratorial smile.

'Thank you, Katie. Someone has to stick up for us married women.' Helen eyed the suitcase, vanity case and pile of boxes stacked by the front door.

'That's right, pick on the outnumbered.' Judy emerged from the kitchen with another box.

'Not for long with an engagement ring that size on your finger,' Helen observed archly.

'We're in no hurry.'

'That's not what Sam said the last time I spoke to him.'

'Sam can wait until I'm good and ready.' Judy slipped on her coat.

'You sure you have everything?' Helen asked.

'My clothes, my books, the coffee set I bought and all my engagement presents. You're welcome to keep the coffee set . . .'

'No, really, you take it,' Helen broke in.

'I'll grant you, your house looks better without my clutter and with all your wedding presents unpacked and on show around the place.'

'I just hope they're all right.' Helen frowned. 'Perhaps I shouldn't have kept everything for two and half years. The guarantee has run out on the toaster and the radio.'

'Once Jack gets here you won't have time to think about guarantees.' Lily helped Katie up from the sofa.

'It only seems like yesterday the four of us were moving in here,' Judy murmured wistfully.

'Some yesterday.' Heavily pregnant, Katie moved awkwardly around the furniture into the hall. 'I've been married nearly two and half years and Lily two.'

Time's flown.' Judy felt in her pocket for her keys.

'I can't understand why you keep putting Sam off, Judy.' Helen picked up a box. 'You two have been going out forever.'

'I like courting and I like my independence, which is why I'm moving into the flat above the salon, but living with Emily Murton Davies won't be like living with you.'

'You'll miss me?' Helen asked, blatantly fishing for a compliment.

'Your mess.' Judy picked up the suitcase, balanced it on her knee and opened the front door. Stepping outside, she set the case down behind the second-hand Morris Minor she had bought so she could drive between the hairdressing salons she and her mother owned.

'You can hardly call the house messy now.' Helen dumped her box beside the suitcase.

'I'll grant you that I've never seen it as tidy as it is at the moment.' Judy opened the car boot. 'But then, you haven't had a husband coming home after two and half years away before.'

'I tidied it because you were leaving, not Jack arriving.'

'And I bet you ten shillings Jack won't even notice the effort you put into getting the place perfect for him.' Judy took a box Lily handed her and stowed it on top of the suitcase. 'I'm going to miss living here. The view . . .'

'You can see the sea from your flat above the salon.' Helen passed her another box.

'Can't swim in Mumbles like you can here.'

'You have a car, it's only five minutes' drive . . . hey, what are you doing?' Helen cried, as Katie came out of the house carrying Judy's vanity case.

'It's light as a feather,' Katie declared.

'Women in your condition shouldn't even lift feathers.' Helen snatched the bag. 'Back in there, sit down and I'll make us a cup of tea.'

'Listen to your stepdaughter.' Judy laughed but none of the others even smiled. It hadn't been easy for Helen to accept their friend Katie's marriage to her father, even after two and half years. Sensitive to the sudden silence, Judy checked both cases and all the boxes were in the car before closing the boot. 'We'll be back in ten minutes.'

Helen shivered in the cold night air. 'You and Lily can unpack if you like. Jack's train won't be in until nine.'

Judy glanced at her watch. 'That only gives you two and three quarter hours of worrying time left.'

'I am not worrying,' Helen countered.

'Pull the other one,' Judy mocked, as she climbed into the driver's seat.

*

'Jack won't have changed,' Katie reassured Helen, after Judy and Lily drove away.

'I wish I could be as sure as you.' Helen wrapped her arm around Katie's shoulders and they walked back up the path to the house.

'He sounded like the same old Jack in all his letters to me.'

'And how many did he send you?'

'Twenty-three besides postcards, Christmas and birthday cards.'

'In two and half years.' Helen closed the front door and led the way into the living room. 'I rest my case.'

'He's only my brother. You're his wife. He wrote to you every week.'

'Sometimes twice and once three times, but writing to someone isn't like seeing them face to face.' Helen unclipped the guard from the grate, set it aside, and heaped half a dozen lumps of coal on to the fire.

'You'll soon get back to where you were before he went away.' Katie sank down clumsily on the sofa.

'You don't look comfortable.' Helen replaced the guard.

'I'm not.'

'I knew I should have bought the three-piece with higher seats.'

'It's not the sofa.' Katie swung her feet on to the pouffe Helen pushed towards her. 'It's me. I feel like the pumpkin after it was transformed into Cinderella's coach.'

'Not long now.'

'No, but the midwife said first babies are often late . . .' Katie faltered, consciously stopping herself from launching into her favourite topic of conversation. Helen had lost a baby the day she and Jack had returned from honeymoon. More sensitive than Judy, Katie knew the pain of that loss had never entirely left her sister-in-law and Jack being called up for National Service practically the day she had been discharged from hospital hadn't helped.

Helen plumped up a cushion and handed it to her. 'I've never asked, do you and Dad want a boy or a girl?'

'We don't care, as long as it's healthy.'

'Everyone says that, you must have a preference.'

'None. I know that when you were pregnant, you and Jack wanted a boy,' she ventured hesitantly.

'Jack wanted a boy.' Helen laughed a little too loudly. She didn't know what was worse, her friends carefully avoiding all mention of the baby she had lost, or times like this when they brought up the subject to show her that they hadn't forgotten any more than she had.

'You'll have children. When Jack's home and you're settled—'

'Want a cup of tea?' Helen interrupted abruptly.

'No, thank you. Judy won't be long and I've prepared a meal for John. I don't want to spoil it. What have you got for Jack?'

'Steak, chips, frozen peas and a chocolate cake.'

'His favourites.'

'They used to be his favourites.'

'If half of what the boys have said about army food is true, Jack will have been dreaming of a meal like that for weeks.'

'I hope you're right.' Helen left her chair and walked restlessly to the window. 'Tell me something, truthfully?' She looked earnestly at Katie.

'If I can.'

'Do you think I've changed much since Jack left?'

'Yes. You've much better dress sense for a start. That black sack dress looks great on you.'

'You don't think it's plain and shapeless?'

'It's certainly not shapeless with you inside it and I'd describe it as elegant and sophisticated, not plain. Jack will love it,' Katie assured her confidently. Helen had gone through seven changes of clothes earlier in search of the ideal welcome home outfit and it had taken the combined efforts of Judy, her and Lily to persuade her to settle on her newest and most fashionable dress.

'I couldn't have had worse dress sense.' Helen smiled ruefully. 'Do you remember that awful frock I stole from Dad's warehouse and wore down the Pier Ballroom the night Jack first asked me to dance?'

'I don't think I'll ever forget it.' Katie looked critically at Helen for a moment. Her friend had changed radically from the wild girl her brother had married. Her long blonde hair was smoothed into a neat French pleat instead of hanging loose to her shoulders. The bright red lipstick, rouge and vivid blue eye shadow she had favoured in her teens had been replaced by softer shades, subtly and discreetly applied, that highlighted her classical features and flawless complexion. But the greatest change of all was in her personality. All trace of the defensive belligerence she had employed to disguise her lack of confidence had long since vanished. 'You've learned how to make the best of yourself and you've a lot to make the best of,' Katie complimented sincerely. 'You are more sure of yourself and your judgement, and it shows. You only have to look at the difference you've made to the fashion department in the warehouse since you took over as buyer. Half the teenage girls in Swansea are wearing clothes you've chosen, the turnover's skyrocketed and it's all down to you.'

'Whatever a wicked stepmother is supposed to be like, you're not it.'

'I wish Judy would stop joking about that. I never think of myself as your and Joe's stepmother. I'm two years younger than him for a start and we've been friends for ever.'

'She is only teasing.' Helen closed the curtains against the night.

'You don't mind?'

'Not any more.' Helen walked back to her chair. 'I've been meaning to say this to you for some time but somehow there's never been the right moment. I've never seen Dad as happy as he's been since he married you.'

'You're not just saying that,' Katie blurted uneasily.

'No.'

'He worries about me and the baby so much and he's not well. You know what he's like. He never complains about the scars he got in that fire, or his damaged leg and arm, but I know he's in pain—'

'Katie, he's had those scars since before I was born. And as for worrying, if he worries, it's good worry about someone he loves very much. And now that Joe and I are off his hands, it's just as well he has someone else to fuss over.'

'Have you heard from your brother lately?'

'Hasn't Dad?'

'He had a letter last month. Joe seems to be doing well at the BBC and we listened to his last radio play.'

'So did I.' Helen glanced sideways at Katie and they both burst out laughing. 'Did you understand it?'

'To be honest, I preferred the ghost story and thriller he wrote.'

'So did I. Perhaps it's just as well he's living with all the other intellectuals in London and not with us.' Helen sat back and stared into the fire. 'I've been wondering if Jack will find Swansea and me boring after all the excitement of Cyprus.'

'I should think after being shot at, blown up and spending two months in hospital he'll welcome a little peace and quiet.' Katie closed her eyes against the memory of the telegram that had caused so much upset and worry.

'I wish I could have visited Jack then. His letters were strange around that time.'

'Is it surprising when three of the men he was with were killed?'

As the coal began to glow, Helen knelt on the hearthrug, removed the guard again and layered small coal over the lumps she'd put on earlier. 'I tried asking

Jack about it but it was as though we were writing in different languages. There was me going into the warehouse six days a week, coming home every evening, hardly ever going out except to visit you and Dad, or Lily and Martin, or going to the pictures with Judy. And there was him, fighting terrorists, having bombs thrown at him . . .' She bit her lip and hooked back the guard. 'He's bound to have changed. We were both so young, so crazy . . .'

'We all were.'

'Not you,' Helen contradicted. 'You were born sensible.'

'That's not what people said when I married your father.'

'But you didn't take any notice of them and you can't get any more sensible than that.' Helen glanced at her hands to check that they were clean, as she rose to her feet. 'I'm sorry, I shouldn't be dumping my worries on you, especially now with the baby due next week. It's just that I can't help thinking that if Jack had come home six months ago when he should have, instead of having his term extended because of a shortage of troops, everything would have been so much better. He was expecting to come home. I had everything ready. It was just so unfair that he had to stay on and get caught up in that attack—'

'He's fine now,' Katie reminded, 'and he'll be home in a couple of hours.'

'Yes, he will.' Helen hesitated. 'I don't suppose you'd like to look over the bedroom and the rest of the house and tell me if I've done anything Jack will hate?'

'Bearing in mind that you know him better than me, I'm flattered you asked.'

'You grew up with him.'

'And you married him.' Katie took the hand Helen offered to help her up.

'Not a word to Judy,' Helen pleaded.

'I promise.'

*

'You sure you don't want to unpack this lot?' Lily carried the last box up the stairs and into the lounge of Judy's flat above her Mumbles salon. 'We've plenty of time before Jack's train gets in.'

'I'm sure.' Judy dropped her suitcase and vanity case on to the floor of her bedroom and closed the door. 'Sam's coming over later, he can help me. Besides don't you and Katie want to get home to your husbands?'

'Katie has a casserole all ready to go in the oven for John and, as Martin won't be home until after he's picked Jack up from the station and dropped him off at Helen's, I've plenty of time to prepare something.'

'I'm surprised Helen didn't want to meet the train.' Judy picked up a box marked 'Kitchen' and carried it through to the narrow galley.

'According to Martin, it was Jack's idea he meet him alone.'

'So Helen isn't the only one who's nervous.'

'Wouldn't you be nervous if you were in Helen's position?' Lily asked, as Judy returned to the living room.

'I can't imagine having a husband, let alone seeing him after a long absence.'

'You haven't given a thought as to what it will be like to have a husband after you and Sam have been engaged for eighteen months?' Lily questioned incredulously.

'I've been too busy opening the new salons and building up trade to think about weddings and marriage. Mam did what she could to help, but frankly it wasn't much. Not that I'm complaining. She didn't expect Billy's arrival, not at forty.' Judy referred to her twenty-month-old half-brother who had been born nine months to the day after her mother's wedding to Lily's Uncle Roy.

'Billy's gorgeous and worth any number of salons, and considering you and your mother now have eleven . . .'

'Ah hah.' Judy gave Lily a knowing look, as she heaved a box of books on to the table.

'Ah hah, what?'

'I detect a hint of broodiness in the bank manager's high-flying secretary.'

'I am not broody.' Lily opened the box and lifted out half a dozen books.

'Then you don't envy your uncle and my mother Billy, or Katie and Mr Griffiths's "forthcoming happy event" as Mrs Lannon and the rest of the Carlton Terrace "gossips" so coyly put it. And you never go all gooey over Billy and buy him toys . . .'

'And you, of course, hate Billy.'

'I adore him.' Judy took the books from Lily and stacked them on to an empty bookshelf. 'But that doesn't mean I want a baby of my own.'

'You and Sam don't want children?'

'I told you I haven't had time to think about anything other than the salons for the last couple of years.'

'There's nothing wrong between you and Sam, is there?' Lily asked perceptively.

Judy couldn't remember a time when she hadn't known Lily, Helen and Katie. Even in the babies' class in primary school, Helen had been the wild one, always up to her neck in trouble, Katie the quiet one and Lily the one who could be trusted never to betray a confidence. 'We're fine,' she answered slowly, 'but . . . well, you know how it is. You almost got engaged to Joe before you married Martin.'

'I almost got engaged to Joe because I didn't know the difference between wanting to be in love and being in love.'

'Wasn't it more exciting with Joe?'

'What?' Lily questioned, genuinely bewildered by Judy's train of thought.

'Joe was your first boyfriend, he took you on your first date, gave you your first real kiss . . .'

'Every minute I spend with Martin is a million times more exciting than the time I spent with Joe and that's without bringing kisses into it.'

'Come on, don't try telling me that your heart still

turns cartwheels every time you see Martin when you've been married to the man for almost two years?'

'Cartwheels and handstands.' Lily had fallen in with Judy's flippant mood but there was an underlying gravity to her voice.

'And you never think about Joe?'

'Only when Helen, Katie or his father mentions him and, when they do, I thank my lucky stars that I married Martin.'

'You're serious, aren't you?'

'Very.' Lily handed Judy another pile of books. 'This conversation wouldn't have anything to do with you and Brian Powell by any chance, would it?'

'I haven't seen Brian in almost three years.'

'The fact that you remember how long it's been says a lot.'

'All it says is that I remember my first boyfriend,' Judy retorted. 'And you know what people say about first love.'

'Tell me.' Lily dropped the empty box to the floor and lifted another on to the table.

'It's like your first party dress, better remembered than kept.'

'And Sam?' Lily queried. 'Do you love him?'

'Of course I do,' Judy asserted, 'in a seeing him every day kind of way.'

'But not in a breathless, heart-pounding, floating on air . . .'

'We just agreed those kind of feelings can't last.'

'You said they can't, not me.' Lily ripped the box open and handed her another half a dozen books.

'Then you don't think I'm in love with Sam.'

'You just said you were.'

'I am.' Judy paused thoughtfully. 'It could be that we're just different people . . .'

'Of course we are, you've auburn hair for a start,' Lily joked.

'You really never wonder what Joe is like now or what you'd do if you bumped into him?'

'Never. Do you wonder about Brian?'

'Sometimes.' Judy gave a wicked smile. 'I picture him fat, bald, toothless . . .'

'Sounds as if the poor man's aged eighty years in three.'

'London's not the healthiest place to live.' Judy pushed the last few books on the shelf. 'That's enough. I'm not sure why we started this when I had no intention of unpacking. Let's go and get Katie.'

'Thanks for coming round and helping.' Helen opened her front door.

'I'm not sure how me sitting on your sofa and chatting helped, but thanks for the invitation.' Katie kissed Helen's cheek.

'It helped by keeping me sane.' Helen squeezed Katie's hand as she climbed into the front seat of Judy's car. 'And thanks for clearing out your things, Judy.'

'There's no way I could have allowed my rubbish to clutter up Jack's homecoming.'

'Is there anything I can do for the party tomorrow?' Lily asked, as Judy slotted the keys into the ignition.

'Just bring yourself and Martin around about seven.'

'And some beer, sherry and food.'

'I won't refuse any contributions.' Helen closed the car door and Judy started the engine. She turned and looked back at the house when Judy drove off. Would it be better to open the shutters and curtains and switch on all the lights so Jack could see the home she had created for both of them the moment Martin drove up to it? Deciding it would, she checked her watch and ran back inside.

'Lily, are you there?' Sam called, as he walked up the internal stairs that led from the basement flat he and his fellow policeman, Mike, rented from Lily and Martin.

'No,' she shouted.

Ignoring her denial, he walked down the passage and into her kitchen. 'We've run out of tea. I don't suppose you've a quarter you can spare?'

She shook her head despairingly but went to the cupboard where she kept her dry goods. 'It's getting to the stage where I buy double rations every week to cater for you and Mike. The only wonder is Swansea's streets are safe, the way you two organise your lives.'

'We make better policemen than housewives.'

'I hope you're right.'

'Thanks, Lily.' He took the packet of Barbers tea she handed him. 'You know we'll give it back.'

'Only until the next time you want to borrow it.'

Sensing exasperation behind her flippant comment, he sniffed the air and looked from the saucepan simmering on the stove to the table where she was rolling pastry. 'If that's one of your meat and potato pies, lucky Martin.'

'Judy told me you're going over to her new flat tonight.'

'So?' He looked quizzically at her.

'I'm sure she'll make something for you.'

'You don't know Judy. I'll get fish and chips, and only if I go to the fish shop to fetch them.' He watched as she opened the oven and took out an apple flan. 'You enjoy torturing me, don't you? You know that's my favourite dessert. If your husband doesn't appreciate you . . .'

'He does.' She set the flan on a rack to cool.

'I'd give a week's wages for a slice of that. And,' he opened the fridge door, 'I just knew it, real clotted cream.'

'Don't you dare touch that bowl. And that flan is staying in one piece until Martin gets home.'

'You hard-hearted woman.'

'That's me.'

'Can I at least smell it?' He stood over the flan and sniffed theatrically.

Relenting, she reached for a cake tin. 'There are some rock buns in there that I made yesterday.'

'With sultanas and currants?'

'And candied peel.'

'If I get Judy to give me back my engagement ring, will you take it?'

'No.'

'That's what I was afraid of.' He opened the tin and took out a bun. 'Any tea going?'

She picked up the rolling pin and dusted it off with flour. 'Only if you make it.'

He lifted the kettle from the stove and carried it to the sink. 'Has Judy taken everything from Helen's to the flat?'

'Yes, but it's not unpacked. She said you were going to help her do that tonight.'

'It's not my idea of a perfect way to spend an evening but,' he paused as he lit the gas hob and put the kettle on to boil, 'what else can a man do when his woman gives him orders but obey?'

'You make it sound as though you're Judy's slave.'

'I am.'

'Poor, hard-done-by Sam.'

'You think I like living with Mike when he can't even remember to buy the essentials?'

'You could try buying them yourself.'

'I do, sometimes,' he qualified. 'But I still have to do every single little thing for myself and it hurts when I come up here and see Martin's whims, never mind needs, lovingly catered for by you. The man lives like a lord, eats like a king . . .'

'And works almost every hour God sends.'

Although Lily had inherited the house from her aunt, Martin worked all the overtime he was offered in the council garage where he was employed as a mechanic. Sam had found that strange, until he realised that Martin felt he had to bring as much money home as he could because the house and furniture had been Lily's, not his.

'We all work hard, even you in the bank.' He lifted the teapot from a shelf, poured a little boiling water in it, and swirled it around to warm it.

'What do you mean, even me?'

'You're a woman.'

'And women are?'

'Chattels and homemakers. Face it, Lily, you're built to be men comforters.'

'If I were you, I wouldn't say that around Judy, not even as a joke.' Lifting the pastry from the table, she folded it over, eased it into the pie dish and patted it down.

'I don't need the warning, I know my woman. Has she said anything to you about opening another salon?'

'Not since she opened the last one.'

'She won't be happy until she has a dozen and maybe not even then.' He poured milk into her cup. 'No sugar, right?'

'Right.' She took the tea he'd made her and put it on the table. 'Help yourself to another bun, if you like.'

'I would like, very much indeed. You know, as landladies go, you're the best I've ever had.'

'I'm the only one you've ever had.'

'I was hoping you wouldn't remember that.' Sinking his teeth into his second bun, he looked around the kitchen. Lily and Martin had made a lot of changes since they had taken over the house after Lily's Uncle Roy had married Judy's mother and moved out, and all of them were for the better. Martin had bought Lily every labour-saving gadget on the market, like the Bendix washing machine, Hoover, gas cooker, electric toaster and brand-new, sixty-six guinea, Everest blue Frigidaire he had presented her with on her last birthday, yet somehow Lily had still managed to make the room look warm, cosy and inviting. 'Good rock buns.' He pushed the last few crumbs into his mouth.

'If you eat any more, you won't have room for those fish and chips.'

'You're right. Goodbye, dear buns, I hope to see you tomorrow.' He pushed the top back on the tin and returned it to the shelf. 'Any messages for Judy?'

'Only that I'll see her at Jack's party tomorrow. Is Mike going?'

'He's on shift.' Sam grinned. 'It was mine but I persuaded him I needed the night off more than him. Do you think Jack will have changed much?'

'Don't you start, that's all Helen can talk about.'

'Poor beggar. Two years National Service was more than I could bear. Those extra six months must have felt like a life sentence. Well, no peace for the wicked – and ever hopeful.' He picked up the packet of tea. 'Thanks for this.'

Martin stood outside the gate at Swansea station and watched passengers stream off the London train. Considering it was a freezing cold evening in March, a surprising number had made the journey. Young men and women who worked in the 'Smoke' returning for the weekend, an elderly couple burdened with so many parcels they were either bringing presents for half the people in Swansea or had been on a mammoth shopping spree, a couple of students wearing college scarves. He stared at a young man who strode confidently down the platform. He was Jack's height, colouring and build, but the army had changed radically since his day if they allowed National Servicemen to wear their hair that long.

'Marty.'

He whirled around as someone tapped his shoulder. 'Jack?' he muttered tentatively, staring at his brother.

'Have I changed that much?'

'Only grown a foot and a half and put on about six stone.'

'Four stone and four inches.'

'And with a suntan a Hollywood star would envy and an almost bald head.'

'By army standards this is long.' Jack ran his hand over

his regulation short back and sides. 'If I buy you a pint in the Grand, do you think you could shut your mouth long enough for it to go down?'

'Try me.' Taking one of the bags Jack was carrying, Martin shook his brother's hand before leading the way across the station yard to the hotel.

Chapter Two

'So.' Jack moved along the bench seat to make room for his brother when Martin returned from the bar with two pints of beer. 'What's been happening in Swansea since I left, apart from you marrying Lily, and Katie, Mr Griffiths?'

Too taken aback to absorb Jack's question, Martin continued to stare at his brother. 'I would have passed you in the street . . .'

'Or at a railway station,' Jack broke in dryly.

'Helen's going to have the shock of her life. She'll never believe it's you.'

'She'd better.' Jack took the pint Martin gave him. 'Cheers. And how is my wife?'

'Fine, or she was last night when I gave Sam a hand to move Judy's dressing table out of your house; that is apart from being in a cleaning frenzy. Everything around her is gleaming. I think Judy only moved out today because she was afraid that if she stayed, Helen would polish her along with everything else.'

'My house!' Jack sipped his pint. 'I've only been in it once and that was just after Helen inherited it. It was in a bit of state.'

'It's not now, but I'm not saying any more or Helen will kill me for spoiling her surprise.' Martin fell serious. 'She's missed you, Jack. You wouldn't believe how much.'

'I might.' Jack replaced his glass on the beer mat. 'I missed her too, you know.'

'All she's done since you left is work in the warehouse

and on the house. Papering, painting, sanding off floorboards and woodwork, sorting the garden . . .'

'No trips to the Pier?' Jack's voice was casual but there was a keen look in his eye.

'Not since the last time we were all there together. I think we outgrew dance halls that night.'

'I can understand you and Lily doing that,' Jack grinned. 'You landed on your feet there, boy. Pretty wife with brains enough to work in a bank, furnished house all paid for . . .'

'Just like you with Helen. And it was Lily I wanted, not the house or her money.'

'Keep your hair on. I was only ribbing. I watched you fall in love with the woman when you were six years old. You would have married her when you were still in short trousers if you could have.'

'We're lucky, Jack,' Martin murmured soberly. 'Both of us, I don't know what Helen told you in her letters—'

'I should hope not,' Jack interrupted.

'I don't mean anything personal. She's done wonders for the trade in her father's warehouse. Expanded the teenage fashion side beyond even her own expectations and they were high.'

'She wrote me.'

'I rode your bike over to your house yesterday and put it in the garage. I cleaned it off and gave it a full service. Although I haven't used it much this last year, it's in surprisingly good nick. Not that you'll be using it much either now that Helen has a car.'

'A car?'

'She hasn't told you.' Martin hit his forehead with the heel of his hand. 'That's me in the doghouse for opening my big mouth and saying too much. It's not exactly hers, it belongs to the warehouse, but as she needs it for her job no one else drives it. You won't tell her I told you?'

'That depends.'

'On what?'

'What other secrets you're keeping from me.'

'Judy and Sam are engaged.' Martin deliberately moved the conversation on.

'Still? Helen put that titbit in her Christmas letter the year before last. What's the bloke waiting for?' Jack offered Martin a cigarette.

'I think if it was up to him he'd marry her tomorrow. It's Judy. Since her mother had the baby, Judy's been running the hairdressers. They've opened ten more shops and she insists she hasn't time to think about a wedding let alone plan one.'

'Sam obviously needs a few hints on how to keep her in line. Women should be in the kitchen not opening shops.'

'And with Helen working all hours in the warehouse you're the one to give them to him?'

'Perhaps, after I've had time to remind Helen of her wifely duties.' Jack flicked his lighter and lit Martin's cigarette before his own.

'I hope, for your sake, you're joking.'

Jack winked. 'How is Katie?'

'Happy, and,' Martin took a deep breath, 'pregnant. The baby is due in a few days.'

Jack scowled. 'I was in shock for a week after Katie wrote and told me she'd married Mr Griffiths.'

'Believe me, I went through all the arguments with her at the time.'

'I would never have given my consent to their marriage.'

'I don't remember Katie asking for it, or mine come to that.'

'You gave her away at her wedding. For Christ's sake, Martin, he's my father-in-law.'

'And brother-in-law.'

'Don't remind me.' Jack pulled an ashtray towards them.

'I can't say I was happy about it at the time. It certainly wasn't what I wanted for Katie, but she forced me to accept that it was what she wanted for herself, so I went along with it. And now I can honestly say that since she married Mr Griffiths, I've never seen her happier. Except . . .'

'What?' Jack broke in eagerly, too eagerly for Martin's liking.

'I don't know what you wrote to her because she never showed me any of your letters.'

'I told her that he was old enough to be her father.'

'Hardly tactful when she was already married to him. And as I said, they are very happy.'

'You said "except",' Jack reminded.

'She's worried about you and how you'll react when you see them together. She doesn't want anything to change between the two of you, but more than anything she wants you and John Griffiths to be friends.'

'That's going to be difficult seeing as he's my father-in-law and boss, as well as brother-in-law.' He looked at Martin. 'Do I still have a job in the warehouse?'

'Do you still want one?'

'To be honest, I don't know. I enjoyed learning to drive in the army and I gained a HGV licence as well as an ordinary one, but I'm not sure I want to carry on working as a driver in civvy street, especially if it means travelling long distances and being away from home for days at a time. I was hoping to use the next couple of weeks to get reacquainted with my wife and think about what I'm going to do with the rest of my life.'

'The warehouse might be boring after the army.'

'After the last couple of years I can live with boring.' Jack sank half his pint.

'Was Cyprus as bloody as everyone says it is?'

'As I haven't been here, I don't know what they're saying.'

'I'm sorry about what happened. Have your wounds—'

'I'm fit,' Jack broke in tersely, 'which is more than can be said for some of the poor buggers I was with.'

'I'm sorry.'

'Everyone was – at the time.' Jack emptied his glass

and stubbed out his cigarette. 'Much as I've enjoyed our brotherly chat, I've a wife waiting.'

Following Jack's lead, Martin finished his beer and rose to his feet. 'Do me a favour, call in on Katie and John.'

'Now?'

'You don't have to go in the house. It will only take a minute to tell Katie that you're happy for her and wish them well. Helen will understand.'

'You're taking a lot upon yourself, speaking for my wife.'

'She's spent a lot of time with Lily and me since you left, and it wasn't easy for her either, Jack, seeing one of her closest friends marry her father.'

'So Helen and Katie . . .'

'Are still the best of friends.' Martin held the door open for his brother. 'Please, Jack, don't say anything that will upset anyone, especially Katie in her condition.' He pulled his keys from his pocket as he halted next to a green Hillman Minx parked in front of the Grand.

'This yours?' Jack asked, as Martin unlocked the driver's door.

Martin failed to hide his pride. 'I bought it second-hand.'

'How old?'

'Eighteen months,' he grinned proudly.

Jack let out a long, low whistle and tossed his bags into the boot. 'I didn't expect to come home to find my brother with the trappings of the crache.'

'Hardly.' Martin gunned the ignition as Jack climbed in beside him

'First stop Carlton Terrace,' Jack said flatly.

'Then you'll see Katie.'

'As she's having my nephew, I suppose I'd better.'

'Or niece. Thanks, Jack.' Martin glanced at his brother as he halted at the junction between High Street and Alexandra Road. 'It's good to have you back.'

'It's good to be back.' Jack settled into his seat and

absorbed sights that had been familiar to him all his life. They seemed oddly strange after two summers spent in the blazing sun of Cyprus. But he wasn't missing the warmth, not even on a cold, Swansea, March night.

'So you think you'll be getting married soon?' Judy tried not to sound overly enthusiastic as she took the cup of coffee Emily handed her. Four out of the five salons she and her mother had bought on mortgages, as opposed to leased, had flats above them and she would have preferred to have taken sole possession of one, but the only empty room was in the one Emily rented.

'Robin and I have been engaged for fourteen months and with things the way they are . . . you do know about my father?' Emily sat in the easy chair opposite Judy's.

'Yes, I'm sorry,' Judy murmured mechanically. The whole of Swansea had heard about Ernest Murton Davies. A year ago he had been counted among the town's wealthiest and most respected citizens, a bank manager who lived in a large house with vast gardens overlooking Caswell Bay, a picturesque and expensive Gower beauty spot. His wife, daughters and son had lived in a style few could aspire to and everyone envied. Helen's brother, Joe, had been briefly admitted to the 'Murton Davies set' when he had studied at university alongside Emily's brother Laurence. He had talked about their lavish hospitality, servants, swimming pool and trips abroad, but all that had come to an abrupt end when Ernest had been arrested for fraud and embezzlement. It had taken the case six months to reach court. Ernest pleaded guilty and was sentenced to eight years imprisonment, but by then his family had lost everything. The house, furniture and even Mrs Murton Davies's jewellery had been sold to meet the demands of Ernest's creditors. Mrs Murton Davies had retreated to Bournemouth to throw herself and her younger daughters on her sister's charity leaving Emily and Laurence to fend for themselves.

Both Emily and Laurence had been forced to abandon their studies, Laurence in university and Emily at the art college. Now the closest Emily came to anything resembling art was a walk past the Glynn Vivian Gallery on her way to her sales assistant's position in Lewis Lewis's department store, two doors down from the tailor's where Laurence worked.

'It's been awful for all of us,' Emily confided, 'but worse for Larry and me because we stayed in Swansea. But I couldn't bear to move away from Robin. I don't know what I would have done without him. He and his family have been marvellous.'

'I'm sure they have.' Judy couldn't help wondering why Robin Watkin Morgan's family hadn't invited Emily to live with them. It wasn't as though they were cramped for space. Joe had been a frequent visitor to their house and said that besides their twelve bedrooms there was a whole attic floor, which had once been servants' quarters, they never used.

'Of course, I'll give you as much notice as I can.' Emily set her coffee mug on the shelf next to her. 'You'll need to get someone else in.'

'I'm not sure I will.'

'I thought you'd need the money,' Emily blurted thoughtlessly.

'I can afford to live alone.'

'I didn't mean to suggest you couldn't.'

'No offence taken,' Judy said evenly.

'And,' Emily looked at the solitaire on Judy's left hand, 'you'll be getting married yourself soon.'

'Possibly.'

'That will be Robin.' Emily jumped to her feet as the doorbell rang, and ran down the stairs to the front door.

Judy carried their cups through to the kitchen. Her flatmate's babbling was interspersed with a slow, masculine drawl. The door closed and Emily darted back up the stairs ahead of a more ponderous step. Judy returned to her chair just as the living room door burst open.

'Judy, I'd like to introduce my fiancé, Robin Watkin Morgan. Robin, this is my landlady and flatmate, Judith Hunt.'

'We've met before,' said Judy, stepping back as Robin leaned forward to kiss her cheek. Extending her hand, she kept him at arm's length while he shook it.

'I hate to disagree with a lady but I would have remembered someone as beautiful as you, Judy.' He gave her a charming smile that didn't quite reach his eyes.

'And I hate to disagree with a gentleman, but you were at Joe Griffiths's and Lily Sullivan's engagement party. Not that they were engaged at the end of it.'

'They weren't, were they?' His smile broadened. 'Ems said you'd been living with Joe's sister. It must be a hundred years since I've seen the old boy. How is he?'

'Fine from what I hear.'

'Living it up in London, eh?'

'Presumably.'

'I've just had the most fantastic idea. Why don't you come to the pub with Ems and me? You can fill me in on what's been happening with Joe.'

'Much as I'd like to, I'm expecting my fiancé.' Judy did something she had never done before; wave her engagement ring under a man's nose.

'Too late, eh? Well, come on, Ems, you're wasting good drinking time.'

'I only have to get my coat.'

'Goodbye, Judy.' Robin reached for her hand. Before she could stop him he lifted it to his lips and kissed it. 'I hope this is the beginning of a long and beautiful friendship.'

'That rather depends on how soon you marry Emily.'

Raising one eyebrow, he winked at her and followed Emily out through the door.

'My wife won't like it if you strangle me,' Jack smiled, disentangling Katie's arms from around his neck.

Moving away from him, she looked him up and down. 'I didn't hurt you, did I?' she asked anxiously. 'Your wounds—'

'I was joking.'

'I can't believe it's you. You've changed so much, I wouldn't have recognised you. Would you have known him, John?' She turned to her husband, who had retreated to the other side of the room.

'No, I wouldn't.' He took the hand Jack offered and shook it warmly. 'Helen's in for a surprise.'

'Which I'd better be on my way to give her.' Despite Martin's assertion that he wouldn't have to go into Katie and John's house, Katie had dragged him into her living room as soon as he and Martin had knocked at the door. And after seeing her swollen figure, the shadows beneath her eyes and the troubled look on her face, he hadn't the heart to refuse.

'I wish . . .'

'Let him go to Helen, love,' John demurred.

'Of course, I'm being selfish, especially when we'll be seeing you tomorrow.'

'You will?' Jack asked, as she and John walked him and Martin to the door.

'Pretend I didn't say that.'

'You girls have arranged a surprise party,' Jack guessed.

'You won't tell Helen I told you?' she begged.

'Absolutely not. They train you to keep secrets in the army.'

'I'll open the car.' Martin walked on ahead.

Jack looked at John standing on the doorstep with his arm around Katie and understood what Martin had been trying to tell him about their sister's marriage. He would have been hard pressed to decide who looked the more besotted, John or Katie. 'I know it's a bit late but congratulations.'

'Thank you, Jack.' Katie's eyes shone with gratitude.

'Take care of yourself and my nephew.' He kissed her cheek.

She looked up at her husband. 'That's John's job.'

'See you tomorrow,' he called, as he went to the car.

'Bit of a nuisance, you having a flatmate, Ems. It's going to curb our style,' Robin complained, unlocking his sports car.

'We could go to your place,' she suggested, as she lifted the hem of her duster coat clear of the sill.

'Drive all the way up Gower Road when we're meeting the crowd in the George in half an hour?'

'It will only take ten minutes.'

'There and back makes twenty and that only gives us ten minutes in the house.'

'We could be late.'

'And if everyone moves on, we'll never find them.' What Robin hadn't told Emily was that since her father had pleaded guilty to the charges against him, his parents had been nagging him to break off his engagement and that nagging invariably increased in frequency and intensity after one of her visits to his home.

He'd delayed doing so for two reasons. First, as he'd explained to his father, he'd look a right heel if he dropped Emily the moment she and her family became social lepers. And second, he was loath to give her up after he'd expended a great deal of time and effort persuading her to extend her sexual repertoire into realms most girls refused to explore. Something he'd discovered from personal experience, because even when he'd intended to marry Emily, he'd never been entirely faithful to her.

As he drove away from the kerb, he pushed up her skirt and rested his hand on her knee. 'We could park by the big apple.'

'It's freezing.'

'A quick onc, just to keep me going until I take you home.'

'You heard Judy, her boyfriend's coming round for the evening.'

'Lucky boyfriend,' he griped.

'Why do I have the feeling that you don't want to take me to your house any more?'

'We're always going to my house,' he countered irritably.

'Not since my last flatmate moved out.'

'Only because I want to spare your blushes. You know how embarrassed you get when we waltz in, say hi to Mums and Pops, and disappear up to my room.'

'They must know we're sleeping together.'

'There's a difference between knowing and our rubbing their noses in it.' He headed up the road that led to the car park on the headland between Mumbles and Bracelet Bay.

'So when are you going to take me home with you again?'

'Sunday,' he replied, aware that his parents had made plans to go away for the weekend. 'Come for lunch. I'll warn the housekeeper.' He pulled up in a row of spaces facing the sea and turned off the engine.

She saw half a dozen cars dotted around the car park, all with their windows steamed up. 'Whenever you do this, I'm terrified we'll get caught.'

'A peeping tom would die of frostbite.'

'A peeping policeman in a warm car wouldn't.'

'Then I'll keep my eyes open for police cars,' he retorted irritably. Unbuckling his belt, he unzipped his trousers and sat back. As she moved closer, he murmured, 'Knickers and bra off.'

'Robin, it's freezing.'

'Off!'

'There's no room to undress.'

'I'll help.'

'I'll look a mess in the pub.'

'You can go to the Ladies as soon as we get there. Stop moaning, Ems, and get on with it.'

*

'Looks like Helen's switched on the illuminations to welcome you home.'

'So it does.' Jack opened the car door and stepped out as soon as Martin drew to a halt. He stood outside the garden wall and looked through the windows. The lamps glowed golden, illuminating beautifully furnished and decorated rooms that could have served as an illustration for *Home and Garden*.

This was the house his wife had prepared for him to return to, his home, yet the more he tried to visualise stepping inside and living there, the less he could imagine doing so. He caught a glimpse of movement in the upstairs bay and strained his eyes, hoping to catch sight of Helen. But if she was there, she was remaining resolutely out of sight.

'She's done a great job, hasn't she?' Martin dropped his bags at his feet.

'Yes.' Jack fought a lump in his throat, as he continued to gaze at a place that seemed far too magnificent for the likes of him.

'You going to stand there all night?'

'No.' Jack turned to his brother. 'You coming in?'

'No fear, I've my own wife waiting at home.'

'Thanks for the lift.' Jack shook Martin's hand. Picking up his bags, he pushed opened the gate and walked to the front door. It opened ahead of him. Dropping his bags to the floor, he closed the door and looked behind it. Helen stared back at him, open-mouthed and wide-eyed. 'No kiss for the returning hero?'

As her eyes grew round in disbelief, he realised that Martin and Katie hadn't exaggerated how much he'd changed. Picking her up, he swept her off her feet and hugged her.

'You're, you're . . .' She continued to stare at him, as he lowered her gently back on to the floor.

'Handsome?' he suggested deprecatingly.

'Big,' she whispered, shivering in the draught of cold

air he'd brought into the house. 'I can't believe it's really you.'

'In the flesh.'

'Why didn't you tell me you'd changed?'

'Because I didn't realise I had.'

Suddenly and unaccountably shy, she opened the door to the living room. 'Look at us standing in the hall. I lit a fire first thing this morning. I hope the house will be warm enough for you after Cyprus.' She walked over to the grate, lifted the guard and poked the fire, setting the coals ablaze. 'You must be hungry. I've a meal ready, your favourite, or what used to be your favourite, steak, chips, peas and a chocolate cake for dessert. Take off your coat, make yourself at home. What am I saying? This is your home . . .' She paused as she replaced the guard, realising that she was blurting out anything and everything that came into her head to hide her nervousness.

He made a show of looking around, although he could have described the room in detail after studying it through the window. 'This is very nice. You've even bought a television.'

'We all have, my father and Katie, Lily and Martin . . . Do you really like the room? I almost left everything as it was so we could chose the colour schemes together, but then I thought it would be awful for you to come home to a scruffy house. And after two and half years away, the last thing you probably want to do is start decorating.'

'You did all this by yourself?'

'Most of it, but not by myself. Judy, your brother, Lily and Sam helped.' Still staring at him, she backed into one of the easy chairs. As her knees connected with the seat, her legs buckled from under her and she sat down abruptly. 'I . . . I'll get the meal on, shall I?'

'I'd rather see around the house.'

'Of course, you probably don't remember it.'

'I remember it all right, just not like this.'

Glad of something to do she led the way back into the hall. 'I painted the kitchen walls pale green.'

He looked around the door. 'Very nice.'

'This is my aunt's original furniture. I remembered you saying that you liked it. But the cooker is new, and the washing machine and fridge.'

'There's a fridge and washing machine?'

'You think I shouldn't have bought them?' she asked anxiously, stepping back so he could see them. The one thing they had never discussed in their letters was money. She hadn't touched her army wife's allowance but she hadn't needed to. Judy's rent money and her wages from the warehouse had been more than enough to keep her and pay for the improvements she'd made to the house.

'Of course you should have, sweetheart. It's just a bit much for me to take in all at once. I never thought we'd live as grand as this.'

'Sweetheart.' That one single word spoken in Jack's voice brought back a flood of memories. 'We wouldn't be, if my aunt hadn't left us this house.'

'You.'

'It's ours now.' She ran her hand over the pine table. 'Judy and I ate in here, but I thought we'd use the dining room. I kept my aunt's mahogany dining-room suite as well, but as you saw, the three-piece suite and coffee table in the living room are new.'

'Why eat in the other room when it's warm and comfortable in here? It would be less work as well. You wouldn't have to carry dishes and food through.'

'Yes, but . . . all right, if you want to, we can eat in here, but not tonight. I've laid the table in the dining room.' She walked back into the hall and down a passageway. 'I've had the downstairs cloakroom tiled,' she opened the door on a narrow cubicle that held a wash hand basin and toilet, 'and the floor of the back porch. It's a bit dark to see the garden, coalhouse, garage and shed.'

'I'd rather see them in daylight,' he agreed.

Realising he'd either developed a new and rather dry sense of humour, or she'd forgotten it, she avoided his gaze as they returned to the hall. 'There are four bedrooms and a bathroom.'

'I remember.'

She ran up the stairs and opened every door on the landing in turn without taking the time to show him the rooms.

'Where are we sleeping?'

Her heart began to pound from more than just the exertion of running up the stairs. 'In here.' She trembled as she entered the master bedroom and walked to the window. After closing the shutters she'd opened only an hour earlier, she turned to find him watching her.

'It's a beautiful room, Helen.'

'You don't think it's too prissy.'

'Prissy?'

'Too like a girl's room; Martin and Sam weren't keen on the flowered wallpaper when they first saw it, although Martin said he liked it better when it was up.'

'The paper suits the room.' He ran his hands over the wardrobe doors. 'Nice furniture.'

'I used some of the money I earned in the warehouse to buy two new bedroom suites as well as the furniture downstairs. Martin and Sam moved the suite that was in here into one of the other bedrooms. Do you remember those two walnut horrors? I threw them out.' She opened the wardrobe door. 'I had your suits cleaned and I bought you new underclothes and socks. Not that many, I wasn't sure how many clothes you'd have.'

'Not many and most of what I have is summer stuff.'

'Shirts.' She lifted down a box and showed it to him.

'Can you change it?'

'You don't like it.' She was crestfallen. 'It's the latest . . .'

'I'm not fifteen and a half collar any more, sweetheart.'

'Oh!' She sat on the bed only to leap to her feet when he moved towards her. 'I bought them in the warehouse so there won't be a problem. It's just as well I didn't unpack them.'

'It is.' Taking the box from her, he pushed it back on top of the others.

'What size are you now?'

'Seventeen and a half.'

'You're so different. I would have never—'

'Recognised me. That's what Katie and Martin said.'

'You saw Katie?'

'Only for a few minutes. Martin said she'd been worrying about my reaction to her marriage to your father.'

'She has.' She turned to him. 'You're not angry?'

'I wasn't pleased when I received her letter telling me about it, but I've had time to get used to the idea. They seem happy.'

'They are.' She looked away self-consciously when she realised he was still watching her.

'Underneath the extra pounds and inches I'm the same Jack you married, Helen. Come here.' He opened his arms and she went to him, but she couldn't stop herself from trembling when he kissed her.

'I'm so glad you're back. It must have been horrible in Cyprus.'

'It was.'

'Your wounds—'

'Have healed.' There was a note in his voice that warned her not to probe further.

'I'll make us something to eat.'

'Do you mind if I have a bath first?'

'No.' She jumped away from him. 'There's towels in the bathroom.'

'I saw them. You expecting a platoon?'

'There's more in the airing cupboard if you need them,' she continued, undeterred, returning to the landing and opening both the airing cupboard and bathroom doors. 'Soap, toothbrushes, toothpaste, shampoo, razor blades.' She slid back a mirror in the bathroom and revealed well-stocked shelves. 'I bought you hair cream – I hope Brylcreem is all right – shaving soap and aftershave. I wasn't sure you'd still be using Old Spice.'

'Helen.' He slipped his fingers beneath her chin and lifted her head, forcing her to look him in the eye. 'It's perfect. Everything is absolutely perfect.'

'I'll start running your bath.'

'You don't need to do everything for me.'

'Then I'll go downstairs and . . .' Ducking under his arm she almost ran away from him. Deciding she needed a little time to grow accustomed to the idea of him being in the house, he went into the bathroom and turned on the taps.

Robin pushed his shirt into his trousers, buckled his belt and pulled his zipper. 'Fit for the pub.' He looked at Emily who was struggling to fasten her bra. 'Here, you're hopeless.' Tugging her blouse free from her skirt, he slipped his hands beneath it and hooked it for her.

'Thank you. Can we talk for a minute?'

'In the pub.' He reached for his keys.

'Please, Robin, here.'

'It's bloody freezing.'

'We need to set a date for the wedding.'

'Not until everyone's stopped talking about your father.'

Knotting her hands together, she looked down at her lap. 'That will be too late.' She paused before finally finding the courage to say what she had been trying to tell him for weeks. 'I'm pregnant.'

He turned off the engine and stared at the sea. Dark, gleaming, a narrow silver path glittered to the horizon reflecting the light of the moon. 'I don't understand . . . How can you be?'

'We have sex every time we meet.'

'I always use something.'

'They're not infallible.'

'I've been telling you to get a Dutch cap for years.'

She began to cry, great, fat tears that splashed on to her lap. She hadn't been able to predict how Robin would respond to her news, but the last thing she'd expected was this cold, controlled anger.

'Are you absolutely sure?' he demanded harshly.

'I've just missed my fourth period.'

'That doesn't mean anything. All girls are irregular, the magazines say so.'

'Not me.'

'You've seen a doctor?'

'No. How can I when my doctor knows I'm not married?'

'Then it could be something else. The shock of your father, or your mother moving away – having to work long hours in that shop. That's it,' he cried fervently. 'You're not used to working or standing on your feet all day.'

'I don't think so. I've talked to some of the girls in work . . .'

'You told them you're pregnant?' He was horrified at the thought of her discussing a possible pregnancy with a stranger, perhaps even mentioning his name.

'Of course not. But they talk about having babies all the time and one of the older women said your breasts are tender for the first couple of months and mine are.'

'I haven't noticed.'

'There's no reason why you would. And I've been sick in the morning.' Her voice rose precariously. 'Robin, I'm frightened. You will marry me, won't you?'

'First we need to find out if you really are pregnant. I could get Pops—'

'No, Robin, not your father. I'd die of embarrassment if he examined me.'

Robin hadn't been about to suggest any such thing, but his father was a doctor and if anyone would know how to get him out of a jam like this, it would be a doctor. Then he realised his father was the last person he could go to. He'd been advising him to break off with Emily for months.

He leaned forward over the steering wheel so Emily couldn't read the expression on his face. One thing was certain; on top of what had happened to her father, this would keep the Swansea scandal machine in juicy titbits for months. None of the Murton Davies's reputations had survived the ignominy of the court case. He could almost hear the Swansea matrons, his mother among them, rejoicing at yet another scandal that would prove the family weren't the crache they'd pretended to be.

'Robin, please say something,' she begged in a small voice.

'Like what?' he snarled.

'That it will be all right,' she pleaded, needing to believe it.

'Of course it will.' He dismissed brusquely. 'Leave it to me.'

'We'll get married—'

'I said, I'll sort it, Ems.' He started the engine. 'But for now, let's go to the pub.'

As soon as Helen heard the plug being pulled in the bath, she left the living room and went into the kitchen. The steaks were already in the pan; all she had to do was light the gas under them. The frozen peas were defrosted in water in a saucepan. The chips were peeled. It was time to heat the fat fryer. Or was it too soon?

Did Jack shave before or after a bath? Or did he need to shave at all? His cheek had felt smooth when he'd kissed her. She walked to the foot of the stairs and called, 'Jack.' When there was no answer, she walked up the stairs.

The light was off in the bathroom but she could feel the air, hot, clammy and steamy, as it blasted through the open door on to the landing. She looked down the passage to their bedroom. It was in darkness.

'Jack.' She switched on the light in the master bedroom. Too late she realised he'd opened the shutters and was standing, naked, in front of the window.

Chapter Three

'That's the last of the kitchen things you brought from Helen's, washed and dried.' Sam strolled into the bedroom where Judy was busy sorting through her clothes.

'And put away?'

'I don't know where you want to keep them.' He sat on the edge of the bed, avoiding the underwear she'd stacked in neat piles on the eiderdown.

'I would have thought that was obvious.'

'Not to me,' he replied, disingenuously.

'For pity's sake, the kitchen only has three cupboards.' She pulled out a drawer and dropped one of the piles of underwear into it.

'Exactly.' He moved back as she swooped on a second pile. 'I didn't know which one you wanted them in.'

'This may sound astonishing but the china goes in the china cupboard, saucepans in the saucepan cupboard and food in the food cupboard. Why are men useless at all things domestic?' She picked up the last pile and dropped it into the bottom drawer of her dressing table.

'We're not, just clever enough to recognise that women are better at running a home than us.'

'More like clever enough to get most women to do everything for you. Well, I have news for you, Sam Davies. If you try using that ploy on me again, you'll find yourself getting enough practice to run a home more efficiently than any woman.'

'I do my share,' he protested mildly.

'That's debatable.' As she closed the last drawer with her hip, she allowed herself a small smile of satisfaction.

All her clothes were away, her brushes, comb, scent and dusting powder neatly laid out on the dressing table, her make-up hidden out of sight in the top drawer, the bed made with fresh sheets and blankets . . .

'Stop rushing around and sit down for a minute.' Sam patted the bed beside him.

'I want to find a place for my record player and records in the living room.'

'Find it tomorrow.' Reaching out, he grabbed her waist and pulled her down on top of him.

'I'll scream.'

'You do, and I won't get us fish and chips.' Pushing her back on to the bed, he slid his hand beneath her sweater and kissed her. 'I'm going to like you having your own place.'

'I have a flatmate,' she reminded, as his fingers closed around her bra cup.

'She won't come into your bedroom, will she?' He kicked the door shut with the heel of his shoe.

'Not unless she's invited.'

'And as she's out . . .' He tried to lift her sweater over her head.

'I'm hungry.' Pushing him aside, she pulled down her top, straightened her clothes and sat up.

'Judy . . .'

'I really am hungry,' she repeated, realising she'd annoyed him.

'I offered to take you out for a meal.'

'I'd rather eat in.'

'All right, I can take a hint.' He tucked his shirt into his trousers as he left the bed. 'But after we've eaten, we are going to do some serious talking.'

There was an odd look in his eye that perturbed her. 'What about?' she asked warily.

'I'm saying nothing beyond I'm reserving the right to choose the topic of conversation. Do you want hake or cod?'

*

'Oh God, I'm sorry.' Acutely conscious of Jack's nakedness, Helen switched off the light.

'I was admiring the view. I'd forgotten how spectacular it is. Join me.' He held out his hand.

'I have to make the meal.' She stood transfixed in the doorway, shocked that Jack was making no attempt to cover himself. Didn't he realise there was enough light shining in from the landing for her to see him?

'It's all right, Helen.' He spoke quietly, but there was suppressed mirth in his voice. 'We are married and we have the certificate to prove it.'

'I . . .' She stammered and backed away as he turned towards her.

'You're shocked at my barrack room manners.'

'No. I . . .'

'I'm disturbing you.'

'It's been a long time.' She crashed into the wall.

'Long enough for you to forget our honeymoon – and before? Your father's sofa in your basement? All those baths we took together in the hotel in London?'

She shivered as he drew closer, then she saw the scars, a long one that began at the top of his thigh and snaked down past his knee, puckering his skin. And another that slashed diagonally across his abdomen. 'When I got the telegram saying you'd been wounded, it didn't say your injuries were this serious.'

'They're healed.'

'They don't hurt?'

'Not any more,' he said dismissively.

'Jack . . .'

'Forget about them, Helen. I have.' He reached out to her.

'I know I'm being stupid, but I can't help feeling shy.'

'You're not stupid and, if my memory serves correctly, you won't be shy for long once we get into that bed.'

'You want to go to bed – now?' Her voice wavered at the thought.

'Not if you don't.'

'I . . . We haven't eaten, we . . .'

Folding his arms around her, he kissed her, slowly, tenderly, waiting for her to respond before pulling her even closer. As her fingers closed around his neck, he whispered, 'I would undress you but I've lost touch with women's clothes.' He fingered her sack dress. 'I wouldn't know how to get into that or you out of it.'

'I'm glad to hear it,' she whispered.

'There doesn't appear to be any fastening that I can see.'

'It goes over my head.'

'If you raise your arms, I'll pull it off.'

As she did as he suggested, he peeled it gently from her. 'Now, this I do remember.' He slipped the straps of her petticoat over her shoulders. 'And this.' Unclipping her bra, he dropped it to the floor before caressing her breasts. 'You are beautiful, so beautiful I'm having trouble believing this isn't one of the dreams that has kept me going for the last two and half years.' Pulling the clips from her French pleat he ran his fingers through her thick blonde hair as it tumbled to her shoulders. 'And thank you for not cutting this.'

'You always liked it long.'

'And loose.'

She shuddered as his hands moved lower.

'Pretty panties and suspenders, are all your underclothes like this or did you buy them for me?'

'I bought them especially for you,' she confessed.

'I'll turn back the bed while you slip them off.'

'More apple flan?' Lily picked up the cake knife.

'No, thank you.' Martin sighed contentedly, pushing his chair back from the table. 'That was a fantastic meal but I couldn't eat another thing.' He handed her his plate, as she cleared their dishes and stacked them on top of the cupboard next to the sink.

'Just as well; I more or less promised Sam that he could have a slice tomorrow.' Covering the flan and cream dishes with greaseproof paper, she opened the fridge door and set them on a shelf.

'You're too soft with him and Mike, they take advantage.'

'I know, but he begged nicely. Do you want tea or coffee?'

'Perhaps later.' Catching her hand he pulled her on to his lap. 'But for the moment, I want to talk to my wife.' His grip tightened as she struggled.

'We have been talking,' she laughed.

'Only about my brother and Helen. I want to talk about us. Someone I know got a promotion today.'

She stopped fighting him. 'You've been given the foreman's job?'

'As of Monday, I will be a salaried not waged employee of Swansea Town Council.'

'And you sat there for the last hour without saying a single solitary word?'

'You didn't ask.'

'I was afraid to. I knew how much you wanted it. You can be the most exasperating man when you want to, Martin Clay.'

'But you love me,' he beamed.

'Only sometimes. I don't know whether to kiss or hit you.'

'I'd prefer the kiss.'

She linked her hands around his neck and kissed him, long and lovingly.

'It might not make much difference to the money I'll be bringing home because there'll be no overtime payments,' he warned. 'But it does mean a higher basic rate and more security.' His smiled broadened. 'So, if you'd like to discuss that family you want . . .'

'*I* want!'

'All right, we want.' Releasing her, he grabbed the table to stop his chair from toppling over, as she flung her arms around his neck and kissed him again. 'Given the way Sam and Mike treat all of this house as their own, I think we'd better continue this conversation in our bedroom,' he muttered, coming up for air.

'You are serious?' she asked earnestly.

'I've never been more serious in my life.' He brushed a tear from the corner of her eye with his thumb. 'Hey, this is something to celebrate not cry about.'

'I know. I'm just so happy . . .'

'Surely you didn't believe that I hadn't noticed how broody you get around Billy, or seen the envious glances you've been sending my sister's way since she's expanded.'

'I wasn't envious; I just wanted our own baby. I wonder what he'll be like.'

'Or she. You do realise that you will have to give up work.'

'Yes, but not until I begin to show.'

'You won't miss the bank?'

'A bit perhaps at first, but,' she hugged him again, 'it will be wonderful to stay at home and look after the house, you and the baby, and in a year or two we'll have another one – won't we?' She gave him an anxious look.

'How about we have them one at a time?'

'But you do want more than one?'

'I'll let you know after the first,' he hedged.

'Auntie Norah and Uncle Roy were marvellous to me, but I always thought it would have been fantastic to have had an older brother or sister. That's the only thing I ever envied Katie and Helen. I'd hate for our baby to be an only child.'

'He or she will be for a while.'

'And afterwards?'

'One step at a time, Mrs Clay.' He picked her up, swinging her high in his arms as he left the chair. She looked over his shoulder as he carried her out of the kitchen.

'Wait, I haven't finished clearing the table.'

'Is there anything that needs to go in the fridge?'

'Move round and I'll tell you. No, there isn't.'

'Then, as I have tomorrow off, I'll do it in the morning.'

'I love you.'

'You might not be saying that nine months from now. From what I've heard, women curse their husbands when they're in labour.'

'I won't be one of them.' She almost blurted out the secret she'd been carrying for weeks but decided against it. Tomorrow would be soon enough and hopefully then he'd completely forgive her for not telling him that he was going to be a father and two and half months sooner than he thought possible.

'Good fish and chips.' Sam set down his knife and fork.

'Very.' Judy picked up their plates and carried them into the kitchen. 'Do you want coffee?'

'Please.' Sam left the table and sat in an easy chair and Judy put the kettle on to boil. She returned to the living room with a tray. 'Cigarette?' he offered. Judy rarely smoked but Sam knew she occasionally enjoyed one after her evening meal.

'Yes, please.'

He lit two and handed her one.

'Thank you.' She set his cup of instant coffee on the tiled hearth next to him.

'Ready for that talk?'

'As I'll ever be, although I've a feeling that I'm not going to like what I'm about to hear.' She took the chair opposite his.

'Most women can't wait to set the date of their wedding.'

'Sam, I—'

'Am – are – have been busy,' he derided. 'You've been giving me that excuse for over eighteen months and I'm not prepared to listen any more.'

'So, what do you expect me to do?'

He looked her in the eye. 'Fix the date.'

'I've just taken on a couple of good stylists. One has

the makings of an excellent manager but she will need time to settle in. It will get easier, perhaps in a month or two . . .'

'I won't be around in a month or two,' he said quietly.

'I didn't know you were up for a transfer. You know there's no way that I can move out of Swansea.'

'The only place I'll be going is away from you if you don't set a date,' he broke in brusquely.

Unnerved by the expression in his eyes, she studied her hands. There was a chip on her varnish and her nails needed filing. 'I need more time.'

'You've had all the time I'm prepared to give you, Judy.' He flicked the ash from his cigarette into an ashtray on the mantelpiece.

'Can't we at least discuss this over the weekend?' she begged.

'No.'

'We could go into the bedroom . . .'

'So you can wind me up and tease me like you did earlier?' He drew on his cigarette. 'No, Judy, I've had enough of teasing and enough of waiting.'

'You agreed that we shouldn't make love before we were married.'

'I didn't think you were going for the longest engagement on record at the time.'

'I hate ultimatums—'

'And I love you, but I won't settle for this half life any longer,' he interrupted. 'I'm earning good money. I could get a police house tomorrow. I want to get married and have children before I start drawing my old age pension.'

Her eyes blazed. 'We're not even married and you're talking about having children. You never said—'

'I never said, because it seemed more important to discuss setting a wedding date than to make a booking in a maternity clinic.' He looked at her over the rim of his coffee cup. 'I take it from that outburst that you don't want any. No, don't tell me, I know – you haven't had time to think about it.'

'I haven't,' she snapped defensively, and not entirely truthfully.

'So what's it to be?'

'I need to talk to my mother.'

'Fair enough.' He finished his coffee and set his cup on the tray. 'You'll be seeing her tomorrow night at Helen and Jack's. I'll give you until then.'

'That's not enough time.'

'It will have to be, because that's all I'm going to give you.'

'You're not going!' she cried out in surprise, as he stubbed out his cigarette and went to the door.

'I am. Think about what I said, Judy.'

'You'll pick me up tomorrow, for Jack and Helen's party?' she asked apprehensively.

'I'll be here. Seven o'clock, isn't it?'

'Yes.'

'And I'll have my answer as soon as you've spoken to your mother.' Without waiting for her reply, he shrugged on his coat and kissed her cheek. 'Don't bother to come down, I'll see myself out.'

John switched off the television as the evening news ended. 'Would you like cocoa, love?'

'No, thank you.' Katie patted her swollen stomach. 'I'll be glad when this one's born. He's not leaving much room, even for a cup of cocoa.'

'Is he kicking?'

'All the time.'

'If you are in pain . . .'

'I am not in pain and I promise you, he won't be born tonight.' She set the bootie she'd been knitting aside. 'I am quite happy on my own, John, you don't have to stay in every evening with me.'

'I know.'

'Then why don't you go down the pub occasionally? Before we married you used to meet Roy Williams in the

White Rose a couple of nights a week. He must think I'm locking you up.'

'He doesn't think anything of the kind because, like me, he's discovered the pleasures of staying home at night.' He rested his hand lightly on her smock. 'Don't tell me that didn't hurt.' He gave her an uneasy look as he felt the baby move inside her.

'It didn't, honestly. It's a peculiar feeling, I can't explain it other than to say it's good to know he's well enough to move about.'

'You look tired. If you don't want any cocoa, at least let me help you to bed.'

'Please, John, don't wrap me in cotton wool.'

'We'll have a late night tomorrow,' he reminded. 'I can't see you leaving Jack and Helen's much before midnight.'

'As usual, you're right, and I want to get up early to buy flowers for Helen and something for Jack. Can you think of anything?' She struggled to her feet.

'Let me get the flowers and I'll buy some beer for Jack. Seeing as it's a party I could have a crate or two delivered to their house.'

'You can buy the beer but I want to choose the flowers myself.'

'Stubborn creature.'

'Do you think Jack still drinks beer?' She opened the door.

'Judging by the weight he's put on, I'd say almost definitely.' He walked slowly up the stairs behind her, smiling when she opened the door of the first bedroom she came to, instead of walking on to the master bedroom.

The room was papered in a pretty primrose paper patterned with cartoons of nursery rhymes and fairytale characters. A plain white wood cot stood along the back wall, carefully screened from draughts and the direct heat of the radiator he'd recently had installed as part of a central heating system. A chest of drawers and wardrobe that matched the cot were ranged along the opposite wall and the single bed set in front of the window held a changing mat and plastic bath filled with tins of baby cream and talcum powder. Walking to the chest of drawers, Katie opened it and looked down on the hand-knitted layette she'd spent the last few months making.

'If there's anything else I can do in here, love, you only have to ask.'

'There's nothing. It's perfect.' She closed the drawer and drew the primrose cotton curtains she'd made, before sitting in the rocking chair he'd bought her the day she'd discovered she was having their child.

'Nothing you want to add to your case for the nursing home, or the baby's?' He looked at the two cases that stood at the foot of the bed.

'No.'

He stood behind the chair; wrapping his arms around her, he kissed the back of her neck. 'Then all we want is for him to put in an appearance.'

'The sooner the better,' she agreed.

'You afraid?'

'No,' she lied stoutly. Realising she'd spoken too quickly, she added, 'It's the most natural thing in the world for a woman.'

'I wish I could do more to help.'

She smiled and patted her swollen body. 'I think you've done your share, John.'

'Remember me?' Jack hugged Helen as he cradled her in the bed next to him.

'Now I do.' Turning on her stomach, she looked into his eyes. 'You hungry?'

'Starving, I could eat a horse.'

'I have no horses, only beef steaks.'

'Then they will have to do.'

'Bags I bathroom first.' Flinging back the bedclothes, Helen grabbed her dressing gown and ran naked into the bathroom.

'It didn't take you long to lose your shyness,' he laughed.

'You always were a bad influence on me,' she shouted back.

Folding his arms under his head, he lay back feeling happy and just a bit smug. Martin was right, they were both lucky. Beautiful wives, ready made homes, life couldn't get any better.

'Lazy bones.' Helen walked back in wearing a red silk dressing gown.

'You look wonderful and,' he sniffed the air, 'smell exactly as a scarlet woman should. New perfume?'

'Like the underclothes, I bought it for my husband.' She picked up the sack dress from the floor, folded it on to a chair and lifted another from her wardrobe.

'You're not going to dress?' he objected.

'I can't walk around the house in a dressing gown at this time in the evening.'

'Why not?'

'Someone could call.'

'If anyone dared, I'd send them away.'

She hesitated, then unable to think of a single reason why she should dress, hung the frock back in the wardrobe.

'I'll go down and get my bags from the hall.'

'The curtains aren't closed,' she warned.

'I'll give the neighbours a thrill.'

'Jack . . .'

'Don't worry, not too much of a thrill.' Picking up the bath towel he'd draped on the window seat, he tied it around his waist. 'Go cook, woman. If I like the result I may give you a reward.'

'I thought you just had.'

'You don't want another one?' he teased, chasing her down the stairs.

'You can be extraordinarily stupid at times,' Angela Watkin Morgan railed at her brother.

'Come on, Angie,' Robin cajoled. 'It's the sort of thing that could happen to anyone.'

'No, it's damned well not. And don't try exercising your charm on me, I'm your sister, not one of your tarts. If you'd listened to Pops and dropped Emily when he told you to months ago, she wouldn't be pregnant and you wouldn't be in this mess.' She went to the drinks tray set on a table in the corner of the billiards room and poured herself a small brandy.

'I should have known better than to hope for sympathy from you.' Robin filled a glass with whisky and downed it in one.

'You should have,' she agreed caustically. 'No one knows Ems better than me and there was a time when I was fond of her, but after what happened with her father I had no choice other than to drop her. You should never have carried on with your engagement.'

'I was waiting for the right time to break it off.'

'Any fool could have told you that was the day her father went to prison.'

'I would have looked a right bastard if I'd dumped her just as her family had lost everything.' He'd given the explanation as to why he'd carried on with his engagement in the face of scandal so often, he was almost beginning to believe it.

'More like you were afraid that you wouldn't find another girl to do the things Emily does for you.' She looked him coolly in the eye as his face darkened. 'Surprised I know about your weirder habits? I don't know what Ems is like now, but she used to talk too much, especially after a couple of drinks. And she wasn't so stupid that she didn't realise that some of the things you asked her to do were bizarre. So, you carried on in your own selfish way, never once giving a thought as to how the gossip about the two of you would affect Pops and Mums.'

'Not to mention you and Julian Pickering Jones,' he broke in acidly. 'Your darling boyfriend never shuts up about the money his family entrusted to Ems's father and lost.'

'It was more than fifteen thousand pounds.'

'And I've heard about it every day for the last year.' Reaching for the whisky, he replenished his glass.

'Forget Julian, me, Pops and Mums, and think about yourself. Have you any idea what people will say about you once this gets out?'

'I'm not the first boy to get his girlfriend pregnant,' he muttered defensively.

'It wouldn't matter if she was from an acceptable family. You knew everyone was cutting the Murton Davieses. If Emily and Larry had one ounce of sense they would have gone to Bournemouth with their mother and the others. I don't know of a single girl who'll go near Lewis Lewis's or that tailor's in case either of them is serving. It would be so humiliating.'

'For Ems and Larry, or your socially acceptable friends?' Robin enquired cuttingly.

'Everyone concerned. I just don't understand why you can't see it.' She sipped her brandy. 'What are you going to do?'

'I haven't a clue.' Robin finished his second shot of whisky and refilled his glass.

'Getting drunk won't help.'

His hand shook as the full impact of his predicament hit him. 'I know,' he mumbled miserably.

'For all our sakes, Robin, break off your engagement tomorrow.'

'How can I when she's having my kid?'

'You can't be thinking of marrying her?' She was aghast at the idea.

'What else can I do, Angie? We've been engaged for over a year.'

'Marry Ems and you'll be finished at the BBC,' she predicted callously. 'A good social life is essential these days and you'll never have that with her. As it is Pops, Mums and I have been hard-pressed to persuade people to invite you to some of the more vital functions this year because of your engagement. Turn that into marriage and you'll become a pariah like her.'

Robin's hand shook as he finished his third shot. 'Do you think she really is up the duff?'

'You'd be better placed to answer that than me. I haven't seen Ems in ten, eleven months. Not since she moved from Caswell.'

Setting down his glass, Robin lifted a cue from the rack behind him and sent the billiard balls scattering over the table. 'But girls do sometimes lie about being pregnant to get a chap to marry them.'

'If they're desperate about the boy,' Angela conceded.

'Exactly, and Ems is desperate,' Robin gushed, wanting to believe she'd lied to him. 'She hates having to work and living in that poky flat in Mumbles after the house in Caswell.'

'On the other hand, you two were always at it like rabbits. And Ems was always complaining how careless you were.'

Knowing it was more likely that Emily was pregnant than not, Robin reached for the whisky bottle again. 'Even if I don't marry her, she hasn't a bean so I'll have to keep her and the kid. And after all the money Pops has laid out on me lately, he'll go ballistic.'

'Has Ems threatened to take you to court for maintenance?'

Robin stood back and studied the table. 'No, I told you, she expects me to marry her. I don't suppose you know anyone who can help?'

'Like who?' she questioned suspiciously.

'Like one of those women you read about in the papers. The kind girls visit when they have a problem,' he suggested coyly.

'The same kind who hit the headlines when they kill a girl.' She shook her head. 'You really should have been more careful. But then that was never easy with Ems. When she came around with us she was always stripping off at the drop of a hat.' Taking the whisky bottle from him just as he was about to fill his glass for the fourth time, she stared at him thoughtfully.

'Why are you looking at me like that?' he snapped.

'Can you be one hundred per cent certain that this baby is yours?'

'You said it yourself, everyone's dropped Ems; she hasn't seen anyone else in months.' He snatched the bottle back.

'Mums and Pops are away this weekend.'

'That's why I invited Ems to lunch on Sunday. She was moaning that I never bring her here any more.'

'Not lunch, Robin. A party, we'll round up some people and invite her to stay over tomorrow night.'

'None of the girls will come if they know Ems will be here.'

'But the boys will.' She refilled her glass.

'I can't see how that will help.'

She thought rapidly. She had an idea, but she knew Robin wouldn't like it and it might not work. But if it did . . . 'First things first, Robin, you need to find out if she is pregnant.'

'And how do you propose I do that? Ask Pops to stay so he can examine her?'

'Of course not. I'll talk to her.'

'And you think she'll tell you after you've cut her for almost a year?' he sneered.

'We were close. And, as I said, she could never keep a secret once she'd had a couple of drinks. But we'd better make it look like a real party. Invite the old crowd, that boy with red hair . . .'

'Thompson.'

'That's the one.' The only thing Angie could recall about Thompson was that he'd had the most enormous crush on Emily.

'And if she tells you she really is up the duff?'

'We'll cross that bridge when we come to it.'

'I suppose even if it's bad news at least I'd know where I am with her. You're a brick, Angie. Thanks.'

'Phone,' she prompted.

'We'll need some girls and if they know Ems is coming . . .'

'I won't tell them until after they arrive. Then, if anyone cuts Ems or is foul to her, it will give her all the more reason to drink and me the chance to worm the truth out of her.' She picked up the cue and returned it to the rack. Robin went into the hall.

Emily had been her closest friend and as a consequence knew more about her than was desirable in view of the Murton Davieses' fall from grace. She hadn't been comfortable with Robin's refusal to ditch Emily or Emily's insistence on remaining in Swansea. There was nothing quite so embarrassing as meeting someone who presumed on old friendship when that friendship no longer existed. And Robin was right about one thing; her boyfriend, Julian, didn't like her brother's liaison with Emily any more than their parents did. Much as he and his family adored her, they would never welcome the sister-in-law of Emily Murton Davies into the Pickering Jones family.

But – and it was a huge 'but' – if tomorrow's party went according to her plan, Emily would have to leave town and they'd never move in the same social circles again.

Robin looked in on her from the doorway. 'Thompson's coming and bringing a couple of friends.'

'Good.'

'I'd better get back to it.'

'The more the merrier,' she called after him, as he returned to the telephone.

'Jack, they're beautiful.'

'Real gold and sapphires,' he said proudly.

Helen kissed him. 'Could you afford them?'

'No, but I did. Put them on.'

'They'll look wonderful with my dressing gown,' she joked.

'They'd look better without it.'

'I'll reserve that fashion show for our bedroom.' She kissed him again before slipping the plain gold studs from her ears and replacing them with the sapphires. 'Help me with the necklace.'

As he fastened the clasp, she slid the ring on to her finger. 'It fits.'

'I remembered your size.' He took her hand and fastened the bracelet around her wrist. 'I told you I'd give you a reward if the meal was good.'

'You did,' she smiled, 'but I wasn't expecting anything like this. Thank you.'

'You can thank me properly later.'

'Would you like another piece of chocolate cake?'

'No, it might interfere with the plans I've made.' Picking up the tray she'd loaded with their dishes, he carried it into the kitchen. 'Leave those,' he said, as she began to run a sink full of water. 'I'll do them in the morning.'

'You?' She looked at him in surprise.

'Yes, me, I'll have nothing else to do. I was hoping you could take some time off.'

'I have, two weeks.' Untying the apron from her waist, she hung it on the back of the door. 'Dad said you can go back to the warehouse whenever you want. You can talk to him about it tomorrow night.'

'I'm not sure I want to go back.'

'You want to do something else?' She followed him into the living room.

'I've had two and half years of taking orders. That's more than any man should put up with.' He sat on the sofa facing the fire.

'Working for my father wouldn't be like being in the army.'

'I know, sweetheart.' He slipped his arm around her

shoulders as she nestled close to him. 'But with Katie married to him . . .'

'They're happy.'

'Can't you see it's all too neat and convenient? Me married to you, your father married to my sister. I don't want a job that's reliant on family charity.'

'You were good in the warehouse. The stockroom manager said you were one of the best boys he's ever had working under him. He's been looking forward to you coming back.'

'Anyone can put stock out in a warehouse, Helen.'

'Then what do you want to do?'

'Spend all the time I can with you, while looking around to see what else is on offer. I'll find something.'

'I don't doubt you will. And if whatever it is doesn't work out, you can always go back to the warehouse.'

'Perhaps.' He nuzzled her ear. 'When are you going to tell me about the party tomorrow night?'

'Party—' Her eyes blazed as she moved away from him. 'Martin said something, didn't he? And he promised he wouldn't. I'll kill him.'

'It wasn't Marty, it was you.'

'Me!'

'You just said I could talk to your father tomorrow night, you wouldn't have invited him without everyone else.'

'Oh.' Anger deflated, she moved close to him again. 'You don't mind, do you?'

'No, sweetheart, not as long as you've kept the next two weeks free. This evening's reminded me just how much I like being married to you.'

Chapter Four

'Those look even better than they smell.' Martin glanced around the kitchen door at the trays of cheese straws, oyster patties, miniature Cornish pasties, and choux cream and chocolate buns that Lily had spent all morning baking.

'Thank you.' Lily recalled the night before and gave him a quick, self-conscious smile. 'You were up early.'

'The car needed servicing and I couldn't sleep. You looked so peaceful I was afraid I'd disturb you if I stayed in bed.'

'I could have taken a little disturbance.'

'Can I take that as permission to do just that on some future occasion?'

'We'll discuss it when you're clean.' She wrinkled her nose at his grease-spattered and oil-stained overalls.

'I don't even get to sample anything,' he complained, eyeing the trays.

'I'll feed you two of anything you want on condition you stay that side of the door.'

'Fine way to treat me after I've spent all morning working on the car you ride round in.'

'Is there any oil left in your car engine or did you pour it all over yourself, Martin?' Sam peered over his shoulder.

'Don't you ever knock?'

'I heard you talking as I came up the stairs.' Sam stared at the trays. 'Oh my! And all I was hoping for was a slice of apple flan.'

'And that's all you're getting,' Lily warned. 'Marty?'

'You can put one of those pasties in my mouth.'

'Wonderful, he gets fed and I have to beg for yesterday's leftovers,' Sam complained. Martin demolished the pasty Lily held out to him in two bites.

'You can eat all you want, Sam,' Lily slapped his wrist as he reached for the nearest tray, 'tonight, at Helen and Jack's.'

'More please,' Martin mumbled through a full mouth. 'A cheese straw this time.'

'Want me to get that?' Sam asked, as the doorbell rang.

'Please. I'd better have a bath before I contaminate any more of the house.' Munching a mouthful of cheese flavoured pastry, Martin headed for the stairs as Lily attacked a greasy finger mark he'd left on the kitchen door with a cloth and neat Quix.

'Lunch will be ready in half an hour,' Lily called after him, 'so don't start reading in the bath.'

'I won't.'

'And don't you dare touch any more paintwork until you've washed your hands.'

'Turned out bossy, hasn't she?' Sam said to someone behind him. He moved and Lily stared, dumbfounded.

'Think she recognises me.' Brian Powell nudged Sam with his elbow.

'It's been a long time,' Sam mocked. 'Over two and half years – Jack and Helen's wedding.'

'Sorry I couldn't make yours,' Brian apologised to Lily.

'Thank you for your present.' The phrase 'speak of the devil and he appears' sprang to mind, as she recalled the conversation she'd had with Judy only the night before. 'The towels were just what we needed.' She pulled him into the kitchen. 'This is such a surprise, but it's lovely to see you. Martin will be thrilled. He's been complaining that he hasn't heard from you in months.' She hugged him and he kissed her cheek.

'I see you were expecting me,' Brian joked, indicating the trays of food.

'These are for Jack's homecoming party tonight.'

'When did he get back?'

'Last night.' She handed him a chair. 'Sit down; I was just about to make a meal. You will join us?'

'If this is any indication of what's on the menu, I'd love to.'

'Great,' Sam moaned. 'He comes back after years away and gets an instant invitation while you make your lodger, who pays his rent every week without fail, beg for crumbs from your table.'

'If you made yourself useful instead of grumbling, Sam, I'd invite you as well.' Lily pulled down the flap on the kitchen cabinet and stacked the trays of food inside.

'I'm putting the kettle on even as I speak.' Sam went to the stove.

Lily pushed a casserole dish into the oven and switched it on. 'So, what are you doing in Swansea, Brian? Are you down for a couple of days, or longer? Are you still working in London?'

'That's a lot of questions. Do you want me to answer them in order?'

'Still the same old, aggravating Brian.'

'Not quite.' He winced as he lowered himself on to a chair. 'I've been invalided out of the Met.'

'What happened?' Sam set three cups on the table.

'I had an argument with a man carrying a switchblade. I lost.'

'But you are all right?' Lily sat next to him.

'As you see.' Brian smiled, but Lily could detect pain lines around his eyes and mouth.

'Couldn't they find you a desk job?' Sam poured boiling water into the teapot.

'They offered, I turned it down. After three years in London I wanted to come home.'

'So, you're back in Swansea.' Sam set the teapot on the table.

'Not as a copper. You know the force, they like their officers fighting fit.'

'What will you do?'

'Take it easy, see a few mates, admire their wives, see if I can entice them away,' Brian winked at Lily, 'drink a couple of beers. But that's enough about me,' he added, closing the subject. 'How about filling me in on what's been happening here since I last heard from Martin. If Jack's only just got back he must have served more than two years.'

As Lily told him about Jack's extended National Service, injuries and return, Katie's pregnancy, Helen's career as a buyer in her father's warehouse, the changes she and Martin had made to the house, she noticed the one person Brian didn't ask about was Judy. But with Sam sitting in the room, she didn't dare mention her, and from the look on Sam's face, she wasn't the only one who remembered how close Brian and Judy had once been.

'Sam has a point, Judy,' Joy suggested mildly, as she lifted a noisy, wriggling Billy from her lap and set him on the floor next to a wooden toy truck filled with plastic bricks. 'You have been engaged for over eighteen months.'

'Exactly, which is why I can't see that a couple more months will make much difference. The salons—'

'Are doing fine,' Joy said. 'We have good girls in every one of them and provided we keep paying them well and treating them fairly, they're not going to be in a hurry to move on.'

'But we could open more,' Judy began heatedly.

'I was happy with one salon for eighteen years; you've opened ten in the last two and half.'

'They bring in a good income, which we both need.'

'You can only spend so much money in a lifetime.' Joy looked fondly down at her son who was running his truck along the edge of the hearthrug.

'It will soon go, between Billy's education and the house I want to buy . . .'

'You've seen a house you want to buy?'

'Not yet,' Judy conceded, 'but I will want a house one day and they are expensive.'

'And when the time comes, Sam will get a mortgage. And as for Billy,' Joy smiled as Billy looked up at her, 'the state schools were good enough for you and they will be for him.'

'Billy might go on to university.'

'Not for seventeen years.'

'I'd still like to pay my share of any deposit Sam and I put on a house.'

'So you and Sam have been talking about houses?'

'We haven't,' Judy retorted irritably.

'I see.' Joy sat back in her chair. 'Do you want a full church wedding with a big reception or a small affair in a register office?'

'I haven't a clue.' Judy chewed her lip. 'Damn Sam, he knows I hate threats and ultimatums.'

'He doesn't strike me as the kind who would make them lightly.' Joy looked at her daughter. 'Are you sure you love him?'

'Of course I'm sure.' Judy didn't want to elaborate after Lily's reaction to her definition of 'everyday love'.

'Then why the reluctance to set a date?' Joy questioned gently.

'Because Sam is pushing me into it when I'm not ready.'

'You're not making much sense, Judy.'

'You and Roy carried on for years before you were married, and that's not meant nastily,' Judy added hastily, realising how her comment could be misconstrued. 'In fact, I rather admired you for it. Independent successful businesswoman able to keep her clients and lover happy while successfully bringing up and grooming intelligent, talented daughter to take over from her,' she joked.

'Thank you for the compliment, but my biggest regret is that I was too stupid to give your father the divorce he wanted years ago, when you were a baby.'

'Really?' Judy questioned seriously.

'Really,' Joy reiterated solemnly. 'Given how fond you are of Roy and he is of you, the three – four,' she handed Billy back a brick he had given her, 'of us missed out on years of what could have been happy family life.'

'Brum . . . Brum . . .'

Joy bent down and tickled Billy as he made car noises. 'There might even have been more like this one.'

'There still could be.' Judy opened her arms, as her brother headed towards her.

'Perhaps.' Joy fell serious again. 'If you are one hundred per cent sure that you love Sam and he loves you, and you want to spend the rest of your life with him, then marry him, Judy, and my advice is the sooner the better. But if you have any doubts, any at all . . .'

'Which I haven't.'

'Mam!' Billy rolled his truck back to Joy.

'Then I can't understand why we are having this conversation. You clever darling.' Joy scooped her son into her arms, as he pulled on her skirt to show her the pillar he'd made out of the bricks.

'Don't you resent staying at home with Billy? You must miss running the business . . .'

'Miss what?' Joy hugged Billy. He threw his arms around her neck and planted a sticky kiss on her cheek. 'The smell of peroxide, hair lacquer and perming solutions; standing on my feet all day trying to soothe cantankerous old women who want to look like Hollywood stars while griping about the time it takes to set their hair.' She wiped Billy's mouth with her handkerchief before he dribbled over her blouse. 'I wouldn't go back to that for all the tea in China.'

'How's my favourite son?' Roy opened the door and strode towards Billy, who screamed with delight at the sight of him. Scooping the toddler from Joy's lap, he tossed him, squealing with laughter, into the air. After he caught him, he bent his head to Judy's and kissed her cheek. 'And my favourite stepdaughter?'

'I'm fine.' Judy felt strangely embarrassed as she intercepted a look between Roy and her mother, a loving intimate glance that spoke volumes about their marriage. She rose to her feet. 'Time I was off.'

'Stay and eat with us,' her mother offered. 'It won't be much, just toasted sandwiches.'

'I want to check on the Morriston salon.'

'It will still be standing after lunch.'

'Please stay, we hardly see anything of you,' Roy pressed.

'Perhaps some other time.' Taking Billy from Roy, she kissed him goodbye.

'You work too hard,' Roy commented, walking her to the door. 'And it's not just us who are complaining, Sam—'

'Sam talks to you about me?' Judy whirled round.

'Only to say nice things. You don't mind, do you? After all, he will soon be my step son-in-law.'

'Yes.' Judy looked back at her mother as she opened the front door. 'Yes, Roy, he will.'

'Thanks for the meal, Lily.' Sam left the table.

'When are you and Mike going to invite Lily and me down to your place to sample your cooking?' Martin asked.

'The next evening we're both free and off shift.'

'And we'll be eating what exactly?' Lily questioned.

'The fish and chip shop in Hanover Street does a great battered cod and chips.'

'Judging by the number of times you eat here, I'm surprised you know,' Martin retorted.

'A man builds up an appetite pounding the freezing winter beat in Swansea. Not that a grease monkey who works in a nice, dry, comfortable garage would know anything about the effects cold, rain, damp and snow have on a man.'

'I'll expect afters as well as fish and chips.' Lily stacked their empty dessert bowls.

'I'll get you the cake of the day from Eynon's.' Sam turned to Brian. 'Great seeing you again, mate. You'll be at Jack's tonight?'

'Hardly, I'm not invited.'

'Only because Jack and Helen don't know you're here.' Martin handed Lily the empty custard jug. 'You have to come, it'll be great, a reunion of the basement flat boys.'

'One of us still lives there.' Sam glanced at his watch. 'If I don't get a move on, I'll never get to my mother's and back in time to pick up my missus. See you, Brian. Thanks again for the meal, Lily. Next time I promise I'll wash up.'

'If I thought you wouldn't take advantage, I would say come again.' She carried on clearing the table.

'Sam's married?' Brian asked, as Martin ran a sink full of hot water.

'Engaged, has been for eighteen months.' Martin caught Lily's eye and remembered that it had been serious enough between Judy and Brian for Brian to follow her up to London, only for their relationship to end when Judy had returned to Swansea a few months later. 'I'll wash, you dry,' he suggested to Lily.

'I've a better idea; you take Brian into the living room while I wash the dishes and leave them to drain. When I've finished, I'll make us coffee.'

'That's hardly fair,' Brian protested.

'I'll enjoy the peace and quiet. Go on,' Lily ordered, hoping Martin would have the sense to tell Brian about Judy and Sam. 'Out of my kitchen, both of you, now.'

'Sam is right,' Brian said, when he and Martin were in the living room.

'About what?' Martin turned on the gas fire.

'Lily, she's turned out bossy.'

'So you'll stay over?'

'Yes, please.' Emily glanced around the shop floor to check a supervisor wasn't watching her. She had been reprimanded twice for talking to Robin in the store and didn't want another dressing down.

'I'll pick you up around eight, you'll be ready?'

She nodded and moved towards a woman who was hovering at the lower end of the counter.

'Wear something special. That red dress with the low neck.'

She smiled assent. It was as much as she could do to keep from laughing aloud as she recited the store's approved opening gambit: 'Can I help you, madam?'

After almost a year of being frozen out by her old friends, she was finally back in with them. A party – Robin had invited her to a party – and he had said that it had been Angela's idea to ask her to stay overnight. She couldn't wait to tell Larry.

'You and Lily have given me a welcome fit for a king, but you must be wondering why I'm here.'

Martin offered Brian a cigarette. 'Old friends don't need an excuse to call.'

'I have a proposition to put to you.' Brian took the cigarette and flicked his lighter, lighting Martin's cigarette before his own. 'I don't know if I ever mentioned my . . .' He hesitated.

'Your?' Martin looked at him in amusement.

'My family's a bit complicated – my cousin and half brother-in-law would probably be the most accurate description.'

'I didn't know you had a half sister to have a half brother-in-law.'

'I have a half sister and a half brother, both years older than me, but Ronnie isn't married to my half sister, the half sister he married died years ago when I was a baby. Anyway, he's married to my cousin now.' He frowned at the confused look on Martin's face. 'That probably didn't make sense.'

'None,' Martin concurred cheerfully.

'You don't have to agree with everything I say.'

'I won't if you try to explain your family again.'

'The ones I want to tell you about are Powell and Ronconi.'

'The garage people! That Powell is you?' Martin exclaimed. 'The ones who own the biggest garage chain in South Wales?'

'Before you get too excited, that Powell is my cousin, not half brother. Anyway, to cut a long story short, my family is the kind that rallies round when one of us hits trouble. After I was invalided out of the Met, Will and Ronnie came to see me—'

'Will and Ronnie being Powell and Ronconi?'

'I just said they were,' Brian reprimanded. 'Pay attention! They suggested that I might like to manage a car dealership they were in the process of buying in Swansea.'

'Good God!'

'Yes, me, the car salesman.' Brian made a wry face. 'I never saw myself selling anything, but I said I'd give it try and as it's Fords . . .'

'The cars will flood out without any effort on your part.'

'That's what they're hoping. They're putting up half the money; the other half is part my compensation and part bank loan I've taken out. Now, I'm going to need a mechanic and I thought, who do I know who loves dirt enough to spend half his life under a bonnet covered in grease and muck?'

'You want me to run the service and maintenance side for you?' Martin tried to rein in his enthusiasm long enough to consider the implications of Brian's offer, but it was impossible. Ever since the morning he'd received the letter offering him an apprenticeship he'd dreamed of opening his own business.

'To be honest, no,' Brian prevaricated. 'When I said that the other half of the money was coming from my compensation and a bank loan, I exaggerated. I'm looking for a partner not an employee. Powell and

Ronconi have bought the garage, we have a dealership, showroom, office, petrol pumps, yard and two large workshops, but the workshops will be empty. The mechanic who is running the service side at the moment is retiring and he has sold his tools to his nephew who is setting up in Carmarthen. So if you want to manage the service and maintenance side, the first thing you'll have to do is equip both workshops because all you'll be left with is the inspection pits.'

'There'll be no tools at all?'

'None. I won't lie to you, Marty, it won't be easy. From the figures we've compiled, you'll have to lay out the best part of a thousand pounds on equipment and that's without paying your share of the loan on the buildings. Of course, you'll get to keep all the profits from that side of the business, but it's going to be a while before you recoup your outlay, let alone make anything, and I won't be able to help you financially. There'll be staff to pay. I'll need at least one other salesman and a girl to run the office and I doubt if you'll be able to cope with everything on the repair and servicing side on your own, so you will have to find enough to pay one apprentice, two might be better. And it will take time to get everything up and running. My cousin warned it always does after a change of ownership. I've some costings based on other Powell and Ronconi garages. Two years and we should break even; three and we'll be making a modest profit. Five, we won't be rolling in it but we will own the garage outright and be making more for ourselves than we could expect to earn working for anyone else.'

'How much money are you looking for besides the tools?' Martin questioned cautiously.

'Another thousand pounds before we break even, but I reckon you could finance two apprentices out of that.'

'Two thousand in total!'

'Not all upfront but don't forget you won't be bringing in much of a wage for the first couple of years.'

Martin's hopes sank. 'Thank you for thinking of me, Brian, but I couldn't come up with anything like that kind of money.'

'Yes, you could.' Lily stood in the doorway holding a tray. 'Brian's offering you a chance to make your dream come true, Marty. You'll be working for yourself, partnering a friend you trust. I can't thank you enough for thinking of us, Brian.' Lily set the tray of coffee and biscuits on the table in front of them.

'Be realistic, Lily, where would I get two thousand pounds?'

'We have savings.' She poured the coffee and handed Brian a cup.

'Last time I looked there was nearer two hundred than two thousand pounds in our savings account.'

'There's the money Auntie Norah left me.'

'Oh no, we're not touching that,' Martin protested heatedly.

'And if that's not enough we'll mortgage the house,' she continued blithely.

'Over my dead body,' he declared vigorously. 'And if you were eavesdropping long enough—'

'I was not eavesdropping. I just happened to overhear a few things Brian said as I came in.'

'Did you hear him say that there wouldn't be any profits for the first two years?'

Recalling just how much money her aunt had left her, she pushed all thoughts of her pregnancy to the back of her mind. This was a chance in a million and she was determined Martin wasn't going to lose out. 'We'll manage. We have the rent money Sam and Mike pay . . .'

'And, if they move out?'

'We'll rent to someone else. There's never been any problem finding lodgers, with the housing shortage. And we could turn the top floor into a flat. There are four rooms up there. It wouldn't take much to convert one into a kitchen and another into a bathroom.'

'It would cost a fortune.'

'We'll borrow it from the investments Auntie Norah left us and make it back in rent money within six months, just as we did when we had a proper bathroom and kitchen installed in the basement.'

'Whether you come in with me or not, any chance of me renting the flat?' Brian asked.

'There.' Lily smiled triumphantly, sugaring Martin's coffee and handing it to him. 'We've already found another lodger and one who wouldn't mind sharing our kitchen and bathroom until we organise a conversion.'

'You really want me to do this?' Martin asked Lily. 'Just after I've been promoted to foreman?'

'Foreman, congratulations.' Brian looked uneasily from Martin to Lily. 'The last thing I want to do is cause an argument between you two. Foreman's a good position.'

'But it's not like owning your own business, which is all Marty's talked about ever since I've known him.' Lily looked intently at her husband. 'You could go your whole life without getting another offer like this. You'd be insane to turn it down.'

'You really think I should take it?'

'Absolutely.' Lily sat on the arm of his chair.

'It would mean putting some things on the back burner, including what we talked about last night.'

She looked down at her hands wondering how much longer she could keep her pregnancy from him. Hopefully long enough for him to sign all the legally binding papers. 'I know.'

'All right, but I have conditions. First, I make an appointment with the bank manager and I'll raise a loan. Me, not you,' he glared at Lily. 'I am not touching your inheritance from your aunt and the deeds to this house stay locked in the bank vault.'

'The money from my aunt and the deeds to the house are as much yours as mine.'

'I am not touching the money or the deeds,' he repeated sternly, looking her in the eye. 'And I don't want you breathing a word of this to anyone until I get the loan.'

'Yes, oh masterful one.'

Brian exploded with laughter. 'You've got yourself a handful there, Marty.'

'You don't know the half of it.'

Brian extended his hand. 'Partners.'

'If I get the loan,' Martin qualified. 'Partners.' He shook Brian's hand. 'And you'll stay over tonight and come to Jack's with us this evening?'

'I'd like to, thank you.' Brian thought for a moment. 'Is Jack going back to the warehouse?'

'He wasn't keen on the idea when I spoke to him last night.'

'Don't suppose . . .'

'He's no mechanic,' Martin warned.

'But he might make a salesman.'

'He might at that.'

'I'll ask him.' Brian rose to his feet. 'Do you mind if I use the telephone to let my family know that I won't be returning to Pontypridd tonight?'

'It's still in the hall,' Lily said. 'Sam and Mike pay the bill as they need it for work. Looks like we'll have to revise that arrangement once you two become businessmen.' She kissed Martin's cheek. 'Congratulations.'

'I haven't got the bank loan yet,' he warned.

'But you will. I just know it.'

'Stunning,' Judy complimented, Emily walked into the living room in a strapless, red satin, ballerina length evening dress and black silk stole.

'Party in my fiancé's house.' Emily glowed with excitement, dropping an overnight case next to the door. 'His sister has invited me to stay over.' She hoped the mention of Robin's sister would make the arrangement sound more respectable. 'I have no idea what time I'll be back tomorrow.'

'Does it matter?' Judy smiled. 'Enjoy yourself.'

‘I will.’ Emily drew back the curtain and looked out of the window. A car horn sounded outside. ‘That’s Robin.’ She picked up the case and ran to the door. ‘Have a good weekend,’ she called back as an afterthought, before slamming the door.

‘I’ll try,’ Judy murmured disconsolately and went into the bedroom. Kicking off her shoes, she wandered into the bathroom, put the plug in the bath and turned on the hot tap before returning to her bedroom and opening her wardrobe door. Emily had looked so glamorous that most of her evening frocks looked dowdy by comparison. She flicked through the rail before settling on a dark green taffeta.

Back in the bathroom she tipped a handful of salts into the water, stripped off and lowered herself into the water. Despite all the duty visits she had made to the salons that afternoon, she had spent more of the day thinking about Sam than the business. Her mother was right, if she loved him there was no reason for her not to marry him and soon – and if she didn’t . . .

She lay back and allowed the hot water to wash over her. If she didn’t, what the hell had she been doing with him for the last eighteen months?

‘The beer was delivered this afternoon, thank you.’ Jack took John’s overcoat and hung it in the hall cupboard.

‘Katie’s idea, not mine.’ John watched Helen settle his wife into an easy chair with a cushion at her back.

‘I thought you might have come with Martin and Lily.’

‘We travel everywhere alone these days in case we have to make a dash to the nursing home.’

‘Helen said the baby could come at any time.’

‘A week to go according to the midwife.’ John gave his wife another anxious look. ‘I’m not so sure. Does Katie look well to you?’

‘Tired,’ Jack said, ‘but that’s only to be expected, isn’t it?’

‘I suppose so.’

John looked so concerned, Jack searched for something reassuring to say. 'Katie's always been stronger than she looks.'

'I hope you're right.'

'Glass of beer.'

'Yes, please,' John nodded, as he joined Katie in the living room.

'Surprise.' Martin pushed open the front door and walked in with Lily, Brian, Roy, Joy and Billy, whose head was lolling sleepily on Roy's shoulder.

Helen rushed over to them. 'I've a bed all ready made up for Billy upstairs. I've piled bolsters around the middle so he won't roll anywhere.'

'Thank you, Helen, that's thoughtful.' Joy took Billy from Roy.

'Third door on the right,' Helen whispered, following Joy up the stairs.

'Good God, Jack, where did they change you?' Brian looked his old friend up and down. 'You used to be such a skinny little runt, I had to be careful not to tread on you when I walked around the flat.'

'One more comment like that and I won't pour the beer I was about to offer you.'

'I see you've picked up more cheek too.'

'Come down from the Smoke especially to insult me?' Jack jibed.

'Of course. Couldn't risk you getting too big for your boots, now could I?'

As Jack went into the kitchen to get the beer, Brian accompanied Martin and Lily into the living room. 'Helen,' he kissed her cheek as she returned from upstairs, 'you look more beautiful than ever. Any time you want to run away from your husband, give me the nod and we'll go off together.'

'Not when I've just got him back. It is good to see you, Brian. Thank you for coming.'

'Thank you for allowing me to gatecrash.' He glanced round the room.

'Looking for someone?' Helen asked.

'No, the old crowd are all here.'

'Except Judy and she's always late for everything these days.'

'Any reason.'

'Haven't you heard? She's running the salons now.'

'Salons,' he repeated in surprise.

'She and her mother own eleven.'

'Good for her. They must keep her busy.'

'They do,' Helen agreed, as he looked round again.

'You have a beautiful house and fantastic views.'

'Thank you.'

'Don't suppose you'd like to show me round,' Brian asked Jack, as he carried a tray of glasses and bottles of beer into the room.

Jack looked at Brian in surprise. Martin gave him an almost imperceptible nod. 'Just as soon as I get rid of these.'

'We're going to be late,' Sam grumbled, staring out of the lounge window of Judy's flat.

'I know.' She opened her bedroom door and twirled around in front of him. 'But I hoped you'd say the wait was worth it.'

He walked towards her. 'You look good enough to eat.'

'Can you eat me when you bring me home? I won't mind you messing my hair or smudging my lipstick then.'

'Promises, promises.'

'Emily's away for the night.'

'Is she now?' His smile reached his eyes.

'Yes, and she has no idea what time she'll be back tomorrow.'

'You'll be lonely.'

'And you, I saw Mike when I visited the town salon this morning. He told me you'd offloaded your shift on to him tonight.'

'Did he now?' Sam's smile broadened. 'Is that an invitation for me to stay over?'

'I was thinking more of coffee on the way home.'

'Why stop at coffee?'

'Maybe a little more than just coffee.' Her mouth went dry, as she realised what he was thinking.

'You promised you'd have a date for me.'

'After I've spoken to my mother.' She conveniently forgot that she'd called in on her earlier.

'Then you can give it me when I bring you home.' Taking her mohair stole from her, he dropped a kiss on to her naked shoulder before draping it around her.

'You know what Robin is like at a party, Ems. He and the boys always hole up in the billiards room.' Angela went to her dressing table, picked up her atomiser and sprayed the toilette water she had bought on her last visit to France behind her ears.

'I know.' Emily blotted her eyes with a handkerchief. 'It's just that – well, you know how foul everyone's been to me . . .'

'That's why Robin and I threw this party to get you back in with the crowd.'

'So they can cut me like Cicely just did.'

'Cicely's a bitch,' Angela commiserated. 'I'm here, aren't I?' Replacing the atomiser, she went to her bedside cabinet. Opening it, she lifted out a bottle of brandy, poured two stiff measures, and handed Emily one. 'Come downstairs.'

'You won't leave me.'

'Not for one minute.'

'And Robin?'

'I'll do what I can to entice the boys out of the billiards room, but you know what they're like when they get together. Come on.' Angela picked up Emily's overnight case from the foot of her bed and carried it into the spare room. Emily trailed behind her, still dabbing her eyes. 'I hope you'll be comfortable in here.'

'Yes,' Emily mumbled tearfully.

'It's important to keep up appearances. I know you and Robin are engaged but with a house full, we don't want to risk any gossip. That's why I asked Mrs Jones to put you in here. Robin's only next door, he can slip in and out without anyone noticing.'

'Thank you.' Emily's eyes shone with gratitude.

'Now drink that down and I'll get you another one.'

Chapter Five

'You'll love it in the nursing home, the staff are marvellous and nothing is too much trouble for them. Billy's birth there was wonderful, so calm and relaxed it was a completely different experience to having Judy in hospital,' Joy confided to Katie.

'Medicine has advanced in the last twenty odd years, love,' Roy reminded her gently.

'Seeing as men know absolutely nothing about having babies, you're not allowed into this conversation,' Joy rebuked.

Not in the least offended, Roy wandered off, beer glass in hand.

'So how are you keeping?' Joy whispered to Katie. 'Not that I don't know exactly how you're feeling. Between the backaches, the cramps, the baby kicking lumps out of your insides every time you try to eat, the heartburn, the varicose veins . . .'

'I haven't had the varicose veins,' Katie smiled.

'Lucky girl, but I'll talk to you again when you are having your second.'

'I feel incredibly well,' Katie insisted. 'But then John hardly lets me lift a finger in the house. Mrs Jones does most of the housework and prepares the evening meal, and we eat out most Friday and Saturday nights.'

'Lucky you. I wish Roy and I could go out more than once in a blue moon.'

'If ever you need a babysitter . . .'

'Between Judy and the neighbours I'm never short of a babysitter. Just a husband who works regular hours. I'd forgotten what a bind police shift work can be. Now where was I?' Joy thought for a moment. 'I find it difficult to talk to anyone over two years old these days. I'm so used to spending all my time with Billy, I get the urge to show everyone picture books or talk about Moo Cows and Bunny Rabbits. So beware, your brain could go the same way.'

'You were telling me about the nursing home,' Katie prompted shyly.

'Of course I was, it's a splendid place, but be sure you allow the staff to wait on you hand and foot after the baby's born. Make the most of your ten days there because, once you get home, between seeing to the baby and John, and running the house, you won't have a minute to yourself.'

'I'm looking forward to that part.' Katie set her orange juice on the coffee table.

'You're not worried about the actual birth, are you?' Joy asked.

'Just a bit. You hear such terrible stories.'

'Invented and spread by old wives who enjoy scaring young girls because it makes them feel important. Thank you, Helen.' Joy took the bottle of Pony Helen handed her and poured it into her glass. 'I won't say having a baby is easy because it's not, they don't call it labour for nothing.'

'Is there a lot of pain?' Katie asked apprehensively.

Joy thought for a moment before answering. 'Yes, but it varies enormously from one woman to another. It's also a peculiar pain, it hurts at the time but once you're holding your baby for the first time you forget all about it.'

'And that's how you felt after Billy was born.' Helen sat on the arm of the sofa.

'And Judy. If I hadn't forgotten what it had been like to give birth to her, I might not have had Billy.'

'And you honestly can't recall the pain now,' Helen pressed.

'Only the good bits,' Joy asserted. 'Holding Judy and Billy for the first time, seeing what they looked like after spending so many months wondering whether I was going to have a girl or a boy. It's a feeling like nothing else I've ever experienced and impossible to explain, other than to say it's wonderful.'

'Then Billy's not going to be your last baby?' Katie ventured.

'I think having Billy was pushing it a bit at my age, not that I'd mind having another one,' Joy said quickly, 'but I think it's time you girls did your bit to repopulate the world. Katie's baby needs a few playmates and now Jack's home . . .'

'Excuse me, I have to check there's enough food laid out in the dining room.' Helen left the sofa and went to the door.

'Trust me to put my foot in it,' Joy murmured guiltily.

'Now Jack's home I'm sure they'll try again,' Katie sympathised.

'I hope you're right.' Joy looked through the open door into the dining room. Jack had slipped his arm around Helen's waist, as he carried on talking to Martin and John. 'They look happy together.'

'Helen was worried that Jack would have forgotten her. I told her there was no chance of that but I'm not sure she believed me.'

'From the way she's looking at him, she does now.' Joy took an oyster pattie from a plate Lily was handing round. 'These are good, you must give me the recipe.'

'I will.' Lily glanced at the door. 'I hear Judy.'

'At last. I was worried she had stopped off to buy another salon on the way here,' Joy quipped, and not entirely humorously.

'You persuaded Brian to stay then.' Sam looked from Martin to Brian, who was gazing intently at Judy. To his annoyance, he realised Judy was staring back.

'You look as beautiful as ever, Judy.' Brian found his

voice, sensing the sudden silence had something to do with him and Judy.

Acutely aware of Sam's grip tightening on her arm, Judy replied, 'I didn't expect to see you back in Swansea, Brian.'

'You know me, a sucker for punishment.' He forced a smile, as he glanced from Judy to Sam, who looked as though he was trying to weld himself to her. 'Still breaking men's hearts?' The flippant remark fell like lead shot into the heavy atmosphere.

'I hope not,' Sam answered caustically. 'Judy and I are engaged – and soon to be married,' he added, giving Judy an uncompromising look.

'So where's Julian tonight?' Thompson leered at Angela, as she topped up his glass of whisky.

'I haven't a clue,' she answered blithely.

'I thought you two were courting strong.'

'We are, when we're together,' she concurred.

'And when you're apart?' He flushed, as she gave him a dazzling smile.

'We go our own way. I'd find anything else stifling and you know how I hate being stifled.'

'I'd jump at the chance to find out.' Encouraged by her flirtatious smile he dared to run his fingers down her bare arm.

'I thought you were seeing Cicely.'

'Were being the operative word.'

'I'm sorry.'

'I'm not; she's a tease. Don't suppose you'd consider showing me around upstairs,' he suggested artfully. 'I've always wanted to see over this house.'

'You don't suppose right. But . . .' Angela eyed Emily who'd stuck to Robin like glue since he'd emerged from the billiards room, which was undoubtedly the reason why he was demanding that the boys return there with him.

'But,' he repeated, running his tongue suggestively over his lips as she turned back to him.

'I might change my mind if you are good.' She pulled him towards her by his tie. 'Very very good,' she whispered.

'And what do I have to do to be considered good?'

'Look after Ems for me.' She scowled at Robin, as he stalked out of the room leaving Emily fighting back tears.

Thompson followed her line of vision. 'She has nerve coming here, I'll give her that.'

'Have you spoken to her?' she asked. Emily turned her back on the room and looked out of the window.

'I said hello, which was more than most people did,' he retorted defensively.

'As you see from his absence, Robin's a pathetic host, so while I check on people's drinks, you,' she poked his chest, 'can start being good by being nice to Ems until I'm free.'

'And if I do, you'll reward me?'

'Possibly.'

Angela joined Emily at the window. Taking her by the hand she led her to Thompson. 'He'll look after you while I see to everyone's drinks.' She folded Emily's hand into Thompson's. 'Take this.' She handed Thompson a bottle of whisky. 'I'd hate for you or Ems to be thirsty.'

'I didn't have the chance to congratulate you and Sam earlier.' Brian had been waiting for an opportunity to speak to Judy ever since the embarrassing scene in the kitchen, so the minute he saw her walk into the empty dining room he followed.

'Thank you.' She looked into his eyes, a deep rich brown, intensely and overwhelmingly familiar even after the years they'd spent apart. He seemed taller than she remembered and she wondered if it was because he'd lost weight. Lily had said something about him being injured and not wanting to talk about it . . .

'I'd also like to apologise for some of the things I said

to you when we split up. My only defence is that I was angry, young and stupid at the time.'

'Both of us were.'

'But now we're grown-ups it's good to know that we can remain friends.'

'Is it?' Judy found it difficult to control her resentment. Since Brian had walked away from her almost three years ago on Swansea station, he had never once tried to contact her, never sending her as much as a Christmas card, although she knew full well that he sent them to Martin and Lily, Katie and John, and Helen and Jack. And now he dared to presume that they could remain friends!

'You haven't changed. I would have known you anywhere.' His eyes crinkled at the corners. 'Same green eyes, same red hair, same temper . . .'

'Temper,' she blazed, before realising he knew exactly how much the 'friends' remark had incensed her.

'Sam is obviously better at handling you than me. Martin mentioned you'd been engaged for eighteen months. We barely lasted a third of that time, probably a sixth if you take out the days and weeks we spent sulking and quarrelling. Do you remember?'

'I'm so busy these days, I can't remember what happened three weeks ago let alone three years,' she said loudly for Sam's benefit as he joined them.

'I hear you've become quite the entrepreneur.' Brian helped himself to a cheese straw. 'Helen told me you have eleven salons now.'

'My mother and I,' she corrected. 'We do.' She took the glass of orange juice Sam handed her and promptly abandoned it on the table to show him she resented his intrusion.

'Martin said you're moving back to Swansea permanently, Brian.' Sam slipped his arm proprietorially around Judy's shoulders.

'Yes,' Brian confirmed, reaching for another cheese

straw. 'Have you tried these?' He handed Judy one. 'They're delicious.'

'You're renting the top floor of Lily's house.' Sam watched Judy bite into the straw.

'Yes, we'll be housemates again. It will be like old times.' Brian was finding it increasingly difficult to remain pleasant in the face of the antagonistic looks Sam was sending his way.

'Not for long.' Sam squeezed Judy so hard she winced.

'Then the big day's imminent?'

'We're setting the date this weekend, aren't we, darling?'

'Mm, sorry, I wasn't listening.' Judy was furious with Sam for allowing his jealousy to show. She and Brian had been over long before she and Sam had gone out together.

'I said we're setting the date this weekend,' Sam repeated tersely.

She looked up and saw Brian watching her. His smile broadened and she had an uncontrollable urge to wipe the grin from his face and hurt him every bit as much as he had hurt her. 'Yes, we are,' she confirmed, sliding her hand around Sam's waist.

'So, what are you going to do in Swansea, Brian?' Sam asked.

'Open a laundry.'

'I didn't know you were a washerwoman.'

'There are a lot of things you don't know about me, Sam. Congratulations again to both of you, I hope you will both be very happy.'

'We will,' Sam declared forcefully.

'If you'll excuse me, I'd like to speak to Katie and John and wish them well with the baby. I haven't had a chance to talk to either of them all evening. And,' Brian lifted his eyebrows, 'they'll soon have a lot of nappies that will need washing.'

'Ems is plastered,' Thompson announced, as he walked

into the conservatory where Angela was mixing cocktails for an appreciative and tipsy audience.

'Since when have you joined a Temperance Society?' Cicely drawled. 'None of us are exactly sober.'

'The rest of us aren't lying flat on our faces under the dining-room table,' Thompson rejoined.

'I'll see to her. Take over here, Cicely.' Angela tossed Cicely the cocktail shaker before following Thompson into the dining room. He hadn't exaggerated. Emily was lying face down on the Turkish rug under the table. 'Roust Robin out of the billiards room.'

'My pleasure.'

Angela had turned Emily on to her back and pulled her out from beneath the table by the time Robin appeared.

'I should never have listened to you, Angie,' Robin groused. 'It was a stupid idea of yours to invite Ems. Everyone's cut her and, as if that's not enough, she's made a complete fool of herself.'

'Just give me a hand to get her out of here and into bed,' Angela ordered tartly.

Robin picked Emily up; slinging her over his shoulder, he hauled her up the stairs. 'There's no way she's sleeping in my room in this state,' he said unequivocally.

'I've put her in here.' Pushing past him, Angela opened a door.

'Mums' favourite guest room. She'll kill you if Ems throws up in here.'

'If Ems does, I'll get Mrs Jones to clean it up before Mums gets back.'

He tossed Emily on top of the bed. 'Did you find out if she is preggers?' he whispered, after glancing over his shoulder to make sure that no one had followed them up the stairs.

'I didn't get a chance.'

'You're bloody useless.'

'Give me a hand to undress her.'

'I'm not her bloody maid.'

'We can't leave her in what she's wearing, she'll ruin

it.' She turned Emily on to her side and unzipped her frock. 'Here, you hold her up and I'll pull it off.'

He did as she asked, watching as she hung the frock in the wardrobe. 'What am I going to do, Angie?' he questioned plaintively.

'See to our guests and not hide in the billiards room.'

'I meant about Ems.' He stared at Emily's bare midriff, imagined it ballooning, swelling . . .

'Leave her to me.'

'I haven't a clue which way to turn or what to do. I'm at the end of my tether . . .'

'And bleating.'

He continued to stare at Emily, hating her in a way he would have never believed possible a few days before. 'I'd do anything to get out of this bloody mess.'

'Anything?' Angela gazed coolly at him.

'Anything,' he repeated angrily, slamming the door as he left.

Angela unclipped Emily's suspenders and rolled her stockings from her legs. Emily continued to lie, limp and comatose, as Angela unhooked her suspender belt and bra and peeled them from her. Her knickers were a little more difficult. Switching off the main light, Angela left a small lamp burning on the dressing table. It shed little light and did nothing to dispel the shadows cast around the bed. Pulling the eiderdown out from underneath Emily, she covered her, hiding most of her hair under a pillow. She went to the door and looked back. Anyone entering the room would see that someone was in the bed, but they wouldn't see who until they turned down the eiderdown and, if everything went according to plan, by then it would be too late.

'Cyprus still hot and pretty?' Brian asked Jack, watching him open bottles of beer in the kitchen.

'I'd say bloody would be a better description than pretty.'

'I read the newspapers; you had a rough time.'

'Rough enough for me to want to forget it.' Jack's eyes were frosty. He refilled Brian's glass.

'We ran into trouble when I was posted there, but nothing like what's happening now. The worst things Martin and I came up against were women who wouldn't take no for an answer.'

'And where exactly did you and Marty meet these women, Brian?' Lily handed Jack half a dozen empty Babycham and Pony bottles.

'The Cypriot equivalent of the Pier ballroom.'

'Really?' she queried sceptically.

'We were under orders to visit there to further relations with the locals.'

'And what kind of relations would those be?' Lily pressed mercilessly.

Jack took advantage of their altercation to slip from the room. He went into the cloakroom and ran a sink full of cold water. Splashing it over his face, he looked into the mirror. The longer he was home, the easier it would become. People would eventually stop asking him what had happened in Cyprus and he'd be able to forget it. Put it behind him, hopefully for ever and, hopefully without Helen finding out about the one thing he wished had never happened.

'You are enough to try the patience of a saint.'

'And you are no bloody saint, are you, Judy?' Sam shouted. 'I saw the way Brian Powell looked at you tonight and the way you looked back at him.'

'What way?' She glared at him before turning back to concentrate on the road. 'He's a friend,' she muttered through clenched teeth.

'Like Martin and Jack.'

'Exactly.'

'Then why haven't I seen you look at them the way you looked at Brian when we walked into Helen's tonight?'

'All you saw on my face when I looked at Brian Powell

tonight was surprise. He was the last person I expected to see.'

'But you wanted to. You've been wanting to see him again for years, haven't you, Judy?' he taunted.

'You're being ridiculous and what's even worse you made *me* look ridiculous tonight. You couldn't have made it any plainer that you were jealous of Brian if you'd dyed your face green.' She grated the gears to negotiate the hill.

'You did go to London together,' he reminded her pointedly.

'Three years ago and we lived in single sex hostels.'

'And when you got together.'

'We held hands in the pictures.'

'And that's all.'

'What do you want me say, Sam?' She parked the car outside her flat, turned off the ignition and looked fiercely at him. 'That we slept together? Fine, if that's what you want me to say, I'll say it. I took my clothes off every time Brian and I met. We made mad passionate love in Trafalgar Square, Piccadilly Circus, even outside the gates of Buckingham Palace. And you know something, even if we had, it shouldn't matter a fig to you, because whatever I did or didn't get up to with Brian Powell happened before I even met you.' Thrusting open the car door, she climbed out of the car and slammed the door behind her.

He followed her to her front door. 'You promised you'd give me a date for our wedding.'

'The only thing I feel like giving you is this.' Tearing her engagement ring from her finger, she thrust it into his hand. Turning her back, she unlocked her door and ran up the stairs.

Deciding there was no way they could end the evening like this, Sam followed her inside, closed the door and climbed the stairs. She was standing, holding on to the mantelpiece, staring down at the cold gas fire.

'If I embarrassed you by letting my jealousy show, I'm

sorry,' he apologised. 'But I love you and I'm terrified of losing you.'

'Peculiar way you have of showing it.' As she lifted her head, he saw that her eyes were brimming with unshed tears.

'I look at Martin and Lily, Jack and Helen, and I want what they have,' he said softly. 'Is that so unreasonable of me?'

'No.' All she could see, all she could think about was the expression on Brian's face as he'd congratulated her and Sam and hoped they'd be happy together. It was as if he revelled in the power he possessed to hurt her. And all she'd done was return to Swansea three years ago because she could no longer bear to live in London – even with him there – because she had suspected that she needed him far more than he needed her.

He'd hurt her, he knew it, and despite his apology, she suspected he didn't give a damn. If he had any consideration for her, he would never have come swanning back into Swansea and her life, laughing and joking with Martin and Jack, flirting with Helen, Katie and Lily . . .

'July!' she exclaimed suddenly.

'July?' Sam repeated dully.

'It's the perfect month for a wedding. The weather will be warm, the chances are it won't rain, and that augurs well for the honeymoon as well as the day.'

'July's months away.'

'It's almost the end of March and that only gives us April, May and June to plan the wedding. We could be married fourteen weeks from now.'

'You mean it?'

She nodded.

Folding his arms around her, he crushed her close to him as he kissed her. 'I'm sorry about earlier, but I suppose it was inevitable that we'd have our first real quarrel.'

'As opposed to spat.' As he bent his head to kiss her

again, she whispered, 'Did you close the door downstairs?'

'Yes.' He looked into her eyes. 'I think we'd be more comfortable in the bedroom.'

'You don't want to wait any longer?'

'There's no reason to, now you've set the date.'

'You have something with you?' She blushed. 'I don't want to get pregnant . . .'

'I won't get you pregnant,' he assured her, 'not yet and not for a while. It may be selfish of me, but I want you all to myself for some time yet.'

'You really know how to get a man going,' Thompson breathed heavily, as Angela unzipped his trousers and slipped her hand inside his flies.

'You don't like what I'm doing?' she questioned innocently.

'God, Angie, can't we go somewhere more private?' he pleaded, as the door opened behind them and an, 'Oops, sorry,' was followed by a burst of feminine giggles.

'Third bedroom on the left at the top of the stairs, give me five minutes to get undressed.'

'Five minutes,' he groaned. 'I'll never last that long.'

'There are conditions.' She moved her fingers downwards. 'Both of us have to be naked, the light off and,' she slid her fingers even lower, 'you have to get into bed without saying a single word.'

'I can do that,' he gasped.

'Mind you do, I'd hate to be disappointed.' She slipped away from him and blew a kiss through the door as she closed it behind her.

Sam was already lying in Judy's bed when she left the bathroom. Determined to blot all thoughts of Brian from her mind, she smiled resolutely, closed the door and walked across the room.

He folded back the bedclothes. 'I've never seen you in a dressing gown before,' he commented. She untied the belt from her blue quilted nylon housecoat and slipped it off to reveal a sleeveless, blue nylon nightdress.

'You'll be seeing me in nothing but, most evenings when we're married,' she warned. 'I like relaxing in comfort at the end of the day.'

Moving towards her, he fingered the bodice of her nightdress and helped her into the bed.

'You've nothing on.' She shuddered as his bare legs brushed against hers.

'Clothes, even pretty ones,' he unbuttoned her nightdress, 'get in the way of what we'll be doing in a few minutes.'

'I know, I . . .' She continued to tremble. He reached down and lifted the hem of her nightdress to her waist.

'There's nothing to be afraid of, Judy.'

'I know . . .' The sentence hung, unfinished in the air. She closed her eyes and swallowed hard. He lifted her nightdress over her head and pulled it out from beneath her. She continued to keep her eyes closed, as he turned back the bedclothes and explored her tense and quivering body with his hands and lips. His knees pushed between hers, separating her legs. She gasped as he heaved himself on top of her and entered her.

Steeling herself, she continued to accept his kisses and caresses, all the while consciously making an effort to clear her mind. But Brian's image persisted in intruding. Smiling, laughing, as he flirted with Lily and the other girls, beer glass in hand, as if they had never meant anything to one another.

'I don't see—'

'Quiet, Robin.' Angie held her finger to her lips, as she led her brother and Cicely up the stairs. She halted outside the door of the guest room. After checking that Robin and Cicely were standing directly behind her, she flung the door open and switched on the light.

Cicely gasped.

'Emily!' Robin stared at his fiancée, spreadeagled beneath a naked Thompson.

'I've been wanting to tell you for a while, Robin, but I just couldn't bring myself to do it, knowing how much it would hurt you.' Angela brushed a handkerchief across her eyes. 'It's been going on from the very beginning. Not Thompson,' she added swiftly, as he opened his mouth. 'It wasn't his fault; none of the boys can resist Ems once she sets to work on them. But then you'd know more about that, than me. In the end, I thought you simply had to see it for yourself.' She swung forward, as if she was about to faint, incidentally opening the door wider to give Cicely a better view.

'Robin . . .' Emily slurred, her voice thick with whisky and sleep, as she fought to push Thompson off her and cover herself with the sheet at the same time.

'I think we've seen enough.' Closing the door to the sound of Emily's hysterical cries and Thompson's hurried retreat from the bed, Angela went to her own room.

'Angie . . .' Robin tried to waylay her.

'You'll have to deal with Emily on your own, Robin.' Angela continued to blot her eyes with her handkerchief. 'I simply can't bear to be near her. Not after all you've done for her. Standing by her when her father was sent to prison, insisting on continuing with your engagement, allying our family to her disgrace when all the while she was sleeping around . . .'

'I'll see to Angie.' Cicely pushed Robin aside. 'Just get Emily out of the house as quickly as you can.'

'That was fantastic.' Sam gazed lovingly at Judy, as she emerged from the bathroom in her nightdress and dressing gown. 'I never thought we'd hit it off so well the very first time. It was all right for you too, wasn't it?' he asked anxiously, slipping on his shirt.

'Yes.'

'And we'll improve with practice, lots of practice.'

Buttoning his shirt, he pushed it into his trousers, before taking her into his arms and kissing her. 'Happy?'

'Yes.'

'I'll go and see my mother tomorrow and tell her that we're getting married in July. You'll come with me?'

'Yes.'

'Pick me up in your car in the morning and we'll have lunch with her. She always cooks masses of food on a Sunday so she won't mind one extra, especially when she hears our news. She'll be in her element organising a great big white wedding. It will be important to her. You don't mind, do you?'

'No.'

'She'll want my cousins to be bridesmaids. There are six of them, but you can choose the dresses, and we'll have to decide where to hold the reception. The Mackworth did a great job on Helen and Jack's, and Lily and Martin's.'

'Yes.'

'So we'll go there. There's just one other thing.' He drew her back to the bed and sat beside her. 'Tonight – well, it was great but it would be even better without me having to use a French letter.'

'I don't want children yet and you agreed.' Her eyes rounded in alarm.

'We can use something else. There's something called a cap that women can use. They push it inside them . . .'

'How do you know about it?' she asked suspiciously.

'I overheard Lily and Katie talking about it, not long after Lily and Martin got married.'

'I'll remind them to be more careful when you're around.'

'Don't! They'd be mortified and you're the only one I've mentioned it to or am likely to. So, you'll see the doctor because, well,' he beamed, 'tonight is just the beginning for us. There's tomorrow . . .'

'And all our tomorrows.' She forced a smile to hide a sinking feeling in the pit of her stomach.

'Mike's on nights again so we could go back to my flat tomorrow evening if your flatmate is here. Either way I'll see you in the morning when you pick me up. One last kiss.' He slipped his hand inside her gown and nightdress and squeezed her breast. 'Sleep well, my love.'

'Ems, you have to dress.' Robin paced the floor of the guest bedroom. Emily continued to lie face down on the bed, crying hysterically. 'You can't stay here, not after I saw you with Thompson . . .'

'And your bloody sister made sure you saw everything there was to see,' she screamed frantically.

He sat on a chair at the foot of the bed. 'Sorry, Ems, but you can't expect me to ignore you sleeping with other boys.'

'Can't you see Angie set the whole thing up?' she pleaded tearfully, finally lifting her head from the pillows.

'I can understand why you would say that. But you can't expect me to believe you.'

'I'm having your baby . . .' The rest of the sentence dissolved into unintelligible sobs.

'Even if you are having a baby, after what I saw you doing with Thompson, you can't be sure that I'm the father.'

'We're engaged.'

'Were engaged, Ems.'

She turned a red, bloated face to his. 'You won't marry me?'

'Be reasonable, Ems, how can I after what you did tonight? But you can keep the ring, as long as you promise not to wear it,' he added cautiously. 'It's worth a few bob so you could sell it. I know how hard up you are.'

'I'll take you to court, make you pay maintenance . . .'

'Don't be silly, Ems. All I'd have to do is get Angie, Cicely and Thompson to sign statements for you to look a right tart. No judge would order me to pay a penny.'

'You're the only boy I've ever slept with.'

'How can you say that when I just saw Thompson humping you?' he broke in crudely. Unable to stand her whining a moment longer, he went to the door. 'Get dressed. I'll call you a taxi.'

'I haven't any money.'

'I'll pay for it.' He crossed the landing and knocked on Angie's door. Cicely opened it. 'Is Angie all right?'

'Fine,' Cicely bit back sarcastically. 'She loves having a stupid brother who embarrasses her in front of all her friends by insisting she invite his tart to her party. I don't know how you could bring that girl into the same house as decent people.'

'Cicely.' Angela appeared in the doorway, pale-faced, her mascara smudged around her eyes. 'Go and watch Emily dress in case she does anything stupid.'

'Like wreck the room or pack any of your mother's treasures? I'd be delighted.' Cicely gave Robin a withering look and flounced off.

Robin eyed his sister as Cicely left. 'Did Ems really sleep around after we got engaged?'

'That's a peculiar question for you to ask, considering you just caught her in bed with Thompson.'

'She said you set her up.'

'Oh yes, I poured drink down her throat.'

'You did, to get her to talk to you. To find out if she was having my baby or not,' he reminded. 'You even undressed her.'

'In case she was sick over her clothes. I most certainly didn't strip Thompson or put him in bed with her. Ask anyone who wasn't closeted in the billiards room with you. Ems was with Thompson all night. She wouldn't leave him alone for a minute and you didn't help by hiding from her.'

'I couldn't stand seeing everyone cut her.'

'Not quite everyone, Robin,' she countered. 'Anyway, I can't see why you're asking these questions. Earlier on you said you'd do anything to get out of this jam.'

'I wouldn't have done this to her.'

'She did it to herself. No one forced her to go to bed with Thompson and frankly I think it's worked out for the best. Ems may or may not be pregnant, but it doesn't matter one way or the other to you any more, because if she tries to stick you with a paternity suit, all you have to do is get Thompson to say that he knows her as well as you – in the biblical sense. She'll be painted the moral degenerate and you two will be off the hook.'

'That's a bit hard, Angie,' he admonished, conveniently forgetting that she was only repeating more or less what he'd said to Emily himself a few minutes before.

'If you're worried about her, you could always slip her some cash. If she is pregnant, she'll have to have the child adopted anyway, so it's not as if it will cost her anything.'

'And if she makes a fuss? Goes to Pops or Mums?'

'She wouldn't dare after Cicely and I saw her with Thompson.'

'No, she wouldn't,' he mused thoughtfully.

'You'd be a fool to see her again, Robin, alone or in public. After what she's done, you don't owe her anything.' She tossed her mascara stained handkerchief into the linen basket behind her door. 'Do you want me to tell Pops and Mums what happened tonight?'

'They'll be furious.'

'They'll be delighted – and relieved. You'll come out of this smelling of roses. The devoted boyfriend who stuck by his fiancée through scandal for over a year, only to discover she was a trollop who'd been sleeping with his friends all along.'

'And you didn't have anything to do with getting Thompson into her bed?'

'Think for a minute, Robin, how could I?'

Robin considered what Angela had said. She was right; he would come out of the whole sordid mess smelling of roses, his reputation not only intact but enhanced. His parents would be pleased with him for once and there was nothing quite like a sad and broken love affair behind a man to attract the girls.

'You have a taxi to call and I have guests to look after.'

He hesitated. 'You have told me the truth?'

'What's to tell? You saw Ems and Thompson the same as Cicely and me. Now can we please forget that you ever knew Emily Murton Davies?'

'I wish I could.'

'You'd better,' she advised acidly, 'because once this gets out – and it will – there'll be a scandal that will relegate what her father did into obscurity.'

Chapter Six

Jack carried a tray of glasses into the kitchen, set it on the table, crept up behind Helen and dropped a kiss on to the back of her neck. 'Thank you for my party.'

'It seemed to go well.'

'Everyone had a great time, thanks to you.'

'Including you?' She took a couple of glasses and rinsed them in a bowl of cold water, before plunging them into a sink of hot, soapy water.

'It was good to see everyone again, especially Brian.' He set his hands on her shoulders, as she brushed her eyes. 'What's wrong, sweetheart?'

'Nothing. Just something in my eye.' She avoided his searching gaze.

'Come on, Helen, I know you.'

'Not after two and half years, you don't.'

'We were only separated by distance. It would take a lot more than that to drive a wedge between us.' He turned her round, forcing her to face him. 'We promised one another before I went away that there'd be no secrets between us, remember?' Even as he said the words, he blanched. Some secrets were better kept, especially ones that would cause pain.

'It's nothing,' she protested, but another tear fell from her eye.

'It's Katie and her baby, isn't it? Judy's mother and Billy . . .'

A sob tore from her throat and she buried her face in his shoulder. Her tears, hot and wet, trickled through his sweater to his shirt. He held her tight, stroking her hair back from her face.

'I told you when we lost our baby that one day there'd be the right child for us. And there will.'

'An adopted child,' she murmured despondently.

'He will still be ours.'

'No, he won't. He won't have grown inside me. He won't have kept me up nights kicking against my ribs. I'll never know what it feels like to give birth, never have a labour pain, experience anything like the feeling Joy tried to describe tonight . . .'

'Oh, sweetheart.' He had difficulty containing his own emotion.

'Don't try to make me feel better, Jack. It's what you always do and you can't, not about this.'

'The pain will never go away, but it will get more bearable when we have a child, I'm sure it will,' he insisted, needing to believe what he was telling her.

She heard the catch in his voice and realised he was hurting as much as her. 'I'm sorry.'

'I can't forget all the plans we made for our son either. Or the look on your face when you found out that you'd lost him and there wouldn't be any more babies. I know it's no consolation but no matter what, I'll never stop loving you.'

'That's every consolation.' She forced back her tears. 'I'm being selfish. It must be even worse for you, knowing you could have children if you wanted.'

'The one thing I am sure of is that I wouldn't want children without you.' He hugged her tight. 'I love you, sweetheart, you'll always be my girl.'

'Jack, I'm sorry.'

'There's nothing to be sorry about. We're in this together, for better for worse, that's what my mother always used to say about marriage.'

'And you got the worse.'

'I got the best.' He continued to hold her until her sobs lessened and she relaxed against him. 'How about we put what's left of the food away, stack the dishes and go to bed.'

John woke with a start; instinctively reaching for Katie, his hand hit cold empty sheet. 'Katie,' he called, fumbling for the lamp on his bedside cabinet. Pressing the switch, he looked around, blinking as his eyes adjusted to the light. The room was empty. He jumped out of bed as fast as his crippled leg would allow and lifted his dressing gown from the peg at the back of the door. Alarmed, he went out on to the landing. Water was running in the bathroom. He tried the door, only to find it locked.

'Katie?'

'I'm sorry, John, I didn't mean to wake you.'

'Are you all right?'

'Fine, I couldn't sleep, I thought a bath might relax me.'

He glanced at his watch. 'At three o'clock in the morning?'

'I said I'm sorry, darling. Go back to bed.'

'You're sure you're all right.'

'Absolutely fine.'

John returned to the bedroom and climbed back into bed; switching off the lamp, he stretched out, resting his head on his pillow. Katie was usually so sensible, it was lunacy to take a bath at this time of night . . .

He sat up suddenly, banging his head on the headboard. As he clambered out of bed again, his legs became entangled in the sheets and the dressing gown he'd thrown over the bedspread. He fell headlong.

'John, I heard a bang.' Swathed in towels, Katie switched on the main light and looked anxiously at her husband lying on the floor. 'Darling, have you hurt yourself?'

'You're in labour.' He looked up at her accusingly.

'Very early stages and everyone knows first babies take hours and sometimes days to arrive.'

'I'll get the car.'

'Take your time.' Concerned, she watched as he divested himself of his robe and the bedclothes.

He saw her watching him. 'I didn't hurt myself.' He grabbed his suit jacket and searched frantically through the pockets.

'What are you looking for?' she asked gently.

'My keys.'

'They're downstairs on the hall table where you always leave them.'

'You're sure?' He went to the door.

'I saw you put them there when we came in.'

'I'll have the car around the front in five minutes. You will be all right on your own until then?'

'I'll be perfectly fine. It's going to take me more than five minutes to dress, but,' she suppressed a smile, 'you should put some clothes on. You might get arrested if you go out like that, even at this time in the morning.'

It wasn't until he looked down that he realised he was naked.

Helen gazed through the window at the sea in the moonlight. It stretched dark, shimmering, mysterious and extraordinarily beautiful to the horizon, and she wondered why she hadn't slept with the shutters open before Jack had suggested it. After only two nights she was already accustomed to looking out at the sea last thing at night and first thing in the morning. She reached out to Jack sleeping beside her.

'Admiring the view?'

She turned and saw Jack's eyes were open.

'I didn't realise you'd woken too.'

'I haven't slept.' He reached for his cigarettes on the bedside cabinet. 'I like lying here after you've gone to sleep, watching you.'

'That must be pretty boring.'

'No,' he answered seriously. 'After two and half years of sleeping in a barracks full of snoring men, I don't think I'll ever get tired of looking at you, or wondering why, out of all the boys in Swansea, you picked me,' He lit his cigarette and sat up, keeping his arm around her.

'That's easy, you were the only one brave enough to ask wild Helen Griffiths out.'

'Do you want to see the doctor and arrange to adopt a baby as soon as we can?'

'Do you?' She turned the question back on him.

'I'd like us to have children. I'm just not sure when would be a good time for us to adopt, or how long it will take.'

'From what the doctor told my father after I lost our baby, a private adoption wouldn't take more than a few months.'

He set an ashtray on to the floor next to the bed and flicked his ash into it. 'So, to repeat the question, do you want to adopt a baby right away?'

'I'd rather have our own.'

'Sweetheart . . .'

'But I've finally accepted that is never going to happen.'

'Finally – you've seen other doctors?'

'Yes, including a woman doctor who drew diagrams and explained exactly why it was impossible for me to conceive again, as opposed to all the men who said, "You'll never have another baby, Mrs Clay, because one of your fallopian tubes has been removed and unlike most women you never had two to begin with," and expected me to understand what they meant.'

'You never mentioned in any of your letters that you'd seen other doctors.'

Resting her head on his chest, she wrapped her arms around him. 'I knew in my heart of hearts before I started that it was a lost cause, but a tiny bit of me couldn't help hoping that the doctors were wrong. That you'd come home and wham, a miracle would happen and I'd end up like Katie. But as I've been forced to accept that the only way we'll ever have a baby is through adoption, the answer to your question is, yes, I'd like to talk to the doctor and see what can be arranged.'

'When?' He offered her his cigarette and she shook her head.

'I'm not sure. You've only just got back . . .'

'Two days,' he mused, 'and already it feels like I've never been away, apart from the house.'

'What's wrong with the house?' she questioned defensively.

'It's too grand for me. Apart from the army I've lived out all my life in the basements of Carlton Terrace.'

'I'm not digging a basement for you.'

'I wouldn't want you to.'

She ran her fingers through the hairs on his chest. 'So, you're just going to have get used to living here.'

'I've another reason for asking when you'd like to adopt a baby. Brian offered me a job tonight, in a garage he's opening in Swansea.'

'You know nothing about cars!'

'You don't need to know much more than how to drive one in order to sell them. The problem is, Brian warned I wouldn't be earning much money for a couple of years. Three pounds a week basic plus commission on any cars I sell.'

'We own this house, I earn a good wage . . .'

'That's just the point, *you* own this house.'

'That's stupid, Jack, the house is ours. I'll see a solicitor first thing on Monday about putting it in joint names.'

'I'd rather you didn't,' he interrupted.

'I will, if only to stop you saying anything as ridiculous as that ever again.'

'To get back to what we were talking about, your good wage would stop once we adopt a baby.'

'Not necessarily.'

'You'd want to carry on working?'

'You'd want to stop me?' she challenged.

'You can't take a baby into the warehouse.'

'Women do every day.'

'Only to shop.'

'I'm a buyer, Jack,' she said heavily, 'and that is exactly what I do. I look at catalogues, go to fashion shows, meet reps and buy the clothes I think will sell in the warehouse. Most fashion shows are in the evening and I can look at catalogues just as well at home as in the warehouse.'

'I'm not sure I like the idea of my wife working.'

'And I'm sure I don't want to be a full-time housewife. I like my job, I'm good at it and I see no reason why I shouldn't carry on doing it, even if we have a family.'

He stubbed out his cigarette. 'And if the baby has the measles and you couldn't go to a fashion show or meet a rep?'

'Once we adopt, I'll do what my parents did, employ a Mrs Jones to look after him when I can't. I need help in the house anyway now you're home, and I'll need even more when we have a baby.'

'My three pounds a week won't stretch to help in the house,' he said sourly.

'Plus commission,' she reminded.

'Which we couldn't rely on.'

'I have savings.'

'You'll soon have none if we use them for day-to-day living expenses.' He plumped up his pillow and slid back down in the bed.

'So, you want to put off talking to the doctor?'

'No. But if you want to adopt a baby right away, I'll turn down Brian's offer and look around for a job that pays more.'

'If you are a super salesman in the making, you could be turning down a fortune.'

'And I might never earn more than a pittance.'

She wriggled down contentedly beside him. 'I'd still love you. When does Brian want you to start?'

'He thinks he'll be ready to open for business in two weeks.'

'Perfect, that's just when I told my father I'd be back in the warehouse. If you want my advice, give Brian's job a try. We've nothing to lose and you might find yourself doing something you really like.'

'And the baby?'

She kissed his chest as he slipped his hand inside her nightdress. 'Let's postpone making a decision for the next two weeks.'

'Do you, Judith Ann Hunt take this man . . .' Judy looked from the vicar to the dress she was wearing. It was tight, so tight she couldn't breathe, and horror of horrors it was sheer nylon . . . everyone could see her corset, suspenders . . . someone started to cry . . . She had to get out of the church run . . . run . . . She fell swiftly through the air . . .

She woke and found herself staring at the ceiling. Thank God, it was only a dream – partly a dream, her nightdress had wound itself so tightly around her chest it hurt. She glanced at the bedside clock, the luminous hands pointed to four o'clock.

Throwing back the bedclothes she switched on the bedside lamp, left the bed and shook out her nightdress. She was starving; the only thing she'd eaten since lunchtime was the cheese straw Brian had handed her and lunch had been a ham roll she'd bought in Eynon's. It was Brian's fault. He had followed her into Helen's dining room and annoyed her so much she had forgotten about food. Stupid, annoying man!

Slipping on her robe, she went into the kitchen. She would make herself tea and toast. She'd slice the bread thickly and when it was golden brown, she'd saturate it with butter that would sink into every last crumb. Switching on the light in the galley, she cut two slices and popped them into the electric toaster Lily and Martin had given her and Sam as an engagement present. She set the kettle on the hob to boil and went to the bathroom. The door was locked on the inside and then she heard it, just as she had in her dream – the sound of someone crying.

'Emily?' she whispered. 'Are you in there?' She tried the door again but it was definitely locked. She went into the living room; it was exactly as she had left it earlier that evening. She returned to the hall. Emily's bedroom door was open, the light on, her handbag, stole and evening dress tossed on the bed. She banged on the bathroom door and shouted, 'Emily!' When there was no reply, she set her shoulder against the door and pushed with all her strength. The door burst open at her third attempt.

Emily lay on the floor, a sliver of broken glass wedged between her fingers, her wrists covered in blood that had dripped on to the linoleum, staining it a bright, crimson red.

'We'll look after your wife from here, Mr Griffiths.' The nurse took Katie's arm from him as he helped her into the foyer of the nursing home.

'I'll be fine, John.' Katie squeezed his hand and clambered awkwardly into the chair the nurse wheeled in front of her.

He paled as her face creased in pain. 'Please, let me go with her.'

'You'd be in the way, Mr Griffiths. I advise you to go home and telephone in the morning.'

'I am not leaving.' John crossed his arms and resolutely stood his ground.

'I swear, the fathers are more trouble than the mothers,' the nurse muttered under her breath, as Katie desperately tried to conceal another pain. 'Nurse Evans,' she called to a colleague who was crossing the hall, 'take Mr Griffiths to the waiting room and give him a cup of tea.'

'This way, Mr Griffiths.' The nurse took him firmly by the elbow and propelled him down the corridor. As John tried to brush her aside, he looked back and saw that Katie was nowhere to be seen.

*

'It was an accident,' Emily slurred, as Judy wrapped damp towels around her wrists. 'I drank too much . . .'

'I can see that.' Judy twisted the towels, exerting pressure in the hope that it would stop the bleeding. 'Can you stand up? I have to get you to hospital.'

'No!'

'Oh yes,' Judy contradicted vehemently. 'You can't expect me to stand back and watch you bleed to death.'

'All right,' Emily conceded, 'I'll go, but you have to tell them that it was an accident.'

'You want me to lie for you.'

'I fell on a glass.'

'I don't believe you,' Judy countered frostily.

'Please, Judy,' Emily started to cry. 'My Aunt Mary tried to kill herself; it was horrible, they accused her of trying to commit suicide, she was put on trial and sent to prison . . .' Emily gave Judy an imploring look. '. . . I was drunk, that was all,' she whispered hoarsely. 'I didn't know what I was doing. It will never happen again. I was drunk. Please . . .'

John paced the floor of the waiting room. Fifteen steps one way, twenty-two the other, including detours around chairs and tables. Two cold, untouched cups of tea stood on the central coffee table. There was a pile of magazines on a second table set in front of a curtained bay. He picked one up, flicked through it and returned it to the stack without absorbing a single word or photograph he'd seen.

'Mr Griffiths.'

He whirled around and saw that the nurse was smiling. How could she, when Katie was in pain . . .

'You have a son.'

'Katie.' His voice sounded high-pitched, peculiar.

'Mother and baby are doing well after one of the shortest labours on record in this nursing home.' The nurse's smile broadened. 'It is just as well that your wife produced after three hours, Mr Griffiths. I don't think you could have stood any longer.'

John caught sight of himself in a mirror; his hair was on end from the times he'd run his fingers through it while he'd paced. His face was white, his lips bloodless. He reached into his pocket for a comb and discovered he didn't have one.

'Would you like to see them?'

'Them,' he repeated in confusion.

'Your wife and son,' the nurse explained patiently. 'Please, come with me.'

He followed the nurse into the entrance hall. She pressed a button set in the wall and he realised why Katie had disappeared so quickly. He hadn't even noticed the lift when they'd arrived. The nurse led him into the lift, up to the second floor and down a corridor into a large, pleasant room decorated with green sprigged wallpaper. Katie was lying in a single bed, propped on pillows. Her smile faded when she saw him.

'You look awful, John. Are you all right?'

'I should be asking you that.'

'I told you I'd be fine.'

He caught her hand. 'And I will be now that I've seen you.' He sank into a chair the nurse placed next to the bed.

'Would you like to hold your son, Mr Griffiths?' The nurse lifted a shawl wrapped bundle from a cot set the other side of Katie's bed and carefully handed it to him. 'I'll leave you to get acquainted, but not for too long, your wife and son need to rest.'

He gazed from the baby to Katie, as the nurse closed the door quietly behind her. 'Are you really all right?' he pressed earnestly.

'It was just like Judy's mother said, there was pain, but as soon as he arrived and they gave him to me to hold, I forgot all about it.' She looked at the baby lying peacefully in John's arms. 'He's seven pounds six ounces,' she revealed proudly. 'The nurse said that's a good weight, he's fit and healthy, has beautiful blond hair, blue eyes . . .'

'And a wonderful mother.' He kissed her lightly on the lips. 'You don't mind him being a boy?'

'I wouldn't swap him for a million girls.'

He pushed his finger gently into the baby's tiny fist. 'You can hardly call him Daisy, which is the only name you picked out.'

'He would get teased,' she agreed. 'What was the name of your grandfather, the one who brought you up?'

'John, and we're not having two John Griffithses in the house. But my father's name was Glyn.'

'Glyn Griffiths.' She repeated it. 'I like the way that sounds.'

'How about Glyn Martin Jack Griffiths.'

'Glyn Martin Griffiths, we'll keep Jack for the next one.' She laughed when his frown deepened. 'He'll need a playmate.'

'I'll need time to recover.'

'Let me know the minute you do.'

The nurse knocked before opening the door. 'I'm sorry, Mr Griffiths, but you'll have to leave.'

'When can I see them again?'

'Visiting is every evening from six until seven for fathers. We'd rather no one else came for the first week, aside from the risk of bringing colds into the home at this time of year, the mothers need their rest.'

'You will take care of yourself?' Katie pleaded, as John handed the baby to the nurse and left the chair.

'I promise, see you tonight.' He kissed her again.

'Love you,' she whispered, 'and thank you for my son.'

'Miss Murton Davies's injuries looked worse than they actually were. The cuts are mainly superficial, only two needed stitching.' The doctor eyed Judy suspiciously. 'You are absolutely certain that she fell on a glass.'

Unused to lying, Judy recalled Emily's pleadings as she had driven her to the hospital. 'I saw the glass myself when I helped her up from the bathroom floor,' she hedged.

'So it was an accident.'

'That is what Emily told me,' Judy confirmed.

The doctor eyed her as though he hadn't believed a word she'd said. 'And has Miss Murton Davies had any other "accidents" lately?' he enquired cuttingly.

'None that I'm aware of.'

'You live with her.'

'We share a flat, yes.' Judy crossed her fingers, hoping he wouldn't ask her how long they had been living together.

'You know she had been drinking. Far too much for someone in her condition.'

'She'd been to a party.' Judy felt she had to say something in Emily's defence.

'You weren't with her.'

'No, she went with her fiancé.'

'And he knows about the baby.'

'She's having a baby?' Judy exclaimed.

'She's almost five months pregnant. You didn't know?'

'No, but she did say she'd be moving out soon to get married.'

'The sooner the better.' The doctor pocketed his stethoscope. 'You will inform Miss Murton Davies's family and her fiancé about this "accident"?'

'Yes.'

'And should there be any more "accidents" . . .'

'I'm sure there won't.'

The doctor nodded. 'Provided you agree to take care of her, you can take Miss Murton Davies home as soon as the nurse finishes bandaging her wrists. But I warn you, if you are lying, you could find yourself in serious trouble. Suicide is a criminal offence, as is aiding and abetting one.'

'I am certain that Emily didn't mean to do anything of the kind.'

'As long as you are sure, Miss . . .'

'Hunt, Judy Hunt.'

'Take care of her,' he barked abruptly, before striding down the corridor that led to the treatment rooms.

His words echoed in Judy's head. She returned to the waiting area outside the cubicle where they'd taken Emily. It wasn't her place to take care of Emily, it was Robin Watkin Morgan's and she'd see that he did exactly that, just as soon as she reached her flat and her telephone.

'A nephew.' Lily's eyes shone with excitement. She laid out dishes of bacon, eggs, black pudding, laver bread, mushrooms and tomatoes on the table in front of John, Brian and Martin. 'My first real relative,' she observed, remembering Brian's offer to Martin and repressing her instinct to shout the news of her own pregnancy.

'Hey, what am I?' Martin complained.

'Only my husband.' Lily joined them at the table. 'What's he like, Mr Griffiths? How heavy is he? What are you going to call him?'

'One question at a time, Lily. Poor Mr Griffiths has been up all night.' Martin passed John the bacon.

'First, now that my son is your nephew, I insist on all of you calling me John,' John said firmly. 'And to answer Lily's questions, he's beautiful, he has blue eyes, blond hair, he was seven pounds six ounces, and,' he looked at Martin, 'we're naming him Glyn Martin Griffiths after my grandfather and you.'

As Martin beamed proudly, Brian murmured, 'Jack isn't going to like that.'

'I wanted to call him Glyn Martin Jack Griffiths, but Katie insists on keeping Jack for the next one.'

'She's already talking about having another one?' Lily opened the butter dish. Taking a helping, she laid it on the edge of her plate and passed the dish to John.

'Brave girl,' Brian whistled.

'I've asked her to wait until I've recovered from the

shock of this one,' John smiled, 'but I've a feeling that won't take too long.'

'Well,' Brian lifted his teacup in a formal toast, 'here's to Glyn Martin Griffiths, may his life be a long, happy, healthy and successful one.'

'Glyn Martin Griffiths,' they all echoed.

'Formal wetting of the baby's head to take place in my house as soon as Katie and Glyn come home,' John invited.

'What, no pub crawl tonight?' Brian grumbled.

'Maybe a pint or two in the Rose tomorrow evening after visiting,' John conceded. 'This is a great breakfast, Lily, thank you.'

'You're welcome to stay for lunch.'

'I may take you up on that offer but I won't be staying. As soon as I've eaten this, I want to drive to Limeslade to tell Jack and Helen the news.'

'They'll be thrilled.' Lily passed Brian the black pudding.

Martin gave John a quick self-conscious look. John, Jack, Helen and him were the only four people who knew Helen would never have any children and he was far from certain that either Helen or his brother would be thrilled.

White-faced, red-eyed, Emily emerged from the cubicle and walked unsteadily towards Judy. 'The doctor said I can leave if I have someone to take care of me for a day or two.'

'I've told him I will.'

'Thank you.'

'Back to have the stitches out in ten days,' the nurse cautioned, carrying a bowl and bandages out of the cubicle. 'Take care until then and no more falling on to glass.'

'I won't,' Emily assured her, 'and thank you. I'm sorry,' she apologised to Judy, as they left the building by the main entrance.

'Sit in the car before you fall down,' Judy advised, unlocking it.

Emily did as Judy suggested. Covering her face with her hands, she muttered, 'I can't thank you enough.'

'I hate lying,' Judy said sharply, pushing the key into the ignition.

'I'm sorry, really sorry.'

Judy looked across at Emily and felt a pang of compassion. 'Give me your solemn promise that you will never do anything like that again. Promise,' she repeated sternly, when Emily remained obstinately silent.

'I promise never to involve you in anything like that again.'

'Then the minute we get home, I'm going to telephone Robin, your mother, your brother . . .'

'No!' Emily interrupted, her voice wavering in emotion. 'I don't want anyone to know about this.' She turned her face to the window.

'The doctor told me that you are having a baby.'

'He had no right. But then, what does it matter?' she whispered wretchedly, 'the whole town will know soon enough.'

'It's not something you can hide,' Judy agreed. 'Did something happen between you and Robin tonight, because if it did I'm sure it was nothing. All couples quarrel. My fiancé and I had a right royal row—'

'Robin broke our engagement.'

'Once he finds out about the baby he'll come running back.'

'He won't, he broke it because of the baby.' Emily turned a dry-eyed, anguished face to Judy's and somehow it all came out. How miserable her life had been since her father had been imprisoned and the family had lost everything. How all her friends went out of their way to avoid her. How she had been left with only Robin and her brother to turn to, and how Robin's sister had somehow arranged for her to be found drunk and naked in bed with one of Robin's friends.

Touched by Emily's pain and despair, Judy felt sympathy for the girl but couldn't believe anyone would engineer a scene like the one Emily described between her and a boy she referred to as Thompson. She had however, heard enough rumours about the parties held at the Watkin Morgans's house to suspect that it wasn't uncommon for girls to wander around naked, or climb into bed with boys they hardly knew.

'So you see,' Emily finished, as they continued to sit in the car after Judy had driven to her flat. 'Robin will never see me or have anything to do with me ever again.'

'I am so sorry.'

'Why?' Emily asked bitterly. 'You hardly know me.'

'But we are flatmates.' Judy considered what had happened between her and Sam the night before. What if they quarrelled and she found herself pregnant despite all his assurances that he was being careful? 'What happened to you can happen to any girl.'

'You're not just saying that?'

'No.' Judy took Emily's hand into hers. It was cold, icy to the touch. 'Let's go inside and switch on the gas fire before you freeze to death.'

After settling Emily in the living room, Judy went into the kitchen and put the kettle on. Discarding the cold toast in the toaster, she cut more bread and laid a tray for both of them. When she'd buttered half a dozen slices of toast and wet the tea, she carried it through to the living room and set it on the coffee table between them.

'Thank you.' Emily's hand shook as she took the cup Judy handed her.

'I hate to think what might have happened if I hadn't woken up.' Judy finally bit into the toast she'd been craving for and savoured the taste. 'Didn't you think of your family?'

'They were the reason I did it. Another scandal will kill my mother. And Larry's had a terrible time this last year and there are my sisters, they're all younger than me.

Imagine how people will treat them once it gets out that my fiancé caught me in bed with another man.'

'Your mother and sisters don't even live in Swansea any more.'

'You don't know the Watkin Morgan set. They love scandal. People will write to my mother, rub her nose in what happened.'

'Then better they hear it from you.' Judy offered Emily a piece of toast.

She shook her head. 'What am I going to do? I'm already fastening my skirts with safety pins. Another couple of weeks and I'll begin to show. I'll lose my job . . .'

'You can stay here as long as you like and don't worry about the rent.'

Emily looked at Judy in disbelief. 'You mean that?'

'Yes.'

'Why are you being kind to me?'

'Let's just say because no one else seems to be.'

'But I'll still need money for food and help with the baby when it's born. I just don't know what to do.'

Judy glanced at the clock. 'Nothing for the moment because you're exhausted. If you get a couple of hours' sleep I'll take you to see my mother when you wake up.'

'What can she do?'

'I don't know. But I do know that she's the first person I'd go to if I were in trouble. And she's had two babies, one less than two years ago, so she knows all about pregnancy. She may be able to suggest something.'

'You won't tell her about last night, or these.' Emily held up her bandaged wrists.

'I won't tell her about Robin, except to say that he won't help you, but she's not stupid, Emily. Come on, go to bed. I'll wake you around twelve o'clock.'

'Thank you.'

As she watched Emily leave the room, Judy contemplated the burden she'd just taken on. But everyone needed someone they could turn to when they had a problem, and it was just her bad luck that she had found herself saddled with a flatmate who didn't seem to have anyone else.

CHAPTER SEVEN

'A boy, Dad, that's wonderful.' Helen flung her arms around John's neck and hugged him.

'Congratulations, Mr Griffiths.' Jack shook his hand warmly.

'As I just told Martin and Lily, I insist on you calling me John now that I'm the father of your nephew.'

'Does that go for me too – John?' Helen opened the sideboard and brought out a bottle of sherry.

'If you want to call me John, go ahead.'

'I was joking. Here.' She handed her father and Jack two of the small sherries she'd poured. 'To . . .'

'Glyn Martin Griffiths.'

After they'd drunk the toast, John said, 'Sorry, Jack, I wanted to make it Glyn Martin Jack Griffiths, but Katie says she wants to keep Jack for the next one.'

'Tell her it's a silly name for a girl.' Jack was watching Helen. She appeared genuinely pleased by the news.

'She said you, Martin and her were so close when she was growing up, she wants Glyn to have a brother or sister as soon as possible.'

'He'll have a cousin too.' Helen set her sherry aside. 'Jack and I have decided to talk to the doctor about that private adoption we discussed when I . . . before Jack went away.'

'That's good news,' John smiled. 'Would you like me to telephone him for you?'

'No, we'll do it ourselves in a couple of weeks.'

'After the second honeymoon.' John finished his sherry

and handed his glass to Helen. 'Which reminds me, I'm imposing.'

'No, you're not.' Helen set the glasses on the table.

'I promised Lily and Martin I'd have lunch with them.'

'You could have eaten here.'

'Not that you would have had anything other than party leftovers,' Jack warned. 'We're eating out this evening.'

'Jack's booked a table in the Mermaid and now we'll have three things to celebrate – Jack's homecoming, his job in Brian's garage and my new brother.'

'Brian offered you a job?' John asked Jack.

'Yes, and,' Jack looked sideways at Helen, 'it appears that I've decided to take it.'

'He's lucky to get you. If it doesn't work out, you can always come back to the warehouse and not as a stock-room boy.'

'Thank you – John.' Jack smiled self-consciously at his father-in-law.

'So, what's my new brother like?' Helen demanded.

'Perfect, beautiful, small, what there is of his hair is fair and his eyes are blue.'

'Give him and Katie a kiss from me. How soon can we see them?'

'They won't allow anyone other than fathers into the nursing home for the first week, but as soon as you're allowed I'll take you two and Lily and Martin in, I promise.'

'If you need anything, washing done, a meal . . .'

'I'll ask Mrs Jones. Look after yourself and don't worry about the warehouse, love. No one's indispensable, not even the chief fashion buyer.' He kissed Helen's cheek. 'Martin and Roy are joining me about half past eight in the Rose tomorrow to wet the baby's head and I've asked them to invite Sam and Mike if they're off shift. Brian, unfortunately, is returning to Pontypridd today. If you'd like to join us, Jack, you'd be more than welcome. On the other hand, if you prefer to stay with Helen, I'll understand.'

'I'd be glad to get rid of him for a couple of hours,' Helen said lightly. 'It will give me a chance to wash my hair.'

Jack glanced at Helen, and realising she meant it, said, 'Thank you, John; count me in.'

'See you then.'

'I've never seen such a mixture of exhaustion and elation on a man's face.' Jack wrapped his arm around Helen's shoulders, as they stood on the doorstep watching John drive away. 'And I'm proud of you.'

'It would be mean to envy Katie and my father's happiness just because they have the one thing I want more than anything else in the world – after you.'

'And soon will have.' Jack closed the front door. 'I think it's a great idea of yours to see the doctor in two weeks, but if we do get offered a baby soon and I accept Brian's job, money will be tight until the garage is established.'

'I told you we'd manage.'

'Not at the expense of your savings.'

'Our savings.'

'I suppose I could give the garage six months,' he said thoughtfully. 'If I don't make a reasonable wage by then, I'll go back to the warehouse.'

'I'd rather you gave it a year.'

'We'll talk about it in six months. So, when do you want to make the appointment to see the doctor?'

'Tomorrow for a fortnight's time, then we can forget about it until it's time to go.' Blocking his path, she pulled his shirt from his trousers.

'Helen,' he warned, as she slid her fingers beneath his waistband. 'You know what that does to me.'

'Yes.' Her eyes glittered.

'You're for it,' he shouted, as he chased her up the stairs.

*

'We arranged to visit my mother to tell her that we've finally set the date.' Sam's voice sank ominously low. He faced Judy in his basement kitchen.

'I didn't know Emily was going to have an accident.' Judy had given Sam the sanitised version of events that Emily wanted the world to believe. 'She is so upset I thought I'd take her to see my mother.'

'For pity's sake, Judy,' he snapped. 'You hardly know the girl.'

'She is my flatmate,' Judy retorted.

'I still don't see why you have to take her to see your mother.'

'Emily has a problem.'

'Haven't we all,' he griped, 'and mine is you.'

'My mother might be able to help her. Please, Sam, don't be difficult. It's not going to make any difference to your mother whether I visit her this weekend or next. It's not as if she's expecting me. And,' Judy reined in her irritation and gave him a strained smile, 'we'll have more definite news to give her next weekend if we go to see the vicar of St Mary's and the manager of the Mackworth hotel tomorrow evening.'

'*We* can't visit anyone tomorrow evening,' he stressed caustically. 'From tomorrow, I'm on the two till ten shift for two weeks.'

'Then we'll visit the vicar and the hotel first thing in the morning and tomorrow night after your shift, you can come over to the flat and I'll make us a meal.'

'You, cook for me?' he questioned incredulously.

'I may amaze you.'

'Knowing you, not in a way I like.' Refusing to be mollified, he crossed his arms across his chest and sat back in his chair.

'There's always tonight.'

'Tonight! How long do you and Emily intend to stay with your mother?'

'As long as it takes, but you said that Mike won't be starting his shift until ten.'

'You'll really go with me to see the vicar and the manager of the Mackworth tomorrow morning?' he asked in a marginally softer tone.

'I'll pick you up in the car at nine o'clock.'

'I suppose that's something,' he accepted, although she could still detect resentment in his voice.

'I'll drive Emily home as soon as she's talked to my mother, then I'll come straight back here if you like.'

'I'll visit my mother, if it's all the same to you.'

'You're hardly dressed for riding your bike. It's tipping down out there.' She looked at the pale grey lounge suit he was wearing.

'Yes, well, we had arranged to go to Neath in your car, remember?' He left his chair. 'I need to change into my bike leathers.'

'I'll be round this evening about eight o'clock then.'

'I won't hold my breath.'

'I'm sorry, Sam, but I promise I'll make it up to you later.' She waylaid him before he reached the door to the passage and kissed him. 'That's on account.'

'I'll hold you to that.' Giving her one final look of exasperation, he left her to see herself out.

'I hope you haven't quarrelled with Sam because of me,' Emily said, as Judy ran up the outside steps of Lily's basement to the car she'd parked in the street.

'Sam and I spend more time arguing than we do talking. Some say it's a sign of a healthy relationship.'

'It could be,' Emily agreed despondently. 'Robin and I hardly ever argued – until last night.'

'I still think you should get in touch with him. If you don't want to telephone you could always write.'

'No!' Emily's reply was so fierce and finite Judy dropped the subject. As soon as Emily left the car, she locked it and led the way up the path to her mother's front door.

'I saw you coming.' Joy handed Billy to Judy and kissed her before turning to her companion. 'You must be Emily, it's good to meet you.' Primed by a telephone call from Judy earlier, she opened the door to the front parlour. 'I thought we'd sit in here.'

'Where's Roy?' Judy asked.

'Working. As he would say, a policeman's life is a hard one.'

'I didn't know your father was a policeman.' Emily took the easy chair Joy offered her.

'Both of them,' Judy answered. 'Roy's my stepfather and my real father is a policeman too, in London.'

'Roy's my second husband,' Joy explained. 'Have you two had lunch?'

'We had scrambled eggs on toast.' Judy tickled Billy and he giggled and squirmed in her arms.

'Is that all?' Joy reproved.

'As we slept late after being up most of the night, we didn't want anything else.'

'There's a quiche in the fridge. Why don't you warm it up in the oven and make some tea for us, Judy?'

'Should I make anything special for Billy?' Judy suddenly realised that Emily was staring at him.

'He likes quiche too.'

'Come on then, monster.' Swinging Billy on to her shoulders, Judy left for the kitchen.

Joy sat opposite Emily. She watched her for a moment, saw how uneasy she was, and decided to come straight to the point. 'Judy tells me you're pregnant.'

'Yes.' Emily stared at her hands and played with the gloves she'd kept when Judy had taken her coat.

'Is the baby's father going to help you?'

'He doesn't want anything to do with me.'

'You could take him to court.'

'No!'

'I hate to ask this, Emily, but you have to be practical in a situation like this. Do you have any money?'

'Not much.' Emily felt the room closing in around her.

'And the baby, do you intend to keep it after it's born?'

Emily looked at Joy through glazed, frightened eyes. 'Without money or a husband, how can I?'

'I had a word with my husband before he went to work. I didn't mention your name,' Joy reassured. 'Just told him that one of my friend's daughters was in trouble. He said there are all kinds of organisations that can help women in your situation. The Salvation Army, the Catholic Church and the Church of England all run homes where unmarried mothers can live board and lodge free until their babies are born and for six weeks afterwards. Then the babies are handed over to adoptive parents.'

'And the mothers?' Emily asked apprehensively.

'Are free to get on with their lives.'

'What kind of life can I have after this?' Emily questioned pessimistically. 'Everyone in Swansea will soon know I'm pregnant, that is if they don't already, and no one will want to have anything to do with a girl who's had an illegitimate baby. I'll be ostracised even more than I have been since . . . since . . .'

'Swansea isn't the only place in the world. After your baby has been placed with adoptive parents, you'll be free to go wherever you want. No one need know about your past unless you tell them.'

'It's not just the baby . . .'

'I know what happened to your father, Emily, and I admire you and your brother for staying in the town and facing the gossips.'

'I wish now that I'd gone to Bournemouth with my mother.'

'Hindsight is a wonderful thing. But life goes on, and your first priority has to be your welfare and that of your baby.'

'You're not shocked,' Emily challenged.

'By you being pregnant and not married?' Joy shook her head. 'It can happen to any girl who puts her trust in the wrong man.'

Emily bit her lip in an effort to contain the tide of

emotion that threatened to engulf her. 'You and Judy are being so kind . . .'

'You'll soon discover that the world is full of kindness. Lots of people will be prepared to help you and your baby.' Sensing Emily's precarious state, Joy deliberately turned the conversation back to practical matters. 'Have you seen a doctor?'

'Only this morning in the hospital.' Emily flushed as she stared at her bandaged wrists. 'He said I was four and half months pregnant.'

'You haven't seen your own doctor.'

'I couldn't . . . it would be horrible, so embarrassing.'

'I know a very good woman doctor. I could make an appointment for you to see her. I'll even go along with you if you like. She'll be able to tell you what your options are.'

'Thank you.'

'I'll try to make it for tomorrow if possible. As soon as I have a day and time, I'll telephone you in the flat. In the meantime, I suggest you stop worrying. You have your whole life ahead of you, and so does your baby. And whichever home you opt to go into, I'm sure they'll find him or her a perfect set of parents. Now,' she brushed down her skirt as she rose from her chair, 'I'll go and see what Judy's doing to that quiche that's taking so long.'

'So, you meant what you said about visiting me?' Sam said when Judy walked into the basement.

'I said I would.'

'I thought Emily needed you.'

'She is going to be fine. She'll also be moving out shortly.' Judy handed him her coat.

'How soon is shortly?' he probed transparently, hanging her coat next to his on the back of the door.

'Before we get married, but that doesn't mean you can more or less move in with me.' She sat at the table and pulled a box of shortbread biscuits towards her.

'No,' he grinned, 'but it does mean that we won't have an audience when I call in on you now and again.'

'Between the salons and organising the wedding, there won't be too many "now and agains",' she cautioned.

'But there is one now.' Taking the biscuit tin from her, he set it aside and pulled her from her seat.

'It's only half past eight,' she protested. 'Mike—'

'Is having tea with some girl he met last week and going straight to the station from her house, which means . . .' He opened the door that led to the passage, bathroom and bedrooms, and flung open his bedroom door. A warm tide of air greeted her and she saw that he'd left the electric fire burning. He'd also turned back the bed.

'You don't give a girl time to get her breath,' she complained, as he led her into the room and closed the door.

'Not this girl, not after last night.' He unbuttoned her cardigan. 'Come on, Judy,' he coaxed.

'Just give me a moment,' she pleaded, wishing she'd never offered to call on him and wondering if this was what their life together was going to be like from now on – sex without preliminaries every time they met.

'Judy . . .'

'If you undress in the bathroom, I'll be in bed by the time you get back.'

'You're being ridiculous.'

'Just five minutes,' she begged.

'You're behaving as if we've just met,' he grumbled, but to her relief he left the room.

She stared at the back of the door when he closed it behind him. She had never been so tempted to run out of a house in her life and couldn't understand why. She loved Sam, and as Lily and Helen said, they had been engaged forever. Did every woman feel like this at the beginning of married life, or was there something seriously wrong with her?

*

'I was engaged to Ems for over a year.' Robin abandoned all pretence at playing billiards and confronted his father.

'And you caught her in bed with one of your friends.' His father eyed him sternly, daring him to say otherwise. 'Didn't you?' he challenged.

'Yes, but—'

'I will not tolerate any excuses,' his father raged. 'And neither should you. A decent girl would have handed you back the ring. You – or rather I – paid over seven hundred and fifty pounds for it. Damn it, Robin, can't you see it's not the money? If you don't retrieve it, there is no saying what use the girl will make of it.'

'I told her she could sell it. A gentleman doesn't go back on his word.'

'And a gentleman's fiancée doesn't service his friends,' his father remonstrated crudely. 'The thing that infuriates me most about this mess is that if it hadn't been for your sister, you probably would never have caught Emily out. You would have allowed her to go on duping you right up to the altar and beyond. And now you have the gall to stand there and tell me that you want to give the girl a seven hundred and fifty pound ring!'

'She'll need money to keep herself until the baby's born.' Unable to meet his father's eye, Robin chalked the tip of the billiard cue he was holding.

'Let's get one thing straight.' His father lowered his voice but his anger was just as apparent. 'It's as you said, *the* baby, not your baby, *the* baby. And from what Angela told your mother, the child could have been fathered by any one of a dozen boys in your set.'

'Including me,' Robin broke in. 'I was the one who was engaged to her for over a year.'

'You were the one who was used, abused and fooled by her more like.' His father filled a glass with whisky and drank half of it straight off. 'Damn it, Robin, I blame myself as much as you. I should have insisted you break off with the girl when I discovered what her father was. It's clear now that the whole family have the morality of guttersnipes. Now, go down to Mumbles, confront her and get that ring back.'

'I told her last night that I don't want to see her again.'

'Then get one of your friends.'

'No.' Taking a glass from the tray, Robin followed his father's example and poured himself a whisky. 'I'll write her a note and tell her to post it back to me.'

'And if it doesn't reach here and she says it was lost in the post?'

'She works in town. I could ask her to leave it at our solicitors.'

'As long as she does.' His father capitulated before emptying his glass. 'Just do it, boy. The sooner this engagement is over and all the loose ends tied up, the better.'

'But if the baby is mine . . .'

'And if it's another man's bastard?' his father interrupted brusquely. 'One day you'll discover, Robin, that it's hard enough bringing up children you can be one hundred per cent certain you've fathered, without taking on another man's leavings.'

Robin pictured Emily and Thompson together the night before. Who was to say how long it had been going on? Or even if Thompson was the only one? Lost for words, he turned to the window.

'You'll write that note and take it to Mumbles tonight. Put it in her letterbox so Emily can't say she never received it.'

'Yes.'

'Once the ring is back, the subject will be closed. I never want to hear the name Murton Davies mentioned in this house again. Is that clear?'

'Perfectly, Pops.'

'Time you found yourself a decent girl, preferably one who won't sleep with anyone before she's married. Not even you.' His father went to the door. 'One last thing,' he turned back to Robin, 'don't bother putting announcements in *The Times* and *Evening Post* cancelling the engagement. I'll get my receptionist to do it first thing in the morning. "By mutual agreement" is the phrase that springs to mind. Is that all right with you?'

'Yes, Pops,' Robin said meekly.

'Not that it will fool anyone for a minute after what went on here on Saturday night, but,' he shrugged his shoulders, 'the only things you can be accused of are being too loyal, blinkered, generous and soft-hearted. Not an entirely bad reputation for a young man to have – apart from the blinkered.'

'You seem tense. Is anything the matter?' Sam rolled off Judy into his half of the bed.

'Besides all this being new to me, no.'

'You'll get used to it,' he assured her confidently. 'You won't forget what I said about going to the doctor and getting a cap?'

'I'd rather do it after we are married,' she demurred.

'This is the nineteen-fifties, Judy. Engaged couples are allowed some leeway.'

'I wouldn't call what we've just done leeway and I've known my doctor all my life. I'd be embarrassed to ask him about birth control before we're married.' Holding the sheet over her breasts, she reached for her slip.

'You're not dressing?'

'I'd better get an early night if I'm picking you up at nine.'

'Ten more minutes.' He tugged the sheet from her hands and pulled her back into the bed, running his hands down her arms. 'You're shivering. If you're cold, I could turn up the fire.'

'I'm not cold.' She covered herself with the sheet again and he yanked it away.

'What's the matter with you? I've seen you naked from the waist up dozens of times.'

'There's a difference between that kind of seeing and the kind of seeing that leads to what we've just done.'

'You don't like making love?' he questioned sharply.

'I need time to get used to it, Sam,' she explained, in response to the hurt expression in his eyes.

'I thought last night was fantastic. Are you saying it wasn't for you?'

'It's probably guilt. All my life I've had it drummed into me that decent girls only make love after they are married.'

He lay back on the pillows and stared up at the ceiling. 'We've been engaged for over eighteen months, we'll be married in three.'

'I know, Sam. All I'm asking is that you be patient with me.'

'And stop making love to you?'

'No,' she whispered, not wanting to hurt him any more than she already had.

'What we need is more practice.'

She tried to return his smile and braced herself to meet his caresses without flinching. While he kissed and fondled her, she wondered how other women coped. Her mother, Katie, Helen, Lily – perhaps they could tell her how long it took to become accustomed to this intimate, painful and grossly humiliating side of marriage.

It was after midnight when Robin parked his car on the Mumbles Road. He removed an envelope from his pocket and turned it over. The words, *Miss Emily Murton Davies*, scrawled in his handwriting, glared back at him.

Despite everything his father had said, he couldn't still a nagging doubt that something wasn't quite right. Why had Emily claimed that Angela had arranged for her to be found in bed with Thompson when she must have known that no one would believe her? It was obvious Angela couldn't have arranged anything of the kind if she hadn't known that Emily had been sleeping around all along. The only wonder was that he hadn't realised what Ems was up to. After all, they had been together a long time . . .

He turned the envelope over. Inside was a cheque for

fifty pounds, the entire contents of his deposit account, which he'd have to transfer to his current account in his lunch break tomorrow. If Ems was careful, fifty pounds should go some way towards keeping her until the baby was born and, once she'd had it adopted, she wouldn't have any more expenses. Besides, fifty pounds was a lot to pay out when there was hardly any likelihood of the baby being his.

What had his father called him? Loyal, blinkered, generous and soft-hearted. His father was right, he was being generous giving Emily fifty pounds considering the position he had seen her in the night before. Wasn't he?

Taking a pen from his pocket he tore a blank page from the back of his address book and scribbled a note.

> My people don't want me to see you again. Please send back the ring. You can drop it off it at my solicitors, Thomas and Butler in Christina Street.

He paused for a moment, then scrawled.

> Thanks for the memories, Robin.

Trite but final. There was no mistaking the message. He pushed the page into the envelope, giving himself no time for second thoughts. Leaving his car, he walked around the corner to the flat and thrust the envelope through the letterbox. He resisted the temptation to look up at the window before retracing his steps. He was free. He'd behaved impeccably and seen to it that Ems had enough money to last her until the baby was born. But he knew he'd feel a whole lot better if he could blot the image of Emily as he had last seen her, wretched and tearful, from his mind.

'I'd be delighted to advance you a bank loan for two thousand pounds, Mr Clay.' Mr Hopkin Jones beamed magnanimously at Martin and sat back in the substantial leather chair behind his desk. 'Just one note of prudence. Are you certain that two thousand pounds will be sufficient for your needs?' He pulled a file towards him and flicked through it. 'Given your assets, I would be happy to arrange a two thousand five hundred pound loan or a two thousand five hundred pound overdraft facility, to be repaid over ten years, whichever you think will best suit your needs.'

'What assets?' Martin queried suspiciously.

'Your house, investments . . .'

'The house is my wife's and she was left the investments by her aunt.'

'She put them in your joint names, Mr Clay. You signed the papers.' The manager checked the date next to the signatures at the bottom of a page. 'Two years ago.'

Martin vaguely recalled Lily bringing a pile of papers home from the bank for him to sign shortly after they were married. She had told him they were related to their bank accounts and the wills they had made, each favouring the other. Trusting her implicitly, he hadn't even given the papers a cursory glance before scribbling his signature alongside hers.

'I want the loan, Mr Hopkin Jones, not my wife.'

'The bank would never consider advancing an unsecured loan or overdraft of that magnitude, Mr Clay.'

'You have my word . . .'

'Forgive me for saying so, but your word would be worth very little should the garage that is offering you a partnership become bankrupt.'

Martin fell silent.

'Your wife has worked for us for over three years, Mr Clay. I don't think I am speaking out of turn when I say I feel that I know her. She would have never put her property in your joint names if she hadn't full confidence in your abilities and judgement.'

'I'll not mortgage Lily's house or touch her investments, Mr Hopkin Jones.' Martin rose to his feet.

'You could miss a golden opportunity if you don't, Mr Clay. The location of the garage is excellent and coupled with the Powell and Ronconi name and the prospective figures in this,' he tapped the file Brian had given Martin the day before, 'make this as sound a business venture as any I've seen in years.'

'But not sound enough to advance me the money I require?'

Mr Hopkin Jones gave Martin a tight smile. 'Not without security, Mr Clay.'

'Thank you for your time.' Martin picked up the file from the bank manager's desk.

Mr Hopkin Jones removed his pocket watch from his waistcoat and opened it as he walked Martin to the door. 'It is twelve-thirty, Mr Clay. Why don't you take your wife to lunch and discuss this with her?'

'There is nothing to discuss, Mr Hopkin Jones, and I have to be back at work in ten minutes.' Martin held out his hand. 'Thank you and goodbye.'

Chapter Eight

'That's the wedding booked for eleven-thirty on the first Saturday in July, banns to be called for three weeks before, when we'll have to be in church for at least one service a day and six meetings booked with the vicar starting mid-May.' Sam noted the dates Judy had scribbled in her diary and put them in his own. 'Why on earth does the vicar want to see us so many times before the wedding?'

'You heard him.' Judy sat back as the waitress set a bowl of tomato soup in front of her. 'To discuss the gravity of the step we're taking.'

'It's enough to make me wish that we'd opted for the register office.' He crumbled his bread roll over his soup.

'You were the one who insisted on a church wedding.'

'It's what my family will expect. My mother was thrilled when I told her we were setting a firm date today. I'll write to her to tell her we'll be up on Sunday. Do you think your mother and Roy will be able to come?'

'I'll ask them.'

'I'll also ask my mother to check around my family so she'll be able to give us a rough idea of the number of people who'll be coming from my side.' He blew on his soup as he spooned it to his lips. 'And I still say twenty is optimistically low for your side.'

'There's only Roy, my mother, my real father if he wants to come . . .'

'What about his family?'

'I've only met them once and I'm sure they wouldn't expect an invitation.'

'You must have other relatives.'

'None alive and that only leaves close friends, Helen, Katie and Lily, Martin, Jack and Mr Griffiths, and perhaps one or two of my old school and college friends.'

'The girls from the salons,' he reminded.

'Invite one and we'd have to invite them all, and I'm not closing the salons on a Saturday, it's our busiest day.'

'There were two hundred people at my brother's reception when he married five years ago.'

She paused with her soup spoon halfway to her mouth. 'I hope you don't expect my mother and me to pay for two hundred of your relatives to lunch in this place?'

'No, there were only a hundred from our side of the family.'

'A hundred! That is ridiculous, Sam. No one has a family that big.'

'I do.' He finished his soup and pushed his bowl aside. 'But you can talk it over with my mother on Sunday. The manager said he didn't need definite numbers until eight weeks before the wedding.'

'Which barely gives us five weeks.' She was alarmed at how imminent the wedding suddenly seemed.

'I thought I'd ask Martin to be my best man, if that's all right with you.'

'Of course.'

'Are you going to ask Lily to be matron of honour?'

'It might be an idea if Martin is the best man.'

'In the meantime, you have to buy a dress and veil, and I'd better get measured for a morning suit.'

'You want me to wear a white wedding dress?'

'What else?' He looked at her in amazement. The waitress cleared their bowls.

'I haven't—'

'Had time to think about it,' he finished acidly.

'We also have to decide where we're going to live.' She deliberately changed the subject.

'I could put in for a police house.'

'We'd have people knocking at the door day and night

if we move into one of those. Couldn't you move into the flat?' She looked down at the gravy smothered pork chop, mashed potato, cabbage and apple sauce the waitress had set in front of her. Breakfast had been half a slice of toast five hours before, and she was ravenous.

'I'm not sure I want to live in your flat.' Sam took his plate from the waitress, almost dropping it as it burned his fingers.

'Why not? Emily will have moved out by then. It's perfectly comfortable . . .'

'For someone who is not married,' he interrupted brusquely. 'It's hardly a permanent home.'

'I'm not expecting it to be. Eventually we'll buy a house.' Cutting a slice from the eye of the chop, Judy dipped it into the apple sauce and popped it into her mouth.

'So it will only be a stop gap?'

'Until we find the right place, yes.'

'All right,' he agreed, 'but we'll still have to get some new furniture.'

'Why? It's fully furnished.'

'In a rented flat style.'

'It has everything we need.'

'You're talking about our first home, Judy.'

'Only until we find a house.' She looked from him to his meal. 'If you don't start eating, it will get cold.'

He finally picked up his knife and fork. 'Then you think we should start looking for a house straight away?'

'Not straight away, I'd like to concentrate on the salons for a while.'

'Not the bloody salons again, Judy.' Sam only realised he'd sworn when two middle-aged women sitting behind them started tutting. He turned to them. 'I'm sorry,' he apologised contritely.

'I should think so too, young man. It would serve you right if we complained to the manager and he called a policeman.'

'I said I'm sorry,' he reiterated testily, seeing the irony

in the threat. Turning back to Judy, he propped his elbows on the table and looked at her.

'For the second time, eat your meal before it gets cold.'

'Is that your way of telling me that you intend to keep on working after we're married?'

'Of course I'm going to carry on working,' Judy hissed indignantly. 'Who else do you think is going to run the salons?'

'Your mother.' He finally cut into his chop.

'My mother has to look after Billy.'

'And you have to look after me.'

'You're looking after yourself now. Most of the time.'

'Most of the time?' he reiterated icily.

'When you can't persuade Lily to cook, bake and generally run around after you and Mike. And before you say another word, Lily and Helen both work, and Katie did until a few weeks ago.'

'In her husband's warehouse.'

'So, what's the difference between Mr Griffiths's warehouse and my mother's salons, they're both family businesses.'

'The difference is Helen, Lily and Katie's husbands don't work shifts. You know full well that sometimes I need my meals at odd hours and there's my laundry . . .'

'Carry on like this and you'll find yourself going back to see the vicar – alone – because I will have called the whole thing off,' she warned.

'You really intend to keep on working?'

'Yes.'

He looked over his shoulder and saw the two women were still watching them. 'We need to talk about this.'

'Yes, we do,' Judy agreed, 'and I mean just that, talk and nothing else. When you come round for a meal tonight might be a good time.'

'I can't make it tonight.'

'You said you'd call after your shift. I've bought steak, potatoes, salad and a cake.'

'Martin invited me to the White Rose to wet Katie and John's baby's head. Everyone's going, even Jack.'

'I see.' She pursed her lips.

'It's no different to you spending yesterday with Emily and your mother instead of me.'

'You hadn't bought food specially.'

'Feed it to Emily,' he bit back childishly.

'Finish your meal,' she ordered sharply.

'You were in and out of the bank in no time.' Lily set two brown paper and string carrier bags on to the hall floor and closed the door.

Still dressed in the oil-stained jeans, old shirt and pullover he wore to work, Martin replaced the telephone receiver. 'I had to get back to the depot.'

'I was hoping we could have had lunch.' She folded her gloves into her coat pocket.

'Did the manager tell you that he wouldn't give me a loan?'

'He's not allowed to discuss clients' business, it's confidential.' Her face fell. 'Oh, Marty . . .'

'Not even allowed to discuss it with the client's wife when she works in his bank?' he broke in cuttingly.

'Especially when the client's wife works in the bank,' she confirmed. 'Marty, I'm so sorry. I really thought there wouldn't be a problem. We grant loans every day and bigger than the one you asked for. I'll have a word with him.'

'You most certainly will not.'

'Why not? He's not allowed to turn down a loan application without good reason. We can appeal to head office.' She hung her coat on the stand. 'Did he say why he refused you?'

'Yes.' Martin leaned against the stair post.

'And?' she looked at him expectantly.

'I wouldn't allow him to use your house or investments as security.'

'That's stupid . . .'

'Now I'm stupid,' he challenged icily.

'Not you, your pride. The house isn't mine, it's ours, as are the investments,' she corrected quickly, sensing an uncharacteristic anger. She crossed her fingers behind her back, hoping that he hadn't found out about the baby. Then she realised he couldn't have. No one knew except her and the doctor, and the doctor had assured her that he hadn't the right to tell anyone, not even Martin.

'So I discovered today. Why didn't you tell me that you'd put everything in our joint names?'

'Surely you're not cross about that? I asked you to sign the papers just after we were married.'

'Routine paperwork, you said. Joint bank accounts, wills leaving everything to one another, sensible precautions,' he taunted.

'They were, and if you'd taken the time and trouble to read the papers you would have known what you were signing.'

'Oh, I will from now on,' he snapped caustically. 'I'll read every single thing you give me twice over, don't you worry.'

'But, Marty, it's not as if we'll be risking anything,' she asserted. 'Brian has all the figures worked out.'

'And going by those, we stand to lose two and half thousand pounds if the garage folds.'

'Which is the exact amount of the investments my aunt left me. And we won't lose it. Brian has the backing of the biggest garage chain in South Wales so the sales side is certain to take off, and the repair, service and maintenance side is bound to be profitable soon afterwards. So why not use our money to finance a business that will secure our future and the future of our family?'

'As if we can possibly consider having a family when I can't even raise a loan to go into business,' he bit back resentfully.

'But you can, Marty,' she murmured persuasively. 'There's no point in us owning this house and having investments if we don't use them to make a better life for ourselves, and if you go for the overdraft option, we may not even need all the money. What can possibly go wrong?'

'Nothing,' he informed her curtly, 'because I've just told Brian that I can't raise the money.'

'Marty—'

'I've said all I am going to say about it.' Turning, he climbed the stairs. 'I'm going up for a bath.'

Knowing Martin too well to try arguing or winning him over when he was in a stubborn mood, Lily picked up the carrier bags. 'I'll have tea on the table when you come down,' she called after him and she walked into the kitchen. She unpacked the sausages, onions and carrots she'd bought on the market and set them on the draining board before returning to the hall. She waited until she heard the sound of the bath taps running. Opening the drawer in the hall table, she took out her address book. Flicking through until she came to P, she checked the telephone number Brian had given them, lifted the receiver and began dialling.

'So.' Joy passed Judy a tureen of Welsh cawl. 'You and Sam have finally fixed the date.'

Judy spooned a small portion into a bowl for Billy before helping herself to the lamb stew. 'He's writing to his mother to tell her we'll visit her on Sunday. Do you think Roy will be able to come?'

'I believe he's on nights, so if we're invited for late afternoon or early evening it should be fine. But I thought you said Sam was on afternoons?'

'He is, but Mike's agreed to swap with him.'

'Poor Mike, he seems to do more of Sam's shifts than Sam does.'

'So he does,' Judy mused, not quite suppressing the thought that Sam always seemed to get people to do things he wanted them to. Her, Mike . . .

'Have you any thoughts on a wedding dress?'

'Sam wants the full white wedding, the dress, the veil,

morning suits for the wedding party, the church, bells, choir, a reception in the Mackworth . . .'

'And you, of course, always do what Sam wants?' Joy teased, as she diced half a slice of bread and sprinkled the cubes on top of the stew in Billy's bowl.

'No, if he'd had his way, we wouldn't have had an eighteen-month engagement.'

Joy tied a bib around Billy's neck, lifted him into his high chair and wheeled it closer to her own. 'Most girls dream of their ideal wedding dress from the age of six. You only have to look at Lily, she knew exactly what she wanted.'

'Yards and yards of lace over gleaming white satin.' Judy smiled at the memory. 'Now you mention it, I think I'm more of a costume girl, like Helen and Katie.'

'Helen had no choice, she could hardly have worn virginal white when everyone knew there was no way that her father would have given his consent to her marriage at eighteen if she hadn't been pregnant. And with John being divorced, Katie had little choice either, but people will think it extremely odd if you walk down the aisle of St Mary's in a costume.'

'Sam did warn me that there may be as many as a hundred expecting invitations from his side of the family.'

'What?' Joy dropped the ladle back into the stew, splashing her blouse. 'Please tell me you're joking.'

'He comes from a large family, but I warned him we're not made of money. No, pet, you're supposed to eat it, not hit it.' Judy turned Billy's spoon around in his chubby fingers and helped him scoop up a helping of potatoes, bread and meat.

'I'd forgotten this age.' Joy mopped up the stew Billy had spread over the wooden tray of the highchair. 'Too old to feed and too young to feed themselves without making one almighty mess.'

'I made this much mess?'

'More, you wanted to be independent from the day

you were born and knew exactly how to throw a tantrum when you didn't want to be helped. Billy's an angel in comparison. Aren't you, my darling, clever boy.' Joy beamed as he managed to ferry most of a spoonful of stew to his mouth. 'I hope you told Sam that we can run to a decent reception. After all, it's not every day my only daughter gets married, but if you can find a tactful way to suggest he limit the invitations to close family I'd be grateful.'

'I've already tried, perhaps it's something we should discuss with his mother on Sunday?'

'I'd say definitely, not perhaps. Roy has tomorrow off, would you like me to visit a few bridal-wear shops with you?'

'I suppose I'd better start thinking about a frock.'

'Such enthusiasm.' Joy wiped the surplus stew from around Billy's mouth with a tea towel. 'But at least after you've seen what's on offer, you'll have a better idea of what might suit you. Ten o'clock all right? I will have Billy sorted by then.'

'I have to check on the salons.'

'Ring round in the morning and tell the girls to do their own banking for once.'

'And if there are problems?'

'The girls will have to sort them. That's what we pay them for. Besides, Tuesdays are never that busy. We could go to the printer's as well to look at invitations and orders of service, and call in at Eynon's to see about a wedding cake. I'm not sure how long in advance that has to be ordered. And there are the cars, the flowers – we'd better check what will be available at the beginning of July. Have you thought what you're doing for your honeymoon?'

'Sam's calling round tomorrow night after his shift. We have a few things to discuss.' Judy decided against telling her mother that one of those things was Sam's objection to a working wife.

'The last thing I want to do is muscle in on your and

Sam's big day, but if there's anything that I can do to help organise things, I'd be delighted.' Joy grabbed Billy's spoon before it hit the floor. 'And it will be nice to spend a whole day with you.' She turned to Billy. 'No, you are not getting down until you've eaten all your dinner,' she warned. 'We'll lunch in the Mackworth, my treat.'

'You can leave Billy that long?'

'Roy will enjoy having Billy to himself and he's as good, if not better, with him than I am.'

'Even at changing nappies?' Judy asked doubtfully.

'Even changing nappies,' Joy said. 'And before you say anything, he asked me to show him how to do it. Sometimes I think he's more domesticated than me. He seems to enjoy cooking and cleaning. He even complained that Norah and Lily would never let him near the kitchen when he lived with them.'

'Any chance of him trying to impart some of his enthusiasm in that direction to Sam?'

'From the way Sam's always turned out, he must know how to cook and do his own laundry.' As Billy refused to hold the spoon, Joy spooned cawl into his mouth only for him to spray it into her face seconds later.

'From what I've seen, his and Mike's cooking is limited to using a tin opener, and Lily, his mother or the laundry do his washing and ironing, not him.'

'You think you'll have problems in that direction?' Joy mopped her face.

'I know I'll have problems in that direction.' Judy had trouble keeping a straight face as the second spoonful Joy fed Billy joined the first. 'I think Billy's trying to tell you that he's had enough.'

'I think you're right.' Joy picked up the tea towel and attacked the tray. 'You know, Norah used to complain Roy didn't know one end of a dishcloth from another and look at him now. Sam will change after you're married.'

'I'm not too sure.'

'It will be different once you're living together. There's

more give and take when you're both under the same roof, if only because it's too exhausting to argue with someone when you see them last thing at night and first thing in the morning. There's nothing more tiring than a quarrel that lasts from one day to the next.'

'I can't imagine you and Roy quarrelling.' Judy poured herself a glass of water. 'He's far too easygoing.'

'We had a row that lasted five days when I told him I was expecting Billy. He expected me to give up work—'

'You wanted to,' Judy cut in.

'But I didn't know I wanted to until after Billy was born,' Joy dismissed. 'But yesterday, when I suggested that Mrs Lannon come in and take care of Billy a couple of mornings a week so I could help you with the accounts and check that the salons are being run properly, he thought it was a good idea.'

'But you said—'

'I said I didn't miss the salon and I don't. But thanks to your expansion of the business I don't have to go back to the drudgery of day-to-day hairdressing. Doing the books, supervising the banking and checking the salons a few hours a week is nothing like standing on your feet up to your armpits in perming solutions all day. And I'd like to take some of the load off you, especially now you're getting married. You've been run off your feet since I stopped working.'

'I didn't expect you to come back, and Mrs Lannon is—'

'A kind, capable old lady who can't wait to get her hands on Billy and start playing grandmother. She's been round here twice a week for coffee ever since he was born, so it's hardly as if I'll be leaving him with a stranger. Is it, poppet?' Wiping the last of the stew from Billy's hands and face, Joy lifted him down from his high chair.

'So it's all settled.'

'You don't want my help?' Joy asked keenly.

'Of course I do.'

'Perhaps I should have discussed it with you first.'

'I am absolutely sure,' Judy repeated earnestly.

'And you don't mind me interfering with your wedding?'

'You never interfere.'

'That's not what you used to say before you left home.'

'I've grown up since then.'

Joy studied her for a moment. 'I know you, Judy. I changed your nappies the same as Billy's. There's something wrong.'

'No, there isn't.'

'What is it?' Joy questioned flatly.

Judy looked at her mother. Joy had always been open with her about sex. And in all the years they had worked together in the salon she had never seen her shocked by anything any of her customers had told her, which was why she'd suggested Emily go to her mother for advice. And, as always, Joy had given sound practical guidance without making any moral judgements. 'How long does it take to get used to . . . ?' She hesitated, searching for the right words.

'Making love?' Joy supplied quietly.

'Yes.' Judy took Billy's bowl and stacked it in her own.

'That rather depends on how often you and Sam have tried.'

'Twice.'

'After being engaged for eighteen months?'

Judy was taken aback by the stunned expression on her mother's face. 'I thought we should wait until after we were married, but once we set the date Sam thought—'

'Sam thought,' her mother repeated. 'What did you think, Judy?'

'I was curious and it wasn't as if we hadn't done anything.' She skirted over the details.

'He did use a French letter?'

'Yes, and that's another thing, he wants me to see the doctor about getting fitted with a Dutch cap.'

'That makes sense if you don't want any little accidents like Billy.'

'You didn't want Billy?'

'Of course we wanted him, but he wasn't planned. He is the result of me thinking that I was too old to get pregnant, not that I'm in the least sorry. We simply thought it was impossible. But you and Sam are young. You've all the time in the world to have a family.'

'That's what Sam says, and,' Judy caught her mother's eye, 'I made it clear to him that I'm not ready to be a mother yet.'

'I'm glad.' Billy toddled back from the corner where Joy kept his toys with a picture book. Tugging at Joy's skirt, he waited for her to lift him on to her knee. 'I often wonder if things would have been different between your father and me if I hadn't become pregnant practically on my wedding night. When he wasn't working, he was out, drinking with his friends, who were all unmarried, and most of their nights out ended with a visit to a dance hall. If I'd been with him instead of stuck at home with a baby, I might have stopped him from developing a wandering eye.'

'I'm sorry.'

Joy laughed and Billy snuggled close to her. 'I didn't say that to make you feel guilty. As it happened we would have been separated by the war no matter what, and no doubt he would have become enamoured by the same WAAF who eventually snared him. You kept me sane. The best daughter a mother could wish for and fantastic company. And just look at me now. I have you, Roy and Billy.' She frowned. 'Not that I want to hear the details, but how serious is this problem between you and Sam?'

'He knows I don't like him making love to me and he's upset by it.'

'Making love should be something you both do, not one doing it to the other, but if you've only done it twice after such a long engagement, I can see that it's going to take some getting used to.'

'Then it will get better?' Judy questioned hopefully.

'I can't answer that. All I know is that it was wonderful for me from the start with your father. Probably,' Joy made a wry face, 'because he practised with every willing girl every chance that came his way, before and after we married and, from what I heard, he wasn't short of chances. As well as being very good-looking, he could have charmed the knickers off a nun.'

'And Roy?'

'It just worked out between us from the start, which doesn't help you at all. Do you think part of the problem could be that you've waited too long and subconsciously you think it's wrong to make love before you're married? Not that I've ever subscribed to that view,' she added swiftly, lest Judy think she was judging her.

'That's what I told Sam.'

'Try inviting him over one evening when Emily's not around, cook him a meal, have a few drinks, relax and take things slowly from there. But don't relax enough for him to forget to use a French letter and another thing; don't get caught up in wedding preparations to the point where you forget the serious purpose behind all the razzmatazz. A wedding is just a day, marriage is for life.'

'I'm all too aware of that. I only hope Sam will remember it before he books any more extravagances for the church or the Mackworth.' Judy picked up the dishes.

'Leave them,' Joy ordered. 'I can do them after I put Billy to bed.'

'It's the least I can do.' Judy looked back at her mother from the doorway. 'Most mothers would have shouted and created the most awful scene if their daughters had asked them what I just asked you.'

'I doubt it.' Joy closed the picture book and set Billy on the floor. 'Most mothers want their daughters to have a good and successful marriage, and in my experience, that's impossible without a first-rate sex life. It's worth working at it to get it right.'

Judy nodded, but didn't return her mother's smile. As Joy watched her walk into the kitchen, she couldn't help wondering if there was another reason behind Judy's reluctance to make love to Sam. Could it be that he was simply the wrong man for her?

'I am not prepared to discuss it, Lily. Brian made me an offer. I can't afford to accept it, end of story.' Martin set aside the plate of pork sausage, fried onion, carrot and mash he'd barely touched.

'I wish—'

'I'm going to the garage. The points need adjusting on the car.' Pushing his chair back from the table, he rose to his feet and walked into the scullery.

Lily waited for the outer door to open and close. When she heard the sound of Martin's step ringing on the metal staircase that led down to the garden, she took a pen and notepad from the drawer, and started scribbling. Whichever way she calculated, she came to the same conclusion. With careful management, she, Martin and the baby would be able to survive for as long as five years without her wages and on half of Martin's plus the rent money from the basement and the attic if they cashed in all of her aunt's investments. And if there were any unexpected bills they could always mortgage the house. Tearing off the paper, she screwed it into a ball and tossed it into the bin before picking up their plates and carrying them to the sink.

She was scraping the uneaten food into the pigswill bin when the bell rang. Wiping her hands on her apron, she went into the hall and opened the door. Judy was on the step.

Sensitive to the fraught expression on Lily's face, Judy backed down the path. 'I came to ask a favour but if it's a bad time . . .'

'No, it's a very good time. I could do with a cup of tea

and a shoulder to cry on. Come on in.' Lily led the way into the kitchen and set the kettle on to boil.

'Martin out?' Judy enquired warily, taking off her coat.

'Playing with the car in the garage. He won't be back until bedtime.'

'You seem very sure.'

'I am.' Lily filled the kettle and set it on the stove to boil.

'Is this a private quarrel or am I allowed to know what happened?'

'I'd rather not say any more than it's about money.' Lily cleared the table and picked up the tablecloth.

'Then leave me out of it. It's bad enough trying to deal with my own and the salons' finances without anyone else's. I'm dreading the day when I come home loaded with shopping and Sam shouts at me for spending too much. It's bound to happen. You know what I'm like once I go into a dress shop.'

'Seeing as you only have time to shop about twice a year, Sam can hardly complain and it's not as if you'll be spending his money when you're earning your own.' Lily shook the cloth out of the window before folding it.

'Doesn't it become joint money once you're married?'

'Try telling Martin that.' Lily set two cups and saucers on the table. Boiling mad, she suddenly realised she was in danger of taking out her anger on Judy. 'Promise you won't tell a soul,' she relented.

'I swear,' Judy agreed solemnly.

'Brian offered Martin a partnership in the garage, where he'd be in charge of the car maintenance and repair side of things.'

'That's marvellous. Martin's always going on about opening his own business.'

'It would be marvellous if he'd use this house and the investments Auntie Norah left me to raise a bank loan to buy into it.' Lily spooned tea into the pot.

'He won't?'

'No.' Lily wet the tea and set the teapot on the table. 'I've tried telling him what I have is his, that he'll soon pay it back and we have enough money coming in to meet the bills and buy the essentials, not only from the flat downstairs but upstairs as well, now that Brian is moving into the attic.'

'I didn't know Brian was moving in with you.' Judy's voice rose in alarm. Brian back in Swansea and running a garage was one thing; Brian living with Lily and Martin and picking up where he'd left off with the old crowd, including her closest friends, was quite another.

'Yes, and that will only make it worse.' Lily was too preoccupied with her own problems to sense Judy's unease. 'The garage is bound to be a success and I know Martin, he'll never forgive himself for missing a chance in a million. Men! They're stubborn, pig-headed creatures.' She sat across the table from Judy and poured out the tea.

'What are you going to do?'

Lily turned to Judy.

'You've already made up your mind, haven't you?' Judy reached for the sugar.

'Martin is so furious with me anyway for putting the house and investments in our joint names, I decided it couldn't get any worse. I telephoned Brian earlier this evening and told him I'd raise the money. Tomorrow I'll ask the bank manager to give me the loan Martin needs to buy into the business. As the property is in joint names he'll lend it to either of us. As soon as it comes through, I'll present it to Martin, then if he wants to waste it, that will be his decision.'

'He won't like it,' Judy warned.

'I know,' Lily mused, 'but he will just have to get over it, won't he? Among other things,' she whispered softly.

'Trouble with the car, Martin?' John glanced over the wall, as he locked his garage door.

'Just routine maintenance.' Martin only just stopped himself from addressing John as Mr Griffiths, but he couldn't bring himself to say 'John' – it simply didn't seem right. 'How are Katie and the baby?'

'Very well. Katie sends you and Lily her love.' John couldn't stop smiling. 'I can't wait to get them home. You haven't forgotten about tonight?'

'Tonight?' Martin looked blank.

'The Rose, wetting the baby's head,' John reminded. 'You said you were going to ask Sam and Mike. Roy and Jack are coming.'

'I'm sorry, I forgot. Mike said he'd be there and Sam will join us when his shift finishes at ten. Give me five minutes to wash my hands and change, and I'll meet you out front.'

John looked thoughtfully after Martin, as he ran back into the house. It wasn't like him to be forgetful. He made a mental note to take Martin aside in the pub. If Katie's brother had problems, the least he could do was offer to help.

'You finished working on the car?' Lily said in surprise when Martin opened the kitchen door.

'No, but I said I'd go down the Rose with Mr Griffiths. We arranged to wet the baby's head.'

'So you did.'

'You could have reminded me.' Martin made an effort to control his temper when he saw Judy sitting at the table. 'How's it going, Judy?' He couldn't help feeling Lily had invited her over just so she could discuss their argument with someone.

'It's going fine. Have you seen Sam?'

'Not since yesterday.' He opened the door that led into the hall. 'If you'll excuse me, I have to change. Mr Griffiths is waiting.' He ran up the stairs.

'I see what you mean.' Judy gave Lily a look of commiseration.

'Would you like another cup of tea?'

'Yes, please.' Judy handed Lily her cup.

'This wasn't just a social call on the off-chance that I'd

need your shoulder, was it?' Lily filled Judy's cup and handed her the milk jug.

'No, as I said, I wanted to ask a favour. Seeing as I was your bridesmaid I was hoping you'd reciprocate and be my matron of honour.'

'You and Sam have set the date?'

'First Saturday in July.'

'That's wonderful and I'd be honoured.' They both laughed at the unintentional pun.

'I only hope Martin calms down before he meets Sam in the pub tonight.' Judy sipped her tea. 'Sam wants him to be best man and, in his present mood, Martin will more likely bite Sam's head off than agree.'

Chapter Nine

'Glyn Martin Griffiths!' The toast echoed around the lounge bar of the White Rose as all the men in the room lifted their glasses to John, who had bought a drink for everyone in the pub.

'And to Judy and Sam.' Roy gave Sam a sly glance, lifting his glass for a second toast. 'Joy mentioned that you two have finally set the date.'

'More like I wore Judy down. The big day's set for the first Saturday in July and you are all invited with your wives, children and in Mike's case, girlfriend.' Sam was grateful for Brian's absence. The last thing he wanted was one of Judy's old flames at their wedding. 'Which reminds me,' he turned to Martin as the landlord collared John to offer his congratulations, 'would you return the favour and be my best man?'

'I'd be delighted.' Martin looked anything but, as he offered his cigarettes to the group at their table.

'Is anything the matter with Martin?' John whispered to Jack.

'Not that I know anything about.' Jack eyed his brother.

'Is he going to work in Brian's garage as well?'

'Brian hinted on Saturday that he'd like him to,' Jack murmured, taking care to keep his voice low. 'But Marty bit my head off when I asked him about it earlier.'

'I thought Martin would have jumped at the chance.'

'He said something about being promoted in the council garage. Perhaps he doesn't want to move from there.'

John moved his chair closer to Martin's. 'I've been talking to Jack about Brian's garage.'

'Oh, yes.' Martin gave John a suspicious look.

'Sounds like it's going to be a great success. Being a mechanic, I'm surprised you're not joining them.'

'I already have a job,' Martin answered tersely.

'I've often heard you say that you'd like to be your own boss. I know that working for a garage the size of the one Brian's about to open wouldn't exactly be working for yourself, but it would be more like it than working for the council.'

'Have you been talking to Lily?' Martin narrowed his eyes.

'No, why do you ask?'

'Nothing.' Martin picked up his pint of beer. 'I'm happy as a foreman in the council depot.'

'Should you ever think of going self-employed, give me a shout. I'm always on the look out for sound investments.'

'The last thing I need is your money, John,' Martin refused curtly, so curtly John allowed the matter to drop.

'As your boyfriend's coming round, I'll make myself scarce.' Emily closed the locks on a trunk and heaved it upright.

'Here, let me do that.' Judy grabbed the handle and carried it to the corner closest to the door. 'You shouldn't be lifting anything this heavy and there's no need to go to your room. Sam cried off to go to a stag night.' She unbuttoned her coat and threw it on to the sofa before collapsing into an easy chair.

'I'm sorry.'

'I'm glad to have some peace.' Judy looked at the trunk. 'You packing already?'

'I saw the doctor this afternoon.'

'The one my mother recommended?'

'Yes.' Emily sat in the chair opposite Judy's. 'She said I'm nearer five months than four, and the three inches I put on around my waist this week is a sign that I'm about to expand even more, and soon. She rang a home after she examined me and they're prepared to accept me on Saturday. We . . . I . . . thought it best I take up their offer of a place.'

'Don't you have to work your notice at Lewis Lewis's?'

'I handed in my notice this afternoon after I left the doctor's. I have a couple of days' holiday due to me, so they said I could leave straight away. All I had to do was wait for the office to make up my wages.'

'Had they . . .'

'Heard about what happened at Robin's on Saturday night?' Emily finished for her. 'I don't think they would have paid me off and given me my cards if they hadn't. No respectable shop wants a slut who is carrying a bastard to serve their customers.'

'Please, don't talk or think about yourself that way. You're anything but a slut.'

'Thank you for saying that, but face it, Judy, everyone who knows me, including you, will be relieved when I leave on Saturday.'

'I'll be sorry to lose you as a flatmate.'

'You can't mean that.'

'Yes, I do.' Judy suddenly realised that it would be lonely to return to the empty flat after living with Helen for over two years. Emily wasn't Helen, but she felt close to her, even though they'd only lived together for a short time. And she felt sorry for her. Pregnant, abandoned by her boyfriend and so friendless she'd been forced to confide her problems to someone she hardly knew. 'Is the home far?'

'Not too far. It's in a big house outside Llandeilo.'

'How are you going to get there?'

'The doctor gave me directions. I get a train to Llandeilo and a bus from there.'

'I could take you.'

'I couldn't possibly put you to all that trouble. The doctor said it's over twenty miles.'

'I'd enjoy the drive,' Judy insisted. 'I haven't been to that part of the world in years and from what I remember it's quite pretty. Besides,' Judy nodded to the trunk, 'you're in no condition to lug anything that size around.'

'I won't have to. I saw Larry after work. He's decided to leave Swansea and join my mother in Bournemouth.'

'He's heard you're pregnant?' Judy suggested perceptively.

Emily nodded. 'The old crowd didn't waste any time in telling him.'

'I'm sorry.'

'Now can you understand why I can't wait to leave?'

'Yes, but what you have to remember is that none of these people are your real friends.'

'As I've found out.' Emily forced a strained smile. 'Larry told his boss my mother's ill. She's not of course, but he's leaving for Bournemouth tomorrow. He offered to take anything I won't need for the next couple of months to my aunt's house. She has plenty of room so one trunk won't be a problem. I packed most of my clothes. There's no point in taking them with me because I can hardly get into any of them now, let alone in a few weeks.'

'You'll need clothes in the hostel.'

'I bought a couple of things on the market today, enough to see me through. I told the woman on the stall that they were for my sister. I'm sure she didn't believe me . . .' Emily bit her bottom lip to stop it from trembling.

'Emily . . .'

'No.' Emily left her chair before Judy could reach her. 'I'm all right, really.' She went to the window and pulled back the curtain. The street outside was deserted, rain was falling, the street lights puddling the damp pavement with pools of yellow light and sepia shadows. 'Thanks to you and your mother, I have somewhere to stay, people to look after me when the baby is born and help me place it for adoption.'

'Do you have enough money?'

'Robin dropped a cheque through the door last night.' What Emily didn't tell Judy was she'd returned the cheque together with his engagement ring to his solicitor's that morning. 'So you see, I'll be fine. I really will.'

'You'll let me drive you to the home on Saturday.'

'You have the salons . . .'

'My mother told me today that she'd like to start working again. Besides, if we leave early, I can still be back to check on them before they close.'

'If you're sure.'

'I'm sure. You'll need a contact number for the home. Is Larry . . .'

'One of the reasons he's leaving tomorrow is to try to intercept any letters sent to my mother from Swansea. I telephoned my aunt at lunchtime. She's keeping an eye out until Larry arrives and she's agreed to set any that come aside for him to deal with. I only hope no one telephones her, but Larry and I don't think anyone here has my aunt's telephone number.'

'You're not going to tell your mother and sisters that you're pregnant?'

'Larry and I decided it would be better to keep it from them. He's going to tell them that I've taken a position as a receptionist in a country hotel. That way, after the baby's born, I can move on.'

'To Bournemouth?'

'No.' Emily kept her back turned to Judy as she shook her head. 'I have a couple of testimonials. I hope they'll be enough to get me a live-in job in a real hotel somewhere far from here and Bournemouth. Then, when I've saved some money, I can start thinking about what I want to do with the rest of my life.'

'You can tell the people in the home that I'm your next of kin if you like,' Judy offered.

Emily didn't even try to protest. 'Thank you.'

'And if ever you need a character reference from an ex-landlady, you know where to come.'

Emily finally turned to face Judy. 'I wouldn't have coped without your help, you do know that.'

Embarrassed by Emily's gratitude, Judy muttered, 'You would have coped fine.' Anxious to steer the conversation back to the practical, she added, 'If you'd like to leave anything here until you're settled again, you're welcome. I won't be letting out your room.'

'Everything I'm not taking to the home is in my trunk.' Emily wrapped her arms tightly around herself. 'Please, don't take this the wrong way, Judy, but after the baby's born and been adopted, I never want to see Swansea again.'

Lily was sitting in the living room, embroidering a blue teddy bear on a white pram blanket she'd crocheted for John and Katie's son, when she heard the front door open and close. Seconds later the basement door banged shut. She glanced up at the clock, it was only just after half past ten and it took ten minutes to walk from the White Rose to the house. The men hadn't even stayed in the pub until stop tap.

The door opened but Martin remained in the doorway. Any hopes she'd had of patching up their quarrel before they went to bed faded when she saw the thunderous expression on his face. Weaving the needle into the blanket she set it aside.

'Would you like some supper?'

'No.'

'Is anything wrong?' It was an idiotic question, but she felt she had to say something.

'You tell me.'

'Martin, all I want is for you to have a chance—'

'So much so, you discussed our personal affairs with John Griffiths.' Martin gripped the doorframe so hard his knuckles turned white. 'Damn it, Lily, isn't it enough that he bought Katie without him trying to buy me?'

'It's not like that between John and Katie, and you

know it.' For once, Lily allowed her temper to rise to meet her husband's. 'They love one another.'

'Whatever,' he dismissed frostily. 'That still doesn't give you the right to discuss our private affairs with him, or him the right to offer me money as if I'm a bloody pauper.'

'I haven't discussed anything with John Griffiths.'

'No?'

'No!'

'And, I suppose you and Judy just talked about the weather when she called in earlier?'

'We discussed her wedding. She wants me to be her matron of honour.'

'My name never came up in the conversation.'

'Of course it came up,' she countered irritably. 'Sam wants you to be his best man.'

'I don't want to talk about Sam and Judy's wedding!' His hands tightened into fists. 'Did you tell Judy that we'd quarrelled?'

'After the way you stormed through the kitchen, I rather think she worked that out for herself.'

'So what did you talk about?'

'A lot of things.' She met his glare defiantly.

'Including Brian, the garage and his offer of a job.'

'What if we did? Judy and I have been friends all our lives.'

'And I am your husband.'

'There are times like now when I wish you weren't,' she retorted, allowing the full force of her anger to erupt into words.

Silence closed in, glacial, raw with tension. Instead of shouting back at her as she'd expected him to, Martin clenched his jaw and grew visibly paler.

'Marty . . .'

'Thank you for letting me know where I stand.' Turning on his heel, he walked up the stairs.

Too upset to think of anything other than the bitter words they had flung at one another, Lily set the blanket aside. An hour later she calmed down enough to tidy the living room. When she'd finished, she switched off the fire, checked that the front and back doors were locked and the kitchen was tidy before climbing the stairs.

Hoping Martin was asleep, she opened the door to their bedroom quietly. The room yawned cold and empty in the subdued light from the landing. Their bed was neatly made, just as she'd left it that morning. She checked the linen cupboard. A set of sheets, pillowcases, two blankets and a pillow had disappeared. With two spare bedrooms next to theirs and four on the attic floor, she had no way of knowing without opening the doors, which room Martin had elected to move into. Her hand shook as she closed the cupboard door. It wasn't worth escalating their argument to find out.

'Mrs Clay,' Mr Hopkin Jones indicated the chair in front of his desk, 'please, sit down.'

'Thank you, sir.' Lily took the seat he offered her.

'The overdraft facility was cleared this morning, two and a half thousand pounds secured against your investment properties, repayments variable in accordance with the amount borrowed, as we discussed.'

'I didn't expect it to come through so soon, sir.' Lily did a quick calculation. She had applied first thing on Tuesday morning and it was only Friday. She had anticipated that the formalities would take at least two weeks and had been worried in case Brian returned before she had an opportunity to tell Martin what she had done. Although it was going to be difficult to tell Martin anything. They hadn't exchanged a single word since their argument on Monday night.

She cooked their breakfasts and evening meals, but after Tuesday morning when the strain of sitting in the same room as him had been more than she could bear, she had taken to eating hers alone in the dining room and leaving his on the kitchen table. She had no way of knowing how much he ate, or if indeed he ate at all because she made a point of not returning to the kitchen until he had left the room and by then he had washed, dried and put away his plate. But if the amount of food in the pigswill bin was anything to go by, neither of them had much appetite.

Even Sam and Mike had stopped their scrounging visits and came up the stairs only when she invited them, which was hardly surprising. She found the atmosphere between her and Martin hideous and, if she had the choice, she wouldn't visit their house either.

'You can begin drawing on the overdraft whenever you like, Mrs Clay.'

'Thank you, sir.'

'As you instructed, I've taken the cost of arranging the facility from the funds in your savings account. There are a few papers for you to sign.' He pushed them across his desk. 'I've marked the relevant lines, but you should go through everything carefully to make sure you understand exactly what you are signing.'

'I will, sir. I'll return them after my lunch break.'

'Good. When do you anticipate that you'll need the first advance?'

'Next week, sir. We need a thousand pounds to buy into the business.'

The manager scribbled a note on a pad on his desk. 'You may sign a cheque for that amount today if you wish.'

'It won't be that soon, sir.'

'Don't forget it takes four working days for a cheque to clear,' he warned. 'The rest of the money you can access as and when you require it.'

'Thank you for arranging everything, sir. I am very grateful.' She left her chair.

'You have talked to your husband about this, Mrs Clay?'

'Of course.' She crossed her fingers and hid them in the folds of her skirt. She hated having to lie to anyone, especially her boss.

'It's just that when I spoke to him, he adamantly refused to use your investment bonds as security for either a loan or an overdraft.'

'I persuaded him that it is too good an opportunity for him to miss, Mr Hopkin Jones.'

'You can tell him from me that he is fortunate to have such an understanding and financially astute wife.'

'I will, sir.'

He gave her a rare smile. 'I'm only glad the bank could be of service.'

'What time do you have to be there?' Judy carried Emily's suitcase through the front door of the flat and opened her car.

'The letter said, any time after ten o'clock.'

Judy glanced at her watch. Even allowing for traffic they would be at the hostel before half past nine. Stowing Emily's case into the boot, she slammed it shut and turned up the collar of her coat. It was a cold, dark, dismal morning. Rain was falling in a steady, unremitting downpour, drenching the street and greying the pavement and slate roofs to a shiny pewter.

'We're going to be early, aren't we?'

'Yes.' Judy gave her flatmate a sympathetic smile. Ever since Emily had made the decision to go into a hostel she had been restless, unable to concentrate or settle to anything. It was as though she'd already relegated Swansea to her past. 'But we could always stop off for a walk on the way if this rain stops and, if it doesn't, we'll settle for a cup of coffee. There's bound to be a café open somewhere.'

'That would be good,' Emily agreed enthusiastically.

Judy opened the driver's door. 'You did lock the flat?'

'Yes.' Emily folded her umbrella and climbed into the passenger seat. 'Here are your keys.' She pressed them into Judy's hand.

'I don't need an extra set. You could hang on to them.'

'No,' Emily refused resolutely. 'I told you. I'm not

coming back to Swansea.' She glanced back at the street, as Judy drove away. 'Not ever.'

'I hope you don't mind.' Brian carried a record player into Lily's hall and set it down gently at the foot of the stairs. 'I've arranged to meet a painter I hired to spruce up the garage today, so I thought I'd take the opportunity to drop a few things off. If I leave everything until next week the car will be groaning. I don't know how I've managed to accumulate so many things.'

'According to Helen, possessions breed.' Lily walked to the porch with him. 'Judy, Katie and I moved into her house with a couple of cases and boxes apiece, but we all moved out with cabin trunks and dozens of boxes.'

'I don't have dozens of boxes, but I do have a few.' He returned to his car and Lily whistled.

'Very nice.'

'You like it?' He beamed with pride. 'My cousin insisted that the garage manager should always drive a top-of-the-range model to instil customer confidence.'

'I love the colour. They'll see you driving down the Mumbles Road from Ilfracombe.'

'That's the idea. And Swansea girls can't say they weren't warned. Red for danger!' He lifted his eyebrows suggestively. 'No, don't try and take this,' he swung an enormous box away from her and carried it into the house. 'It's heavy. Books,' he explained, setting it down.

'I'll take the record player upstairs.'

'Leave it, it's heavy.'

'Not that heavy,' she contradicted, picking it up. 'I want to check the rooms in the attic anyway. I aired and made up the bed in one of the bedrooms earlier in the week, and Mike and Sam gave Uncle Roy a hand to sort out the other rooms but I'd like your opinion on what we've done.'

'Knowing you, I'm sure everything's more than fine.'

'I hope so.' Clearing the attic would have been something that she and Martin would normally have done together, but it had been impossible for her to discuss converting the attic into a self-contained flat with Martin when he wasn't talking to her, so she had enlisted her uncle's help. If Roy had heard about her argument with Martin, he was too tactful to mention it, and, with Sam, him and Mike all working shifts, it had been easy enough to arrange for them to move the furniture about when Martin had been at work. 'The builder called this morning.'

'I don't want you to go to any expense on my account,' Brian demurred.

'It's something we've been meaning to do for a while. It's crazy to shut off the top floor of the house when there is such a shortage of housing in Swansea, and we want you to be comfortable.'

As Brian returned to his car, Lily carried the record player up the two flights of stairs. With her help, Martin had decorated the entire house, including the rooms on the top floor, shortly after they'd married. The attic room she'd chosen to keep as a bedroom had pale blue wallpaper spattered with white polka dots. The linoleum was grey, the bedroom suite of wardrobe, chest of drawers, tallboy and bedside cabinets a light, unadorned pine. It wasn't luxurious but it was clean and comfortable and the new blue, white and grey cotton curtains, rug and candlewick bedspread she'd bought at Swansea market gave it a fresh, modern look.

Brian glanced in and she set the record player at the foot of the bed. 'Someone's been working hard.'

'Martin did most of the work just after we moved in.' She opened the curtains wide before she crossed the landing and opened another door. 'I thought this would make the most suitable living room, not only because it's the largest room but because it has a view of the sea.'

'A good one,' he commented appreciatively.

'The electric fire used to be in Auntie Norah's front parlour. It's old but it works perfectly.'

'I like the coffee table. But please don't tell me you bought a new three-piece suite on my account.'

'We didn't,' she admitted. 'It was Judy's mother's, but she wanted to change it. I didn't like the original covers so I made these to match the rug and curtains and, before you ask, the rug's not new either. It was in my bedroom before I got married.'

'It goes well with the suite and the wallpaper.'

'I know the suite's small and the room looks a bit bare, but Uncle Roy and the boys packed all the leftover furniture into the box room on the floor below. As well as beds and bedroom suites, there are a couple of cupboards, tables and a sideboard. Most of them are old-fashioned but if you want anything, all you have to do is ask Sam or Mike to help you carry it up.'

'I'll take a look. You have good taste, Lily,' he complimented. 'I wouldn't have thought of orange and green as a colour scheme but this looks good.'

'I'm glad you think so.' She left the room and walked along the landing. 'This room is directly on top of our bathroom, it's also small, so I thought it would make an ideal bathroom and the builder agrees. He measured up and it will take the same size suite that we put into the basement bathroom.'

He looked in and saw a pine kitchen dresser, table and chairs. 'I'll give you a hand to clear it.'

'This is Auntie Norah's old kitchen furniture. We thought we could use it in your kitchen. It's solid enough but it will look better after a coat of paint. Martin or I can do that . . .'

'Or me,' he broke in.

'You are a paying guest, as Auntie Norah would say.'

'Did say,' he smiled, recalling the day he had moved into the house just before joining the Swansea police force. 'But I'm also a friend and you've gone to enough trouble on my account as it is.'

'This,' she opened the last door on the landing, 'will be the kitchen. As you see, it's empty. The builder said it was best to leave the cupboards until after he's plumbed in the sink. I bought an electric cooker in the warehouse, it's small but it has three rings and a decent size oven and it's being delivered on Monday. Uncle Roy's on shift and he's taking it in for me.'

'I don't expect to be doing much cooking.'

'You'll be doing some.'

'Possibly,' he agreed.

'So, with Auntie Norah's cupboards, table, chairs and a sink, it should do.'

'It will more than do, Lily, it's going to be extremely comfortable. You sure you and Martin won't mind sharing your bathroom and kitchen with me until it's sorted?'

'I'm sure,' she murmured. It was a relief to talk to Brian after a week of strained silences from Martin, but Martin only worked until midday on alternate Saturdays. If Brian stayed until Martin arrived home he would soon discover that they weren't speaking to one another. And she couldn't help feeling that if she were Brian, she'd sort out other lodgings and as quickly as possible.

The house was neither as large nor as imposing as Emily had been led to believe by the doctor who had examined her in Swansea. Set at the side of a country road, it was the kind of residence her father would have dismissed as belonging to a 'jumped up' country tradesman – a grocer or butcher too insignificant to warrant his attention as manager of the largest bank in Swansea – but it was a lifeline for someone in her condition.

'Ten o'clock on the dot.' Judy drove into a small courtyard at the side of the house, pulled on the handbrake and turned off the ignition.

'Thank you for the coffee.'

'It was disgusting.' Judy wrinkled her nose. 'It was more chicory than coffee and that café was rough, even for the lorry drivers.'

'It passed the time.' Emily's hand shook as she reached for the door handle.

'Every girl in there has the same problem as you,' Judy reminded her.

'I know, but . . .'

'Would you like me to go inside with you?'

'Would you?'

'I'll get your case.' Judy took Emily's arm and they walked to the front door. Before they reached it, Judy heard a baby crying and as soon as she pushed open the outer door and stepped into a covered porch, she could smell 'babies', that peculiar cocktail of odours that ranged from sour milk to talcum powder, with overtones of damp clothes, washing soda and bleach.

'Can I help you?' A stern looking women in a navy blue dress that was almost, but not quite, a nurse's uniform, opened the door a few minutes after Judy rang the bell.

'I'm Emily Davies,' Emily murmured, dropping the Murton.

'You're early, Davies.' The woman looked Emily up and down as if she was an inferior exhibit in a best of breed show.

'It said any time after ten on the letter.'

'It should have been eleven.' The woman turned her attention to Judy. 'And you are?'

'Judy Hunt, Emily's cousin and next of kin.' After setting up ten salons Judy had become accustomed to dealing with officialdom and wasn't even faintly intimidated by the woman's imperious attitude. 'I'd like to see my cousin settled and check on visiting times.'

'Sunday, two until three in the afternoon, any other time has to be by special arrangement,' the woman snapped in a marginally politer tone, ushering them into a large, square, gloomy hall, painted institution green and floored with black and white tiles. She turned to Emily. 'You have been allocated a bed in the third room on the left at the top of the stairs. Your bed is the only one not made up. As soon as you've made it – properly – and put your clothes away, bring your suitcase down here for storage. And, as you're here early, you can see the doctor. He calls every Saturday morning but quick sharp, he's only here until eleven. After he's examined you, one of the staff will take you through the admission procedure. There will be forms for you to sign. Lunch is at twelve, sewing class at one.'

'Yes . . . thank you . . .' Emily stammered, fighting a lump in her throat, as she tried to commit everything the woman had said to memory.

'I am the matron and I expect to be addressed as "Matron" at all times.'

'Yes, Matron.'

'Well, get along then. I'll tell the staff to expect you in the examination room in ten minutes. Second door on the right through the double doors.' The matron pointed down the corridor. 'Just one quick word before you go,' she added, as Judy and Emily stepped on to the staircase. 'This is a home for unmarried mothers, not a rest home. You will keep the areas you live, work and sleep in, clean and tidy. You will be expected to do your share of the housework and cooking until your baby is born and for six weeks afterwards. In return for antenatal care, board and lodge, the staff will expect you to be polite, respectful, willing and helpful towards them and your fellow residents at all times. Do I make myself clear?'

'Perfectly,' Emily whispered.

'Visitors are not allowed into the bedroom, Miss Hunt,' she reprimanded, as Judy followed Emily.

Judy turned back on the staircase. 'I was hoping to see my cousin settled.'

'We will take care of her from here on, Miss Hunt.'

'Thank you.' Realising that if she argued, the matron could take out her displeasure on Emily, Judy hugged her flatmate goodbye. 'I'll visit you a week tomorrow.'

'You'll be busy.'

'Not that busy. If you want me to bring anything, or discover that you've left anything in the flat, write to me.'

'I will. I can't thank you enough . . .'

'No more thank yous.' Judy stepped back. 'You'd better go,' she whispered, as a telephone rang and the matron disappeared, presumably to answer it. '"Quick sharp".'

'And I have to learn to jump to it.' Emily gave Judy a sad little smile. 'Have a good journey back.'

Judy stayed long enough to watch her friend walk up the stairs. Emily looked so small, lost and alone, she couldn't help feeling that she was abandoning her. She recalled Robin Watkin Morgan's good looks, swaggering self-assurance and flirtatious manner. No doubt he had already moved on to the next girl. It was so unfair. If her own experience was anything to go by, all the 'fun' involved in conceiving a child was purely on the men's side and they could walk away any time they chose to, leaving the woman quite literally holding the baby.

Chapter Ten

'You've done me proud,' Brian reassured Lily, running down the stairs behind her.

'Do you have time for tea? If you don't, you could come back for a meal, or stay the night?'

'Once I've sorted things with the painter, I have to drive straight back to Pontypridd.'

'Oh, yes.' She smiled.

'And you can wipe that knowing grin off your face when you like, Lily Clay. I'm meeting Will and Ronnie to talk about business, not a girl to talk about . . . remind me what is it boys talk about to girls?' he enquired disingenuously. 'It's so long since I've had a date I've forgotten.'

'I don't believe it. Not of you.'

'The last date I had with a female of the species was in London. Since then, Ronnie and Will have taken up every minute of my spare time.'

'No nurses in hospital?' she teased.

'They were so bossy when I was ill, I didn't fancy any of them when I recovered.'

'And when did they change you for the Brian Powell that I remember?'

'The Brian Powell you remember was young and foolish and I'm old and wise, but to get back to your question and away from my non-existent private life, I could murder a cup of tea.' He joined her in the kitchen. 'I confess, I also had an ulterior motive for coming here this morning. Martin mentioned that he works alternate Saturday mornings and I calculated that this would be one of them. I wanted to find out if you're absolutely sure about this partnership. One minute Martin was on the phone telling me in no uncertain terms that there was no way that he could afford to take me up on my offer. The next, you ring up to say it's all fine and you have the money.'

'And it is and I do.' She lifted the kettle to check there was enough water in it before lighting the gas. 'The overdraft facility came through yesterday, two and half thousand pounds. I can give you a cheque for one thousand now, if you like. A thousand was the amount you mentioned to Martin, wasn't it?'

'For tools and equipment. And that's the other reason I'm here. There's an auction of second-hand tools and garage equipment in a bankruptcy sale in Cardiff next week. If Martin can get the time off, I could go down there with him. If the stuff's any good he might be able to pick up what he needs cheap.'

'And if it's outdated or damaged?'

'He'll have to fork out full price.' He nodded as she held up a homemade apple pie. 'Yes, please.' He sat at the table.

'But he'll need money to buy into the business.'

'Five hundred pounds for his share of the buildings.' He cut himself a large slice of the pie and laid a dollop of cream on top.

'Then I'll give you a cheque for that amount now.'

'It would help, because my cousin and brother-in-law have already put up the cash for the dealership and the buildings, and it would be nice to pay them back.'

Lily was glad that she had opted to take the extra five hundred pounds the manager had offered. Fifteen hundred pounds going out immediately on tools and buildings only left a thousand for other expenses and the wages of the apprentice Brian had said Martin would need. She went to a cupboard and pulled out a drawer. Removing the chequebook and a writing pad, she wrote out a cheque for five hundred pounds and signed it. 'Who do I make it out to?'

'Powell and Ronconi.'

She filled in the rest of the details, tore the cheque from the book, and handed it to him together with the notepad.

'What's this for?' he enquired suspiciously.

'You, to write a receipt. If you fill in exactly why I've given you the money, there'll be no misunderstanding when Martin reads it.'

He eyed her carefully. 'Martin doesn't know you've raised the money.'

'No.'

'Then he hasn't even given in his notice at the council garage?'

'I checked his diary, he has two weeks' holiday due.'

'If he walks out and leaves them in the lurch, they won't give him a reference worth reading and they'll never take him back, Lily.'

Her blood ran cold at the thought that something might go wrong and Martin would need his old job back. For the first time she understood his reluctance to stake every single penny they owned and possibly even their house on Brian's venture. 'If both of you and Jack put everything you have into this garage, Martin won't need to go back,' she said determinedly, setting the alternative from her mind.

'Lily . . .'

'It's a chance in a lifetime and we can't afford to miss it, Brian. I'm only sorry Martin is too blinkered and stubborn to see it.'

He wrote out the receipt. 'Do you think that Martin is going to see this as a good surprise or a bad one?'

'That's entirely up to Martin.'

'You haven't even discussed it with him, have you?'

'That's a bit difficult when he isn't talking to me.' She set the tea she'd made in front of him.

'The last thing I want to do is drive a wedge between you two.'

'You haven't. I have.' She pushed the pie towards him, as he finished the slice on his plate and set the notepad in the centre of the table.

'You're not even going to give Martin the receipt.'

'I promised my uncle I'd babysit Billy. Joy is looking after the salons today because Judy had to do something or other, so I won't be seeing Martin until Judy's mother comes home this evening.'

'You haven't even told Martin you're babysitting?'

'How could I when he's not talking to me? Mind you,' she gave Brian a wry look, 'I've a feeling that he will have a few things to say to me after reading that.'

'I've seen Martin angry. A couple of hours won't be enough to calm him down when he finds out what you've done.'

'It doesn't matter. This house is big enough for both of us to live in without seeing one another,' she answered, with more courage than she felt.

Emily trailed up the stairs and down a passageway into a room that resembled a dormitory more than a bedroom. Eight beds and lockers lined the three inner walls. The fourth was dominated by an enormous window that looked out over a garden of damp lawns and flowerbeds filled with spring bulbs. In the distance she could see a range of softly rolling hills, their summits shrouded in the misty rain that hadn't let up since she had left Swansea. As Judy had said, the countryside was pretty, but she couldn't help feeling that she would derive little comfort from it.

'Hello, welcome to Cartref.'

A woman was lying stretched out in the bed behind the door. She wasn't at all the sort of person Judy had expected to find in a home for unmarried mothers. Her face was lined and careworn, her curly, blonde hair streaked with silver.

'I'd get up and shake your hand if Matron hadn't ordered me to lie here until teatime and, if you've met Matron, you'd know why I dare not move.'

'I've met her,' Emily said dryly.

'I'm Maggie, and I can tell by the look on your face that your first impression of this place isn't a good one.'

'It's different from what I expected.' Emily studied the only unmade bed in the room. She had never seen such a thin mattress or narrow bed. The locker next to it was considerably taller than it. Divided into two, there was a cupboard and three drawers on one side and a hanging rail on the other. 'Not much storage space,' she commented.

'When you're this shape,' Maggie stroked her bump, 'you don't need much besides a couple of changes of clothes.'

'I suppose not.' Emily lifted a pile of bedding from the foot of the bed on to the top of the locker.

'Don't let Matron or anyone else upset you,' Maggie advised. 'They think it's their duty to show us poor sinners who is in charge from the minute we step over the door, but,' she watched Emily unfold a sheet, 'not all the staff are like her. And she's far too grand to mix with the likes of them, let alone us. She spends most of her time holed up in her office.'

'That's a relief to hear.'

'Not that way,' Maggie warned, as Emily tucked the base sheet over the mattress. 'Any girl caught without hospital corners on her bed gets extra scrubbing duty, and given the length of the corridors in this place, that's the last thing you need.'

'Hospital corners?' Emily queried, mystified by the term.

'Here, I'll show you.'

'You're not supposed to get up.'

'I'm relieving cramp in my leg. Besides, I only fainted. Hardly surprising when you consider that we have to get up a full hour and a half before breakfast.' Maggie pulled the sheet away from the mattress and deftly folded the corners squarely around the thin pallet.

'Where did you learn to make beds that way?' Emily asked.

'My mother was training to be a nurse when she met my father, but they fell in love and that put paid to her career.' She gave Emily a hand to finish making the bed before returning to her own.

Emily opened her suitcase on the bed, lifted a hanger from the cupboard, and folded her dressing gown over it. 'They don't give us many hangers, either.'

'They don't give us much of anything except lectures on morality. But the other girls in this room are friendly and the sewing, knitting and cookery teachers are human. Don't worry.' Maggie broadened her smile, which made her look even more drawn. 'You'll be fine and it's only for a couple of months. Then you'll be able to walk away and be your own person again.'

'I hope so.' Emily gazed at the dismal room. 'I really hope so.'

Brian took a deep breath, as he left his car and walked up the short path to Martin and Lily's house. Bracing himself, he rang the bell and waited. His meeting with the painter had dragged on but it was still only three o'clock and he suspected that if Martin hadn't read the receipt until twelve-thirty he would still be angry and, knowing Martin, very angry indeed. A few seconds later he heard footsteps echoing over the tiled floor of the passage and a shadow appeared behind the frosted glass in the door. The door opened and Martin glowered at him.

'Can I come in?'

'As you seem to have more of a say in my affairs than I do, please yourself.' Despite his hostility, Martin stepped back.

Resisting the temptation to walk away, Brian entered the porch and closed the outer door. 'Look, Marty—'

'No, you look!' Martin confronted him head on. 'I told

you there was no way that I could afford to take you up on your offer. Yet, you still went to Lily behind my back just so you could raise the finance for your bloody garage.'

'I did not go to Lily behind your back.'

'She went to you.'

Trapped, Brian fell silent.

'Dear God! I've been blind and stupid. It was her, not you, wasn't it?' Without waiting for an answer, Martin turned and strode into the living room.

Brian hovered uneasily in the doorway. He saw the receipt he'd written lying abandoned on the coffee table, a cup of cold tea, milk curdling on the surface beside it. The room was freezing; the gas fire switched off. As Martin sank down on the sofa, Brian reached inside his jacket pocket and pulled out his wallet.

'If you want the cheque back, you can have it.' Stepping into the room, he laid it on the receipt.

Martin picked it up. 'Presumably Lily has already paid the arrangement fee for the overdraft.'

'That's peanuts compared to what you stand to lose if the garage fails, as you're so damned sure it will.'

'I never said the garage was going to fail,' Martin retorted hotly.

'It must be what you think, otherwise why would you be so reluctant to come in with me?'

'Because two thousand pounds is more money than I have, or can raise.'

'You're holding part of it,' Brian pointed out mildly.

'This,' Martin slapped the cheque back on the table, 'is Lily's money.'

'And a person can do what they like with their own money. Unless that is, they are married to you.'

'I've never told Lily what to do with her money.'

'You're telling her now.' Brian dared to sit on one of the easy chairs.

'I don't want her to throw it away.'

'Then you do think the garage is going to fail.'

'No . . . damn it . . . I . . .' Lost for words, Martin pulled his cigarettes and lighter from his pocket and laid them on the table.

'Lily has faith in the garage – and you,' Brian added quietly, steeling himself for another outburst.

'It's a risk. She could lose everything. All the investments her aunt left her, possibly even this house . . .'

'It's more likely that you stand to make a good living,' Brian interrupted.

'You expect me to gamble every penny my wife owns on a "likelihood"?'

'If you came in with me, you'd control your own business. You said yourself, you're a good mechanic.'

'There's a world of difference between being a good mechanic and a good businessman.'

'I agree, but you're careful and honest, two qualities in short supply in the motor trade. Believe me, I know. You'll soon have more work than you can cope with from word of mouth alone. People will flock to have their cars repaired and serviced by you once they realise you charge a fair price for reliable work. And there are enough cars being bought every day in Swansea for the accounts of your repair and maintenance side to go into the black and stay in the black.'

'There are also other garages.'

'Who don't have mechanics with your expertise to run them.'

'You said yourself that we won't make any money for the first three years.'

'And after that we'll make a very good living.' Brian looked at his friend. They had lived in the same army barracks for two years when they'd done their National Service and, on their return, shared a flat in the basement of Roy Williams's house. During that time they'd grown close. And although they hadn't seen one another for the last couple of years, Brian sensed that Martin hadn't changed. Not even his close, loving relationship with Lily had blotted the past from his mind. Somewhere beneath the surface of the happily married man lurked the ragged, insecure child who'd been beaten and half-starved along with the rest of his family by his father. 'Lily said—'

'What?' Martin interrupted defensively.

'That she couldn't discuss raising the overdraft with you because you weren't talking to her.'

'That's between me and her . . .'

'Not if I caused the argument. Are you going to offer me a cigarette or do you want one of mine?'

'Help yourself.' Martin pushed the packet towards him.

'I would never have mentioned the garage if I'd known that it was going to cause problems between you and Lily. But I'll tell you one thing.' Brian looked Martin in the eye as he shook a cigarette from the packet. 'I'd give everything I own and twenty years of my life to marry a woman who has the faith in me that Lily has in you. And if you can't see that, you're an even bigger fool than I take you for right now.'

'I can't believe she'd do something like this without telling me.' Martin flicked his lighter and lit both their cigarettes.

'How could she tell you if you weren't talking to her?' Brian reasoned logically.

'Want a cup of tea?' Martin picked up his cold cup.

'I've time for a quick one, but it will have to be quick.' Brian checked his watch as he rose to his feet. 'Ronnie and Will are expecting me back in Pontypridd this evening.'

'You and Lily have boxed me into a corner.'

'Exactly,' Brian agreed as he sat at the kitchen table. 'And you have a choice. You can either tear up that cheque and cancel the overdraft she arranged, or go into work on Monday morning and hand in your notice.'

'I've worked in the depot since I was fourteen.'

'And you want to be working there when you're sixty-five?'

Martin considered the prospect. Getting up six days a week for the next forty-two years, walking to the depot, overseeing the repairs and maintenance of the council's fleet of lorries, vans, cars and buses, coming home every night to Lily . . . Lily!

The last week had been sheer torture. More than anything he wanted to end their argument, but once their quarrel had escalated into silence he didn't know how to set about making amends. He didn't just want Lily – he loved and needed her. And she had proved that she loved him enough to stake everything she owned just so he could realise his ambition of being his own boss.

'No, I don't want to still be working in the depot when I'm sixty-five,' he said finally.

'But you're too afraid of failure to come in with me.'

'Perhaps,' Martin replied honestly. 'But if you were in my position, would you speculate with your wife's inheritance? The only money she has, or is ever likely to have?'

'I wouldn't gamble with it but I would invest it in a business if she wanted me to.' Brian ground the remains of his cigarette to dust in the ashtray on the table. 'It's your decision, Marty.'

'If I hand in my notice on Monday morning, the council will never take me back.'

'So, if the worst does happen and we go bankrupt, you'll have to work somewhere else.'

'I may never get offered another foreman's job.'

'You may not,' Brian agreed infuriatingly. 'But if you do hand in your notice, arrange to take Wednesday off.'

'Why.'

'There's a sale of bankrupt tools and garage equipment in Cardiff. I told Lily about it. You might be able to save a few bob on equipping your workshops.' Brian pushed his hand into his pocket and pulled out a leaflet. 'The address is on there. If you want to go, I'll meet you there an hour before the sale starts.'

'Did Lily say anything else about me when you saw her?'

'Nothing, other than that you two weren't speaking and she'd be out this afternoon. That's why I came back, to try to talk some sense into you. She looked so miserable, I felt guilty for causing the row between you.'

Martin ran his hands through his hair. 'We've both been miserable. I don't know where to start with her.'

'Take Uncle Brian's advice, walk into town, buy her a bunch of flowers and a box of chocolates, and reserve a table in the Mackworth for dinner tonight.'

'I haven't a clue where she is, or what time she'll be back.'

'As soon as Joy comes home from the salons. She's babysitting Billy.'

'She told you.'

'Only in passing. I wasn't here that long. I only called in to drop a couple of things off.'

'Oh God, the attic! I forgot, you're moving in.'

'Lily has everything under control.'

'The furniture.'

'At the risk of sending you screaming mad again, Roy, Sam and Mike moved it for her.'

'You must think I'm a right idiot.'

'Yes,' Brian agreed baldly. 'But to continue with my advice, after dinner, have a couple of drinks. And say you're sorry. But the apologising bit should come at the beginning of the evening, not the end.'

'Why should I say I'm sorry when she was the one who went to you and the bank behind my back?'

'Because you love her and want to be happy?' Brian suggested. He got up.

'The tea . . .'

'Forget it. Do you want me to take the cheque or not?'

'If you do, there'll be no flowers or dinners out for the next three years and that's on your figures.'

'I'll give you as long as it takes for you to walk me to the front door to decide.'

*

'Morning sickness?' The nurse poised her pen over the record card she had made out for Emily.

'It stopped four weeks ago.' Emily tried not to stare at the row of subdued girls sitting around the room in thin cotton gowns, bare legs and feet.

'Sit down, I'll take your blood pressure.' The nurse was older than the matron and every bit as daunting.

Emily removed her cardigan and sat while the nurse fastened the machine to her arm and pumped up the pressure until she felt she was being squeezed in a vice. The nurse recorded the numbers without comment.

'Go behind the screen and take off all your clothes. All,' she stressed. 'Make a note of the hook number you hang them on and put on one of the gowns.'

'I had a full examination this week in Swansea,' Emily protested.

'And you'll have one every week while you're here,' the nurse snapped. 'Take off your clothes.'

The screen was covered in muslin so fine it was transparent. Turning her back to the rows of girls, Emily undressed and slipped on one of the gowns, only noticing that it was open from neck to hem at the back when she tried to fasten it.

'Take a chair and wait your turn,' the nurse shouted, and Emily realised she had been watching her.

The half an hour that elapsed before Emily saw the doctor dragged for an eternity. Too embarrassed to look at the other girls, Emily stared down at the floor, shivering in the thin gown until her name was called. To her relief, she realised she was the last resident left in the room, yet she still clutched the hem of her gown together as she padded barefoot into the examination room. It was small, scarcely large enough to hold the desk, chair and examination couch it contained.

'Lie on the couch.' The doctor checked her notes before proceeding to examine her with a dehumanising thoroughness. Mortified, Emily kept her eyes closed throughout the whole humiliating procedure. When he finished, he removed his rubber gloves, peeled them off and tossed them into a bin. Scrubbing his hands under the tap, he called to the nurse. 'I agree with the doctor in Swansea. She is closer to five than four months.'

The nurse added a few lines to the card.

Almost as an afterthought the doctor glanced up and said, 'You can go.'

Emily climbed off the couch. Averting her eyes from the matron who entered the examination room as she left, she charged across the waiting area.

'Apart from the high blood pressure case, they are all fit and healthy, Matron.'

As Emily began to dress she heard the matron reply, 'They invariably are, Doctor.' Her tone suggested that they had no right to be.

Acting on her mother's suggestion that she cook Sam a meal and have a relaxing evening with him, Judy stopped off in Swansea on her way home. She went to the market and was dismayed to see depleted counters. Most Swansea people shopped early on a Saturday. After studying everything the butchers had on offer she bought a plucked chicken, a bag of ready made stuffing, two pounds of tiny and exorbitantly priced forced new potatoes, a bag of frozen peas, a cauliflower and cheese to make a sauce. She decided on laver bread and bacon as a starter, which only left dessert. Suspecting she wouldn't have the energy or inclination to make anything fancy after preparing the chicken and cleaning the vegetables, she bought a frozen, cream filled sponge.

Sam had said he would call round after his shift finished at ten. She only hoped that his lack of faith in her culinary ability wouldn't prompt him to buy fish and chips for both of them on his way.

'And how is my boy?' Joy opened the door to her living room before she'd even hung up her coat.

'Angelic, as always.' Lily helped Billy down from her lap and he ran across the room to his mother.

Billy nodded enthusiastic agreement and hugged Joy's neck. 'Good,' he chanted.

'How was work?' Lily asked.

'I enjoyed it. I was amazed at some of the things that Judy has done to the salons. It never occurred to me to sell hairbrushes, combs and cosmetics, yet the more I think about it, the more it makes sense. The junior on reception duty always has time on her hands that may as well be put to good use. And every salon was fully booked. I know it's a Saturday and that's always the busiest day, but all of them had healthy bookings for the week as well.' Joy finally managed to unlock Billy's hands from around her neck long enough to take off and hang up her coat. 'Like a cup of tea?'

'No, thank you. I have to go home and make Martin's tea.'

'I told Roy we shouldn't have asked you to babysit, not on Martin's afternoon off.'

'We didn't have anything planned.'

'Everything all right between you two?' Joy was aware of Roy's concern that something was amiss between Lily and Martin, but unlike him she had no compunction about trying to find out what the problem was, in the hope that she could help.

'Fine,' Lily lied unconvincingly. She closed the book she had been reading to Billy. 'We'll find out what happens to the little pigs next week, darling.'

'Huff, puff and blow . . .'

'It's one of his favourite stories.' Joy handed Lily her mac. 'Roy reads it to him nearly every night.'

'I remember him reading to me when I was little. It used to be the high spot of my day. You're a lucky boy, Billy Williams.' Lily kissed first Billy then Joy. Dreading what she'd find waiting for her at home, she left the house.

*

Emily felt lost, friendless and very alone, as she walked down the corridor to the lounge to spend the hour of 'free time' before supper. The medical examination had been followed by a lunch of bacon and egg pie and baked beans. Left too long in a hot tray, the beans had dried and the pie was undercooked and watery. The sewing class had only served to highlight her incompetence when it came to handling a needle. The remainder of the afternoon had been spent in 'domestic duties', which, in her case, had included cleaning the downstairs bathroom. Her hands were dry, they smelled of bleach and she'd splashed cleaning fluid on to her skirt, taking the colour out of it.

No one had spoken to her during the half hour tea break when they'd lined up to receive a cup of weak tea and a scone spread with margarine and raspberry jam, and the cookery class that followed hadn't been any more successful than the sewing class. The only cake that hadn't risen during baking had been hers.

She hesitated at the door and wondered if she'd be allowed to go upstairs. The prospect of a quiet talk with Maggie in the bedroom was more tempting than the thought of braving the room full of chattering girls. There seemed to be dozens of them, although she knew the hostel only accommodated twenty-four.

A well-built girl showing an inch of mousy roots below peroxide blonde hair, beckoned to her. 'I'm Jean, and as the only spare bed in the house is next to mine, I presume you'll be moving into it.'

'I'm Emily.' Emily held out her hand.

'Bit formal, aren't you?' Jean laughed.

'Posh too, if that's the way you always talk. I'm Ann, and I sleep the other side of Jean. Did you see Queen Maggie when you arrived?'

'Yes,' Emily replied warily, wondering what Ann meant by 'Queen'. She sat on the only empty chair at their table.

'Queen Maggie's married.' Ann flicked the cover over

her notepad to conceal the letter she'd been writing. 'That's why she gets special treatment.'

'Maggie has high blood pressure, Ann,' Jean interrupted.

'If Maggie's married, why is she here?' Emily asked curiously.

'Because her husband's dead and she already has four children under six,' Jean explained. 'She says they are enough of a handful without a baby to look after as well.'

'Her father is a vicar and he arranged for her to come in here. That's why she gets special treatment,' Ann carped.

'You never let up, Ann Andrews, do you?' Jean turned her back on Ann and carried on talking to Emily. 'Maggie's husband was killed . . .'

'Months before she started carrying.'

'You've a vicious mouth on you, Ann.'

'I only tell the truth. We're all in here for the same reason and, underneath her airs and graces, Maggie Jones is no different from the rest of us.'

'She was nice to me when I came in this morning,' Emily ventured.

'She could afford to be. Anyone on bed rest is excused domestic duty.' Ann held out her red chapped hands. 'A couple more days of scrubbing and you'll lose that manicured look,' she warned.

'Take no notice of Ann,' Jean whispered, as Ann turned her back and carried on writing her letter. 'Her baby's a week late and she can't wait to get out of here.'

'But they do keep you here after your baby's born, don't they?' Emily asked anxiously.

'Yes, but they move you to a room at the back of the house, where the babies' crying doesn't disturb the rest of us at night.'

'Then we won't see the babies?'

'Not much of them, unless you walk in the garden on a fine day, then they're put outside in their prams. But you'll see more than enough of your own once it's born. For six weeks, that is. You have to do everything for it –

bath it, feed it, nurse it, change it, see to it when it cries in the night.'

Until Emily had seen Judy's brother, she hadn't considered her baby as a being in its own right, simply a disaster that was going to ruin her life. And, although she had younger sisters, she'd had very little to do with them. They had been their nanny's responsibility and, on her mother's orders, the nanny had kept them under control and out of sight until they had reached what her mother called 'a civilised age'. Uncertain as to how she was going to feel when her baby was born, she'd hoped that a glimpse of one of the other girls' babies might have prepared her in some way.

'Ann is right about one thing,' Jean murmured. 'We are all in the same predicament and, while I might not want to remain in touch with the friends I've made here for obvious reasons, I'm glad of their company now.'

Emily glanced around the room. Most of the girls were visibly pregnant, a few, including Ann, looked as though they were about to have their babies at any moment to her inexperienced eye. 'I never thought I'd end up in a place like this,' she whispered despondently.

'It's a world away from the moonlight and romance that got us into this mess,' Jean observed. 'And when I get out of here, I'll never believe a single thing a boy tells me, ever again. Not even if he has a certificate from a bishop to prove he's telling the truth.'

Lily had hung up her mac and was changing out of her shoes and into her slippers when she sensed someone watching her. Turning, she saw Martin standing in the kitchen doorway.

'Hello.'

When she remained silent, he blurted the first thing that came into his head. 'I'm sorry.'

Bursting into tears of sheer relief, she ran to him and wrapped her arms around his waist. He dropped a kiss on to the top of her head and held her tight.

‘I gave Brian a cheque—’

‘I know. He called this afternoon and after telling me how lucky I was to have you for a wife, offered it back to me.’

She pushed him away and looked up at his face. ‘Did you take it?’

‘No.’ He hugged her again. ‘I’m not at all sure that we’re doing the right thing—’

‘I am,’ she said fiercely.

‘Well, either way, we’re committed now.’ He glanced at his watch. ‘Go up and change into your glad rags. I’m taking you out for dinner.’

‘You are?’

‘I booked a table for eight o’clock in the Mackworth. We’ll have a drink first in the lounge.’

‘Can we afford it?’

‘No,’ he sighed. ‘But as we’ll be able to afford it a whole lot less once the garage opens, we’d better make a night of it. I’ve a feeling that we’re going to need the memories.’

Chapter Eleven

'Are we going to eat like this every night when we're married?' Sam forked the last of the slice of cream sponge on his plate into his mouth and pushed his chair back from the table.

'No.' Judy refilled her sherry glass.

'And that's because?'

'I won't have time to cook.'

'We haven't talked about you giving up work yet.'

'And we won't, because the subject's not up for discussion,' she warned. 'I am going to carry on working once we're married, full stop.'

'And what happens when I work odd shifts, like I am now?'

'You'll cope, just as you're coping now.'

'Who says I cope?'

'If you can't, then we'll have to pay someone to do your washing and ironing and cook your meals.' She cleared their dishes into the kitchen and stacked them next to the sink. Much as she hated getting up in the morning to a messy kitchen, she couldn't face washing them. Returning to the living room, she picked her glass and the bottle of sherry, and curled up on the sofa.

'You're serious, aren't you?' he questioned in amazement. 'You'd pay someone to do your housework for you?'

'Just as I pay girls to work in the hairdressing salons, yes,' she answered flatly. 'It makes sense, Sam. My mother and I draw good wages from the salons, so why shouldn't I use some of it to employ someone to do the things I hate, like housework and laundry?'

'You hate housework?'

'That surprises you?'

'Yes.'

'I have no objection to you doing it.' She looked sideways at him. 'Go on, say it.'

'What?'

'It's women's work.'

'It is, isn't it?' He set his glass of beer on the coffee table and joined her.

'That remark doesn't even warrant an answer.' She threw a cushion at him before refilling her sherry glass.

'I've never seen you drink this much before.' He caught the cushion and set it aside.

'I am not drunk.'

'I didn't say you were, but one sherry is usually your limit, you've had five.'

'Now you're counting.'

'I didn't mean it that way.' He slipped his arm around her shoulders. 'Is the bed aired?'

'It was when I slept in it last night.'

'Good.'

'Where did you park your bike?'

'Two streets away and before you ask, no one saw me creep in here.'

'Just because you didn't see any curtains twitching . . .'

'Curtains, nothing, you're talking to an experienced policeman who can sense when he's being watched, so, pretty please, can I stay the night?'

'Not all night.' She finished the sherry in her glass and poured herself another.

'Why not? I don't have to get up in the morning. Mike's doing my shift.'

'I don't want to risk someone seeing you here tomorrow morning.'

'Like who?'

'I have neighbours.'

'Who don't know I'm here. Come on, Judy,' he persuaded, 'as neither of us have to work tomorrow, we could have a lie in, then while you have a long, lazy bath, I'll do the washing up and cook brunch for us before we pick up your mother and Roy, and go to visit my mother. What do you say?'

'All right,' she murmured, too tired and full of sherry to argue. Tomorrow they were going to discuss their wedding arrangements with their parents and in a few weeks they'd be spending every night together. The sooner she became accustomed to sleeping in the same bed as him, the sooner she'd adjust to married life.

Although the duty member of staff had propped the window sash open the regulation three inches before pulling the curtains, the air in the bedroom was fetid and stale. It was also freezing.

Emily shivered beneath a single blanket in her cramped, narrow bed, eyes wide open as she stared blindly up at the shadows that shrouded the ceiling. Around her, the seven other women breathed, snuffled and in one case, snored loudly in their sleep and she hated them simply for being there.

Her mother had insisted that all her children move into a room of their own on their second birthday, and even on the frequent occasions when she'd stayed over with friends, she had generally been given a guest room to herself. The only times she had shared with anyone were on the holidays she had taken with Angie and her other girlfriends when they had doubled up in French and London hotels – and the times that she and Robin had sneaked into one another's rooms at house parties.

Thoughts and memories of Robin tumbled in disarray through her mind, dating back to the time she had returned from her first – and last – London season with her mother. Robin appearing darkly handsome in a dinner jacket at Larry's twenty-first birthday party; Robin asking her to dance on the wooden stage set up in front of the band in the marquee on her parents' lawn; Robin feeding her champagne and strawberries as he had teased her and Angie. She had always liked him but that night she had fallen in love. And when he had invited her to the theatre shortly afterwards, she hadn't doubted that he had been hit by the same thunderbolt as her.

Robin being tender, romantic, undressing her and making love to her for the first time in his bedroom and, from that moment on, every time they met. Robin introducing her to peculiar books full of even more peculiar illustrations and persuading her to join him in what he called 'adventures', which she had agreed to because she was besotted with him.

Robin slipping a ring on to her finger at their engagement party in her parents' house in front of both their families and friends while a band had played 'With This Ring' – his choice. Occasionally afterwards she had felt that he was taking her for granted, but she had assumed that no relationship, even perfect loving ones like theirs, could be sustained on that initial breathtaking plane. And even when he had neglected her when they were out with friends or at parties, he had always ended the evening by making love to her. Even when her father went to prison and the invitations to social functions dried up, he had insisted their engagement continue – right up until the moment she had told him she was pregnant. With hindsight, she realised that after that conversation his whole attitude to her had changed.

A tear fell from her eye. The knowledge that Robin no longer cared for her, and possibly never had in the way that she had loved him, was extraordinarily painful. But she forced herself to face facts. He had abandoned her as soon as she told him she was carrying his child, and that was not the action of the man she thought she knew. If he truly loved her, he would have stayed with her at the party and remained at her side throughout all the snubs and jibes. He would never have left her to Angie and Thompson – or had he been in on their scheming from the beginning? Had the three of them planned the events of that night so he could free himself from the double scandal of her pregnancy and her father's crimes?

She turned over in the bed and buried her face in the pillow, as a second tear fell from her eye.

Maggie stretched out an arm and held out a handkerchief. 'Take it, it's clean.'

Emily managed a wan smile and folded it into her palm.

'You'll get used to this place. When you leave, it will seem like a bad dream. A couple of years and you will find it difficult to believe that you were ever here.'

Clutching the handkerchief, Emily curled into a tight foetal ball, facing away from Maggie's bed. 'I hope so,' she muttered, lacking the courage to look that far forward.

'Judy . . .' Sam muttered sleepily.

'Go back to sleep,' she whispered, as she stole from the bed. She went into the bathroom, locked the door, threw up the toilet seat and vomited the sherry and most of the meal she'd eaten earlier into the toilet.

For all the time and care she'd expended on cooking, decorating the table, and getting in the drinks, her mother's advice hadn't worked. It hadn't been any easier for her to accept Sam's lovemaking than it had been the very first time she had allowed him into her bed.

'I thought pink would be nice for the bridesmaids,' Ena Davies, Sam's mother gushed, as Joy with Billy on her lap, Roy, Judy and Sam sat around the tea table she'd prepared for them. 'And I've found the perfect shade of figured nylon. Sam has six cousins. The oldest is ten, the youngest two. They will look so sweet walking down the aisle behind you in pairs, with crowns of pink rosebuds in their hair and carrying bouquets of pink roses.'

'Don't you think pink crowns, bouquets and dresses will be too much pink?' Judy enquired diplomatically.

'These sandwiches are ham and cress, the ones next to your plate, salmon and cucumber, Mr Williams.' Ignoring Judy's reaction, Ena fussed over Roy.

'Please call me Roy.' He gave Judy a look of commiseration that also managed to suggest forbearance, and took a sandwich from the plate Ena handed him.

'Roy,' she repeated coyly, fluttering her lashes, 'and you must call me Ena.'

'Thank you, Ena.'

Unable to keep a straight face, Joy concentrated on Billy, who was subdued in the unfamiliar surroundings.

'But you must have relatives that you want to invite to be bridesmaids as well, Judy?' Ena passed Joy a paper napkin.

'No.'

'Probably just as well.' Ena poured out the tea and handed cups down the table to her guests. 'Six is a tidy number. I went into town yesterday and picked up a swatch of that material I was telling you about.' She delved into her bulging pinafore pocket and pulled out a square of almost luminous, pink figured nylon. 'Of course you can't see the full flower pattern from this, so you'll have to take my word how pretty it is. If you pull out that drawer behind you, Joy . . . Not that one, the next one down. There's a pattern on top for a bridesmaid's dress that Mrs Howells next door used for her daughter's wedding. The minute I read Sam's letter telling me that you'd been to see the vicar to fix the date, I went round to her house and borrowed it. Have you thought about a dress yet, Judy?'

'No.'

'Of course you haven't,' she broke in blithely, answering her own question. 'How silly of me, you'll want me to help you choose it. And there'll be all the accessories, your veil, headdress and so on. We'll go shopping together.' She beamed at Joy, who was watching Judy intently and wondering just how much longer it would be before she'd lose her temper.

'Please, hand Judy the pattern, Joy.' She waited until Judy took it. 'Isn't it pretty? Mrs Howells's daughter's dress was cut along similar lines . . .'

'It's ballerina length.' Judy set the pattern aside.

'Such a nice length for a bride and bridesmaids, don't you think?' Ena babbled, insensible to Judy's disapproval. 'No long hems to trail in the mud or trip little ones up. Mrs Richards – that's our local dressmaker – made Mrs Howells's daughter's dress as well as the bridesmaids. If you like, I could ask her if she'll make yours. She's very busy of course, booked up for weeks ahead . . .'

'I'd like to buy my dress.'

'Given the short time we have to arrange everything, it might be just as well.' Ena nibbled a crumpet.

'And the bridesmaids' dresses,' Judy added.

Ena giggled. 'Now that would be extravagant. Besides, I've already settled with Mrs Richards that she will make them. Now about the mothers' outfits. I think they should be bought together with the bride's dress to make sure they'll look well on the photographs. Not exactly matching, you understand . . . do try one of those scotch eggs, Joy. I made them myself. I'll give you the recipe. Sam loves my scotch eggs, don't you, Sam?'

Sam grunted agreement through a full mouth.

'Now where was I? Of course, the hotel. Sam said you've booked the reception.'

'In the Mackworth.'

'I hope they have a big room. There'll be one hundred and eleven coming from our side of the family.'

'One hundred and eleven,' Joy echoed faintly.

'We're a big family and everyone loves Sam, so they all want to be there. Of course that figure includes one or two close friends. Now the menu, Judy, I think chicken. Don't you agree, Joy? Everyone likes chicken and it always goes down so much better than pork, lamb or beef at a wedding. And prawn cocktails to start. Your cousin Doris had those at her wedding last year, Sam, do you remember? They looked ever so nice. Smart, different and less messy than soup. Easier for the little ones to eat, although I'm never sure prawns are good for them. Bit too sophisticated, don't you think, Joy?'

'I—'

'Peas and carrots for vegetables, with roast and boiled potatoes, and stuffing, naturally.'

'Naturally,' Judy broke in, wondering if her future mother-in-law's mouth would start unravelling if she talked any longer.

'And ice cream for afters, everyone likes ice cream. Coffee of course. And flowers. Have you thought about the flowers, Joy?'

'Judy and I—'

'Lilies look good at weddings; they would go with the pink rosebuds too, you can have both in your bouquet, Judy. We have ever such a good florist in Neath. She does a lovely bouquet. I can see it now, white lilies and a spattering of pink rosebuds to pick up the colour in the bridesmaids' dresses. You can have them in your head-dress as well. And in vases on the tables at the wedding breakfast. Your cousin Sidney—'

'Who's Sidney?' Sam interposed between bites of pork pie.

'Ernie and Mabel's son, he has a taxi business and he's bought two posh cars that he hires out for weddings. He'll give them to you at discount if you ask him. Oh and I've got the address of that hotel for you.'

'What hotel?' Sam asked blankly.

'The one in Blackpool your cousin Sandra honey-mooned in. She said it was lovely, a real home away from home—'

'I don't want to go to Blackpool.'

Sam's mother looked at Judy as if she'd taken leave of her senses. 'All our family go to Blackpool for their honeymoon, dear. It's a lovely place.'

'I've been there and I don't want to go there again.'

Judy looked to Sam for support, but he appeared to be engrossed in his pie.

'You didn't like it?' Ena couldn't have been more affronted if Judy had insulted her personally.

'Perhaps Sam and Judy have somewhere else in mind, Ena,' Joy suggested smoothly, as Judy began to look mutinous.

'Sam! What do you have to say about this?' Mrs Davies turned to her son.

'We might go to Jersey, Mam.'

'Jersey! I've never heard of anything so extravagant in my life. Going abroad just when you're starting out and have so many things to buy? And that's another thing, Judy. I've lots of odd cups and plates you can have and some old blankets. They've gone a bit – well, bobbly – you know what I mean, but they're perfectly serviceable, good and warm.'

'I have my own things, in my own flat.'

'You've been living as a single girl, Judy. Not a married woman. You have Sam to look after now.'

Judy closed her mouth, as Joy kicked her ankle. Sam still refused to meet her eye, so she did the most politic thing she could think of. Left the table and walked down the garden to the tŷ bach.

'Are you sure you two won't come in for a cup of tea?' Joy asked Judy and Sam, as Roy lifted a sleepy Billy from the back of Judy's car and carried him to his front door.

'No thanks, Mam,' Judy refused. 'I've had about as much tea as I can drink for one day.'

'See you soon then, darling.'

'Yes, see you soon.' Judy revved the engine and her mother closed the door.

'I warned you that my mother would be interested in our wedding preparations,' Sam said, as she drove along Carlton Terrace.

'Interested!' Judy swerved the car around the corner.

'She's taking over. Bridesmaids' dresses, flowers, cars, even the honeymoon.'

'You have to learn to put your foot down.'

'Like you, I suppose. You hardly said a word to her all afternoon and if what you did say was indicative of putting your foot down, I for one, missed the message.'

'It's the only way to deal with her. It's what my father used to do when he was alive and it's the way my brother and I cope with her now. It makes for a quiet life if you listen to what she has to say. Afterwards you can do your own thing.'

'Like boycott Blackpool as a honeymoon venue. And since when are we going to Jersey?' she questioned angrily.

'I didn't say we were going, I said I was thinking about it.'

'You didn't tell me you were thinking about it.'

'Because I only picked up the brochure last Friday and since then we've been a bit preoccupied with other things. Come on, Judy, I know my mother can be overbearing, but don't you think you're being too sensitive? Bridal nerves and all that?'

'No, I don't!'

'She means well.'

'So did Attila the Hun.'

'Are you sure?' He smiled as she glanced across at him. 'As I'm still on afternoons next week, I'll go shopping with you on Tuesday morning and try to keep her under control.'

'We'll be going to dress shops,' she warned.

'It will prove how much I love you.'

As Judy continued to drive along the road that skirted the broad sweep of Swansea Bay, she couldn't help feeling that the world was closing in on her, claustrophobic, constraining. It was almost as though her marriage to Sam was going to mark the end of her life, not the beginning. Time was racing, preparations were being made; in a few weeks she'd find herself married and, if her mother-in-law had her way, honeymooning in a hotel in Blackpool. And she felt absolutely powerless to stop it.

'Jack, is that you?' Helen called downstairs as she heard a key turn in the lock of the front door.

'No, it's the bogeyman,' he shouted, as he stepped into the hall. He caught sight of his rust and grease-stained overalls in the mirror and remained standing on the tiled floor.

'You're late. I promised my father we'd be at his house by half past seven and it's after seven now.' Helen appeared at the top of the stairs. 'You look as though Martin and Brian used you as a mop to clean the garage.'

He bent down and unlaced his boots. 'It wasn't the garage, Brian had that professionally cleaned, it was the second-hand tools Marty bought. They were filthy.'

'I hope you've finished, because if you haven't, you'll be putting those clothes on again tomorrow. There's no way I'm risking clogging my washing machine or staining my mangle with them, they can go in the bin.'

'Every tool is now sparkling.'

'Unlike you.'

'If you think I'm bad, you should see Marty. God only knows why he insisted on cleaning every piece back to the bare metal. They're only going to get dirty again as soon as he uses them.'

'Is everything ready for the opening on Monday?'

'It will be after Brian, Marty and I put in another couple of hours tomorrow. But as it's mainly sorting the office and racking the tools, we shouldn't get into anything like this state again.' Removing his boots, he went to put them on the doormat.

'No!'

'Then where?'

'Leave them on the tiles, they're easier to clean.'

He smiled up at her. 'If you're thinking of going to the party in that petticoat, it's only fair to warn you I can see right through it. And those rollers.' He shook his head,

'I'm not up on fashion but that particular shade of pink plastic doesn't go with blonde hair.'

'It's easy to see who you've been working with all day, you even sound like Brian.' A towel landed at his feet. 'Strip.'

'That sounds hopeful.'

'Forget any thoughts you had in that direction, we're late, remember?'

'After Katie and Glyn's welcome home party?' he suggested.

'That depends entirely on how much you drink. If your feet are clean under your socks, bundle everything you're wearing into your vest, inside out. As it's furthest from those overalls it should be the cleanest and least likely to drip dirt around the place. Then dump everything in the bin in the back porch. I'll start running you a bath. From where I'm standing, it looks as though I should tip in a dozen handfuls of washing soda and the scrubbing brush, and that's just to get the dirt out of your hair.'

'Don't bother to clean the bath after Marty, Lily, I'll do it, and,' Brian gave her a rueful smile, 'I promise to scrub it out again after I've used it.'

'I thought Marty came home from the council depot filthy, but he's never been in this state before.'

'Don't touch the linen bin,' Brian warned as she went to pick it up, 'not until I've cleaned off the greasy finger marks.'

'I'll leave you to it.' Closing the bathroom door, she walked into the bedroom where Martin was towelling himself dry. 'Have you finished cleaning the tools, or can I expect you two in the same state tomorrow?'

'We have to put in a couple of hours tomorrow to get everything ready but it'll be relatively clean work.'

'I know your idea of relatively clean.'

'I'll just be racking the tools and sorting where to put things in the workshops so they'll be to hand.' His face shone as he turned towards her. 'It was a brilliant idea of Brian's to go to that auction. We had some real bargains.'

'Even after all the elbow grease you put into cleaning everything.' She smiled at the expression on his face. He looked like a little boy who had been given his first bike.

'The work we put in was worth it. I knew I'd bought some good stuff, but I didn't realise just how good until we stripped off the rust and grease. Why don't you drive over with us tomorrow and take a look at the workshops? They're not as big as the ones in the depot but thanks to the auction, they'll be better equipped. They're a mechanic's dream.'

'And I'm forgiven for organising the loan,' she interrupted hopefully, as she opened his wardrobe and lifted out a clean shirt.

'You can't blame me for worrying,' he murmured defensively.

'Here, you missed a bit.' Taking the towel from him she dried his back between his shoulder blades.

'I won't be happy about the overdraft until we've repaid every penny, but from the way the place looks, if we fail, it won't be from the want of trying.' He retrieved the damp towel and tossed it on to the bed.

'You'll soak the bed,' she reprimanded, picking it up and folding it over the towel stand.

'Sorry.' He held out his arms and looked down at the bed.

'Dress, or we'll never get next door.'

'There's bags of time. Brian isn't even out of the bath yet and he has to scrub it and dress. And besides, you look fantastically and deliciously plump, just like a wife should.'

'Plump!' Her heart missed a beat. Had he guessed her secret?

'Rounded in all the right places or is it the blouse? I've never noticed it so tight over your bust before. I have this uncontrollable urge to flick the buttons . . .'

'Don't you dare!' She glanced in the mirror as she

backed away from him and realised it had been optimistic of her to hope that Martin wouldn't notice she had gone up two bra sizes in the last two months. 'My blouse must have shrunk in the wash,' she lied.

'Then I advise you to shrink all your blouses.' He caught her and opened the top few buttons.

'Marty,' she protested half-heartedly, laughing as he imprisoned her in his arms. 'I'm all ready . . .'.

'You were all ready.' He pulled her gently down on to the counterpane.

'Am I clean?'

Helen looked critically at Jack and rummaged in the bottom of her handbag. 'I can't see. Turn around. You had a great big black mark on the back of your head when you came in.'

'Has it gone?' He straightened the sleeves on his sports jacket.

'It has. Jack, why don't you wear a suit? Both of them are—'

'Too small.'

'Not your suits as well,' she sighed. 'You only wore them once or twice before you went into the army. Have you any idea how much I paid to have them cleaned?'

'Sorry, love, but the sports coat will have to do until the next wedding.'

'Which is Judy's and only a couple of months away. Damn!'

'Problem?' he asked innocently, as she turned her handbag upside down and tipped the contents on to the hall table.

'I can't find my keys.' She looked at him in exasperation. 'Instead of standing there grinning like a fool, you could help me to look for them.'

'Want me to drive?' He dangled them in front of her.

'Not after what you did the last time you got behind the wheel of my car.'

'Then come on the back of my bike.'

'In this dress, absolutely not! You're infuriating.' She snatched the keys from him.

'You shouldn't leave them where you can't find them.'

'Which was?' She held out her arms so he could help her on with her coat.

'The kitchen table.'

'Blast, I left them there so I wouldn't forget the—'

'Cake you promised to pick up from Eynon's for your father?' He held up the box.

'Think you're so smart.'

'Yes, I do.' He kissed her lips before opening the door. 'Look who I married for a start.'

'Damn!' she reiterated, as she started the car.

'What now?' Jack asked patiently.

'A letter came for you, second post today. I meant to give it to you.'

'Whatever it is, it can't be important enough to make us any later than we already are.'

'You sure?' Helen pushed the gear into reverse.

'I'll read it when we get home.'

'It's nothing but parties for us these days. First Jack's homecoming, now this, and in eleven weeks mine and Judy's wedding.' Teetering on the edge between merry and drunk, Sam beamed benignly at John and every man in the kitchen, with the exception of Brian.

'Pity Glyn isn't old enough to join us, John. This malt of yours is nectar, the best I've ever tasted, and I've tasted some corkers in my time.' Roy sniffed his glass before sipping it slowly and appreciatively.

'From the way the women are fussing over Glyn in the living room, I'd say he's not faring too badly.' Brian offered his cigarettes around. 'And you left one party out, Sam, we'll be organising an event to mark the opening of the garage. At Will and Ronnie's expense,' Brian added quickly when Martin scowled.

'Good idea.' Jack drew his brother aside. 'I've been thinking . . . '

'I thought you were on your second honeymoon.'

'Very funny, Marty. You know that apprentice you're thinking of taking on?'

'After I've sorted just how much work I'll have for him and how much money will be coming in,' Martin qualified.

'I've come up with someone.'

'Who?'

'Me.'

'You?' Martin scoffed. 'You don't know one end of a car from the other.'

'I would if I went to night school.'

'Apprentices only earn a couple of quid a week. You're a married man with a wife to support.'

'And an apprentice's wages will be a nice little boost to the wages and commission Brian will be paying me to sell cars.' Jack opened a bottle of beer and topped up both their glasses.

'You want to work for both of us at the same time?'

'The penny has finally dropped.'

Martin's frown deepened. 'It wouldn't work.'

'Why not? It's not as if the garage is going to be that busy when it opens, at first anyway, and you'd save the cost of a worker between you.'

'Men in suits sell cars, not grease monkeys in overalls,' Martin declared, 'and you can't service cars in a suit. Not if you want to wear it afterwards.'

'So, I'll wear overalls over my suit – when I get one – when I work for you and take them off when I work for Brian.'

'Have you any idea how filthy a mechanic's job is?'

'After today, yes,' Jack said deprecatingly, 'and oil-stained overalls will give the impression that I know what I'm talking about when I recommend a car to a customer.'

'That might be difficult when you haven't a clue what's under the bonnet.'

'How hard can it be to learn?'

'It took me four years of hard graft to get my certificates,' Martin rejoined acidly. 'And you've only ever driven army vehicles.'

'And Helen's car for the last fortnight.'

'And you didn't scrape it on the gate?' Martin crowed.

'How did you find out about that?' Jack demanded. 'Helen swore she wouldn't tell anyone.'

'Lily saw the scratch when you pulled up tonight.'

'Isn't there anything those girls don't tell one another?' Jack griped.

Martin recalled Judy sitting in their kitchen the day he and Lily had quarrelled and Lily's admission that they had discussed his reluctance to go into the garage. 'Not much.'

'I drove all sorts in the army,' Jack boasted. 'Did I mention that I gained a HGV licence as well as—'

'Yes. And please don't try to impress me with the skills you acquired in the army,' Martin implored. 'I know exactly what they're worth and what army drivers are like. They jump in and out of the nearest empty vehicle and leave checking the oil, water, petrol and tyres to the grease wallah. There could be camels under the bonnet for all they know.'

'I've talked to Brian . . .'

'He has.' Brian joined them. 'You're the one who's worried about money, Marty,' he reminded. 'And what's the worst that can happen if Jack grafting for both of us doesn't work out? We'll have to bring in someone else.' He shrugged his shoulders as he answered his own question.

'At practically no notice.'

'That doesn't mean we won't find the right person for the job.'

'And it will give me a chance to find out if I'm more suited to being a salesman or mechanic,' Jack pressed persuasively.

'Stop worrying,' Brian slapped Martin's back. 'Everything is going to work out just fine.'

Chapter Twelve

'Judy, I'm sorry,' John apologised, as she entered the kitchen with an armful of empty bottles. 'I meant to take more drinks in for you girls half an hour ago.' Relieving her of the bottles, he dropped them into a crate.

'You have your work cut out looking after everyone here.' One glance at Sam had been sufficient for her to realise that he'd drunk more than was good for him. As he tried to put his arm around her, she deliberately turned her back on Brian, Martin and Jack, hoping to avoid arousing his jealousy as she had done the night of Jack's homecoming party.

'It's strange how the women always end up in a separate room to the men at parties,' Martin observed, noticing the antagonistic looks Sam was sending Brian's way.

'Not strange at all,' Judy answered lightly. 'The men don't want their wives to know how much they're drinking, and the wives,' she curled her lip mischievously, 'welcome the opportunity to hold an intelligent conversation with someone for a change.'

'It's just as well it's Sam you're marrying, not me,' Jack bit back.

'Here you go, Judy.' As John tried to hand her a dozen bottles in a crate, Brian intercepted it.

Brian swung away from Judy when she tried to relieve him of the load of Babychams and Ponys. 'It's heavy and I need to exercise my muscles.'

'In that case, after you.'

As Brian walked ahead of her down the passage, Judy

saw Sam move from the corner of the kitchen to the sink so he could watch them. She opened the door to the living room and stood back to allow Brian to walk in ahead of her.

'Someone's getting spoiled.' Brian lowered the crate to the floor and set the bottles out on a side table.

'A gorgeous little man deserves all the love and attention he can get. Don't you, angel pudge.' Lily shifted Glyn further up in her arms so Brian could admire him.

'By gorgeous I take it you mean he's not as red and wrinkled as most babies. Here, woman, hand him over.' Before Lily could protest, Brian had pushed the empty crate into a corner and swept the baby out of her arms and into his own. To the women's amazement, the baby looked up at Brian with round, wondrous eyes before settling contentedly.

'I never suspected you were the paternal kind, Brian,' Helen teased.

'I can't wait to tell Roy. He thinks he's the only man in the world who can nurse a baby.' Joy passed Katie her empty glass.

'John is wonderful with him, but Martin and Jack hold Glyn as if he's a bomb that's about to explode at any moment.' Katie set about opening bottles and filling glasses.

'Only because your brothers haven't had any practice since you were born. As soon as Glyn has a couple of playmates,' Joy looked significantly at Helen and Lily, 'they'll become as proficient as Brian.'

'There's nothing to it, is there, Glyn?' Brian addressed the baby solemnly as if he expected him to answer. 'Babies are human; it's only women who don't realise it. That's why they talk to you in noises that even an animal would have trouble understanding.'

'We do not,' Lily protested.

'What's an "angel pudge" when it's at home?'

'Glyn is, you only have to look at him,' Lily responded.

'I rest my case. How is the poor chap ever going to

learn English with you lot gooing and gaaing at him. And don't say you weren't, we could hear you from the kitchen.'

As Glyn continued to gurgle happily in Brian's arms, Judy asked, 'Do you have a dozen babies hidden away somewhere that you practise on?'

'Not quite.' As the baby kicked up his legs, Brian lifted him against his shoulder and rubbed his back. 'Only eleven.'

'Eleven?'

'Nieces and nephews,' he explained, 'although some of them are only a couple of years younger than me.'

'I had no idea you came from such a large family,' Lily said in surprise.

'Of course, none of them are as wonderful as me.'

'Get out of here, this is a women only zone,' Judy interrupted. The comment she'd intended to be light-hearted, sounded anything but.

'That's a vicious lady, Glyn. I think we should run away and hide in the kitchen with the men.'

'Oh no, you don't.' Katie leapt to her feet.

'Why not? I promise to have him back in five minutes and,' Brian gave her a wicked smile, 'I won't allow him to drink anything stronger than beer.' Still nursing the baby, he wandered out of the room.

'Glyn will be fine, Katie,' Joy advised, as Katie went to the door.

'John's in the kitchen as well,' Lily reminded.

'And my father has always been good with children, well, ever since I can remember,' Helen qualified.

'I suppose so.' Katie didn't follow Brian, but she continued to hover in the doorway.

'I can't get over how great you look, Katie,' Joy complimented. 'You've always been thin but no one would think you had a baby two weeks ago. Not like me. A full month after Billy was born, Mrs Morgan asked me when he was due.'

'It's the exercise.'

'You exercise?' Judy asked in surprise.

'I was joking. I can't even claim that I do much in the house. John's only worked mornings since I've come home from the hospital and between what he does and Mrs Jones, I'm almost a lady of leisure.'

'No one with a baby can be that for long. You wait until Glyn starts crawling, he'll be into everything and always the things he shouldn't be.' Joy lifted her glass.

'So, I've been dying to ask.' Helen sat forward on the edge of the sofa and looked at Judy. 'How did the shopping go? Have you decided on a wedding dress?'

'Yes.' Judy glanced over her shoulder. As the door was slightly ajar, she closed it before continuing. 'No thanks to my future mother-in-law.'

'Judy.' Joy sounded a cautious note.

'Even Sam admits she's overbearing, Mam. When we went into the dress shop, she asked the assistant to bring out everything she had in ballerina length, crinoline skirted, white figured nylon.'

'I thought you weren't keen on ballerina length wedding dresses,' Helen interposed. 'When we helped Lily choose hers, you said you would never wear one.'

'I wouldn't be seen dead in one!'

'Sorry I asked.' Helen held up her hands as if to ward off a blow.

'And I'm sorry I snapped like that, but the woman's a nightmare who believes there's only one point of view – hers. She wanted me to wear ballerina length, crinoline skirted, white figured nylon because she'd already picked out the bridesmaids and the material for their dresses and guess what, she wanted them all to wear ballerina length pink figured nylon, all six of them,' she finished caustically.

'And that's what they are wearing?' Helen asked.

'In my nightmares and her dreams,' Judy retorted.

'With six bridesmaids you won't need a matron of honour,' Lily said easily. 'And I won't be in the least offended.'

'That woman is not running my wedding or my life,' Judy snapped. 'And I most certainly will need you.'

'Calm down, love, you're among friends and Ena is nowhere in sight,' Joy soothed.

'I'm sorry,' Judy muttered, taking the glass Katie handed her. 'It's just that every time I think about her I get so mad.'

'Then don't think about her.' Helen helped herself to a sandwich.

'Things became so bad on the shopping trip that Sam had to take his mother into Woolworth's restaurant and buy her a coffee,' Joy divulged.

'At least Sam went with you to chose a dress. Martin would prefer to pull his own teeth than go shopping with me.' Lily set her full glass of sherry aside, hoping no one would notice that she hadn't touched it.

'It was Sam's idea he come with us, not mine. He knows exactly how overbearing his mother can be. But as the one thing that we all managed to agree on was that it was bad luck for the groom to see the bride's dress before the wedding, Sam sat on a chair next to the front door so he couldn't see into the back where I was trying on the dresses. But he could still hear us arguing.'

'And that's when he stepped in and took his mother for a coffee,' Joy continued. 'If nothing else, it gave Judy the chance to pick out a pattern for the bridesmaids' dresses that complemented the bridal gown she chose for herself.'

'Which is?' Lily asked.

'High Tudor collared and styled white satin and silk with a heavily embroidered white silk bodice and an under petticoat ornamented by teardrop pearls,' Judy revealed. 'I know white on white doesn't sound very exciting . . . '

'But it's elegant and absolutely stunning. I had no idea Judy could look so dazzlingly magnificent and that's a mother talking,' Joy enthused.

'And the pink figured nylon?' Helen queried.

Judy made a face. 'I gave in on the colour but not the

material. We settled on pink satin, although Mrs Davies is going to buy it. Needless to say, with my money.'

'She did say it was a shilling a yard cheaper in Neath,' Joy reminded.

'And at least it won't be the same awful shade as the pink figured nylon. It was disgusting, like a Teddy boy's luminous socks.'

'Look on pink satin as a compromise to get the bridesmaids' dresses cut to the pattern you wanted,' Joy advised.

'Anything to keep the peace.'

'One young man who's too tired to join us for a drink.' Jack walked in with Glyn in his arms.

'You taking lessons from Brian?' Katie smiled in relief and went to retrieve her son.

'Just playing pass the parcel. Glyn seems to like it. Here, it's Auntie Helen's turn to hold you.' Jack set the baby down gently in his wife's arms and continued to stand in front of her, blocking her from everyone's view as she struggled to control her emotions. 'You having him christened, sis?' Jack asked, in an attempt to deflect the women's attention from Helen.

'When we get around to arranging it.' Katie gave Judy and Joy an apologetic look. 'The vicar insisted that we couldn't have more than three godfathers and two godmothers. John and I had terrible trouble choosing, but we thought that if we asked Roy, Martin and Jack to be Glyn's godfathers and Lily and Helen to be his godmothers, you two could be godparents along with Sam and Brian next time.'

'I don't mind at all, as long as I can be an honorary aunt.' Judy wondered if the time it took Katie and John to have another child would be long enough for Sam to drop his antagonism towards Brian.

'I can't believe you're already talking about the next one.' Joy shook her head in disbelief.

'My mother always used to say that it was easier to look after three children than one because we played so well together.' Katie offered Jack a depleted plate of sausage rolls.

'Not that she approved of all our games.' Jack sat on the arm of the sofa next to Helen.

'Like?' Judy enquired.

'When we took turns to bury her knives and forks in the garden, so we could pretend it was treasure. Whenever it was Katie's turn, she could never remember where she'd dug the hole, so if Martin and I hadn't found them by the time my mother called us in for the next meal we had to eat whatever it was with teaspoons.'

'Which was nothing compared to the summer you and Martin tried to breed winkles in Mam's washing-up bowl under your bed.' Katie wrinkled her nose at the memory. 'Your bedroom smelled fishy for a month.'

'What about the time you four tried to dye your hair with household bleach?' Jack laughed.

'That was Helen's idea. She wanted to be white not yellow blonde.' Judy took a sausage roll and passed on the plate.

'It wasn't me at all, it was you,' Helen contradicted. 'You were fed up with your red hair.'

'I must admit, that does sound like you, Judy,' Joy agreed.

'You two look good together,' Jack whispered, taking Glyn from Helen. He winked at her. 'Roll on that appointment next Wednesday.'

'I'd forgotten how good Swansea parties can be.' Brian pulled out a chair and sat at Lily's kitchen table.

'Coffee, everyone?' Lily looked at Brian, Martin, Sam and Judy.

'For me, please,' Brian accepted.

'And me.' Martin reached for the mugs.

'Not for me, it will keep me awake and tomorrow I start on mornings, six till two.' Sam glanced at the clock. 'Which only gives me about four and half hours' sleep before I have to get up.' Pointedly ignoring Brian, he turned to Judy. 'I'll walk you to your car.'

'I'm staying for coffee, if it's all right with Lily?' Bypassing Brian's chair, Judy sat next to Martin.

'As if you need an invitation.' Lily turned to Martin. 'And a mug for me as well please, love.'

'I thought you said you wanted an early night, Judy,' Sam snapped.

'Why would I, when Sunday is the one day of the week that I can lie in?'

'Coffee coming up.' Lily poured boiling water into the coffee pot.

'As it's ready, I'll take you up on your offer, Lily,' Sam said tersely. 'That's if you don't object to me changing my mind?'

'Be my guest.' Lily glanced at Martin and rolled her eyes heavenwards. She brought the coffee to the table.

'You lot don't know you're born.' Sam looked from Brian to Martin. 'Tomorrow you'll all be lying in bed until midday.'

'Hardly,' Lily interrupted. 'Martin, Brian and Jack will all be in the garage early tomorrow morning to get it ready for the opening on Monday.'

'And at two o'clock, when you are finishing for the day, they'll still be hard at it and I'll be sitting bored to death at a product demonstration.' Judy realised that Sam had crossed the line between pleasantly merry and argumentative drunk and wished she hadn't followed him into Martin and Lily's. She reached for the milk jug and poured half an inch of cold milk into her coffee to cool it so she could drink it quickly.

'And I'll be doing the washing in secret and hoping that Mrs Lannon can't hear the machine from her back kitchen.' Lily pushed the sugar bowl towards Brian.

'Secret?' Brian asked, bemused.

'Don't you know you'll go to hell if you do any housework other than cook the dinner on a Sunday?'

Judy almost smiled at Brian, realised what she was doing, and looked away quickly, but not before he smiled at her.

'People round here still take that much notice of the chapel?'

'And church,' Lily added.

'They don't in Pontypridd?' Sam enquired sardonically.

'No, I thought you knew we're all Godless savages up there, Sam.' Brian's weak attempt at humour fell flat into the heavy atmosphere. Exhausted by his long day in the garage, the four pints of beer he'd drunk in John and Katie's, but most of all from fencing words with Sam, Brian pushed his chair back from the table. 'I'll set my alarm but given the way I feel, I'm likely to sleep through it. Give me a shout if I'm not up and about by half past seven, Martin.'

'You'd be better off asking Lily, she's the one who kicks me out of bed every morning.'

'After I've woken Martin with a wet sponge, I'll send him in to you.' Lily picked up her own and Martin's mugs and stacked them in the sink.

'I'm off.' Judy left her chair and kissed Lily on the cheek. 'Lunch next Friday if I don't see you before. We have to talk matron of honour dresses.'

'Not pink,' Lily warned. 'I'm too old.'

'You don't have to convince me.'

'I'm on twelve till one break next week.'

'I'll meet you outside the bank. Bye, everyone.' Judy went to the door but Sam reached it before her.

'See you, Judy,' Martin called.

'If you want to lock up, I'll use the basement front door,' Sam shouted.

'Thanks, I'll bolt the front door and put the chain on.'

As Martin went to secure the door, Lily looked to Brian. 'You and Sam have a row?' she asked.

'Nothing I know anything about.'

'I think the expression is "if looks could kill you'd be dead,"' Martin said, returning to the kitchen.

'The bloke's paranoid.' Brian dismissed.

'Only where Judy's concerned,' Lily mused. 'And the last time you were in Swansea, you and Judy were going out together.'

'That was nearly three years ago and it didn't last long. And as she's marrying Sam in a couple of months, I can't see what his problem is. Goodnight, you two.'

'Goodnight, Brian.' As Lily ran water into the sink to wash the mugs, she recalled the look she had intercepted between Brian and Judy, and the dismissive way Judy had talked about her mother-in-law and her wedding preparations. She knew exactly what Sam's problem was; she only hoped for Judy's sake that he had completely misread the situation.

'I'll come round the flat tomorrow about six.'

'No, Sam.' Judy unlocked her car.

'You can't be working?'

'As I said earlier, I'm going to a demonstration of new hair products at a warehouse with the girls from the salons and I have no idea when I'll be back.'

'On a Sunday night?'

'It's the best night for the wholesalers and traders.'

'And you'll be there all night?' he enquired belligerently, swaying in the cold night air, as the beer and whisky he'd downed earlier began to fight in his stomach as well as his head.

'There are refreshments afterwards.'

'Monday?'

'You're on mornings, telephone me about six o'clock.'

'You're angry.'

'Yes, I am.' She climbed into her car. 'And I've every right to be after the way you behaved at the party and just now in Lily's.'

'And you've no right to make eyes at Brian Powell.'

'I don't. And do you want to know why I don't? Because I'm terrified to as much as look at him in case you make a fool of yourself and me the way you did just now.' Seeing a light flick on in Mrs Lannon's bedroom, she lowered her voice to a whisper. 'I don't know what more I can do to convince you that I've made my choice, Sam. I've been to bed with you, I've set the date, booked the church and reception, bought the dress and listened as politely as is humanly possible to your mother's ideas on what a wedding should be, even if I haven't been able to go along with all her insane plans. But I warn you, one more evening like tonight, and I'll cancel the whole damned day.' Slamming the door, she pressed the ignition, put her foot down and drove away, leaving him standing, watching her.

'I can barely keep my eyes open,' Helen yawned, as she walked into the house.

'You go up first. I'll be right behind you, sweetheart.' Jack closed the door, locked it and slipped his keys back into the pocket of his sports coat.

'Promise?' She put one foot on the stairs.

'Promise.' He switched on the light, walked into the living room and checked the fire. The guard was up and there were a few, barely glowing embers. Another hour and the fire would be out. As he rose to his feet, he noticed an envelope on the mantelpiece and recalled Helen mentioning a letter.

He picked it up and turned it over. The envelope was plain, the postmark and the writing unfamiliar. Sliding his thumb beneath the flap, he tore it open, checked the address at the top of the page, which meant nothing to him, and noted that it had been written four days previously.

Dear Jack,

I have thought long and hard about writing to you and I am still not sure that I am doing the right thing, but please believe that I am sincere when I say I don't want to hurt you, your family or upset your life in any way. The problem is, I cannot decide whether I have the right to withhold the knowledge that you are about to become a father.

There, I've finally written the words, yet even now I wonder if you will ever read them. Only if I have the courage to post this and I am still unsure. The one thing I am certain of is that I neither want nor expect anything from you. No moral support and no money. With the help of my parents I am managing reasonably well on my widow's pension.

I told my parents the truth; that the child is a result of an evening when I allowed my grief to spiral out of control and the fault was entirely mine. Even if I could, I wouldn't name you as the father on the birth certificate and I intend for your identity to remain a secret between the two of us. I hope you can respect that wish.

The only reason I am writing to you now is that I talked through my problems with a vicar and he said that if he were you, he would want to know that he had a child somewhere in the world, if only to pray for its well-being. And, you should be aware of the child's existence for the sake of your own children. It would be too horrible if you have a daughter and she brings home an adopted boy . . . however unlikely it might be, it is still a possibility you should be aware of.

I have thought – in fact I cannot stop thinking – about that evening you visited me. If there is an explanation for what happened between us, I think it does lie in grief, yours as well as mine. I wanted Gordon back so much that I was prepared to reach out to anyone to fool myself that he was still alive, if only for a few moments longer. You were mourning him as every soldier under his command did. And, as I tried to tell you that night, the fact that Gordon was called upon to give his life to ensure your safety and the safety of the others in your platoon should not make you feel guilty. Gordon would have seen it as no more than his sergeant's duty. I hope that by now you have had time to reflect on what I said, and realise that neither you, nor anyone else could have stopped Gordon from doing what he did to protect you and the others.

When I left Cyprus, I moved in with my parents. They have offered the children and me a permanent home. When I discovered that I was carrying your child, I realised there was no way that I would be able to claim it as Gordon's, not when he was killed two months before it was conceived. My father called some friends and arranged for me to be admitted into the above church home for unmarried mothers under the name of Maggie Jones. He and my mother are looking after my children and they have told family and neighbours that I have tuberculosis, worsened by shock at Gordon's death and I am recuperating in an isolation hospital in the country.

The baby will be adopted and I have been assured that the church takes great care with the parents it chooses. I trust them because I have no choice, but my father says that the people on the adoption committee are good, well-meaning people.

I will understand if you don't want to reply to this letter, or have any contact with me. Burn this and you have my word that you will never hear from me again. Looking back now, I sometimes wonder if that night happened the way I remember it. If it wasn't for the baby I could so easily believe that I had dreamed the whole episode.

Take care, Jack. You were a good friend to Gordon and to me. Without you I would never have known what his last words or thoughts were. They mean everything to me now.

God Bless.

Maggie

Chapter Thirteen

'Jack, it's not even six o'clock.' Helen wrapped her dressing gown around herself and shivered in the doorway of the living room. Jack sat, hunched on one of the easy chairs, dressed in the dark trousers, white shirt and sports coat he had worn to the party the night before. His tie lay abandoned, still knotted on the coffee table. The room was freezing, the fireplace littered with cold, grey-white ash. 'Surely you haven't been sitting here all night.' She stepped into the room. 'Whatever is the matter?' she exclaimed, when he finally lifted his face. 'You look terrible . . . are you ill?' She crouched in front of him; taking his hands into hers, she rubbed them between her fingers in an effort to warm them.

Numb, cold, exhausted, he continued to stare at her. He loved her far too much to lie to her, but he knew the moment he told her that he had betrayed her with another woman – and that woman was carrying his child – she would never look at him in the same concerned and loving way again. So very, very loving.

Wordlessly he handed her the letter. Then unable to bear the misery it would cause or the contempt it would spawn, he left the house.

Helen sank down in the chair Jack had vacated and read the letter. She continued to scan the closely written pages long after the words had ceased to imprint themselves on her consciousness. Images ran at breakneck speed through her mind superimposing themselves, one upon the other. Fragments of memories she had cherished as magical and sacred.

The first night she and Jack had made love.

'*I'll never let you go, Helen. Not now.*'

The evening she had told him she was pregnant.

'*You're my girl, I'll look after you, Helen, just as I said I would, I promise.*'

Jack attempting to comfort her on the loss of their child as they had both struggled to come to terms with the bitter knowledge that there would never be another, not for them.

'*Don't be angry with me for caring about you more than a baby that never lived. I need you; I'm lost without you. You're my girl, remember?*'

Jack leaving for National Service.

'*How can I prove how much I love you?*'

Jack naked in the arms of another woman. A beautiful, fertile woman who would give him the child she never could. What warm, loving words had he whispered into her ears? Had he even thought of their marriage when he had lain in her bed?

Jack coming home after two and a half years.

'*I can't forget all the plans we made for our son either. Or the look on your face when you found out that you'd lost him and there wouldn't be any more babies. I know it's no consolation but no matter what, I'll never stop loving you.*'

Her own voice echoing back.

'*It must be even worse for you, knowing that you could have children if you wanted.*'

'*I wouldn't want children without you. I love you, sweetheart. You'll always be my girl.*'

'Helen. Helen.' She was suddenly aware of Jack's presence in the room. He retreated to the sofa, recoiling from the anguish in her eyes and the harsh knowledge that he had caused her so much pain.

'Is this true?' She held out the letter.

'Yes.'

'This woman is carrying your child?'

'Please,' he begged, when she remained sitting bolt upright, staring at him. 'I know how much I've hurt you, but please, let me try to explain.'

'All right.' Even her voice sounded cold, remote, as though she had already distanced herself from him. 'Tell me how it happened, Jack. Tell me how you undressed and made love to this woman after you promised to love me and only me for ever.' She sat back in the easy chair and looked at him through chill, dead eyes. 'Tell me.'

'I'm not making excuses – I can't,' Jack began awkwardly, 'but to try to explain, I have to go back to when I was wounded.' He took a deep breath and braced himself before the words began tumbling out.

'Our platoon was out on patrol. The lieutenant was in the first car with his driver, the sergeant – Gordon – was acting as rearguard and I was his driver. We went up into the mountains and hit a terrorist ambush. When they lobbed a bomb at us, the sergeant – he – he deflected it away from me,' he finished quickly. 'He was killed. I was wounded and I didn't come round for several days. Then I was in hospital for two months. When I was discharged, the doctor asked me to visit the sergeant's widow. She was leaving the island the next day and he thought it might help her to talk to someone who was with her husband when he died.'

'You went?' she asked bleakly after a moment's silence.

'I went. I wish to God I hadn't.'

'Stick to the facts, Jack.'

'I took a bottle of wine. She had another . . .'

'You got drunk.'

'Yes.'

'Both of you.'

'Yes.'

'And?' No longer lifeless, her eyes mirrored his image and a revulsion that hurt – almost unbearably.

'I felt sorry for her. She was crying. We both were. I hugged her. I know it sounds stupid in the light of what happened afterwards but it seemed the right thing to do at the time. She needed comforting.'

'Comforting!' Helen's blue eyes darkened.

'She kissed me.' He swallowed hard. 'No, that's not fair – we kissed . . .' The words dried under her unwavering gaze.

'You kissed her back?'

'I kissed her back,' he confessed, unable to compound or excuse what he'd done by lying.

'Would you have ever told me that you'd committed adultery if she hadn't written to you?'

'I thought about it.' He left the sofa and paced to the window. Turning his back to her, he looked down at the beach. 'God, how I thought about it! I couldn't think about anything else for weeks before I came back.'

'And after you arrived, you decided to keep it from me.'

'No . . .'

'You didn't tell me, Jack. You came home after two and half years and climbed into my bed within an hour of walking through that door. You made love to me as if nothing had happened.'

'In one sense nothing did,' he broke in wretchedly. 'Believe me, you can't hate me any more than I hate myself for allowing it to happen. But afterwards it wasn't – it wasn't as if it had been something that I had done. It's difficult to explain, but it's almost as if it had happened to someone else. It meant nothing, Helen, not just to me but her as well. She told me. It meant nothing.'

'We promised one another before I went away that there'd be no secrets between us, remember?'

'I knew you'd be hurt.'

'Get out!' Crumpling the letter into a ball, she threw it at him.

Reeling beneath the force of her venom, he picked it up and backed towards the door.

'Take your things and get out. I never want to see you again.' Helen slumped back in the chair. Silently, Jack went upstairs.

The floorboards creaked overhead as he walked into their bedroom. He ran downstairs a few minutes later and she reflected that he couldn't have packed very much. Then she remembered that almost everything in his wardrobe was too small for him.

She sensed him standing, watching her from the hall, but she didn't look up. She heard the chink of metal, the door opened and closed. A few minutes later his motorbike started up and roared off down the road.

She continued to sit, weak, nauseous, as the seconds ticked off on the grandmother clock that had been her aunt's. The house she had taken such pride in and worked so hard to turn into a home for Jack closed around her like a mausoleum. She felt as though not only her marriage but also her life had come to an end.

When she finally summoned the strength to stand, she made her way into the hall. Then she saw why Jack had lingered for a moment. His keys to the house were lying on the hall table. Taking them into her hand, she sank down on the bottom step of the stairs.

She continued to sit, staring into space, fighting to keep her mind a blank because nothingness was infinitely preferably to the torture of thought and the shattering, soul-destroying knowledge that Jack had betrayed her.

Lily had just left the bathroom when the doorbell rang.

'Who can that be at this hour?' Martin mumbled from the depths of the bed. He squinted at the alarm clock in the half-light from the landing. 'It's not even seven o'clock yet.'

'I'll go down and see.'

'No, you will not. Not in that dressing gown anyway, it shows far too much of you.'

'You've never complained before.' She opened her wardrobe door.

'And I won't while you keep it just for me.' Retrieving his pyjama trousers from the tangle of sheets and blankets at the foot of the bed, he pulled them on.

'Put your slippers on,' Lily advised as the bell rang a second time. 'That hall floor is freezing'

Martin pushed his feet into them. 'Keep your hair on,' he shouted, as the bell sounded a third time when he was halfway down the stairs. Switching on the hall light he walked down the passage and opened the door to see his brother, small suitcase in hand, standing on the step. 'You're keen to get started.'

'Helen's thrown me out,' Jack divulged flatly. 'Can I move in for a couple of days? Just until I get myself sorted.'

'I left him making tea in the kitchen.' Martin removed a set of underwear from a drawer.

Lily folded back the top sheet, blankets and eiderdown to air the bed. 'And you're sure he didn't say why Helen threw him out?'

'No.'

'You didn't ask?' She plumped up the bolster and pillows.

'It's hardly the sort of thing you drop into a casual conversation.' Martin pulled the towel from around his waist, almost dropped it on the bed, saw Lily watching him and draped it over the stand. 'Yes, Jack, of course you're welcome to stay with us for a couple of days. But by the way, why did Helen throw you out?'

'You said he could stay? Helen's my friend.'

'And Jack's my brother. What was I supposed to say to him? Sorry, Lily's a friend of Helen's so go sleep on the beach. I know it's freezing out there but we'll spare you the odd blanket or two.'

'No, but . . .' Lily hesitated, searching for an alternative solution.

'Would you rather he knocked on John and Katie's door when she's just had a baby?'

'All right,' she agreed. 'Jack can stay for a couple of days, but I'm taking the bus over to Helen's this morning.'

'To find out what happened.'

'To see if I can do anything to help.'

'Helen or Jack?' Martin asked.

'Both of them. Wake Brian if he isn't already, I'll go down and start making breakfast.'

'Lily?'

'What?' She turned back.

He pulled her close and kissed her. 'Whatever the problem is between Jack and Helen, promise me it won't affect us?'

'How can I do that, if I don't know what it is?' she questioned logically.

'We can support both of them without taking sides.'

'You think so?'

'We can try,' he murmured, suddenly realising just how difficult that might be.

'I've made a pot of tea,' Jack lifted the teapot, as Lily walked into her kitchen. 'Want a cup?'

'Yes, please. Bacon, sausage, eggs, tomatoes, fried bread and beans do you for breakfast?' She opened the fridge.

Jack debated for a moment. He wasn't hungry but it might be hours before he'd have another opportunity to eat. 'Just toast, please.'

'From what Martin and Brian said, you've a full day's work ahead of you. You have to eat.'

'I can't work in the garage today,' he interrupted.

'Oh?' She looked inquisitively at him.

'There's something I have to do.'

'I see.' She lifted half a dozen eggs out of the fridge and set them on the cupboard next to the stove.

'I asked Martin if I could stay here for a few days. He

said I could, but if it is going to make things difficult for you, Lily, I'll find somewhere else.'

'You're Martin's brother, you're welcome to stay.' She hoped she sounded as though she meant it. 'I'll make up a bed for you in the back bedroom and empty the drawers and wardrobe.'

'Don't bother on my account.' He pushed the small case he'd strapped to the back of his bike into the corner with his foot. 'That's the sum total of my earthly possessions.'

'When you start work, you'll need more clothes.'

'I suppose I will.'

Lily lifted the bacon box and a glass bowl full of sausages from the fridge and closed the door. 'Want to talk about it?'

'No.'

'Fine.' She set her mouth into a narrow line.

'Not until I've talked to someone else,' he clarified, 'and perhaps not even then. It's not just me and Helen, Lily. There are other people involved and I'd rather not discuss what's happened until I get things sorted in my own mind. That's if I ever will,' he muttered, speaking more to himself than to her.

Brian looked from Martin to Lily, as Jack slammed the front door behind him. 'Isn't that the cue for one of us to make a poignant remark?'

'You just have.' Martin sugared his second cup of tea.

'I suppose I have, but it was hardly poignant – or profound. Surely whatever's gone on between Jack and Helen can't be that bad? They seemed happy enough last night. In fact, a lot happier than Judy and Sam.' He wished he hadn't mentioned Judy's name when he saw Martin and Lily exchange significant glances. 'Perhaps we should have tried talking to Jack,' he suggested, bringing the conversation firmly back into line.

'I thought I did,' Martin said, 'but he didn't seem to be in a listening mood.'

Lily rose from the table. 'The sooner you two get to the garage, the sooner you'll be finished for the day and you'll both need to rest afterwards for the grand opening tomorrow. Leave the plates.' She took them from Martin. 'I'll wash them after I've seen Katie.'

'Surely you're not going to tell her that Jack has moved in here?' Martin exclaimed.

'You'd rather she saw him walking in and out of the house and come to her own conclusions? Or even worse, hear the news from one of the neighbours? You know what nosy gossips some of them are.'

'I suppose you're right,' Martin conceded. 'Just don't make too much of a meal of it.'

'How can I, when I don't know anything beyond the fact that Helen has thrown Jack out and he's moving in with us for a couple of days?'

'It's just that I don't think we should worry her. She doesn't look well. She hasn't had time to recover from having the baby.'

'Lily's right, Martin.' Brian drank the last of the tea in his cup. 'Better Katie and John hear it from you than an outsider.'

'I suppose so,' Martin allowed grudgingly.

'And as we're one man short, it's time we were off.' Brian gave Lily a look of commiseration, as she went to the door. 'Good luck,' he mouthed behind Martin's back.

'Lily, how nice, it's a surprise to see you this early on a Sunday morning.' John unrolled his shirtsleeves and fastened his cuffs. 'Katie's bathing Glyn.'

'I'm sorry, I interrupted.' Lily noticed soapsuds on John's hands as he pulled down the sleeves of his sweater.

He closed the door behind her. 'She'll be a little while longer. Would you like to go up and see her?'

Lily hesitated. Until John and Katie's marriage she had always considered John to be first and foremost Helen's father, an adult to her child, and as such, remote from her friends. Katie's marriage had done little to change that. She still felt awkward in his presence, but Glyn's birth had brought them closer and he was Helen's father. 'No, thank you, Mr Griffiths.'

'John,' he smiled.

'John,' she repeated, 'but I would appreciate your opinion on something.'

'If there is ever anything that I can do to help you or Martin, Lily, you only have to ask, surely you know that.'

'It's not Marty or me.' She followed him into his living room. 'Jack came round early this morning, with a case. He said Helen had thrown him out and he asked if he could stay with us for a few days.'

'I see.' If John was shocked he showed no sign of it. 'Please, sit down. Did he say why Helen had thrown him out?'

'No, when I asked, he said he didn't want to talk about it.'

'But he has moved in with you.'

'We had to let him, Mr . . . John. After all, he is Martin's brother.'

'Of course you did, Lily. I wouldn't have expected any less of you or Martin.' He paused for a moment. 'I should go and see Helen.'

'I thought I'd visit her this morning but it would be better if you go. You are her father.'

'No, Lily,' he interrupted. 'You are quite right, if anyone should go, it should be you. Jack has only just come home after years away so the chances are this is nothing more than the sort of stupid, trivial squabble all newlyweds have. And if that is the case, the more people who know about it, the more embarrassed Helen and Jack will be when it's over. She's probably realised by now that Jack has come straight to you, so when you turn up it won't be entirely unexpected. If I stick my nose in, both of them will see me as the heavy-handed, interfering father. Perhaps all they need is breathing space and I could end up doing more harm than good.'

'You really think so?' Lily asked doubtfully.

'You know Helen. This could be nothing more than the result of one of her tantrums. Remember what she used to be like when she was younger? Always off on a tirade against something or someone, without taking the trouble to find out the facts first.'

Lily nodded agreement, but even as she did so, she noticed a troubled look in John's eyes. She hadn't seen Helen lose her temper in two and half years – not since she had married Jack.

Jack slowed his bike to a halt outside a house set a few feet back from the narrow country road. Pulling Maggie's letter from his pocket, he straightened the creases Helen had made and checked the address at the top: Cartref. He'd hated Welsh classes in school and mitched off as many as he could because the teacher had been old, humourless and boring, but even he knew Cartref was Welsh for home. Unoriginal and, given the situation of the girls the place catered for, inappropriate.

Wheeling his bike into the courtyard, he propped it against a wall. He took a comb from his pocket, ran it through his hair then examined his trousers, the same ones he'd worn the night before. They were splattered to the knees with mud, and the leather jacket he'd bought in Cyprus was more practical than respectable, but he would have been frozen as well as damp if he'd ridden his bike in his sports coat. Unzipping the jacket he straightened his collar and tie before climbing the short flight of steps to the porch. The outer door was open but, as he couldn't see a bell on the inner door, he remained on the step, rang the bell and waited.

A tall, thin, sour-faced woman, who reminded him of his primary school headmistress, opened the door. 'Yes.' She eyed him as if he was a potential burglar.

'I'd like to see Mrs Maggie Jones, please.'

'Visiting is two to three Sunday afternoons and then, only for relatives.'

'I am Jack Clay.' As she went to close the door, he blurted, 'Her brother-in-law.'

'Really?' she queried sceptically.

Hoping the woman didn't know too much about Maggie's family, he added, 'I'm married to Gordon's sister. Gordon was Maggie's husband,' he prompted. 'I've only just found out that Maggie is here.'

'Visiting, even from relatives, is from two o'clock until three o'clock on Sunday afternoons,' she repeated, as if she were reciting a mantra.

'Please.' He gave her his most charming smile as he sensed her wavering. 'I've just returned from serving abroad and I haven't had an opportunity to offer my sister-in-law my condolences on Gordon's death.'

'Your wife is not with you?' she questioned suspiciously.

'She is ill. In hospital.' As his lies began to take on a life of their own, he only hoped he would be able to recall what he'd said, should this woman grill him at some future date.

The matron peered at him for a moment. Just as he'd decided that she was about to send him packing, she opened the door wider. 'This is most irregular. Any future visits will have to be made strictly within visiting hours.'

'I understand,' Jack said gratefully.

'You can wait in here while I check that Mrs Jones is in a suitable condition to receive your visit. She has been ordered to rest.' She ushered him into a tiny, freezing cold anteroom set off the porch.

'There is nothing wrong, is there?' he asked, hating himself for being unable to suppress the thought that it might be easier for him, and his pitifully slim hope that Helen might eventually forgive him, if the baby Maggie was carrying never became a reality.

'There is no cause for alarm. Mrs Jones has been

suffering from the effects of high blood pressure. Something not entirely unexpected in a woman of her age, in her condition.'

A stone bench was set against the green distempered wall but Jack didn't sit down. He stood uneasily, listening hard, waiting for the sound of the matron's returning footsteps. In the distance he could hear the clatter of pots and pans. Someone was making a meal. There was no sound of women's chatter or babies crying. Baby – his baby. His stomach lurched at the thought of a child he had been instrumental in making. A child he was responsible for – a child that wasn't Helen's.

The matron reappeared. 'Mrs Jones would like to see you, Mr Clay, but I warned her as I am warning you, that I cannot allow a visit of more than ten minutes duration. Mrs Jones was only discharged from bed rest yesterday afternoon and the doctor left strict instructions that she is not to undertake any heavy work.'

Jack couldn't see how talking to a visitor constituted 'heavy work', but he nodded agreement.

'You can use the residents' lounge. I am aware that you are a relative and this is a condolence visit, but you will, for obvious reasons, have to leave the door open.'

'I'd appreciate privacy.'

'And I have to run this home in an appropriate manner. If it should become common knowledge that I allowed a man, any man,' she gave Jack a steely glare, 'private access to a resident, the committee would quite rightly relieve me of my position.' She opened a door and Jack saw Maggie sitting uncomfortably in a vinyl cushioned wooden armchair. Her figure was swollen and bloated, her face thinner and more lined than he remembered, and her blonde hair heavily threaded with grey.

'Jack, how good of you to come. I didn't expect to see you.' He went to her and she rose clumsily to her feet. As he offered her his hand, she fell sobbing on to his shoulder.

'I will leave the door open, Mr Clay, but as most of the residents are engaged in domestic duties elsewhere in the house, you should not be disturbed.' The matron lingered for a moment. When neither Maggie nor Jack acknowledged that they had heard her, she sniffed loudly and walked away.

Lily rang the bell of Helen's house for the third time and waited. When no answering sound came from within, she looked through the front windows. There was no sign of life in the living room or kitchen. Walking around the back, she peered through the dining-room window and French doors and checked the back door. To her surprise, it opened. She called Helen's name and knocked loudly as she stepped inside but she was greeted by silence.

She found Helen crouched on the bottom stair in the hall.

'Didn't you hear me knock?' she asked apprehensively, concerned by her friend's pallor.

'No,' Helen murmured remotely.

Lily grasped Helen's hand. It was icy. 'Let's go into the kitchen. I'll make you a cup of tea and some breakfast.'

'I don't want anything,' Helen remonstrated, but she allowed Lily to pull her to her feet.

'You will, when it's set in front of you.' Refusing to take no for an answer, Lily steered Helen down the passage and into the kitchen.

'I've pins and needles in my legs,' Helen muttered, lurching clumsily towards a chair.

'I'm not surprised.' Lily filled the kettle. Helen sat at the table. 'It's like an ice-box in here.'

'I haven't lit the fire this morning.'

Lily switched on the electric fire and closed the door. 'We'll soon have this room warm.'

'You know, don't you?' Helen turned a bleak face to Lily's.

'Jack turned up on our doorstep this morning.'

'He's staying with you.' It wasn't a question.

'As Martin said, we could hardly throw him out, he is his brother.'

'He told you what he did.'

'No.'

'Do you want to know?'

'Not if you don't want to tell me.'

Helen sat shivering on the chair. Lily brewed the tea and set a cup in front of her. 'You're a good friend, Lily.'

'So are you.' Lily laid a hand over Helen's. She was still frozen. 'You need a hot bath and to get into some warm clothes before you catch pneumonia. I'll lay and light a fire while you go upstairs. When you're ready, we'll go down to Mumbles. I'll buy you dinner in a café.'

'I couldn't face people.'

'OK then, do you have food in the fridge? I'll make us something to eat.'

'Please, Lily, sit down. If I don't talk to someone I'll go mad.' There was a frenzied look in Helen's eyes that reinforced her words. 'I know that if I talk to you, it will end with you.'

'Of course it will.'

'You won't tell anyone else, not even Martin if he asks you?'

'I promise.' Keeping her grip on Helen's hand, Lily sat next to her and began to listen.

'This is ridiculous. I'm behaving like a fool.' Maggie dried her eyes with a handkerchief and sat back in her chair. 'It's not you, Jack.' She looked to the door to make sure that the matron had left. 'It's seeing you again. You remind me of Cyprus – and Gordon.'

'I'm sorry.' Jack pulled a chair as close to Maggie's as it was physically possible to get and lowered his head next to hers. 'And I am sorry for getting you into this mess.' He whispered so low he was barely audible.

'You couldn't have done anything without me.' She continued to watch the door. 'And there was no need for you to come here.'

'I had to. If you need anything, I'm starting a new job tomorrow . . .'

She shook her head. 'As I said in my letter, I don't need anything, but thank you for asking. Gordon always said you were one of the best National Servicemen in his platoon.'

'I could visit you any time you want me to. They think I'm married to Gordon's sister.'

'I know.' She managed a weak smile. 'It's just as well that you gave the matron your name. If she had told me that my brother-in-law had come to see me I would have denied all knowledge of you. Gordon and I are – he was an only child.'

'I see.' Even as Jack uttered the banality, he couldn't decide what he should do next. From the moment he had read Maggie's letter he had been agitated, disturbed by the thought that he should do something. The journey to the hostel to see her had been the first logical step, but now that he was actually sitting with her, he was at a loss. Not at all sure what he should say, let alone know what he was supposed to do.

'It will all be over in a few months,' she said, as if she had read his thoughts.

'Then you'll go back to live with your parents?' He didn't know why he was asking when she had detailed her plans in her letter.

'I need help with the children, my mother and father enjoy having them, and the children adore living with their grandparents. It's important that the boys have a man around now that Gordon – now that he's gone.'

'It must be.' He watched her struggle to keep her voice on an even keel.

'My parents always said that they wanted a houseful of children. I think they were disappointed when they had to settle for just me. I miss them,' she said earnestly, 'not just the children, my parents. Even if I wanted them to, they couldn't visit me here. I don't know if I wrote that they've told everyone I have tuberculosis and can't receive visitors.'

'You did.' He clenched his hands. 'I really messed things up for you.'

'I'm dreading this one being born,' she said softly, as if she hadn't heard him. 'Having the others only makes it worse. I remember how I felt the first time I held them. How they suddenly seemed the most precious and important beings in the universe. It's going to be hard . . .' She choked back her emotion. 'If not almost impossible for me to give him up. But I have no choice.' She looked to him, seeking reassurance.

'Of course you don't,' he agreed.

'It's not just me, my father's in the church, gossip could ruin his life and my mother's, and destroy his career. And there are the children. I couldn't bear for them to be hurt by the knowledge that they have a bastard brother or sister and with Gordon dying a hero's death everyone will remember the date.'

'You said in your letter that they choose the adoptive parents here carefully,' he reminded, trying to find something positive they could talk about.

She nodded. 'We see them sometimes. When you have your baby here, you are moved to a room at the back of the house in the old servants' quarters. There's only one connecting door between the two halves, so we rarely see the babies, or the girls once they've given birth, except in the garden. But we do see the adoptive parents arriving and they are always well-dressed couples in cars. They look so pleased and happy when they take their baby away . . .' Her voice tailed off. What she didn't tell him was that she had also heard the cries of the birth mothers after their babies had gone.

'I have a new address.' He reached into his pocket and pulled out a pen and his diary. Tearing a page from the back, he scribbled down Martin and Lily's address and telephone number. 'If you need me for anything – anything at all, just phone or write and I'll come.'

She took the paper from him. 'You moved so soon after going home.'

'In with my brother.'

'You said you were married.'

'I am.'

'Oh God!' Her hand flew to her mouth. 'Your wife read my letter?'

'I showed it to her.'

'Jack, how could you?'

'I couldn't lie to her.'

'And she can't forgive you?' Jack's silence told her everything she wanted to know. 'I was afraid that something like this would happen if I wrote to you. I really shouldn't have . . .'

'Mr Clay, I did say ten minutes. You have now been here for fifteen.' The matron appeared in the doorway.

Hoping that the matron hadn't overheard any of their conversation, Jack pushed his chair back and rose to his feet. 'I'll write and I'll come to see you again.'

'You don't have to.'

'Yes, I do,' he contradicted flatly, as he walked away.

CHAPTER FOURTEEN

Helen glanced out of the kitchen window and pushed most of the scrambled eggs Lily had made her to one side of her plate. Darkness had fallen early and the beach was shrouded in misty rain that blurred a car's headlamps into ghost lights as it drove past on the coast road.

'Can't you eat anything?' Lily pleaded, as Helen set her knife and fork down on top of the eggs.

Tearing her attention away from the wintry darkness, Helen said, 'It was good of you to cook for me today. I'm just not hungry.' She checked the time on her watch. 'It's almost five. Martin will be wanting a meal.'

'Martin and Brian aren't incapacitated,' Lily said lightly. 'They can cook their own food for once.'

'They won't thank you for saying that to them after a hard day's work.'

'Sometimes, I think we women run round far too much after our men.'

'I'd agree with you, if I still had one to run round after.'

'I'm sorry,' Lily stacked their plates, 'that just slipped out. It was thoughtless of me.'

'No, it wasn't. You can't watch every word you say from now on just because I've thrown Jack out.' Preoccupied, Helen left the table and walked to the window. 'Thank you for coming. I don't know how I would have survived the day without you, but you don't have to stay any longer. I'll be fine, I really will.' After taking one last look of what little she could see of the beach in the grey-black mist, she closed the shutters.

'I hate leaving you alone like this.'

'You want me to sign a paper to say that I won't kill myself?' Helen grimaced as Lily paled. 'Sorry, bad joke.'

'We could go down to Judy's . . .'

'No,' Helen broke in abruptly. 'It's not that I don't want her to know that I've thrown Jack out. I simply can't face talking about it any more today. All I want to do is crawl into bed, pull the blankets over my head, and shut out the world.'

'I can understand that.'

'Can you?' Helen asked earnestly.

'Yes.' Lily couldn't help thinking how much Helen had changed in one short day.

Dressed in a plain black skirt and polo-necked sweater, her long hair scraped back into a bun, her face devoid of make-up, she looked ten years older than the laughing, smiling girl who had walked into her father and Katie's house the night before with Jack.

'But you were about to say, life has to go on.' Helen returned to the table and picked up a packet of cigarettes.

'No, to be honest, I've been trying to imagine what I would do if Martin cheated on me.'

'What would you do?'

'I have no idea.'

'Well, if your imagination comes up with anything constructive in the next day or two, I'd be interested to hear it.' Helen opened the packet with trembling fingers. Like Judy she enjoyed the odd cigarette, generally after a meal, but she had smoked her way through most of Jack's weekly ration in less than a day.

'Will you divorce Jack?'

'Not if it means I'll have to see him again. I'd be sick if I had to sit in the same room as him at the moment. Frankly I just wish he'd go . . .' Helen clicked her fingers. 'Somewhere – anywhere, so long as it's not near me.' She struck a match and snapped it in two. When she splintered the second, Lily took the box and lit her cigarette for her.

'Want some coffee?'

'Please.' Lost in thought, Helen forgot that she had been urging Lily to leave. 'Do you think Jack went to see that woman today?'

'It would make sense of what he said to me about other people besides you and him being involved.'

'It would, wouldn't it?' Helen flicked her ash into the overflowing ashtray on the table. 'He might even take her out of that home and live with her. Then he'll have her and his baby.'

'I still can't believe Jack did this to you,' Lily broke in fiercely. 'He loves you.'

'Evidently not enough to stay faithful to me, but then, my mother used to constantly warn me that all men are after the same thing and when they get it, they dump the girl. Perhaps I should have listened to her.'

'I can't . . . don't want to believe that,' Lily amended, as Helen gave her a sceptical look. 'It's obvious that Jack loves you from the way he looks at you. He would never have set out deliberately to hurt you.'

'Who knows, perhaps after two and half years he couldn't even remember me. And now there's this baby.' Helen gazed at Lily through grief-stricken eyes. 'I can't have any.'

Unsure she'd heard Helen correctly, Lily stared at her. 'I don't understand . . .'

'The doctors told Jack and me that we wouldn't be able to have any more children after I lost our baby,' she explained impatiently. 'Ironic, isn't it, having to get married at eighteen because a baby's on the way, then losing it and discovering there won't be any more.'

Lily's hands closed instinctively over her stomach. 'Oh God, Helen . . .'

'My father knows,' Helen broke in, unable to accept sympathy for her childless state, even from Lily, 'and Jack told Martin before he went to Cyprus. But I couldn't bring myself to tell anyone. Not even you and Judy, and especially Katie. She's so happy with Glyn.'

'Helen, I am so sorry.' Words had never seemed so inadequate. She was terrified what Martin's reaction might be to the news of their baby, especially in view of the overdraft she had arranged, but the thought of never being able to have any children at all was unbearable.

'It's been hard, especially when people like Judy's mother constantly harp on about you and me having babies. Jack said we'd adopt, but then he doesn't need to, not now.' Helen ground what was left of her cigarette into dust, spilling half the contents of the ashtray on to the table.

'I wish there was something that I could say.'

'There isn't anything anyone can say. And for someone who didn't want to talk any more today, I haven't stopped, and you were going home.'

'I could stay the night.'

'No,' Helen refused adamantly. 'There'd be nothing for you to do even if you did. I'm going to bed.'

Lily picked up their plates and scraped the eggs into the bin. For all that either of them had eaten she may as well not have bothered to make them.

Helen rose from her chair. 'But first I have to change the sheets. I can't bear the thought that Jack . . . that he slept . . .'

'I'll give you a hand,' Lily offered. 'It will be easier with two.'

'Thank you, then I should drive you home.'

'I'll enjoy the walk.'

'It's raining.'

'I won't melt.'

Helen fastened the shutters and closed all the curtains in the downstairs rooms before leading the way upstairs. As Lily followed her, she couldn't help feeling that Helen was shutting herself in, rather than closing out the night.

'Something smells good.' Brian sniffed the air as he hung his coat in the hall. 'Your Lily is a cracking cook.'

'Not, Lily, me.' Jack opened the oven door as Brian

and Martin walked into the kitchen. 'I found some mince in the fridge so I made a shepherd's pie. I hope that's all right.'

'Where's Lily?' Martin asked.

'She wasn't here when I came in a couple of hours ago. I assumed she'd gone to the garage with you.' Jack turned down the oven and closed the door.

'She went to see Helen.' Martin went to the sink and washed his hands.

'When?' Jack asked urgently.

'Just after you left this morning.' Martin reached for the towel. 'I think I'll drive over there and check she's all right.'

'If she's on her way home, you'll miss her,' Brian pointed out.

'There's hardly any buses on a Sunday.' Martin went into the hall to get his coat. 'She'll get soaked in this if she walks home.'

'Helen has the car.' Jack followed Martin into the hall.

'And Helen might not be in a fit state to drive,' Martin retorted.

Chastened, Jack fell silent. The front door opened and Lily stepped on to the doormat, dripping a stream of rainwater. Her nylon mac was drenched, her hair soaked under her sodden umbrella.

'Good evening, Lily, did you swim across the bay?' Brian quipped from the kitchen.

'It might have been quicker if I had.' Lily dropped her umbrella into the stand.

'I've only just got in myself.' Martin ran to peel her sodden mac from her back. 'I was coming to look for you. You should have telephoned the garage. I would have driven over and picked you up.'

'I'm fine, Martin.' Lily looked at Jack. Unable to meet her gaze, he joined Brian in the kitchen.

'Go on upstairs. I'll run a hot bath for you while you get out of those wet clothes,' Martin offered, as she sat on the bottom stair and slipped off her shoes. 'Jack's made tea so there's nothing for you to do.'

'I'm not hungry. But a bath sounds like a good idea.'

'Here, give me those shoes, I'll stuff them with newspaper so they'll dry in shape.' Martin left them on the doormat together with her mac and ran up the stairs ahead of her. Pushing the plug into the bath he turned on the hot tap. As water gushed in, clouding the bathroom with steam, Lily joined him, swathed in a towel.

He closed the door behind her and slid the bolt home. 'How is Helen?' he whispered, although he was certain that neither Jack nor Brian had left the kitchen.

'Devastated, upset, trying hard not to show it. She insisted she wanted to be left alone to sleep. I told her I'd telephone her in the warehouse tomorrow. If she changes her mind about going in, I'll take a bus over there after work.'

'Did she say why she has thrown Jack out?'

'Yes.' Lily tested the water and threw in a handful of bath salts. 'And if you had done what he did, I'd never want to see you again either.' Dropping the towel, she stepped into the bath.

'You're not going to tell me what he's done?' Martin sat on the edge of the bath.

'Ask him yourself. It's something you should hear from him.'

'Want me to wash your back?'

'Please.'

He soaked a sponge in the bath, wrung it out and rubbed soap on to it. 'I'm tempted to climb right in there with you, rose scented bathwater and all.'

She studied him. 'You look cleaner than you were yesterday.'

'I am.' His mouth went suddenly dry. The two years they had been married had been the happiest of his life and had done nothing to diminish the heart-stopping effect she had on him every time they were alone.

'Then why don't you?' she invited.

'Because Jack's made tea and Brian will tell me that I smell like a Turkish brothel if I wash in that scented water, and knowing him, in front of any customers we get tomorrow.'

'A what?'

'A Turkish brothel, it's one of his favourite expressions,' Martin explained. 'God knows where he got it from.'

'Perhaps he's been in one.'

'I doubt it,' he answered casually.

'Have you?'

'What?' he murmured absently, rubbing the sponge between her shoulder blades.

'Been in a brothel?'

'What?'

'Been in a brothel? You were in the army.'

'I have never been a brothel,' he denied emphatically. 'I wouldn't even know what one looked like.'

'Then how would you know whether you'd been in one or not?'

'Is that what Jack's done?' he asked suddenly.

'All I've done all day is talk about Jack and I don't want to, not any more. But as you brought up the subject of brothels, I wondered if you'd been in one.'

'I only mentioned brothels because of one of Brian's crazy sayings, and I haven't, nor do I want to go near one of those places. You're all the woman I'll ever need or want.'

'You don't have to say such a nice thing in such a furious manner, Marty.' She held his gaze as he rose reluctantly from the side of the bath.

'If I stay here any longer, I'll be tempted to carry you back into our bedroom and we'll go to sleep hungry.'

'What did Jack make?'

'Shepherd's pie.'

'Provided it's covered when it's reheated, it won't dry out.'

'You're a temptress, but as he's taken the trouble to

cook, we should make the effort to eat it. That way he might make tea for us again.'

'I ate in Helen's.' She conveniently forgot that neither she nor Helen had eaten much.

'But you'll come downstairs.'

'Yes, I'll be down.' She slid down in the water and ducked her head under, soaking her hair. 'I want to ask Jack how long he intends to stay.'

Despite Brian's attempts to stimulate the flagging conversation with talk about the garage and some of the more outrageous ideas he had to attract customers, most of the meal was eaten in silence. When Lily joined them in the kitchen, dressed in slacks and a thick pullover, her long hair wrapped in a towel, Jack and Martin were washing the dishes and Brian was making coffee. Accepting Brian's offer of coffee, Lily sat down.

'You must come over to see the garage soon, Lily.' Brian took the milk jug from the fridge and set it on the table. 'Everything looks fantastic, especially the workshops. Martin's spent so much time polishing the floors I think he intends to let the place out as a skating rink. Rumour has it he will never allow them to be dirtied by car tyres.'

'Watch me pull in the first car that needs servicing as soon as it drives within grabbing distance.' Martin washed the last plate and set the pie dish into the sink to soak.

'A couple of months and they'll be queuing up to buy their cars from us,' Brian predicted optimistically. 'And get them repaired,' he added in response to the sombre expression on Martin's face.

'You do know that the builder's coming tomorrow to make a start on your kitchen, Brian,' Lily reminded as she poured milk into her coffee.

'Yes, and there's no need to worry. I haven't put anything into the room, like a spare girl or two, so he has plenty of space to work in.' He looked from Jack to

Martin and Lily, as he set their coffee on the table. 'If you don't mind, I'll take this upstairs. There's a radio play on the Home Service that I want to listen to, and as tomorrow's the big day I should get an early night.'

'There's no need to go on my account.' Jack sat opposite Lily at the table.

'I'm not.'

'You know what's happened?'

'Yes, Jack.' Brian opened the door. 'And some things are best discussed within the family.'

'You're almost that.'

'Thank you for the compliment, but I sense a conversation coming that this distant cousin would rather opt out of. Good night, everyone.'

Judy allowed herself a smug smile of satisfaction, as she studied her living room. Trusting that Sam had believed her lie about a non-existent product demonstration, she had spent the day giving the flat a thorough clean. It looked a little sparse with only her books on the bookshelves and her records on the rack next to the record player, but at least everything in the room was hers and after years of sharing her living space she felt independent and marvellously free – until she glanced at Sam's photograph in its silver frame on the mantelpiece.

Only another few months and she'd be back to organising her life around another person again. Eating meals when Sam wanted to eat, listening to his favourite radio programmes and music, even if she hated them, going to bed when he wanted to . . . suppressing the thought of her and Sam in bed together, she straightened the mirror over the mantelpiece. It was as her mother had said. She needed time to adjust, that was all.

She went to the bookcase, intending to push one of her photograph albums back in line; changing her mind, she lifted it from the bookcase, sat at the table and opened it. The first photograph had been taken with a box camera her mother had given her for her sixteenth birthday.

Judy, Lily and Katie were sitting on Swansea beach, towels modestly wrapped around their swimsuits, their hair on end, sticky with seawater. She flicked through various shots she had snapped on the beaches and an Easter funfair. There was even one of the four of them together, although she had no memory of handing her precious camera over to anyone. A picnic on the hill of Cefn Bryn, various day trips to Cardiff, Porthcawl and Barry Island – then she realised the album was a visual record of the last summer the four of them had spent together before boys had entered their lives.

She turned to the last page and froze when she saw a print of her and Brian that had been taken by a professional photographer at a police ball in London. They looked happy and relaxed, Brian smiling and darkly handsome in a grey lounge suit and white shirt. As memories flooded back, she could even recall the exact shade of blue in his tie, the smell of his aftershave, the rustle of the taffeta skirt of her dress as she had danced with him.

The bell rang shrilly, shattering her recollections. Startled, she dropped the book, picking it up hastily as the bell rang a second time. Returning it to its place on the shelf, she ran down the stairs and opened the door.

'You're back,' Sam said.

She looked at him in bewilderment.

'The product demonstration,' he reminded.

'I got the date wrong, it's next Sunday.'

'And you didn't drive down to tell me.'

'I thought you were on afternoons.' She retreated up the stairs, as he pushed past her into the tiny hallway to shelter from the rain.

'I was, but one of the boys came round early this morning to ask if I'd swap my afternoon with his day shift. It's only for today because his brother was called in as a reserve to play football for one of the junior teams. I wondered if you fancied going for a meal. I know there's not much open. But we could go to the Italian café. I smelled fish and chips as I drove past.'

'Fish and chips sounds wonderful,' she answered, feeling suddenly and unaccountably guilty. 'Just let me get my coat.'

'Judy,' he called after her, as she ran up the stairs. 'There's nothing wrong is there?'

'Of course not,' she shouted back. 'Why should there be?'

'I take it Lily has told you why Helen threw me out,' Jack said, as he, Lily and Martin sat around the kitchen table.

'No,' Martin answered briefly.

'I thought it would be better coming from you.' Lily picked up the spoon in the sugar bowl and started playing with it.

Jack looked his brother squarely in the eye. 'I had a letter yesterday from a woman I met in Cyprus. She's having my baby.'

Martin's eyes rounded in shock.

'I showed the letter to Helen. I respect her too much—'

'Respect!' Martin's exclamation was full of contempt. 'You—'

'Let Jack tell us about it, Martin,' Lily interposed quietly. 'After spending most of the day with Helen, I'd be interested to hear what he has to say.'

Jack sat in silence for a moment.

'You must have something to say in your defence,' she prompted.

'Nothing,' Jack replied slowly. 'All I can do is try to explain how it happened, that's if you're prepared to hear it.'

'We're listening,' Martin snapped.

'You know what Cyprus is like, Martin. You've been there—'

'Please, don't tell me you were seduced by the beautiful countryside, the beaches, the weather, the wine, the girls,' Martin mocked.

Jack refused to rise to Martin's bait. 'The Cyprus I served in may have had all that to offer, but National Servicemen in my draft weren't free to find out about it. Whenever we left the barracks, we could never be sure we'd be coming back. Or, for that matter, after a bomb was left in a biscuit tin in the NAAFI, whether we'd survive another day in camp.'

'So this baby is the result of you living on a knife edge,' Martin said coldly. 'For God's sake, Jack . . .'

'Please, Marty, I'm not making excuses. Just trying to explain, and very badly. So, please . . .' Unnerved by Lily's hostile glare, Jack struggled to collect his thoughts. 'I don't want to use getting shot as an excuse—'

'Then don't,' Martin interrupted, his anger escalating.

'It's part of what happened.' Jack looked in on a world he'd failed to put behind him. 'You know I was a driver. The sergeant I chauffeured most of the time was a decent man. I don't know what it was like when you were in the army, but it was rare to find a non-commissioned officer who was liked by everyone, superiors as well as other ranks, but he was one of them. He really cared about the men in his platoon, even National Servicemen. Anyway, we went out on patrol in the Troodos Mountains. It was routine but everyone in the column was edgy. Two Greek Cypriots had been sentenced to death for killing an RAF corporal the day before and we'd been warned to expect trouble. They told us to be vigilant, but they didn't tell us how, and it's not easy to make out what's ahead when you're driving along narrow mountain roads. We couldn't see through rock and for all we knew, every bend, every twist, every turn, every ditch could have hidden a couple of dozen terrorists.' Jack pushed his chair back from the table. Sinking his head in his hands, he looked down at the floor.

'When the first shots were fired, it was almost a relief. The lieutenant at the front of the column gave the order to halt and take cover. The driver of the jeep directly ahead of us was shot as he tried to roll under his vehicle. I was hit in the leg when I climbed out of ours. It was weird, until then, the thought of being wounded had terrified me, but all I felt was a peculiar burning. I didn't even realise my leg was shattered until I tried to put weight on it; then I just crumpled. Bullets were flying everywhere. The sergeant risked his life to pull me under the jeep. Then he went out again to haul in the boy who was supposed to be our guard from the back of the vehicle. The kid was so petrified by what was going on he froze.' Jack pulled his cigarettes from his shirt pocket, took one from the packet, lit it and pushed the packet across the table towards Martin.

'By that time everyone in the column had taken shelter under their vehicles. We tried to return the terrorists' fire. We'd see them coming from one direction but as soon as we fired, they attacked from another angle. I'll never forget the screams of the wounded as long as I live. They were high-pitched, unreal. At first it was almost like watching a film, I couldn't believe it was happening, then the longer it went on, the worse it got.' Jack reached for an ashtray. 'Afterwards, they told me we'd been pinned down for twenty minutes. Between the shots, the screaming and the sheer bloody terror of thinking that I'd reached my end and I was going to die there on that mountain road and never see Helen or Swansea again, I would have been prepared to believe it had been months.

'I don't know if the terrorists ran out of ammunition, but eventually they stopped shooting. But just as we thought we'd beaten them off, they started lobbing grenades. One rolled under our vehicle. The sergeant, the boy and me saw it coming. The boy started screaming. The sergeant and I dived towards it, only I couldn't move. My leg wouldn't move . . .' Jack forced himself to go on. 'The sergeant reached it first and threw himself on top of it.'

Lily blanched and closed her eyes.

'He was killed.' Jack drew heavily on his cigarette. 'But not outright. The bloody thing tore a great gaping hole in his stomach, half his insides spilled out but he was still conscious. He knew he didn't stand a chance and I couldn't do a thing to help him. He'd saved my life, and I didn't have anything to give him other than water and that's not much use when a man is screaming in agony. I held his head, tried to get him to drink, listened as he whispered the names of his wife and children, then a second grenade hit us. It blasted the jeep sideways and took the head off the boy we were with. They told me afterwards the force of the blast knocked me unconscious. It was just as well because some of the shrapnel embedded itself in my chest and stomach.' He pulled on his cigarette again. 'I came round in hospital days later. My wounds had become infected and they warned me that I wouldn't be discharged for a couple of months. My first visitor was an officer who was collecting as many accounts of the attack as he could because they were putting the sergeant up for a medal. I told him what I remembered and he suggested that I talk to the sergeant's widow. I didn't want to.' He raised his eyes to Martin's. 'Would you be able to face the wife of a man who had saved your life at the expense of his own?'

Unable to speak, Martin shook his head.

'I felt I'd never be able to look her or her children in the eye. When I was finally discharged from hospital ten weeks after the attack, the doctor said the sergeant's wife wanted to see me. Apparently she'd visited the hospital once or twice to talk to survivors but hadn't been able to bring herself to walk any further than the entrance to the wards. He told me she was leaving for England with her four children the following day. Even that conspired against me; she would have left the island weeks before if her children hadn't been ill with measles. The doctor gave me her address and I buttoned it into my tunic pocket although I had no intention of visiting her – not then. Later, after I'd had a few drinks in the mess, I remembered the sergeant's last words and the officer who'd come to see me telling me that she had a right to hear them.'

'So, you went to see her,' Lily murmured.

'Not until I'd had a few drinks to give me courage. And that was a big mistake. I was weak, I'd just spent months in hospital; the doctors had warned me that a pint of beer could put me flat on my back. I had two and I took a bottle of wine. She had another one. I'm not blaming her, simply saying that neither of us knew what we were doing.' He looked down at the table. 'And it is no bloody consolation that all I can remember about it now is her calling out her husband's name and me whispering Helen's.'

Silence closed in on the kitchen again.

'When I had the letter from her telling me that she was pregnant with my child, I couldn't keep it from Helen. I'd cheated on her enough without lying to her as well. I went to see the sergeant's wife this afternoon. She is in a home for unmarried mothers. Her parents are looking after her children. She doesn't want to give this one up but her husband died a hero's death. Everyone will remember the date and there's no way his child can be born more than eleven months after he was killed so she has no choice. But I do.' He lifted his head again. 'I don't expect Helen to forgive me because what I did was unforgivable, but I can't turn my back on the baby. It's mine and because of what I did, it is going to lose the most important person in any child's life, its mother. I can't allow it to lose a father as well. I'm going back up to the home next Sunday to tell her that I want to keep it.'

'Jack, be reasonable. How can you bring up a baby—'

'I don't know, Marty. I only know that I can't abandon it to strangers. It's my baby. The result of my mistake and I don't want it to suffer for what I've done.'

'Have you told Helen?' Lily asked, choking back tears.

'About the terrorist attack and what happened when I called on the sergeant's wife the day I came out of hospital – yes, but not that I want to keep the baby.'

'And you told her just the way you told it to us now?'
'More or less.'
Lily went to the door. 'You can stay here as long as you like, Jack.'
'Thank you, but I don't want to make things awkward for you two with Helen.'
'You won't, because I won't let you. Goodnight, I'll see you in the morning.'
'I won't be long, love,' Martin murmured softly, as she closed the door behind her.

'Let me know which you'd prefer and I'll pick up the brochures tomorrow.' Sam took the last piece of bread and butter from the plate set between him and Judy and bit it in half.
'Mmm,' Judy murmured absently.
'You haven't heard a single word I've said all evening,' Sam observed irritably.
'Sorry, I was miles away.' Judy sat back, as the waitress placed two cups of coffee on their table.
'Thinking about the salons again,' Sam commented acidly, handing the waitress their empty plates. 'Bill please, when you have time, miss.' He turned back to Judy. 'I was asking where you'd like to go for our honeymoon.'
'Not Blackpool.'
'I gathered that from the way you snapped at my mother when she suggested it.'
'I did not snap.'
'I don't want to argue about it, Judy,' he said wearily. 'Just settle on a place we both want to go. What about my suggestion of Jersey?'
'I don't know . . .'
'Say you haven't had time to think about it and so help me, I'll scream.'
'Jack and Helen had a good time in London,' she ventured.
'You said you hated the place when you lived there.'

'Living in a city is not the same as visiting it on honeymoon. There's so much to do there, we could see the sights, go to a show, visit the shops and the parks.'

'Jack and Helen married in April,' he interrupted. 'London in July is going to be hot and sticky.'

'That's true,' she agreed, realising he was as set against the idea of London as she was of Blackpool.

'Isn't there anywhere you want to go that you've never been to?'

'Millions of places. My mother was so busy running the salon when I was small, the only holidays I ever took with her were the odd day trips she could fit in on Sundays, and always by bus or train. Generally we went down the Gower or to Barry or Porthcawl. I went to Weston once with Lily and her Uncle Roy and Auntie Norah for a week, but apart from my short time in London and a weekend trip to Blackpool, that's as far as I've been.'

'I fancy somewhere warm and sunny, lying on a beach all day, looking at you in a bathing costume . . .'

'Look at me, Sam.'

He propped his chin on his hand and gazed into her eyes.

'I don't mean like that.' She pulled a strand of her hair forward. 'What colour is this?'

'Auburn,' he suggested tentatively, knowing how sensitive she was about her colouring.

'Try red, which means I have white skin. Very white,' she emphasised, 'as in white that burns bright red whenever I sit in the sun for more than five minutes.'

'So no beach honeymoon.'

'Not unless you want an untouchable lobster for a wife.'

'I don't like the sound of untouchable.' He took the bill the waitress handed him. 'One of the boys in work said he had a good time in Butlin's.'

'On his honeymoon?'

'He went with his wife and two children.' He took her coat from the stand and held it out.

'I would hate to honeymoon in a crowded camp.' She turned her back to him and slipped her arms into the sleeves of her coat.

'The schools don't break up until the second week in July so it wouldn't be that crowded, but if you hate the idea . . .'

'I do,' she said firmly. He opened the door for her.

'I'm beginning to wonder if you even want to go on honeymoon. Perhaps you'd prefer to run your damned salons.'

'I only want us to go to the right place,' she explained, in an attempt to pacify him.

'Please, tell me where that is and I'll book it. So far tonight you've turned down the Channel Islands, Blackpool, Butlin's and every beach in Britain, which cuts out just about every holiday resort I can think of.'

'How about I call into the travel agents tomorrow and look at what they've got?'

'How about why didn't you do that weeks ago?' he said crossly, refusing to be placated.

'Because we have plenty of time to book a honeymoon.'

'I have Wednesday and Thursday off this week. I suppose it's out of the question to ask you to visit my mother with me.'

'Sorry, this week's impossible, Sam, but let me know as soon as you have your days off booked for the following week and I'll make a point of clearing them.'

'My mother will want you to check on the bridesmaids' dresses. We also have to decide what to give them as presents. My mother thinks silver bracelets will be acceptable.'

Judy reined in her temper, as Sam continued to repeat the contents of his mother's latest letter. After a while, she didn't even hear his voice. All she could see, all she could think about was the photograph of Brian and her that she had found earlier that evening.

'So can I?'

She looked up and realised they'd stopped walking because they were outside her door.

'Can you what, Sam?'

'Come up?' he snapped furiously, realising that she hadn't been listening to him – yet again.

'I'm tired.'

'Just five minutes.'

'You can have a couple of hours on Wednesday after you visit your mother.' She felt for her keys in her coat pocket and kissed him lightly on the lips. Unlocking and slipping through the door, she closed it quickly behind her.

'Jack, face facts, there is no way that anyone in authority will allow you to adopt a baby when you are living apart from your wife. And that's without bringing things like a house, money and someone to look after the child when you're at work, into the equation.'

'With Maggie's help, I might be able to organise a private adoption,' Jack suggested hopefully. 'And if you and Lily . . .'

Martin shook his head. 'Leave Lily and I out of it. Quite apart from Helen being a good friend to both of us, there is no way that we can afford for Lily to give up work to have our own children at the moment, let alone look after someone else's.'

'I could ask Katie . . .'

'I wouldn't if I were you,' Martin said forcefully, leaving the table. 'Once John finds out what you've done, he's bound to take Helen's side. I'm tired, and as Brian said, it's a big day tomorrow.' He picked up his cup.

'Leave it, Marty,' Jack lit a cigarette. 'I won't be able to sleep so I may as well make myself useful.'

Martin looked back at his brother. 'I'm sorry, Jack. I really am.'

'So am I.' Jack grimaced. 'Remember what Mam used to say when we were kids? If there's a hard way to do things, our Jack will find it.'

'It's a tough way to learn a lesson.'

'It's tougher on Helen than me.'

'You could try talking to her again when she's had time to calm down.'

'There's no point.'

'You don't know that until you've tried.'

'You didn't see her face when she threw me out. Believe me, Martin, there's no point, no point at all.'

Chapter Fifteen

'It's really not so bad in here,' Emily announced unconvincingly to Judy. They were sitting in a corner of Cartref's lounge during visiting hour. 'Most of the girls are nice and friendly.'

Only three other girls had visitors that Judy could see. None looked particularly friendly and the half a dozen residents who were sitting grouped around a table in the centre of the room looked positively sullen. She opened her shopping bag. 'I've brought you some magazines and chocolate and a couple of books. I know you said you didn't want anything in your letter, but I couldn't come empty-handed.' She passed them to Emily.

'It's enough that you visit.' Emily took the gifts. 'After all, it's not as if I'm ill or anything.'

'I won't be able to visit next weekend because Sam has Sunday off and we're going to his mother's. She's organising the bridesmaids' dresses.' Judy wrinkled her nose at the prospect.

'You don't look very happy about it.'

'I'm not,' Judy agreed shortly. She didn't want to discuss her prospective mother-in-law because she suspected that once she started talking about Ena Davies she wouldn't stop. 'But I'll visit you the weekend after and if there is anything you need in the meantime, phone or write to me and I'll post it on.'

'There's nothing.' Emily clutched the books and chocolate close to her chest. 'These books and magazines will last me for weeks. You don't get much free time to read in here.'

'I thought you'd have masses,' Judy said in surprise.

'We spend part of the day cooking and cleaning and the rest in classes. House craft, sewing, knitting – that sort of thing. We have to make a full layette for our babies, three of everything. The adoptive parents expect it.'

Judy thought it harsh to ask unmarried mothers to make clothes for babies they would have to give up but, very aware of the girls sitting around them, she muttered a non-committal, 'I see.'

'I'm hopeless at sewing,' Emily confessed. 'I spend more time unpicking my mistakes than stitching anything new.'

'I could buy a layette and smuggle it in,' Judy whispered conspiratorially.

Emily laughed nervously. 'One girl's already tried that. The matron caught her sister handing it over. The girl was given a telling off and extra sewing classes in the evenings. I dare not risk it, one sewing class a day is as much as I can stand.'

'Have you heard from your family?'

'I've had letters from my mother and sisters and one from Larry. He's managed to keep my condition a secret from everyone except my aunt. A couple of people did telephone her house after I left Swansea, but she told them that my mother and sisters had moved on and she didn't have their address.'

'Is Larry staying in Bournemouth?'

'No, he's taken a job as a bank clerk in London. He couldn't stand Bournemouth. Apparently all my mother can talk about is my father and the disgrace he's brought on the family. She and my sisters hate living off my aunt's charity almost as much as my aunt hates dispensing it. The two eldest are looking for jobs, but according to Larry, not very hard. Thanks to my father's upbringing, they think work is beneath them.'

'They'll learn,' Judy murmured philosophically.

'From what Larry wrote, my aunt is trying to teach

them. The one good thing is that they are all too immersed in their own affairs to think about me. Larry said they weren't pleased when he told them Robin had broken off our engagement because my sisters had ideas of coming back to Swansea to visit after we were married. Once they found out that I wouldn't be able to offer them free board and lodge at some future date, they were happy to swallow his story that I'd taken a job here as a hotel receptionist. It's one less thing for my mother to worry about and I never was that close to any of my sisters.'

Irritated by the muted whisperings of the other residents and their visitors, Judy glanced out of the window. The sky was grey and the wind was blowing piles of dead leaves around the lawns and flowerbeds, but the rain was holding off. 'I know it's cold but it's dry. Do you fancy a walk in the garden?'

'Yes,' Emily answered decisively. 'Yes, I do.'

'You don't need to get permission?'

'Not in free time when it's dry. I'll just put these things in my locker and get my coat.'

As Emily carried the books, magazines and chocolate out of the lounge, Judy picked up her coat and empty shopping bag and wandered into the hall. Her footsteps echoed hollowly over the tiled floor and she wondered how she would cope if she had to surrender her independence and privacy to live surrounded day and night by strangers in a place like this. She suspected not all that well. For all of Emily's assertion that it wasn't so bad, there was a depressing institution feel to the house, a cross between the oppressively disciplined atmosphere of an all girls' school and a hospital. She thought she could even detect the overcooked cabbage odour that she would forever associate with her school days, among the baby smells.

'I'm ready.' Emily ran down the stairs in her green duster coat and a blue knitted hat pulled over her short curly hair. She opened the door and stepped outside ahead of Judy.

'You're behaving like an escaped prisoner,' Judy smiled.

'Just glad to get out for five minutes. I don't know why I didn't think of it earlier. It might be cold, but at least no one can eavesdrop on our conversation, not that we were discussing anything scintillating.' Emily wound a scarf around her neck and took a pair of blue mittens from her coat pocket.

'You sensed that everyone was listening to us as well?'

'As Maggie says, there's nothing else to do in here except gossip and wait. I'll be glad when the next girl comes in, it will take some of the attention away from me.'

'You've made a friend?' Judy and Emily walked through an archway that led from the paved front courtyard into the side garden.

'Maggie – everyone gets on with Maggie. She's more like a sympathetic aunt than a resident. Apart from being at least twenty years older than the rest of us, she's the only one who has actually had a baby and knows what it's like.'

'You afraid?' Judy asked perceptively.

Emily nodded. 'Terrified. I've never been good at dealing with pain and it's supposed to be absolute agony.'

'My mother told me it's an odd sort of pain, you forget it as soon as the baby's born and one of my friends who's just had a baby agreed with her. When she held her son . . . ' Judy faltered, realising that discussing Katie's experience with Glyn was hardly tactful, not when Emily would have to hand her baby over to strangers six weeks after she had given birth.

'Your friend is married.'

'Yes.'

'She's lucky.' There was more sadness than bitterness in Emily's voice.

'Yes, she is. Her husband is years older than her but they are very happy together.' They walked around the corner of the house on to a patio fringed by wrought ironwork entwined with the shrivelled, blackened skeletons of trailing plants.

'Jack!' Judy stared in astonishment. Helen's husband stood in front of her with a blonde, older woman.

He started guiltily and looked from Judy to Emily. 'You're the last person I expected to see here.'

'I came to visit Emily. She was my flatmate.'

'I remember meeting you at a party years ago.' He nodded briefly to Emily. 'If you'll excuse us.'

'Of course,' Judy answered. It was difficult to determine who wanted to put an end to the chance meeting the most, her or Jack.

'Is that going to make things difficult for you?' Maggie asked. Jack glanced back at Judy.

'No more than they already are.'

'I wish you hadn't visited.'

'I told you why I had to come.' He offered her his arm and they walked in the opposite direction to the one taken by Judy and Emily. 'And you still haven't answered my question. Can you arrange for me to adopt the baby?'

'Even if I could, I wouldn't. It's a ridiculous idea, Jack. No one in authority would consider handing a baby over to a man. Especially one who has just left his wife.'

'Not even when the child is his?'

'I know you mean well but you would never cope with the day-to-day practicalities of looking after a child,' she added, in an attempt to soften the blow.

'I could learn. After all, it's my baby too,' he broke in earnestly.

'What would you live on?'

'I have a job.'

'And who would take care of the baby while you are at work?'

'I'd find someone. My sister has just had a baby . . . '

'And she'd welcome the opportunity to look after yours as well?' When Jack didn't answer, Maggie shook her head. 'You have your own life, you should concentrate on trying to save your marriage.'

'I told you it's over. Helen has thrown me out.'

'Which is understandable because she's angry, Jack. But she won't be angry with you for ever. You admit you still love her.'

'I'll never stop,' he said simply.

'Then fight for her.'

'How can I?'

'You can start by going to see her and trying to explain what happened between us.' Emotionally and physically exhausted, Maggie sank down on to a wooden bench set facing the hills behind the house. 'Tell her it didn't mean anything. That it would never have happened if either of us had been in our right minds.'

'I've already tried.' He sat beside her.

'Obviously not well enough,' she retorted impatiently.

'You don't understand Helen, Maggie. I promised to love her and I betrayed her. She'll never believe in me or trust me again.'

'If you two had a marriage half as strong as the one you described to me the night you came to see me in Cyprus, it isn't over, Jack. How can it be when you still love her? No.' She held up her hand as he tried to cut her short again. 'Listen for a moment. Love isn't something anyone can switch on and off, no matter how much they may want to. If it were, the divorce courts would be full and all marriages would end the minute a couple hit their first rough patch. If you want my opinion, I think your Helen is feeling just as wretched as you are right now. So go and see her, talk to her, plead with her to forgive you.'

'She wouldn't even open the door to me.'

'You don't know that until you try. Why be so stubborn?' she persisted irritably. 'All you have to lose is your pride and that's a small price to pay for a good marriage. If I had your chance, I wouldn't throw it away,' she added with brutal honesty.

'Even if Helen took me back, she would never agree to take the baby and I can't give it up.'

'It's not yours to give up, Jack,' Maggie said forcefully.

'It's my child and I will take care of it properly. I'll see that it will want for nothing.'

'I have no doubt that you'll set out to do just that, but I have children. I know just how demanding they can be and how difficult it is to bring them up. They need two parents, a mother and a father.' She faltered, her declaration bringing home the full magnitude of her loss.

Jack closed his eyes against an image of the sergeant as he had last seen him, his body broken and bloody, his lips blue as he had whispered Maggie's name. 'I know I'm years younger than you, Maggie, but Helen will divorce me. Then I . . . we . . . we could . . .'

'Don't even think it, let alone say it.'

'He died for me,' he whispered.

'Don't flatter yourself that it was personal. Gordon died protecting his men. You just happened to be one of them. He was doing his job, nothing more. If you had reached that grenade first, he would have been furious with you for usurping his authority. You do know that, don't you?'

'Yes,' Jack said, realising that his sergeant would have been angry. It was the officer's place to act, the other ranks to stand back until given a direct order. He had a sudden vision of the sergeant shouting, 'No' as he had tried to crawl towards the grenade – memory or imagination?

'I told you in Cyprus that guilt is destructive. You can't keep carrying it around with you.'

'Your children have lost their father and I can't help thinking that he died because of me.'

'He didn't, and my children still have their mother and their grandparents.'

'I could . . .'

'I'm beginning to think the worst thing I ever did was to write to you.' She left the bench. 'All you can do for me now, Jack, is forget me, and forget this ever happened.'

'I can't. Not when you're carrying my baby.'

'You'll just have to, because I have nothing more to say to you.' A bell rang within the house.

'I'll come and see you next weekend.'

'I'll tell them I don't want to see you,' she warned. He looked into her eyes and saw that she meant it.

'Then I'll write. I won't give up.'

'Jack, you're a lovely boy, but you're also a hopeless romantic who won't face facts. If you won't think of yourself and Helen, think of the baby and the kind of life you'd give it, passed from babysitter to babysitter while you work, no security, no continuity, no warm, loving family life. Then think of the adoptive parents the society will find. A couple who can't have children of their own and will love our child all the more because of that. You and Helen should have your own family.' The bell rang again. 'I have to go in.'

'I'll write,' he called after her. 'And I will come again, you can't stop me.' He watched her enter the house. Then, squaring his shoulders, he walked to the courtyard where he'd parked his bike. Judy was standing next to her car.

'Maggie was my sergeant's wife, in Cyprus,' he explained, feeling the need to say something.

'Emily mentioned that her husband had been killed.' Judy unlocked her car door.

'By EOKA terrorists. I was there when it happened.'

'I'm sorry.' She climbed into her car. 'It might be best not to mention that we'd seen one another here. Emily wants to keep her condition a secret and I rather suspect Maggie does too, or she wouldn't be here.'

He nodded agreement and turned towards his bike.

'Jack.' Judy waited until he turned back. 'I hope you and Helen sort out your differences. If there's anything that I can do—'

'There's nothing anyone can do, Judy. But thank you for the offer.'

'See you around,' she called after him.

'Yes, see you around,' he repeated, as he climbed on to his bike.

'If you don't want pink bridesmaids' dresses, Judy, you should come right out with it and tell Sam's mother when you visit her tomorrow,' Lily advised when she joined her at a table in the upstairs restaurant of Woolworth's in the High Street. It was one o'clock and the place was packed with Saturday shoppers. Lily set the ham rolls and glasses of milk she had had bought for herself and Judy on to the table and returned the tray to the stand.

'It's too late, she's bought the material and the dressmaker has already cut them out.'

'Then you should have said something to her sooner.' Lily pulled out a chair and sat opposite Judy.

'I suppose I should have.'

'It's not like you to be backward about coming forward.' Lily picked up her knife, opened her roll and spread the mustard she had dolloped on the side of her plate over the ham.

'It's not just the bridesmaids' dresses,' Judy qualified, 'it's everything. I promised Sam I'd go to the travel agents and pick out a place for us to go on honeymoon over a week ago. We had the most awful row last night when I told him I hadn't had time. It wasn't even the truth. I went there on Monday, Tuesday, Wednesday and Thursday – and again yesterday.'

'And you couldn't decide where to go?' Lily closed her roll and cut it into four neat segments.

'I must have looked a right idiot standing in the middle of the shop surrounded by posters of smiling girls sitting in swimsuits in just about every resort in the country. But the more I looked, the more sure I was that I didn't want to go to any of the places they were advertising.'

'It's not the place that's important,' Lily smiled

artfully. 'I would have been happy with a room next to the gasworks so long as Martin was with me and we were alone.' Her smile widened at the memory of the two days they had honeymooned in a wooden chalet in Oxwich, which Martin had borrowed from a friend.

'You two only went away for a couple of days.'

'Because we couldn't wait to start decorating the house,' Lily explained. 'It seemed more important to get that right and begin our lives together than to have a holiday we could take at any time.'

'I wish Sam thought so. He's not even keen on moving into my flat. He thinks he should apply for a police house so we can have people knocking on the door at all hours of the day and night.'

'You're getting married and you haven't even decided where you're going to live?' Lily asked incredulously.

'We're still arguing about it. He thinks my flat is all right "for a single girl", whatever that means. I can't see what his problem is. It's plenty big enough for the two of us until we buy a house.'

'You're looking at houses?'

'No,' Judy laughed. 'But I will—'

'When you have time.'

'Don't you start. If my friends don't understand how busy I've been—'

'Of course you've been busy,' Lily concurred. 'No one else could have expanded your mother's business the way you have in the last couple of years. But . . .'

'What?' Judy snapped defensively.

'You seem to have lost your sense of humour along the way.'

'Not so much lost it as had it stolen by Sam,' Judy agreed.

Lily surveyed her friend thoughtfully. 'Are you sure it's just Sam's mother and the honeymoon that you're worried about?'

'What do you mean?'

'Nothing.'

'It's bad enough having to second guess everything Sam says to me without you starting,' Judy countered touchily.

'All right.' Lily took a deep breath. 'Are you absolutely sure that you want this wedding to go ahead?'

Judy paused, mid-bite.

'Sorry, I had no right to say that. After all, you two have been engaged and planning your life together for months. If you don't know your own mind by now you never will.'

'No, it's all right.' Judy returned her roll to her plate. 'We've been friends long enough for you to say whatever you like to me.'

'It's just that for a bride you don't seem very bride-like.'

'Which is?'

'Happy, bubbling with excitement, full of talk about flowers, veils, lace, wedding cake and prawn cocktails,' Lily suggested tentatively.

'You're spot on. If that's how a bride is supposed to behave, I feel more like a ranting fishwife.' Judy picked up her milk and sat back in her chair. 'Ever since Sam pushed me into setting the date for the wedding, all we've done is argue. About the bridesmaids' dresses, my dress, the number of guests, his mother's plans for the big day that she seems to be organising more for her benefit than Sam's or mine, and now this blessed honeymoon. I just know we're going to quarrel about it as soon as he comes round tomorrow and I tell him I still haven't decided where we should go. And you're absolutely right, where you honeymoon isn't important. Neither is whether the bridesmaids wear blue, pink or God forbid, luminous green figured nylon. All that should be important is our life together afterwards.'

'Please don't tell Sam's mother that I suggested you elope?'

'Elope?' Judy frowned.

'That was what you were thinking of doing?'

'It's an idea,' Judy smiled.

'Go to Gretna Green and you'll have your mother to contend with after all the plans she's made and deposits she's paid, as well as Sam's.'

'I was actually thinking about the other arguments I've had with Sam. Over the salons and me working after we're married.'

'Sam doesn't want you to?' Lily was surprised.

'He thinks I should be home cooking meals at all hours when he's on shift work. Then there's . . .'

'There's?' Lily looked questioningly at her.

Judy looked around. A crowded restaurant during a Saturday lunch hour was hardly the place to discuss the intimate details of her and Sam's private life. 'It's going to be strange living with Sam, seeing him every day whether I want to, or not,' she finished lamely.

'I think that's the best part of marriage,' Lily enthused.

'Don't you ever wish you could have five minutes to yourself?'

'I can have that any time I want.'

'Except at night,' Judy qualified.

'I love going to bed with Martin.' Lily lowered her voice, as a woman in a large hat glowered in the direction of their table. 'Seeing him last thing at night and first thing in the morning. But you've lived with other people. Helen, Emily . . .'

'I didn't share a bed with them.'

'Have you told Sam how you feel?' Lily asked earnestly.

'Not yet.'

'You should,' Lily counselled strongly.

'Do you actually like Martin touching you?' Judy whispered.

'Yes,' Lily replied thoughtlessly.

'Oh God, then there is something wrong with me!'

'Of course there isn't. It takes time to get to know someone that way.'

'Then you didn't always like Martin touching you?' Judy asked, desperately seeking reassurance.

'Without going into details, can I just say it gets better and better,' Lily hedged, eying the woman in the hat. 'You must talk to Sam, and the sooner the better,' she added quietly.

'I know.' Judy stared at the uneaten roll on her plate.

'And don't make any rash decisions, at least not without consulting your mother and Sam's.'

Judy glanced at her watch as she lifted her glass of milk. 'I must get a move on. I'm picking my mother up in half an hour. We're going over to the Brynhyfryd salon.'

'All work and no play.'

'I know, makes Judy a dull girl. You doing anything this afternoon?'

'I need to pick up a couple of things for Martin in the warehouse, so I thought I'd see if Helen was there.'

'You seen her lately?' Judy mumbled through a full mouth.

'Not since the night she threw Jack out.'

'Me neither. Although I've rung her a couple of times in the warehouse, she's always come up with an excuse as to why she couldn't meet me for lunch. Tell her I'm thinking of her.'

'I will.'

'And if there's anything I can do . . .' Judy picked up her coat and handbag from the back of her chair.

'I'll let you know,' Lily called after her, as Judy sidestepped past the queue in front of the food counter and ran out of the restaurant.

'Lily, how lovely to see you. I trust you've come to spend a fortune.' John greeted her warmly, as his secretary showed her into his office in the warehouse.

'I have, two new shirts for Martin.' Lily held up a bag. 'I was wondering if Helen was about.' She sat in the visitor's chair he pulled close to his desk. 'I haven't seen her in two weeks and every time I've telephoned here offering to call on her or meet her for lunch, she said she was up to her eyes in work and too busy to see anyone.'

'Did she?' John sat behind his desk.

'So, as I had to call in here anyway and Martin's working late, I thought I'd see if she fancied doing something with me this evening.' After looking round to check Helen was nowhere in sight, she asked, 'How is she?'

'Dreadful,' John disclosed. 'She won't talk to me about anything other than work and she's here all hours. Not that there's any more for her to do than she has been doing for the past couple of years. She's just using this place as an excuse to stay away from her house. How is Jack?'

'I don't know because he hardly says a word in the house,' Lily admitted. 'According to Brian, he's the same in the garage. He won't say anything beyond what he absolutely has to, and then only to the customers.'

'He hasn't tried to see Helen.'

'I don't think so, in fact I'm sure of it, because he travels to the garage with Brian and Martin, and he's stayed in every evening since he moved in with us. Martin and I have tried persuading him to go over to see Helen, but he insists that she won't want to talk to him.'

John moved his chair closer to his desk. 'I can't sit back and allow Helen to carry on the way she has been these last two weeks. I suspect she's not sleeping and you only have to look at her to know that she hasn't been eating. Katie's invited her round each night this week for a meal and she's refused every time.'

'Perhaps she's afraid of seeing Jack going in or coming out of our house?'

'Do you know what happened between them?'

'Yes,' Lily murmured, 'but as it's Jack and Helen's business . . .'

'I wouldn't want you to tell me. I've tried talking to Helen about it, but she won't, not to me.' He gave Lily a small smile. 'I'm glad she has you for a friend.'

'I'm not sure Helen is. It's awkward with Jack living in our house . . . Helen.' The smile on Lily's lips froze as Helen walked into her father's office. She would never have believed that someone could lose so much weight in two weeks and it wasn't just the weight. There were dark circles beneath her friend's eyes that she had tried and failed to conceal with make-up. She looked ill, exhausted and, from the way her hand trembled as she lifted a cigarette to her mouth, on the verge of a breakdown.

'Lily, what are you doing here?'

'I came to see if you fancied doing something like going to the pictures or having a meal.'

'I have to—'

'There's nothing that needs seeing to here that I can't sort out, Helen,' John interposed. 'You haven't stopped all week. Lily was just telling me that she was starving. I'll ring the Mackworth, book the two of you a table and get them to put your meals on the warehouse account.'

'I'm not hungry,' Helen demurred.

'You didn't eat lunch,' John reminded.

'The Mackworth's always full. I can't face people.'

Lily left her seat. 'We could pick up something on the way over to your house. If you stop at an off licence, I'll get us a bottle of sherry. Martin's working late. It's a rush repair on a car that's wanted for a wedding tomorrow, so he's not expecting me home.'

'Why don't you telephone and tell him you're going over to Helen's?' John pushed the telephone across the desk towards Lily. 'Make arrangements for him to pick you up from there later.'

Helen looked from Lily to her father. When she didn't say anything, Lily lifted the receiver and dialled the number of the garage.

'I could have made my own plans for tonight,' Helen said tersely.

'You could have but don't try telling me you did.' John left the office and took Helen's coat from the stand.

'How's the garage going, Lily?' he asked when Lily hung up.

'Better than Martin and Brian expected it to, considering it's only just opened. Brian just told me that they've already sold four cars and Martin's had a few repairs and a couple of servicing jobs.'

'I must take a run over there and talk to Martin about servicing our fleet of vans. I'm not too happy with our current provider.'

'That would be wonderful, and a tremendous boost to Martin's confidence. He's still unsure he did the right thing in setting up with Brian.'

'Helen, you're keeping Lily waiting.' John held out her coat.

Helen hesitated just long enough for Lily and her father to wonder if she was going to come up with yet another excuse, then she finally allowed John to help her on with her coat.

Brian switched off the lights in the office, locked the door and walked over to where Jack was polishing a car they'd taken in part exchange that afternoon. 'Is Martin ready to go?'

'He said he needed another half an hour.' Jack shook out the cloth he'd been using, stood back and eyed his handiwork.

'You've done a good job.'

'I try.'

'We could go round the corner to the pub and get in a swift half and a ciggy while Martin finishes up whatever it is he has to do,' Brian suggested.

'I heard that, Powell,' Martin complained from the inspection pit.

'Is there anything we can do to help?' Brian asked.

'No,' Martin conceded reluctantly.

'Then, as you won't allow any of us to smoke in here, I rest my case. I'm gasping for a cigarette. We'll be back in twenty minutes.' Brian eyed Jack. 'Coming?'

Unable to think of a reason why he shouldn't, Jack picked up his coat and followed Brian around the corner and into the pub. The place was deserted. He sat at a table in the back room while Brian went to the bar.

'I thought you were getting halves,' Jack remonstrated when Brian returned with two full pints.

'You know Martin's half hours. They're always more like hours.' Brian flicked open a packet of cigarettes and offered Jack one. 'You think you'll stick working in the garage?'

'You know something I don't?'

'Like what?' Brian asked, confused by Jack's train of thought.

'Like, I'm not up to the job?'

'Come on, Jack, we're all feeling our way. The only one who knows anything about running a garage is Martin and he only knows the repair side. I spoke to Ronnie earlier this afternoon and he's pleased with our sales figures. With what we did today that's four cars this week, and two of those sales were down to you.'

'I suppose so,' Jack allowed grudgingly, sipping his pint.

'How long are you going to carry on like this?' Brian questioned bluntly.

'Like what?'

'Like your world has come to an end. Helen threw you out? So do something about it. Crawl to the girl and beg her to take you back.'

'Suppose I don't want her to take me back?'

'Of course you do, it's obvious to everyone who knows you that you're miserable. And from what Katie said—'

'You've spoken to Katie.' Jack's eyes glittered frostily.

'Yes.'

'About me!'

'It started as a conversation about the weather actually, then she asked how you were because, although you're only living next door, apparently you haven't bothered to call or ask after her and Glyn since the night of the party.'

'I've been busy.' Jack had the grace to look abashed.

'I've seen how busy you are. You have to read the newspaper cover to cover every evening and some evenings upside down. You then have to listen to the radio, polish all the shoes in the house, wash the dishes . . .'

'I try to do my share,' Jack snapped defensively.

'Pull the other one, Jack. Obviously whatever you did to make Helen throw you out is something you're ashamed of, or you wouldn't be hiding from Katie and John. And no, that it isn't an invitation for you to tell me all about it. Agony aunt isn't my line.'

'Then why mention it?'

'My father always used to say if you can do something about a problem, do it; if you can't, forget it. I suggest you do one or the other because I'm fed up of working and living with a misery guts.'

'I'm sorry—' Jack began hotly.

'Apology accepted,' Brian said lightly, ignoring Jack's rapidly rising temper. 'So, can I take it that you're going to be a regular ray of sunshine at home and in work from now on?'

'You're a bastard,' Jack growled.

'Literally.'

'Pardon.'

'My parents weren't married. As a result, I learned to use my fists early in life. When I discovered I couldn't fight all the boys in Pontypridd who insulted me and my mother, I began to use humour as a defence, but the last two weeks with you has just about dried up my entire year's supply. And in case you haven't noticed, Martin and Lily aren't exactly ecstatic about the way you're behaving either.'

'They haven't said anything to me.'

'Only because they're too polite, or afraid of your reaction to tackle you. You're putting one hell of a strain on all of us and I'm fed up with it.' Brian finished his pint and stubbed out his cigarette. 'Time we went back to the garage.'

'That's it, lecture over?' Jack questioned suspiciously.

'I only hope it has the desired effect. If you want to borrow a car to visit Helen, you can take the one you cleaned. On the other hand, there was nothing wrong with your bike the last time I looked.'

'I overheard you telling Martin that Lily was visiting Helen tonight.'

'She isn't going to stay all night. Do you want the car or not?'

'No.'

'Stubborn bugger, aren't you?'

'If I visit Helen, and I'm not saying that I will, I'll go on my bike.'

'It won't happen, Jack.' Brian set down his glass and pocketed his cigarettes.

'You think I won't go . . .'

'Not that. You may or may not. But lightning's not going to strike you down to give you an excuse to keep ignoring her.'

'You think I need an excuse to stay away from my own wife?'

'Don't you?' Brian asked coolly.

Chapter Sixteen

'Is Lily in?'

'No, but Brian is in the kitchen.' Jack turned his back on Judy and ran up the stairs, as she walked into the hall of Martin and Lily's house.

'Charming!' She stared at Jack's retreating figure.

'As you see, Jack's not his usual cheery self,' Brian pronounced insensitively, appearing in the kitchen doorway, spatula in hand and one of Lily's floral aprons tied around his waist.

'So I gather.' As Judy glanced up the stairs, Jack disappeared and Martin crossed the landing, naked.

'Sorry,' she apologised, suppressing a smile as he turned crimson.

'Comes to something when a man can't leave his own bathroom without an audience,' he shouted from behind the safety of his bedroom door.

'Come and help me cook before you create any more havoc.' Brian dived back into the kitchen, picked up a sizzling frying pan and flipped bacon and black pudding that were browning at the edges before turning down the gas.

'Bit late for breakfast, isn't it?' Judy commented, noting sausages and tomatoes keeping warm in a second frying pan, baked beans in Lily's best milk pan and eggs already beaten in a bowl.

'We all agreed that as we want a lie-in tomorrow, it would be wasted if we didn't eat it now.'

'We, being Martin, Jack and you?'

'Lily isn't here.'

'And this has nothing to do with the fact that all you can cook is a fry-up?'

'Anything else involves unwrapping potatoes and vegetables and I hate doing that.'

'Unwrapping?' She raised her eyebrows.

'All right, peeling.' He lit the gas under the beans. 'If you're looking for Lily, she's visiting Helen.'

'She said she was going to call in on her at the warehouse. I'm glad she's made some headway. I've tried and failed to get Helen to have lunch with me every day for the last two weeks.'

'If you'd like to wait, Martin's going to fetch her after he's eaten.'

'No, it's nothing urgent, just wedding details. I'll see her some other time.'

'What are you doing here, Judy?' Sam walked in, dressed for a night out in his best pair of drainpipe trousers and a leather jacket.

'And hello to you too, boyfriend.' Brian poured the eggs he'd beaten into an omelette pan.

'I'm Judy's fiancé, not boyfriend,' Sam corrected.

'I beg your pardon . . .'

'I'm visiting Lily,' Judy interrupted, hoping to stop Sam becoming more pompous or Brian even more absurd.

'And she's busy.'

'In Helen's house,' Judy explained briefly.

'Why is she with Helen if you two have arranged to go somewhere?' He glared at Brian. Apparently oblivious to Sam's antagonism, Brian continued to concentrate on stirring the eggs.

'We hadn't arranged to go anywhere,' Judy informed Sam tartly. 'I called in on the off chance that she'd be here.'

'You here to annoy your fiancée,' Brian mocked, 'or are you after something as usual, Sam?'

'I came up to see if I could borrow some black shoe polish.'

'Borrow?' Brian questioned heavily. 'I'm with Lily on this. You and Mike treat this place like a corner shop.'

'It's not your polish I want to borrow,' Sam snapped.

'Presumably you know where Lily keeps it.' Brian transferred a couple of slices of black pudding on to the sausage pan.

'In the scullery.' Sam gave Judy another hard look before stomping out and banging the door behind him.

'Do me a favour, call Martin and Jack,' Brian asked, ignoring Sam's display of temper. As Judy returned, he said, 'You're welcome to eat with us if you like, there's more than enough for four. That's if his lordship doesn't object,' he added, perfectly aware that Sam had opened the door a crack and was eavesdropping.

'His lordship, as you put it, doesn't own me,' she responded brusquely.

'So, do you want me to lay another place setting?'

She glanced into the two frying pans. 'It's too greasy for my taste, but thank you anyway.'

'How about just scrambled eggs on toast?' Brian suggested. 'There's no fat in that if you don't smother the toast in butter.'

'Judy has to go home.'

'I do?' Judy queried, eyeing Sam as he stood in the scullery doorway.

'We are going to my mother's tomorrow . . .'

'That's tomorrow, Sam.' Judy opened the cupboard next to the stove and lifted down a plate. 'I'd love to have scrambled eggs on toast with you, Brian. Thank you so much for inviting me.'

'You joining us, Judy? Good.' Martin breezed in and began ferrying the bowls of food that Brian had set out on the sideboard on to the table. 'Given the mileage you do around Swansea, I've been meaning to have a word with you about whoever's servicing your car. I could probably offer you not only a better service but a better price.'

'Or even better, a new car,' Brian broke in.

'Lay off, Powell, this is my deal,' Martin warned.

'If I sell her a new car, you'd be the one servicing it.' Brian glanced up at Sam who was still hovering, granite-faced in the doorway. 'Give Jack another shout on the way out, would you, mate? This lot is going to get cold if he doesn't get a move on.'

'I know you're upset, Helen, but you really do have to take better care of yourself,' Lily lectured, as she and Helen left the kitchen and carried the sherry bottle and glasses into the living room.

'Just because there were a few bits of mouldy food in my fridge.'

'Bits! You couldn't have opened it since—'

'Jack left,' Helen finished for her. 'You can say it, Lily; it's the truth. But I've been working long hours in the warehouse so I've been eating in town.'

'That's not what your father said. And before you start on again about how much food you had in the house, I don't count tins of fruit, cream, soups and corned beef as real food.'

'That meal you whipped up didn't taste that bad.'

'Soup and crackers topped by corned beef isn't my idea of a meal. If you don't get in some fresh fruit and vegetables, you're going to go down with some horrible disease.'

'Like the scurvy Miss Smythe used to warn us about in Domestic Science class,' Helen suggested.

'Exactly,' Lily concurred emphatically, refusing to see any humour in the situation.

'I never knew you could be so bossy.' Helen poured two glasses of sherry, handed one to Lily and sank down on the sofa. She had cleaned out the fireplace, re-made the fire and lit it when they had arrived, but although it was burning cheerfully, the room remained cold.

'Someone has to take care of you, if you won't do it yourself.' Lily sat on a chair next to the fire and set her sherry glass in the hearth. She hadn't drunk alcohol in any form since she had become pregnant simply because she couldn't bear the smell, but she had continued to accept it when it was offered to her in the hope of concealing her pregnancy until the time was right to tell Martin. Which, given the way she was putting on weight, had to be very soon.

'I had a letter this week.'

'From Jack?' The expression on Helen's face at the mention of Jack's name tempered Lily's optimism.

'No, that – the woman who is having his baby.'

'What did she say?' Lily wasn't at all sure she wanted to hear.

'More or less the same as Jack, that what happened between them was an accident that only happened once and didn't mean anything to either of them. Although how anyone, man or woman, can *accidentally* take off their clothes and make love to another person is beyond me.'

'If they were drunk . . . sorry,' Lily apologised, as a steely look appeared in Helen's eyes. 'Did she say anything else?'

'That she's sorry she wrote to tell him about the baby because the last thing she wanted to do was wreck our marriage. That she hadn't set eyes on him before it happened and hadn't afterwards until he visited her in the home and she's given him orders not to visit her there again.'

'Jack said that he had visited her.'

'He's been twice apparently.' Helen drank half her sherry and replenished her glass. 'It doesn't help to know that although she's having his baby she doesn't want to see him again. It's almost like, "Thank you very much, I've used your husband, I'm having his baby, but you can have him back now. And by the way, keep him away from me because I can't be bothered with him."'

'It can't be at all like that when she is in a home for unmarried mothers,' Lily remonstrated. 'Did she say why Jack visited her?'

'Guilt.'

'And you don't believe her.'

'I have this image of her and Jack lying naked on a deserted beach, making love and revelling in it like Deborah Kerr and Burt Lancaster in *From Here to Eternity* . . .'

'Deborah Kerr and Burt Lancaster were both wearing swimsuits in *From Here to Eternity*.'

'If it had been real life instead of a film, I bet they wouldn't have been wearing anything. And this woman that I imagine Jack with is beautiful and perfect, just like Deborah Kerr with red gold hair, deep blue eyes and a fabulous figure. She doesn't have my operation scar or fat knees . . .'

'You do not have fat knees.'

'. . . And now she's pregnant,' Helen finished, struggling to control herself. 'It hurts so much I think that if I ever saw her I'd kill her,' she pronounced vehemently. 'Then I get this pathetic letter from a woman in an unmarried mothers' home telling me what a mess she's made not only of her life but Jack's and mine, and how sorry she is for everything and I don't understand . . .' She reached for a handkerchief.

'Jack told Martin and me how it happened.'

'He did?' Helen blew her nose.

'I'm not saying that if it had been Martin I could have forgiven him any more than you can forgive Jack,' Lily ventured slowly, 'but afterwards I did feel as if I understood why they did what they did.'

'What exactly did he tell you?'

'He said the same as he told you.'

'Can you remember?'

Slowly, haltingly, Lily tried to repeat word for word what Jack had said to her and Martin.

'You're not going to go without doing the washing up,' Brian protested when Martin left the table.

'I have to fetch my wife.'

'And I cooked the meal. Fair's fair,' Brian demurred.

'Jack?' Martin turned to his brother who was already pushing his chair under the table.

'I'll do it tomorrow. I have letters to write.' There was such a bleak expression on Jack's face neither Martin nor Brian tried to stop him from leaving.

'Then your wife is going to come home to a messy kitchen,' Brian threatened, pouring himself a second cup of tea. 'I'm downing tools for the day.'

'I'll play the martyr, although I don't see why I should, when I ate less than any of you.' Judy collected the dishes from the table.

'You're a sport,' Brian complimented.

'It's the last time I take you up on an offer of scrambled eggs, Brian Powell. You bringing Lily straight back?' she asked Martin.

'No, I thought I'd buy her a drink in the Mermaid. It seems ages since we had any time to ourselves.'

'In that case, I can promise you a clean and tidy kitchen by the time you get back. Unless you and Jack mess it up again.' Judy kicked Brian's feet out of her way and scraped the plates into the bin.

'See you later.' Martin closed the front door behind him.

'Isn't it sweet?' Brian lifted his feet on to a chair and picked up a newspaper.

'What?'

'Martin wanting to take Lily out for a drink on a Saturday night after two years of marriage.'

'They're practically honeymooners,' she retorted, 'and you can get off your rear end and start washing.'

'I cooked.'

'And I need help.' She glared at him and he dissolved into laughter.

'Is that the best angry look you can manage?'

'Brian Powell . . .'

'I know my name, and that stung,' he complained, as she flicked a tea towel in his face.

'It was meant to.'

'All right, I surrender. I'll wash the dishes as well as cook the meal, but you dry and put everything away.'

'Deal.' She handed him the dish mop.

'I don't get rubber gloves,' he griped, as she peeled them from her hands, clipped them on to a peg and hung them on a hook glued inside the cupboard door.

'They're Lily's. Put your great clumsy paws into those and you'd split them but,' she smiled maliciously, 'I'm sure Lily would have no objection to you buying a pair of extra large and hanging them alongside hers. Then she and Martin would have time to go for more quiet drinks outside of this zoo.'

'If this place is a zoo, it's none of my doing. You saw Jack earlier, and your,' he hesitated for the barest fraction of a second, 'fiancé treats the main part of this house as an extension of his basement flat and the contents of the cupboards as his own personal, private store of goodies.'

'Then it's up to Lily to slap him down and set him right.' Overlooking her own annoyance with Sam earlier, she bridled at Brian's criticism.

'You know Lily, she's far too nice to tell anyone off.' Brian lifted the cleanest pile of dishes and dunked them in a bowl of hot water and SqEzy washing-up liquid. He gave her a sideways look. 'Unlike you these days. Perhaps it's my memory playing tricks but I remember you as being rather sweet and charming . . .'

'I am sweet and charming.'

'You're like a demented wasp around the place. Buzzing and angry, ready to pounce and sting the first person who says a wrong word.'

'I am not angry!'

'If you raise your voice a few decibels, Katie will be able to hear you next door.'

'You are—'

'If you're not careful, you're going to drop those

plates,' he warned, as she snatched three from the dish drainer at the same time.

'It would serve you damn well right if I did.'

'They're Lily's plates.'

'I wouldn't be here if they weren't.'

'If running eleven salons winds you up this much, Judy, shouldn't you consider selling one or two of them?' he suggested airily. 'There's no shame in admitting that not all of us are cut out for business.'

'Like you?' she bit back acidly.

'I have no idea if I am up to running a business or not.' He lifted a bundle of cutlery into the water and swished it around before mopping each piece individually. 'But I have no intention of giving myself an ulcer finding out.'

'And if it gets too much for you?'

'I'll tell my cousin and brother-in-law that I'm not up to the job and walk away from it.'

'To live on the dole, I suppose.' She continued to dry dishes angrily, wiping each plate in turn as if she was punishing it.

'To find something less taxing,' he prevaricated, realising he'd pushed her a little too far. 'So, you girls making any headway with Helen?' He deliberately changed the subject. 'As you see, Martin's and my efforts to talk to Jack have been a dismal failure.'

'As I said earlier, I haven't seen Helen since she kicked Jack out.'

'So you don't know if there's any likelihood of them getting back together?'

'No.'

'To go back to what I said about Martin still wanting to spend time alone with Lily . . .'

'You can't compare Martin and Lily with Jack and Helen,' she argued, still furious with him for his comments about her salons. 'Jack and Helen hadn't seen one another in two and half years.'

'All the more reason for Helen not to throw him out.'

'She wouldn't have without good reason. And while

we're on the subject of happy marriages, what about Katie and John?'

'They're both saints.' He immersed the frying pan in the sink.

'And that means what?'

'Just that, they're saints,' he echoed, turning to look at her.

'And Jack and Helen aren't?'

'I didn't say that.'

'You implied it.'

'Can you imagine Katie throwing John out of the house?' he asked evenly, rinsing off the frying pan and running a fresh sink full of hot water.

'That would depend on what he'd done.' She jerked open the cutlery drawer, picked up a bundle of knives and tossed them in one after the other as she dried them.

'She'd forgive John anything short of murder and, depending on who he killed, probably even that. And, I'm not sure that Lily will thank you for scratching her knives.'

'I am not scratching her knives.'

'No?' He washed the last frying pan and set it on to the drainer.

'As you obviously think that I am drying the cutlery all wrong, you can do it yourself.' She dumped the tea towel and the cutlery it still contained on to the sideboard.

'I wasn't criticising . . .'

'No?' she challenged.

'Want another cup of tea?'

'No.' She felt her resentment and anger dissipating under the steady gaze of his deep brown eyes. 'I should be going.'

'You haven't finished.'

'There's hardly anything left.'

'What's the matter?' he goaded. 'Sam likely to call in on you after his stag party and play Pop if you're not there to open the door to him?'

'If he is, it's hardly any of your business,' she answered frigidly.

'No, Judy, it's not,' he muttered, as she grabbed her coat from the stand and slammed the front door behind her.

The clock ticked loudly into the silence that settled over Helen's living room when Lily finished speaking. Helen leaned back on the sofa and stared into the fire.

'Is that what Jack told you?' Lily asked eventually.

'Not quite.'

'Are you going to reply to Maggie's letter?'

'I don't know.' Helen looked across at Lily. 'What I would like to do is go and see her.'

'Do you think that's wise?'

'I don't know whether it's wise or not, but at least if I see her, I'll have a real woman to hate and torment myself with instead of the Deborah Kerr image I've created.' She fumbled in her skirt pocket for a packet of cigarettes. 'Would you come with me tomorrow?'

'To the home?'

'Please. I'll drive there, but I'm not sure I can walk in there alone.'

They both started at a knock at the door.

Lily left her chair, walked to the curtains and opened them a fraction. 'It's Martin, he's earlier than I thought he would be.' She draped the edges back together. 'It might be easier for both of you if he didn't come in. It's not that he's taken sides . . .'

'Jack and I have put quite a strain on both of you. And we're still asking for more. Will you come with me tomorrow?'

'Yes,' Lily answered decisively. 'Yes, Helen, I'll come with you.'

'You won't have to ask Martin?'

Lily shook her head. She knew Martin and he, like her, would do anything to help resolve the miserable situation between his brother and Helen.

*

Judy opened her eyes as her doorbell rang for the second time in as many minutes and peered at the luminous hands on her alarm clock. It was a quarter past ten and she had only been asleep for half an hour, but exhausted by her long morning and afternoon in the salons, Sam's anger and Brian's aggravating, she hadn't felt up to anything except a hot bath and an early night when she returned to her flat. As the bell rang a third time, she fumbled for her dressing gown and went to the window. Seeing nothing unusual, she stumbled down the stairs.

'Who is it?' she demanded from behind the chained, bolted and locked door.

'Don't be sshtupid, Judy, it's me,' Sam slurred.

'I'm asleep.'

'Yoush can't be ashleep if you're on the shtairs.'

'I can and will be one minute after you leave.'

'I want to talk to youssh.' His speech slipped into incoherency.

'I don't want to talk to you when you're in that state.'

'Issh only shad a few drinksssh . . .'

'Call a taxi, go home and go to bed, or we'll never get to your mother's for Sunday dinner tomorrow,' she shouted.

'Five minutessssh,' he wheedled.

'No, Sam.'

He banged the door. 'Damn issh, Judy, open thish door or—'

'Not until tomorrow, Sam.' She switched off the light but remained, standing on the stairs, as he slammed against the door again and put his hand over the bell. 'If you don't go away, I'll call the police,' she threatened. 'And if Mike's on duty, I don't think he'll enjoy arresting you for causing a disturbance of the peace.'

After an interminable ten minutes she heard Sam's footsteps echoing back along the pavement in the direction of the square. Darting back upstairs in the dark, she groped her way into her bed and pulled the covers over her. Lily was right, she did have to talk to Sam, but she also had to think out what she was going to say. And she was tired. So tired, all she could see was Brian's irritating smile every time she closed her eyes.

'You sure you won't have a sherry?' Martin picked up Lily's empty orange juice glass along with his pint mug.

'I'm sure. Helen and I drank the best part of half a bottle between us earlier,' she lied.

'It's not as if you do it every day. I can't remember the last time we went out for a drink together like this.' Martin went to the bar and returned with a pint of beer and another orange juice.

'It is good to have you to myself for half an hour.' Lily took the orange juice. 'Between Brian and Jack eating with us and the hours you've been working in the garage . . .'

'And Sam and Mike walking in on us at all hours of the day and night.'

'You're getting fed up with them, aren't you?'

'They push it sometimes.' He sipped his pint. 'Perhaps we should bolt the door on the stairs down to the basement.'

'They might take it the wrong way.'

'What wrong way is there to take it? We'd like more privacy and that's one way to get it.' He made a wry face. 'There's something else you should know before you hear it from Judy. She called tonight and we both got more than she bargained for when she saw me walking from the bathroom into our bedroom.'

'You didn't have any clothes on,' Lily guessed.

'You know me so well.'

'That will teach you to walk around in the nude,' she smiled. 'Did Judy say why she called?'

'To see you, but that didn't stop her from joining us for tea. Brian cooked, so be warned we have nothing for breakfast tomorrow.'

'I promised to spend the day with Helen and you can make yourself porridge.'

'That's not worth climbing out of bed for,' he grumbled. 'And much as I'd like my brother and Helen to get back together, I think it's a cheek of her to commandeer you on my one day off a week.'

'You can make yourselves sandwiches for lunch and I'll cook the joint when I come back. I won't be late.'

'It's not the cooking I'm thinking of. You all right?' he asked anxiously. The colour had drained from her face.

'I feel weird, but it's probably too much orange juice on a practically empty stomach. Helen had hardly any food in and, as she wouldn't go out to eat, we shared a can of soup, some crackers and corned beef.'

'If I'd known, I would have brought you some of Brian's fry-up in a paper bag. Want some crisps?'

'I would but there's a restaurant upstairs.' She had a sudden and unaccountable craving for stodge. She felt she could eat a mountain of mashed potatoes or an entire loaf of bread.

He slipped his hand into his trouser pocket and pulled out some change.

'They don't serve snacks at the bar, not even crisps.'

'I could buy you a meal.'

'They stop serving at ten.'

'Damn Helen, if she's made you ill.'

'I'll be fine. I'm just hungry.'

'Tell you what, finish your drink, and I'll buy us pattie and chips in the fish shop round the corner.'

'You're hungry after one of Brian's fry-ups?'

'You know me, I can always eat pattie and chips. Besides, if we drive up on to the headland car park and eat them in the car, it will give us another half an hour of peace and quiet.'

Helen walked restlessly around the house, checking doors and windows that she had checked half a dozen times, straightening perfectly draped curtains, plumping up cushions that didn't need it.

Lily was a good friend and she was grateful to her for

the unselfish support she had given her through every major crisis in her life, through childhood mumps, measles and chicken pox, the untimely pregnancy that had resulted in her early marriage to Jack, the subsequent loss of her baby and Jack's two and half year absence. Until that evening, she would have said that she trusted Lily implicitly, but the account Lily had given her of what had happened in Cyprus was so different from the one Jack had told her, she was no longer sure what or who to believe.

It wasn't at all like the picture her imagination had painted during the last couple of weeks. She had conjured up scenes of Jack cavorting with a beautiful siren on sun-drenched Mediterranean beaches while she had been working hard on the house and in the warehouse. Working and waiting . . .

If he had only made love to the woman once, could she forgive him? Could she ever bring herself to trust him again?

But then, the question was academic when Jack hadn't tried to see her, much less asked her to forgive him or allow him to return to the house. And then there was the baby. Jack's child! Her face contorted in pain. How could either of them attempt to salvage their marriage when they were faced with the reality of a child he had fathered alive somewhere in the world?

A picture intruded through her grief and pain. An image no less real than that of the woman she had fabricated, of a small boy racing across a deserted, windswept cold winter beach on Gower; a boy with Jack's black curly hair and piercing dark eyes.

'You two seem happy,' Brian commented, as Martin and Lily fell laughing through the kitchen door.

'We are,' Martin grinned.

'Want some cocoa?' Brian held up his cup.

'Good God, the debonair, sophisticated Brian Powell drinking cocoa?' Martin teased. 'Next thing you know, you'll be smoking a pipe, leaning on a walking stick, wearing a flannel waistcoat and walking to the shops in your bedroom slippers.'

'Very funny, that's the last time I offer you cocoa. And in case you're wondering, the kitchen's immaculate and Judy left before it was finished, so I'm excused kitchen duties for the next three days.'

'Jack not around?' Lily enquired.

'He hasn't come down all evening.'

'I'll look in on him when we go up,' Martin said in response to the concerned expression on her face.

'How's Helen?' Brian asked.

'Terrible,' Lily murmured. 'Her father's really worried about her.'

'So are you?'

'Yes,' she admitted.

'If you ask me, the pair of them need their heads knocking together.'

'If only it were that simple.' Lily allowed Martin to help her off with her coat.

'I'm only an uncomplicated bachelor who sees things in black and white,' Brian said flatly, 'and after the work I've put in this last week, I'm looking forward to a lie-in until at least midday tomorrow. See you when I see you.' Taking his cocoa, he climbed the stairs.

'You still look a bit peaky, love,' Martin said, as Lily hung away their coats. 'Why don't you go on up. I'll be right behind you as soon as I've talked to Jack.'

Too tired to argue, she followed Brian up the stairs.

'Jack's sleeping.' Martin slid into bed besides Lily ten minutes later.

'It's not like him to go to bed early.'

'He's not actually in it, more like on it and still dressed.'

'He'll freeze.' She winced as the full length of Martin's icy body embraced hers.

'No, he won't. I took a blanket from the airing

cupboard and covered him with it and, before you start worrying about the bedspread, he'd taken his shoes off.'

'Do you think it's a good idea for Helen to meet this woman tomorrow?' she asked suddenly.

'I honestly don't know, love. I suppose it could go either way,' he replied. 'Send Helen rushing to the divorce courts or possibly galvanise her into talking to Jack again.'

'I suppose it's too much to hope that it will do any more than get them talking.'

'Even I can't be that optimistic.' Pulling her tight against him, he kissed the back of her neck. 'Can we forget Jack and Helen and concentrate on us for the next half hour?'

She shivered as his fingers closed around her breasts. 'Do you mind if we wait until after you're warm?'

'Moaning Minnie.'

'That's me.' She turned and kissed his lips, feeling strangely light-headed again.

'You're fantastic,' he complimented, as she wrapped herself around him.

'Because I warm you when you're cold?'

'Among other things,' he answered. 'But I mean it, Lily. I don't know what I'd do without you. Jack and Helen's problems have made me realise just how lucky I am to have you.'

'Not that I'd forgive you either if you had done what Jack did.'

'But after he told us about it, you said you could understand how it happened.'

'Helen and I agreed tonight that there's a world of difference between understanding and forgiving. So if you've any intention of straying . . .'

'Not from this bed.' He kissed her again. 'You're stuck with me, Mrs Clay.'

'I hope so,' she whispered, thinking of her secret, 'I really hope so.'

Chapter Seventeen

Sam ran up the outside steps of the basement and opened the door to Judy's car just as she was about to hit the horn for the second time. 'I wasn't sure you'd come.'

'Neither was I, after the way you behaved last night.' She barely waited for him to close the door before putting her foot down on the accelerator.

'I'd had a few drinks.'

'I noticed.'

'You objecting to me going out with the boys now?' he questioned tetchily.

'You can drink Swansea dry for all I care. It's what you do with yourself afterwards that concerns me.' She braked suddenly at a set of traffic lights, jerking them both forward.

'Christ! You're even driving angry.'

'Can you blame me?' As she turned to glare at him, the driver behind them blasted his horn.

'The lights have changed,' Sam informed her curtly.

'So I see.' She slammed the car into gear and drove off. Before they had travelled fifty yards, the car behind pulled out and overtook them, forcing her to swing over sharply.

As the driver drew alongside he slid back his window and shouted, 'Bloody women drivers!'

'Judy! For Christ's sake, let him go,' Sam shouted, as she revved up speed.

'You saw the idiot. That was dangerous.'

'As my mother's taken the trouble to cook Sunday dinner for us, I'd like to be alive to eat it.'

Realising that Sam had brought out the worst in her, yet again, she slowed the car and headed for the junction that led to Neath Road.

'Look, Judy, about last night—'

'If we're going to discuss last night, I think we should start with the way you behaved when I called in on Lily.'

'Don't you mean Brian?' he corrected.

'No, I do not. I called to see Lily.'

'Who wasn't there,' he pointed out, lowering his voice.

'I wasn't to know that beforehand,' she said irritably. 'I'm not psychic.'

'But you stayed to have tea with Brian.'

'Martin, Jack and Brian.'

'It wasn't Martin or Jack who invited you.'

'It was Brian,' she agreed, 'and I might not have accepted his invitation if you hadn't told me I couldn't.' Fighting anger, yet again, she glanced across to see him sitting as tense and grim-faced as her.

'He was flirting with you and you were loving every minute of it.'

'How many times do I have to tell you that what little there was between Brian Powell and me has long since been over?'

'Shout louder, why don't you?' he goaded. 'You know damn well I've a king-size bloody hangover.'

'Good!' As soon as the retort was out of her mouth, she regretted being so petty and childish.

'Fine bloody day this is turning out to be.'

'And whose fault is that?'

'Mine,' Sam replied icily. 'Everything is always my bloody fault, isn't it, Judy?'

She couldn't let the remark pass. 'This time it is, Sam.' Ten strained minutes later; she sneaked a sideways look at him again. He was sitting back in his seat, a pained expression on his face as he squinted into the bright morning sunlight. For once she found herself in total agreement with him. It was turning out to be a 'fine bloody day' and she couldn't help feeling that the worst was yet to come.

'Helen is picking me up in Mansel Street in a hour and I have to wash and dress, Marty . . .' Lily stifled her laughter, as Martin grabbed her by the waist, pulled her back into the bed and tickled her.

'I am not going to let you go.' Leaning over her, he pinned her down on the mattress and kissed her.

As she kissed him back, she sensed him relaxing. Moving quickly, she slithered sideways out of the bed and landed on the floor with a bump.

'Did you hurt yourself?' Lying on his stomach, he peered anxiously down at her.

'Not much.'

'I could kiss whatever it is better.'

'No fear, you'd pull me back in there.' She retreated to the other side of the room and opened her chest of drawers.

Martin settled back on the pillows and watched her. 'It's not fair of Helen to drag you off. I'll be lonely.'

'You could come with us.'

'I'd cramp your style and Helen's.'

'Probably.' She removed a set of underclothes from a drawer, closed it, opened the next one down and took out a suspender belt and pair of stockings.

'I hope the sacrifice of what could have been our day is worth it.'

'It will be if I manage to persuade Helen to at least talk to Jack.' She flicked through the clothes in her wardrobe. Settling on a dark green woollen sweater and a straight black skirt, she held them up in front of her. 'What do you think?'

'Are they new?'

'Sometimes I think you wouldn't notice if I went around naked.'

'I'd prefer it, provided no one else was about.' He

picked up her nightdress from the floor and threw it at her. 'Just in case my brother or Brian is up.'

'I was going to put on my dressing gown, unlike some people I could mention.' She smiled playfully. 'I can't wait until Judy, Katie, Helen and I get together for our next gossip. After what Judy saw yesterday, we can compare notes.'

'You lot don't talk about things like that, do you?' he asked, horrified.

'No more than you men,' she teased, and ran out of the door.

As Judy pulled up outside Ena Davies's terraced house, the curtains twitched in the front parlour. Like most valley matrons, Ena regarded the room as sacrosanct, opening it only for what she regarded as state occasions, such as funerals, weddings, christenings, and entertaining the chapel minister to tea. She had shown Judy the room the first time Sam had taken her to his home, but only from the passage, and the fact that she was in it now watching for their arrival, suggested she was agitated.

Resigning herself to a day of bickering with Sam and fencing words with his mother, Judy opened the door. Ena appeared on the doorstep before she'd had time to lock the car.

'You're late.'

'It's not half past eleven yet, Mam,' Sam said. Judy's mouth tightened.

'Mrs Richards and the girls have been waiting for over half an hour to show Judy the bridesmaids' dresses.'

'You didn't tell us they would be here.' Judy pocketed her car keys.

'Well, there's no need to waste any more time hanging around out here talking about it.' Ena ushered them into the house and down the passage that led to her back kitchen cum living room.

Half a dozen giggling girls of varying sizes from tiny through medium to large – one in particular was very large, Judy noted sympathetically, having suffered a weight and spot problem in her own early teens – spilled out to meet them.

'These are Sam's cousins, Judy.' Ena took charge of the situation, while trying not to pretend that she was loving every minute of it. 'Susan, Christine, Anne, Gillian, Wendy and Pamela.' She grabbed the nearest girl, a two-year-old who wriggled out of her hand. 'All of you say hello to your new Auntie Judy.'

Overwhelmed by the noise, Judy mouthed, 'Hello,' feeling that any attempt to shout above the din would only make things worse.

'Mrs Richards, this is Judy Hunt, our Sam's fiancée.' Ena pushed Judy towards a small round woman wearing a pair of bright pink, plastic National Health spectacles.

'Pleased to meet you.' Judy extended her hand. Before Mrs Richards could shake it, she lost her balance and fell on her as Pamela shoved Wendy into her back.

'Now, Pamela, behave,' Ena warned severely, 'or you won't be allowed to put on that beautiful dress Mrs Richards has made for you.'

Pamela looked suitably chastened until Ena turned her back, then she poked her tongue out at Judy. Suppressing a laugh, Judy glanced over her shoulder at Sam who was backing down the passage.

'Now Judy has finally arrived, you can all go upstairs and put on the dresses, nicely now,' Ena cautioned, as the girls and Mrs Richards dutifully trooped past Sam to the stairs.

'If you don't need me for anything, I'll nip down the rugby club for a quick one.' Sam went to the front door.

'Must you?' Judy pleaded.

'A man's entitled to a bit of relaxation after working hard all week, Judy,' Ena admonished. 'There's no need to hurry back, Sam. I'm not going to have dinner on the table much before two with everything that needs to be done here. Not even if Judy helps me.'

Ena's last remark was one too many for Judy. 'I think Sam should stay.'

'Don't be silly, Judy,' Ena contradicted.

'It's Sam's wedding too. He should be involved.'

'Not with the dresses.' Ena crossed her arms over her ample bosom and faced Judy. 'It's bad luck for a man to see them before the wedding.'

'That only applies to the bride's dress.'

'It most certainly doesn't. Don't tell me that you're going to turn into one of those wives, Judy.'

'What wives?' Judy asked, striving to control her temper.

'Wives who won't let their husbands out of their sight or off the leash for a moment. Sam works hard—'

'As do I,' Judy interrupted coldly.

'Of course you do, dear,' Ena granted patronisingly, 'but not for much longer. Do you need any help, Mrs Richards?' she shouted, as a crash followed by a scream and high-pitched giggling echoed down the stairs.

'I am going to carry on working after I am married.' Judy gave Sam an imploring look.

'And who is going to look after my son?'

'The same person who is doing it now,' Judy suggested.

'I really don't think it's done for a son to bring his washing home after he's married, or do you expect me to do yours as well?'

'I don't expect you to do anything, Mrs Davies. There are plenty of laundrettes Sam can use in Mumbles and Swansea.'

'Laundrettes! You expect my son to wash his clothes in a laundrette – in public!' Ena couldn't have look more shocked if Judy had suggested that Sam patronise a nudist colony.

'I see no reason why not. Plenty of men do their own washing in a laundrette. My friends' husbands—'

'I am sure that you and your friends think you are being very contemporary and modern,' Ena sniffed. 'But my son hasn't been brought up that way.'

'You brought him up to be idle.'

'Judy, that was insulting to both my mother and me,' Sam warned.

'It was meant to be truthful not insulting.'

'Sam's right, it was insulting,' Ena concurred.

'For the life of me, I can't think of one single reason why a man shouldn't do his share of the housework after he's married,' Judy said in exasperation. 'John Griffiths and Martin do.'

'John can afford to employ a cleaner and Lily does practically everything.'

'She does not. I've seen Martin cooking, cleaning and washing up,' Judy contradicted.

'Then the wife of this Martin, whoever she is, should be ashamed of herself,' Ena reproved.

'Why?' Judy questioned. 'She works all day in a bank.'

'Auntie Ena, am I pretty?' Pamela flounced down the stairs holding the front of her dress up in two hands, revealing an underskirt of pink net. Three other prospective bridesmaids followed, all imitating her prancing walk.

'The dress is very pretty, Pamela,' Ena qualified. 'Well, Judy, as you're the bride, I suppose you'll have something to say about it.'

Judy stared in disbelief as the girls lined up on the stairs. 'You bought the figured nylon.'

'It was much prettier and cheaper than the satin so I thought I'd surprise you.'

'And they're not made up in the pattern I bought,' Judy gasped.

'Mrs Howells's daughter's pattern was much nicer.'

'And ballerina length!'

'As I said, much more suitable and practical than full-length. They could trip over a long skirt and that would be a disaster in church.'

'But these dresses look nothing at all like mine.' Judy visualised the elegant lines of her Tudor collared, lace crinoline, set against the fussy flounces of the girls' ballerina length, almost luminous pink nylon bridesmaids' dresses. She had given in on the colour on the understanding that the style and fabric would be the same as her gown, but instead of high Tudor collars, they had floppy Peter Pan collars, set off by large, inexpertly sewn bows and rows of pink buttons down the front.

'If you had chosen the one I wanted—'

'You wanted!' Green eyes blazing, Judy finally allowed her temper to surface as the girls and Mrs Richards retreated smartly back up the stairs. 'Against my better judgement and in the interests of keeping the peace, I allowed you to talk me into having this menagerie of bridesmaids. For the same ridiculous reason, I allowed you to talk me out of buying the dresses I chose, on condition these were made up to match my dress both in pattern and fabric. I bought the patterns. I paid for the damn material. I paid to have them made by the dressmaker of your choice and you wreck—'

'If that's all the thanks I'm going to get for putting myself out—'

'If this is an example of you putting yourself out, Mrs Davies, please don't ever put yourself out for me again.'

'Judy, you can't talk to my mother like that!'

Judy stepped back and looked from Sam to his mother who was standing, tight-lipped, white-faced and speechless for once. Pulling the glove from her left hand, she slipped off Sam's engagement ring and handed it to him. 'Sorry, Sam, I should never have accepted this from you in the first place.' Opening the door, she stepped out into the street.

Lily stuck her head around the kitchen door and checked the time on the clock.

'I've made tea. Would you like a cup?' Jack looked up from the *Sunday Pictorial* he'd spread out on the table. 'You look smart. Are you going somewhere special?'

'Just out for the day.' Lily felt her cheeks burning. She

hated lying but Helen would be furious with her if she let slip where she was going, or who she was going with.

'That sounds very mysterious.'

Irritated with herself for arousing his curiosity, she answered, 'Not at all. Spring is on the way and a couple of the girls fancied a drive in the country.'

'And a break from cooking Sunday dinner for their long-suffering husbands.' Martin walked in wearing his dressing gown over pyjama trousers. 'Have you made toast, Jack?' He winked at Lily.

'No, but if that's your way of telling me that you'd like some, I'll make you a couple of pieces.'

'Thanks.' Martin rested his hands on Lily's shoulders and kissed her. 'Shouldn't you be on your way?'

'Yes.' She glanced at her watch again. 'I'm meeting the girls around the corner to save time. See you later.'

'Here.' Martin followed her into the hall and helped her on with her coat. 'Another kiss goodbye?'

'No. You've had too many kisses before shaving as it is.'

'You're a heartless wife, no kisses and leaving me to fend for myself all day.'

'We'll have dinner tonight instead of at one o'clock.'

'And a quiet night in, just the two of us in the living room. Good luck,' he whispered, as she ran from the house.

'Your toast is ready,' Jack shouted from the kitchen.

'Thank you, slave.'

'I suppose you want me to pass you the butter and marmalade out of the fridge?'

'Please, seeing as you're closer to it.' Martin sat at the table. 'You off somewhere?'

'Not particularly, why do you ask?'

'You're dressed and it's before midday on a Sunday.'

'I thought I might call round and see Katie, John and the baby. I haven't visited them since the party.'

'Good idea.' Martin opened the butter dish and

attacked the slab with his knife. 'Sometimes, just sometimes, I miss the bad old days when Mam was too poor to afford a fridge. At least then we never had trouble spreading the butter.'

As Judy sat in the front seat of her car, trying to calm herself in readiness for the drive back to Swansea, Sam left the house. She expected him to walk past her car on his way to the club, but to her surprise he tapped on the car window. She wound it down and looked at him warily. He crouched on his heels to bring his face down to her level.

'I think we should talk.'

Bracing herself for yet another argument, she said, 'The passenger door is open.'

He walked around the car, opened the door and sat besides her. 'That was quite a performance you gave in there. My mother is really upset. I left her crying.'

'Crocodile tears?' She looked him in the eye. 'Sorry, that was unpardonable of me.'

'Yes, it was. As I was saying, she is very upset but if you go back in and apologise to her it might help. I'm not saying she'll forgive you but she may talk to you again before the wedding. As Mrs Richards just said to her, all brides suffer from nerves.'

'Nerves!'

'There you go again, Judy, repeating everything I say.'

She took a deep breath and steeled herself. 'I meant every word I said in there and,' she looked him in the eye, 'everything I did.'

'You can't be serious about breaking our engagement.'

'I've never been more serious in my life.'

'But we've booked the church, the Mackworth, the flowers, the car, the cake, the invitations—'

'And tomorrow I'll go around and unbook everything.'

'But my suit's being made. It will be ready next week.'

'As that is the only thing you agreed to pay for and

likely to lose money on, I think you can stand the expense.'

'Just because my mother—'

'This has nothing to do with your mother, Sam,' she said seriously. 'I haven't been happy since we set the date.'

'Please, don't try telling me that you need more time. That's all I've been hearing from you for the last two years. That and your bloody salons.'

'Listen to yourself, Sam, you never used to swear the way you do now.'

'You'd make a monk swear,' he broke in abruptly.

'Can't you see that we're not happy together?' she pleaded, deliberately pitching her voice low.

'Now I'm not making you happy!'

'No more than I make you.' Her hand shook as she accepted a cigarette from him.

'So, what have we been doing together for the last two years?' he asked angrily. 'Wasting our time?'

'Of course not, we had some good times.'

'Did we?'

'I thought so,' she murmured softly. 'And if you didn't, why did you ask me to marry you?'

'Because I thought you cared for me.'

'And you? Did you care for me, Sam?'

'Of course I bloody well did.'

'Please, Sam, let's try and talk about this calmly and sensibly without losing our tempers and swearing and shouting at one another,' she begged.

'The way I see it, we were fine until the night that bastard Brian Powell walked into Helen and Jack's.'

'This is about you and me. It has nothing to do with Brian.'

He slipped his hand into his trouser pocket and pulled out her engagement ring. He held it out to her. 'Put this back on your finger.'

She looked him in the eye. 'No.'

'That is your final word?'

'Yes, Sam.'

'Then go to hell, and take bloody Brian Powell with you.' He wrenched down the door handle and stepped out of the car. Feeling anything but calm, she gunned the ignition and pulled away from the kerb.

'Jack, this is a nice surprise. Don't just stand there. Come in. Katie, Jack's here.' John opened the living-room door. Katie was sitting in the easy chair next to the fireplace nursing Glyn, his pram set in a draught-free alcove next to her. As newspapers were scattered on the floor around the other easy chair, Jack sensed that he had interrupted the sort of quiet, domestic Sunday morning he and Helen would have enjoyed – if they had still been together.

'Jack, it's lovely to see you.' Katie's thin face shone with pleasure. 'Let me make you a cup of tea.'

'I'll make it, love,' John interrupted.

'No, thanks,' Jack refused. 'I've only just left the breakfast table.'

'At least sit down,' John insisted.

Jack sat on the sofa set between the two easy chairs.

'Look, Glyn, it's your Uncle Jack come to visit.' Katie pulled the shawl away from the baby's face so Jack could get a better look at him. She smiled at her brother. 'Would you like to hold him?'

'As long as he doesn't cry.' Jack took the baby from her and cradled him in the crook of his left arm. To his surprise, the baby settled happily.

'I was only saying to Brian the other day that I hadn't seen you since the party.' Katie leaned forward and retied a blue ribbon on one of Glyn's booties.

'He told me.'

'I didn't mean it as a criticism, Jack. I know how busy you are with the garage opening up and everything.'

'Not that busy.' He smiled down at the baby who was staring up at him through enormous, round blue eyes. 'He's going to be a looker, Katie.'

'What do you mean going to be,' Katie burst out with

all the protective enthusiasm of a new mother. 'He's beautiful, aren't you, my precious?'

Excited by the sound of her voice, the baby waved his arms and legs, catching one of Jack's fingers in his hand. 'Some grip you've got there, mate.' Jack fought a tightening in his throat. He had never entirely believed women when they cooed over babies, saying things like, 'He has his father's eyes' or 'That's his mother's chin,' but Glyn's mouth was the exact same shape as Katie's and his forehead was high and broad just like John's. The child was a perfect combination of both parents and he couldn't help remembering the child Helen had lost and wondering what he – or she – would have looked like. And that brought thoughts of the baby Maggie was carrying . . .

'Have you seen Helen?' Katie asked courageously.

'Not since she threw me out of the house. With good cause,' he added, anxious not to give the impression that he had visited to complain about her. 'Has she talked to you about it?'

'No,' John responded. 'She hasn't talked to me about anything other than work for the last two weeks and then only in the warehouse. We've invited her to visit us, but she hasn't. However, you only have to look at her to know that she's desperately unhappy. And if you'll forgive me for saying so, you don't look too good yourself.'

'I miss her.'

'Then why don't you go and see her?' Katie broke in impatiently. 'Surely whatever it is that's happened can't be that bad?'

'It is, sis.'

'Have you come to tell us about it?' John asked intuitively.

'Helen's your daughter. You have a right to know what I've done to hurt her.'

'You two have far more of a right to live your own lives without interference from me or anyone else in the family.' John picked up the papers from around his chair and folded them into the magazine rack.

'It's all going to come out anyway and I'd rather tell you to your face than have you hear it from the gossips.' Jack looked from John to Katie, saw love and concern etched in his sister's face and mustered his courage.

He began by telling them about Cyprus, the ambush and the sergeant's death, just as he had related to Martin and Lily. Neither Katie nor John interrupted him while he spoke and even after he had finished telling them the whole sorry tale they remained silent.

Just as he was wondering if he should leave, rather than wait for them to make a comment, the baby kicked out restlessly in his arms.

'Glyn needs changing and feeding. I'll take him upstairs.' Katie left her chair and lifted Glyn from Jack's arm.

'Katie . . .' Jack found himself talking to a closed door.

'Katie will need time to come to terms with what you've just told us, Jack,' John warned.

'That's if she ever does.'

'Oh, she will, don't worry yourself about that.' John left his chair and went to the sideboard. 'Would you like a drink? We have brandy, or sherry, if you'd prefer it.'

Jack shook his head. 'Nothing, thank you.'

'I hope you don't mind me indulging.' John poured himself a small brandy and returned to his seat.

'Katie will hate me after this.'

'No, she won't,' John reassured, 'but as I said, she will need time to adjust to the fact that one of her big brothers isn't perfect. Not that anyone ever is. It's simply that you and Martin have always been her heroes.' He sipped his brandy. 'Does anyone else know why Helen threw you out?'

'I told Martin and Lily when I moved in with them. I thought it only fair. I think Lily would have thrown me out as well if I hadn't been Martin's brother. I offered to find somewhere else to live and I will start looking. Given the circumstances, I can hardly carry on living next door to you.' He rose to his feet. 'I'm sorry. I've intruded enough.'

'I'll say this much for you, Jack, you've never lacked courage. I remember the night you told me you'd made Helen pregnant. You faced me man to man, almost daring me to hit you. You accepted responsibility for your mistakes then, just as you are now.'

'I thought you'd be furious and I don't just mean then, I mean now.'

'I was and I am,' John said shortly. 'But I'm also an expert at concealing my feelings.'

'I'm sorry for messing up Helen's life, and upsetting you and Katie. I know that sounds pathetic, but I mean it and I'll understand if you don't want me to call again and see Katie and Glyn.'

'You can't throw someone out of a family the way you can throw someone out of a house,' John said wryly. 'Katie won't forget what you did, but in my opinion she will forgive you – eventually – and given my age and disabilities, Glyn will be grateful for a young uncle who can run alongside his bike when he's learning to ride one.'

'Thank you.'

'What are you going to do?'

'Work hard in the garage and make as much money as I can. If Helen wants to divorce me, as the one who fouled up I think I should be the one to pay the bill. And, if I can, I'd like to adopt the baby when it's born. I've hurt enough people without hurting him.'

'You think they'll let you adopt the baby?'

'Maggie said they won't, but that's not going to stop me from trying.'

'Have you thought how Helen will feel, if by some miracle you do manage to adopt this baby?'

'Yes, and I also know she's never fully recovered from the pain of losing our baby. You know we talked about adopting one when I came home, but much as I love

Helen and don't want to hurt her more than I already have, I can't turn my back on this child.'

'So you have no intention of trying to save your marriage to my daughter?'

'If I thought there was anything to save, I'd crawl back to her on my hands and knees, and spend the rest of my life trying to make her happy. But I saw her face when she threw me out of the house. There is nothing left.'

'I'm sorry, Jack.'

'So am I,' Jack opened the door. 'More than I can say.'

'You don't have to go in,' Lily comforted Helen as they sat outside Cartref.

'I know,' Helen murmured.

'Do you want me to come with you?'

Helen looked at the front door. 'She'll think it strange that I want to see her. If we both go in, she might feel threatened.'

'She might.'

'But I feel awful to have dragged you all the way up here. I can't just go in and leave you sitting in the car.'

'Yes, you can.' Lily opened her handbag. 'I brought a book.' She held up a copy of Wilkie Collins's *Woman in White* that she'd borrowed from the Central Library. 'I've been trying to finish it for a week but I don't seem to get a moment's peace at home. Between Martin, Brian—'

'And Jack.' Helen opened the car door. 'You sure you don't mind?'

'I'm sure.'

'Here goes.'

Lily watched Helen ring the bell and walk into the house. Just as she was settling to her book, the door opened again and a girl she recognised walked awkwardly down the short flight of steps into the courtyard. Without thinking what she was doing, Lily opened the car door and shouted, 'Emily?'

Emily turned in the direction of the car. When Lily saw

her blush, she realised how indiscreet she had been, but she could hardly ignore her after she had called her name.

'It is Emily, isn't it?' Lily asked.

'Yes.' Emily dragged her step as she walked over to the car. 'And you used to be Joe Griffiths's girlfriend.'

'A long time ago. I've been married to someone else for two years. I'm sorry.' Lily looked back at the house. 'I didn't mean to embarrass you.'

'I rather think I did that to myself.' Emily looked down self-consciously at her bump. 'Are you visiting someone here?'

'Just keeping a friend company on the drive.'

'It's a long way from Swansea.' Emily looked around at the hills. 'In fact it's a long way from anywhere.'

CHAPTER EIGHTEEN

'You're sure that's Mrs Maggie Jones?' Helen asked the member of staff who had shown her to the residents' lounge.

'That is Mrs Jones, Mrs Clay,' the woman confirmed. 'But surely you know your own sister-in-law?'

'We only met once and that was years ago,' Helen fabricated, wondering what other lies Jack had spun when he'd visited Maggie.

'Are you better, Mrs Clay?'

'Better?' Helen asked in confusion.

'Your husband mentioned that you were in hospital the first time he visited Mrs Jones.'

'Yes . . . yes, I'm fine now,' Helen stammered.

'If you'll excuse me, I have to supervise the tea.'

'Yes, of course. Thank you,' Helen watched the woman walk away before turning back to the lounge.

The image she had conjured of a beautiful seductive siren who had cavorted with Jack against the backdrop of a sun-drenched Mediterranean beach, faded as she stared at the plump, dowdy, middle-aged woman who sat knitting a tiny white garment. Her fair hair was more silver than blonde. Her skin was creased with wrinkles, sallow with a faded tan, and there was a defeated, beaten expression in her eyes. She looked more like a grandmother than a woman about to become a mother and, Helen realised with a start, probably was more of an age to be just that.

Grateful that Maggie had chosen to sit alone and in a secluded corner, Helen walked across the room and stood in front of her chair. As Maggie looked up nervously, Helen saw that she already knew who she was.

'I hope you don't mind me coming to visit you.'

'No, Mrs Clay, I don't mind you coming to see me,' Maggie answered apprehensively. 'Please, won't you sit down?'

'Are you sure you didn't give Sam his ring back just because you lost your temper with his mother?' Joy asked Judy bluntly. They sat facing one another across Joy's kitchen table.

'No,' Judy asserted. 'It's as I said to Sam, I should never have taken it in the first place.'

'Roy and I agree the woman's an absolute nightmare and considering she had the gall to have those bridesmaids' dresses made up the way she wanted, after you paid for the pattern and material . . .'

Judy shook her head. 'She is a nightmare and I was furious about the dresses, but it's not her, it's me. I don't think anyone would willingly opt for a mother-in-law like Ena Davies, but if I loved Sam I'd put up with her, and I won't because I don't love Sam. I realise now that I never did and I simply can't understand why I took so long to see it.'

'Better you realise now than after the event, I suppose,' Joy said philosophically, lifting the teapot and topping up both their cups.

'I'm sorry, it's going to cost a fortune.'

'Whatever it costs, it will be cheaper than a divorce both financially and in emotional wear and tear.'

'It would have been cheaper still if I'd never agreed to marry Sam in the first place.'

'Money's not the issue, Judy. Your happiness is, and it's only a few lost deposits.'

'Not to mention the dress, the veil, the accessories and those . . .' Judy only just managed to stop herself from swearing, 'pink flock bridesmaids' dresses.'

'Ena liked the material and Mrs Howells's daughter's

pattern so much I'm sure she'll keep them until Sam finds himself another bride.'

Despite the guilt that gnawed inside her, Judy laughed. 'I suppose I'd better go home and pack up the engagement presents.'

'The ones that were given by Sam's family,' Joy agreed. 'I certainly don't want mine back and I can't see Lily and Martin, or Katie and John taking theirs back either. It's just as well that the wedding presents hadn't started coming in.'

'I'll write to everyone we sent an invitation to and tell them the wedding's been called off.' Judy finished the tea in her cup. 'The sooner I start, the sooner I can post them.'

'Why don't you move in here for a couple of days?' Joy suggested. 'That way I can help you to organise everything that needs to be done. You know Roy and Billy would love to have you stay.'

'No,' Judy refused, 'but thank you for asking.'

'You're afraid of seeing Sam in the street?'

'I'm not afraid of seeing Sam anywhere now that I've finally said what I needed to say to him. I live on my own, I like living on my own, and I don't need to run home to mother every time something goes wrong.'

'It wouldn't be like that, Judy.'

Judy left her chair and kissed her mother's cheek. 'Thank you for asking, but I really am all right. In fact,' she gave her mother a tight smile, 'I am more all right than I have been in a long time.'

'This place is set in pretty countryside,' Helen observed lamely, as she removed her gloves, folded them into her coat pocket and draped her coat and scarf over an empty chair.

'Yes,' Maggie concurred, 'it's also isolated. How did you get here?'

'I drove.'

'You have a car?'

'Yes, but it's not mine; it belongs to the warehouse where I'm a buyer in ladies' and children's fashion.' Helen made a conscious effort to stop talking. She felt that the conversation between her and Maggie was ridiculous given the circumstances, but she couldn't bring herself to mention Jack – not yet.

'It sounds like an interesting job.'

'It is.'

They sat opposite one another for a moment, both staring out of the window. Helen was surprised to see Lily walking with a pregnant girl in the grounds but she was too preoccupied to recognise Emily.

'I . . .'

'I . . .'

They both fell silent as they tried to speak at the same time.

'You first.' Helen summoned enough courage to look Maggie in the eye. Maggie couldn't meet her gaze for more than a couple of seconds.

'I was going to say I'm sorry, but that sounds pathetic in view of what I've done to you.' When Helen remained silent, she added, 'I know how hurtful this is for you and how you feel.'

'You can't possibly know how I feel!' As Helen's anger erupted, she realised that despite her initial pity for Maggie, she couldn't forgive her – or Jack for betraying her.

'Yes, I do – a little,' Maggie divulged bleakly. 'When Gordon received his posting to Cyprus, he went on ahead because I had just given birth to our fourth child. By the time I arrived with our children two months later, he was having an affair with a Greek woman fifteen years younger than him and ten years younger than me. I could have scratched her eyes out – and his.'

'Did she have Gordon's child?' Helen enquired acidly.

'No, but it was still devastating to discover that my husband had committed the most intimate and sacred act of married life with another woman.'

'Yet, that didn't stop you from committing the same act with my husband.'

'No. I'm—'

'Very sorry,' Helen interrupted curtly, unwilling to listen to another apology.

'Jack came to see me.'

'So you wrote.'

'He's been twice,' Maggie continued quietly. 'If I'd had any idea of the damage my letter to him would do to your marriage, I would never have let him know that I was having his child.'

'Then why did you write to him?' Helen questioned starkly. 'From what both of you have said, it wasn't as if you had an long-standing affair or even meant anything to one another.'

'We didn't have an affair and we don't mean anything to one another.'

'But you do now.' Helen glared at Maggie's bump.

After another interminable silence, Maggie asked, 'Are you religious?'

Taken aback by the question, Helen took a few seconds to answer. 'Not especially. I used to go to church when I was younger and I still go now and again.'

'Easter, Christmas, weddings and funerals.' Maggie deliberately omitted christenings.

'That's about it.'

'My father is a vicar. The first lesson he taught me was to be constantly aware of my human weakness and frailty because if I didn't fight the temptations of the flesh I would become a sinner in the eyes of God. He was right. If I hadn't defied God and broken one of his commandments, this would never have happened and I wouldn't have hurt you and Jack, sullied Gordon's memory, and risked my own and my children's reputations. And now all I can say is that I am truly sorry and beg your forgiveness.' Her eyes were tormented, tortured as she finally looked across at Helen. 'Do you think that you will ever be able to forgive me?'

Not trusting herself to come up with a coherent answer, Helen shook her head.

'When I discovered I was pregnant, I was appalled. My one consolation was that at least I'd moved out of military circles so Gordon's fellow officers wouldn't find out that I'd betrayed him so soon after his death. But there was my parents' friends, neighbours and family, and I was terrified of having society's damning finger pointed not only at me, but my children.' She knotted her fingers together and stared down at her hands. 'I am ashamed to admit that I tried to kill myself. My only excuse is that I thought my death would be preferable to my shaming Gordon's memory and blighting the lives of our children. If I hadn't been living with my parents, I probably would have succeeded in doing it.'

'What did you do?' Helen wasn't sure why she was asking, but it seemed important.

'The doctor prescribed sleeping pills for me after Gordon was killed. I waited until I was due to pick up a new bottle from the chemist, then I took them all. I didn't realise that my mother had been worried about me since my return from Cyprus and was watching everything I did. It wasn't until I was in the hospital having my stomach pumped that I discovered she had spoken to the doctor and there wasn't even enough in the bottle to kill me, just make me ill. Then it all came out, although my mother had already guessed that I was having a baby and it wasn't Gordon's.'

'But she stood by you.'

'As you see.' Maggie glanced around the sterile lounge. 'She and my father were disgusted and disappointed with me, but my father prides himself on practising Christian forgiveness and charity, even when it comes to his own errant daughter and a scandalous sin that could have adverse repercussions on his career.'

'That must have been hard for you to take.'

Maggie gave Helen a sharp look. 'Yes, it was. But

along with exacting my gratitude, he and my mother also made me see that it was not only Gordon and my children's lives I should consider, or even my own, but this child who has a right to life. How did my father put it?' She pursed her lips as she tried to recall the exact phrase. 'The fruit of transgression who might still live a useful life provided the sin of his conception is kept from him.'

'By lying.'

'Basically,' Maggie agreed wearily. 'But it was easier to allow my parents to take control. I have four other children to consider. They are taking care of them and they arranged my admission here. And it was only when I arrived here that I had time to think about the father of my child. Until then I hadn't even considered him, only my children, Gordon's memory and myself. It was easy for me to find out Jack's address. The doctor who looked after him in the military hospital had been a friend of my husband. He knew how devastated I was by Gordon's death and it was he who suggested I meet Jack, because Jack was the last person to talk to Gordon . . .' She blinked hard in an effort to stop tears from forming in her eyes. 'I talked it over with a vicar who calls here and he persuaded me that Jack had the right to know that he had fathered a child.'

' "If only to pray for its well-being",' Helen quoted.

'Jack said you'd read my letter.'

'Jack gave it to me.'

'I would never have written it if I'd known that Jack would take the responsibility of the child so seriously.'

'Then you don't know Jack very well.'

'I don't know him at all,' Maggie conceded.

'He hasn't told you that I can't have children?'

Maggie stared at Helen, horror struck. 'I had no idea. Jack talked about you, of course. That day he came to see me when he was released from hospital. He said how much he missed you and how he couldn't wait to go home and be with you again . . . I am so sorry, so very, very sorry . . .'

'I look at those hills after living on the cliff above Caswell and I feel as if they are hemming me in,' Emily confided to Lily, as they walked along the path that marked the border between the garden and the fields behind the house. 'I'm used to great big open spaces, the sea, the beach . . .' Lily stumbled. 'Are you feeling all right?'

'Just a bit faint,' Lily confessed, lagging behind. 'I forgot to eat breakfast this morning.' She took a deep breath and the world wavered around her. There was a bench in front of her. She reached out, intending to grab it, then fell headlong into a grey-black, buzzing world.

'There's a commotion in the garden.' Helen rose to her feet and looked through the window.

'Probably one of the girls going into labour. Jean is due this week.' Resting her hands on the arms of her chair, Maggie heaved herself up. 'I'll walk you to the door.'

'There's no need.'

'Mrs Clay!' One of the staff burst through the door. 'Your friend has been taken ill outside.'

Helen ran headlong through the door and up the corridor into the hall in time to see Lily being wheeled into the house by a girl she vaguely recognised and a member of staff. Lily's head was lolling at an uncomfortable angle in the wheelchair and it took a moment for Helen to realise that she was unconscious. Then she looked down at Lily's legs and saw blood trickling down her stockings.

'Mrs Jones, go into my office and call an ambulance. Then call the doctor. His number is pinned on the board to the right of the door. If he's home, he'll get here before the ambulance,' Matron shouted. 'You,' she snapped her fingers at the member of staff. 'Wheel her into the treatment room. Now!'

*

'We were born too soon, Jack.' Brian fumbled blindly for the plate of chocolate biscuits from behind the *Sunday People*. 'It says here that the last National Service call up will be in nineteen-sixty.'

'If I'd known, I would have gone to ground for a few years.'

'Like where?'

'One of my mate's brothers joined a travelling fair.' Jack picked up his cup.

'They'll catch up with him sooner or later and I wouldn't like to be him when they do.' Hearing the clink of crockery Brian handed Jack his cup. 'Pour me one too while you're at it, mate. Only more sugar this time.'

'I put in three last time.'

'Then I obviously need four.'

Too depressed after his talk with John and Katie to argue, Jack went into the kitchen. The teapot was cold so he filled the kettle and set it on the gas to boil. While he was emptying and rinsing the pot he looked out of the window. Martin was in the garden forking over the vegetable plot that Roy had so carefully tended and nurtured when he'd lived in the house. His face, jeans and sweater were covered in dirt but even from that distance Jack could see that he was smiling. But then he wasn't an idiot who'd cheated on his wife.

The telephone rang and Brian shouted, 'I'll get it.'

'About time you did something around here,' Jack called back, rinsing the teapot in warm water. He heard Brian talking. As Brian's voice pitched higher and grew more anxious, he hoped it wasn't anything to do with the garage. If he lost his job on top of everything else, he'd have nothing left.

'Where's Martin?' Brian ran through the door.

'In the garden. What's wrong?'

'That was Helen on the telephone.'

'Helen . . .'

'She's fine,' Brian said impatiently. 'But Lily's ill. It sounds serious.'

*

Helen set the receiver down on the telephone in the matron's office and steadied herself on the desk.

'The staff here are good here in an emergency. I've watched them dozens of times,' Maggie reassured her.

'If Lily had said that she felt ill . . .'

'Emily said she collapsed without warning.'

'Mrs Clay?' The matron walked into the office. 'Your sister-in-law is haemorrhaging. The doctor is doing everything he can to try to stabilise her, but her condition is too critical at present for her to be moved, even to hospital. However, her baby still has a strong heartbeat.'

'Lily's pregnant?'

'You didn't know?'

'No.' Helen shook her head and she remembered how sensitive Lily was. Lily, even more than Katie and Judy, had felt for her when she had lost her baby and that was before she had confided that she couldn't have any more children. She would have been the last person Lily would have broken her good news to.

'Would this be a wanted child?' the matron asked.

Resenting the woman's implication, Helen retorted, 'Very much so. Lily and Martin have been married for two years. They have everything, a house all paid for . . .'

'I am sure that the doctor will do everything he can to help your sister-in-law and her baby. Did you manage to get hold of her husband?'

'Yes, he's on his way.'

'How long will it take him to get here?'

Helen tried to recall how long it had taken her and Lily to drive to the house. 'An hour and a half at the most.'

The matron glanced at the clock. 'We should know more by then.'

'I still say I should drive Marty to this place.'

'For Christ's sake, Jack, Helen is with Lily,' Brian reminded, 'and the last thing Martin and Lily need right now is for you and Helen to start quarrelling.'

'We wouldn't!'

'Whatever, but you'd make a bad situation even worse.' Brian looked up, as Martin stampeded down the stairs in clean trousers, his shirt and belt flapping, his fly open. He grabbed his jacket.

'Ready?' Martin demanded.

'I will be when you zip up your trousers.' Brian pulled the car keys from his trouser pocket and checked that he had his wallet and chequebook. 'Let's go.'

'You'll let me know what's happening,' Jack shouted, as they ran through the front door leaving it wide open behind them.

Neither Brian nor Martin answered. Jumping into Brian's car, they drove off at breakneck speed.

'And that's all Helen said?' Martin pressed Brian for the tenth time in as many minutes.

'That Lily had collapsed and it looked serious. She then gave me the address – you have looked it up?'

'Yes,' Martin folded the map back on the square around Cartref. Try as he might, he couldn't make the miles between Swansea and the house any less than twenty-four. 'I should have insisted on going with her. She said I'd cramp her style, or perhaps I said it and she agreed.'

'If you don't sit back in that seat and take it easy, Marty, you are going to drive yourself mad or to the point of collapse, and then we'll have two sick people to cope with.' When Martin continued to sit poised on the edge of his seat, one hand on the door handle as though he were about to jump out of the car at any moment, Brian tried to distract him. 'Why did Helen and Lily drive up into the wilds of Carmarthenshire anyway?'

'To see the woman who is having Jack's baby.'

As Brian turned to Martin, he momentarily lost concentration.

'Watch out!' Martin grabbed the wheel and turned it seconds before they would have hit the kerb. 'Perhaps I should drive.'

'In your state?'

'Yours is so much better,' Martin retorted sardonically.

'Run that sentence by me again. The one where you said something along the lines of a woman having Jack's baby.'

'You heard it.'

'Christ! No wonder Helen threw him out.'

'Can we please just get there,' Martin shouted, as Brian slowed the car.

'As soon as I can, Marty,' Brian checked his rear-view mirror to make sure there wasn't a police car behind them. 'Just as soon as I can.'

'You are going to wear yourself out, Helen, and your tea's getting cold,' Maggie advised, as Helen paced restlessly from one side of the lounge to the other. All the residents were in the dining room eating their 'high' Sunday tea, which meant the addition of a round of meat paste sandwiches to the usual cake or scone. But as Maggie was supposed to be Helen's sister-in-law and Helen had asserted that Lily was hers, the matron had given permission for Maggie and Helen to eat their tea in the lounge, an unheard of privilege that neither recipient was in a state to appreciate.

'You can't expect me to sit and drink tea when Lily could be dying.' Helen tensed her fists impotently. 'I'll never forgive myself if anything happens to her. I had no business asking her to come here with me. I had no right . . .'

'You weren't to know that she was going to be taken ill, and if you don't mind me saying so, you are not helping your sister-in-law by getting yourself into a state,' Maggie said decisively. 'The best thing you can do for her now is to be strong when her husband arrives. He may need you.'

There was an authoritative tone to Maggie's voice that

suggested she was used to making decisions and being obeyed. As Helen stared at her, she blushed.

'I'm sorry, that's the sergeant's wife coming out in me. We are – I was – expected to look after the wives and children of the ranks.'

'You're right,' Helen said shortly. 'I am not helping Lily by getting myself into a state and I won't be any use to Martin if I carry on like this. It's just that I hope . . . that she doesn't lose her baby as I lost mine,' she finished quickly, fighting emotion as memories of the worst time in her life came flooding back.

Maggie moved instinctively closer and almost put her arm around Helen, but remembering the situation between them, thought better of the idea. 'You heard the matron, the doctor is doing everything he can for your friend and her baby.' She pulled a chair next to Helen and, to her relief, Helen finally sat down. 'I can't tell you everything is going to be fine, because it might not be, but at least she has you for a friend and because you've been through the same experience you will be able to help her.'

'You must have been good . . . as a sergeant's wife,' Helen said. 'Good at dealing with the problems of the wives and children of the other ranks.'

'I'm not sure I was good at giving advice, but I liked trying to help people. It was a peculiar life in a way, not really mine or even my choice, it just went with what my husband did for a living. And I did love him. Very much, perhaps in a way too much.'

'Because of the other woman.'

'Other women,' Maggie corrected, with a touch of resentment.

'More than one?'

'It was an accepted part of army life and no wife I knew dared question it, publicly that is. Plenty, including me, tackled our husbands in private about their behaviour. But the men frequently went away for months at a time and during those months they always seemed to manage to organise themselves a social life of sorts that included women amongst the recreational activities, even when they were posted to the wilds of Africa. We wives on the other hand were stuck in married quarters with the children, immersed in trivia and domesticity. The highlight of our social calendar was the odd coffee morning or bring-and-buy to raise funds for the children's Christmas party.'

'So you're saying it's normal for soldiers to have affairs with other women?'

'More like one night stopovers than affairs,' Maggie answered thoughtlessly, not realising the implication of her words in relation to her own predicament until it was too late.

'So Jack . . .'

'From what he told me, Helen, there wasn't anyone else for him except you and if it hadn't been for the grief and the wine . . .'

'If you don't mind, I'd rather not hear any more.'

Maggie looked up at the clock. It had been half an hour since Helen had telephoned Swansea and twenty-five minutes since the matron had left them to return to the treatment room. Her father had told her she had always been too impatient. Waiting for events good or bad was, for her, the worst possible kind of torture.

'You just passed it,' Martin shouted.

'You sure?' Brian asked.

'There was a plaque on the wall that said Cartref,' Martin bellowed angrily.

'All right, no need to yell, I'm doing my best.' The brakes screeched in protestation as Brian slammed to a halt. Ramming the car into reverse, he executed a hair-raising three-point turn and hurtled back along the road they'd driven.

Martin had the door open before Brian stopped the car. Diving out, he charged up to the front door and rang the bell, keeping his finger on the button until he heard footsteps. 'I'm Martin Clay, Lily Clay's husband,' he blurted breathlessly to the women who opened the door. 'I had a call to say she'd been taken ill.'

'Martin.' Helen ran down the corridor and into the hall. The member of staff moved back, as she flung her arms around his neck and hugged him.

'How is Lily?' he enquired urgently, drawing away from her.

As Helen tried to tell him in as few words as possible that the last she'd heard, Lily was unconscious, Brian joined them.

'Mrs Clay is extremely ill and needs to rest, which is totally impossible given the noise level in this hall.' The matron looked disapprovingly from Martin to Brian. 'I take it that one of you is Mr Clay.'

'I am.' Extricating himself from Helen, Martin stepped closer to the matron. 'How is my wife?'

'Not at all well,' the matron replied with irritating imprecision.

'Can I see her?'

'The doctor is with her.'

'I am her husband.'

There was a resolution in Martin's demeanour that unsettled the matron. 'I'll check with him as to whether or not it is advisable for you to see her.'

'I will see her,' he called after her, as she walked away. 'She is my wife. You can't stop me from seeing her.'

'Martin, there is something that you should know.' Helen stood beside him.

'Not now, Helen,' Martin stared after the matron's retreating figure, noting exactly where she was going.

'Lily is pregnant.'

'What?' He whirled around.

Helen swallowed hard. 'The matron told me. She asked if the baby was wanted.'

'The bitch!'

'Marty, come out here for a minute.' Unlike Martin, Brian was aware of whispering behind closed doors. He had no idea how many people were listening in on them, but he felt that any inmate, staff or resident, who overheard Martin call the matron a bitch wasn't likely to be sympathetic. He led Martin back through the main door into the anteroom set off the porch.

'Lily never said a word . . .'

'She wouldn't, Marty,' Brian said softly, as he pushed him down on to the cold stone bench and sat beside him. 'She wanted you to buy into the business and she had enough trouble persuading you to take up that overdraft she organised as it was. She knew that you would never have done it if she'd told you that she was pregnant.'

'You're right. I was so terrified of failing her. If I'd known she was pregnant and would have to give up work, I would have walked away from the whole proposition.' He looked at Brian accusingly. 'Did she tell you that she was going to have a baby?'

'No, I had no idea.'

'Helen?' He looked to where she stood, hovering miserably in the doorway.

'She didn't confide in me, but given what's happened between Jack and me, she wouldn't have, Marty.'

Martin sat forward and sunk his head in his hands, running his fingers through his hair. 'All the signs were there, only I was too stupid to see them. She was putting on weight; she wouldn't even have a glass of sherry the other night. Why on earth didn't she tell me?'

'Because she thought you wouldn't want a baby now, of all times,' Brian suggested brutally.

'Of course we want a baby. We talked it over, we even . . . but that was before you turned up with the garage proposal . . .'

'Mr Clay.' The matron appeared in the doorway.

Martin rose to his feet. 'Can I see my wife?'

'Yes, but only for a few minutes and only if you promise not to upset her.'

'She is my wife . . .' Martin fell silent, realising his voice had risen – again.

'She only regained consciousness a quarter of an hour ago. She needs to be kept very quiet.'

'The baby?' he asked.

'It's too early to say yet whether or not the baby can be saved. If you'd like to come with me.'

As Martin followed the matron into the house, Brian looked at Helen. 'I would offer to buy you a cup of tea but there doesn't appear to be a café around here, not that I can see anyway.'

'I don't think there is one.' She took Martin's place on the stone bench beside him. 'You got here quickly.'

'If Marty'd had his way, we would have been here half an hour earlier with a smoking engine.'

'He lives for Lily. I'm not sure he'd cope if anything happened to her.'

'Like Jack isn't coping without you.'

'Jack doesn't even know I'm not there.'

'I've never seen him so miserable.'

'Which is why he hasn't even bothered to contact me.' She looked Brian in the eye. 'Has he told you what he did?'

'No, but Martin explained on the way here.'

'Lily wouldn't even be here with me if Jack had managed to keep his trousers zipped up.'

'We all make mistakes, Helen, and from what Martin told me it only happened once.'

'And that makes it all right?' she challenged. 'How about if I make a mistake just once and get pregnant by another man?'

'It's different for a woman . . .' He faltered and considered what he was about to say.

'It is, Brian,' she agreed bitterly. 'We're the ones left holding the baby.' She rose from the cold seat and paced to a tiny mullioned window set with thick, opaque glass. 'Lily's only here because of the bloody awful mess Jack made and I had no right to ask her to come here with me . . .'

'Lily's your sister-in-law as well as one of your closest friends; you had every right to ask her to come here with you. And there was no way of knowing that anything like this was going to happen.'

'Please, you're making things worse.'

'Then I'll keep my mouth shut.' Leaving the seat, he stood beside her and took her cold hand into his.

'I'm glad you're here,' she murmured after a while. 'Do you think Lily will be all right?'

'She had better be.'

'But if she isn't?'

'Don't even think it, Helen.' He led her back to the bench. 'Please don't even think it,' he repeated fervently.

'I have given her morphine,' the doctor warned Martin, drawing him aside outside the treatment room. 'It is a risk but she needs to be kept as quiet as possible if this child is to have a chance of surviving to anything like full term.'

'We want the baby, doctor, but it is Lily I am concerned about . . . she will be all right, won't she?' Martin demanded.

'That's impossible to predict at this stage.'

'Shouldn't she be in hospital?'

'It's a long journey from here to the nearest hospital and she's had a slight haemorrhage. Move her and we risk further blood loss. If that turns into a full-blown haemorrhage, there is a real possibility that she could die on the way there. Our best hope is to stabilise her by bed rest here. If she remains quiet and settled, we can move her into hospital in a few days' time.' The doctor was old but something in Martin's face reminded him of what it was like to be young. He patted him on the shoulder. 'Twenty-four to forty-eight hours and we'll know a lot more, son. They have some medical facilities here. I've taken a blood sample and once we find out her type we'll be able to order some in case we need to do a transfusion here.'

'There's nothing else you can do?'

'Not here. Go and see her, but remember she needs to be kept calm and quiet.'

Lily was lying on an examination couch covered by a white sheet and a red blanket that made her pallor all the more noticeable. The woman who had been sitting with her moved away as Martin walked in, and withdrew with the matron. Martin was too concerned with Lily to notice that the matron had left the door ajar. He walked over the couch and clasped Lily's hand. Lily opened her eyes and smiled. Then the smile died on her lips.

'I'm having a baby, Marty, I'm sorry I should have—'

'It's all right, darling.' He smoothed her long, dark hair away from her forehead. Someone had unclipped her French pleat and it tumbled around her shoulders. 'The doctor said you have to rest. I'll stay with you.'

'No, Marty, you have to work in the garage.'

'I'm not leaving you, Lily, not like this.'

'You don't mind about the baby,' she mumbled, her eyelids drooping from the effects of the morphine.

'We'll teach him everything we know, darling,' he promised. 'Everything will be all right. You'll see. Everything will be all right.'

Chapter Nineteen

Martin sat back in the visitor's chair in Matron's office and looked her in the eye. 'I am not leaving this house until Lily is out of danger.' His voice was low but steady, and there was no mistaking his determination.

'Danger or not, you cannot stay here, young man,' she refuted officiously in the tone of voice she used to address the residents. 'This is a women's hostel. I cannot allow a man to remain in the house overnight.'

'And if my wife should be taken worse?'

'There is a pub a couple of miles down the road,' the doctor suggested, overhearing the impasse. 'I believe they have a couple of rooms they let out. If Mr Clay books in there and telephones you with the number, you can contact him if there is any change in Mrs Clay's condition during the night, Matron.'

'As long as he leaves this house in the next five minutes,' she sniffed, clearly annoyed by the doctor's proposal. 'I am answerable to the committee for the moral welfare of the residents . . .'

'You must grant that the circumstances are exceptional, Matron.' The doctor scribbled a note on a pad and handed it to her. 'If you don't need me during the night, I will be back to check on the patient first thing in the morning. If you'd care to call in around nine o'clock tomorrow morning, Mr Clay, you can see your wife for a few minutes.'

'Provided she is well enough to receive visitors,' the matron cautioned, ensuring they both understood exactly who was in charge.

Realising from the obdurate expression on the matron's face that he wasn't going to receive a more generous offer, Martin muttered a conciliatory, 'Thank you.'

'Telephone as soon as you book a room, Mr Clay,' the matron ordered. 'Our residents go to bed early. I don't want them disturbed after their nine o'clock curfew.'

As he left the office and closed the door behind him he overheard the doctor say, 'I'd almost forgotten what it feels like to oversee a pregnancy where the baby is not only wanted but actually welcome.'

'Can you come up with a better idea?' Brian questioned. He, Martin and Helen sat in a corner of the pub lounge drinking tea, all that the landlord would serve them on a Sunday, although Martin had booked a room for the night.

'No,' Martin admitted.

'Then it's settled. You keep my car and I drive Helen back to Swansea. She shouldn't be driving while she's upset.'

'I am not too upset to drive,' Helen protested angrily.

'All right, you are not too upset to drive,' Brian conceded, ignoring her hysteria, 'but I can't think of any other way that will give Martin the transport he needs while he's stuck out here in the wilds. There's no train and no station for miles and if this road is on a bus route, I didn't see any stops and shelters when we drove here.'

'You are not driving me home,' Helen insisted dogmatically. 'I am an adult, not a child to be looked after.'

'You can drop me off on Walter's Road. I'll walk to Carlton Terrace from there,' Brian compromised.

'Then I'm driving . . .'

'From Walter's Road to Limeslade and, before you say any more, I make a lousy passenger. I shout, I curse, I swear, I unnerve even experienced drivers. Ask Martin if you don't believe me.' He turned to Martin, hoping for confirmation, but his friend remained sunk into his own thoughts – or more likely, misery.

'You're not insured to drive my car. It belongs to the warehouse.'

'As manager of a garage, I am insured to drive anything.' Brian gave Helen a tight, conciliatory smile before tapping Martin's shoulder. 'Cigarette, mate?' He offered Martin the packet.

'Thanks.' Martin took one.

'Do you want me to come back up here in the morning with some clothes for you and Lily?'

'There's no point you bringing anything until I know what's happening. And as it's unlikely they'll let me see Lily for more than a few minutes, I'll have enough time to go back to the house and fetch whatever we need if she has to stay here.'

Brian picked up Helen's car keys from the table. 'Phone me in the morning, or sooner if there's any change. I'll either be at home or the garage.'

'The garage . . .'

'Don't worry, Jack and I will keep the place standing until you're in a position to come back to work,' Brian assured him.

'As long as you don't try to do any servicing or repairs.'

'We know our limitations.' Brian glanced at his watch. 'It's nearly eight o'clock. You'd better give that matron a ring. As soon as you've given her the number of this place and checked how Lily is, we'll be on our way.'

'"Resting" has to be good, doesn't it?' Helen asked Brian after they had driven in silence for ten minutes.

'It has to be better than not resting.'

'How you can make jokes at a time like this?'

'I was being serious,' he countered softly, realising that although both their nerves had been frayed by the traumatic events of the afternoon, guilt had driven her perilously close to breaking point. 'The doctor said Lily needed rest. She is resting and that has to be good.' He slowed the car as they approached a humpbacked bridge. 'You hungry?'

'I ought to be, but I'm not.'

'There might be a fish and chip shop open somewhere.'

'I doubt it, not on a Sunday in this Godly, chapel ridden area of Wales. Besides I couldn't eat a thing.'

Brian glanced across at her. 'You do have food in your house?'

'Yes, and don't you start.'

'Start what?'

'Telling me I've lost weight.'

'You have, haven't you?' he challenged.

'Some,' she conceded abruptly.

'Did you have a chance to say goodbye to the lady you went to visit?' Brian was aware that he was broaching a difficult subject, but he was also too tired to think of a less controversial topic of conversation, and talk – even strained and difficult talk – had to be less wearing than the silence that had blighted the outset of their journey.

'No,' Helen replied shortly.

'Tell me to mind my own business if you want, but I find it difficult to understand why you went to see her.'

'Curiosity.'

'I heard that killed the cat.' Brian passed Helen his cigarettes and lighter. 'Light one for me, please.'

'I wanted to know what she was like.' Helen lit two cigarettes, kept one and handed him the other.

'And was she what you expected?'

'She was much older than I thought she would be, nice enough I suppose, but plain and dowdy. She's probably old enough to be Jack's mother,' she revealed, more shocked by the thought than she had been in Maggie's presence.

'So, what happens to you and Jack now?'

Helen considered Brian's question. She didn't have to imagine life without Jack when she had only spent five weeks with him in the last two and half years. Three before he left for Cyprus and two after he'd returned. The last two had been wonderful from the moment he had shattered the awkwardness and embarrassment of their reunion by persuading her to climb into bed with him, but now she felt that even the memorable night of his homecoming was tainted. 'I don't know. I divorce him, I suppose.'

'Is that what you want, Helen?' he asked gently.

'It's not a question of what I want,' she retorted. 'More like a question of what Jack did.'

'And you can't forgive him.'

'No,' she rejoined vehemently.

He glanced across at her silhouette, dark against the streetlights of Ammanford. 'Not even if it means giving up what could be fifty years of happy marriage?'

'You think I could be happy with Jack after he cheated on me?' There was raw anguish in her voice.

'Only you can answer that. But before you do, I think you should know that two of the happiest people I've seen in my life were you and Jack on the night of his homecoming party.'

'Appearances can be deceptive.'

'Yes, they can, and I've said more than I should have on a subject I know nothing about.'

'Marriage.'

'I can't even make a go of courtship.'

'There wasn't anyone else after Judy?' she fished.

'Dozens,' he laughed, deliberately lightening the atmosphere. 'That was the problem. I couldn't make up my mind which one I wanted.'

'Then you didn't really want any of them.'

'That's what my mother said.'

'Wise woman, your mother.'

'She is.' He blew a smoke circle as they stopped at a road junction. 'Perhaps you should have a word with her about your problems with Jack some time,' he suggested.

'I don't think so,' she said politely.

'So, do you want me to telephone you at home or in

the warehouse when Martin rings me tomorrow with news of Lily?' he asked, changing the subject.

Jack had finished cleaning the kitchen cupboards and was mopping the floor when he heard a knock on the connecting door between the basement and the rest of the house. He opened it to see Sam standing halfway up the stairs.

'Why the knock?'

'Because this is an official visit.'

'I see no uniform.'

'Not police business.' Sam pushed past him and looked around the kitchen. 'Where's Brian?'

'Somewhere in Carmarthenshire.'

'What's the stupid bugger doing there?'

'He went with Martin – on business,' Jack prevaricated, sensing Sam was in a belligerent mood. 'Did you drink the pub dry?' he asked, inhaling beer fumes.

'I had a couple of drinks before dinner in my mother's house. That's not a crime, is it?' Sam bit back nastily.

'You're the copper, you tell me.' Jack lifted the mop head into the sink, rinsed it under the running tap and squeezed it dry.

'So when is he coming back?'

'Who?' Jack emptied the bucket, washed it out and dropped the mop into it.

'The King of Sheba,' Sam growled. 'Bloody Brian, of course.'

'I have absolutely no idea.' Jack opened the door to the scullery and pushed the mop and bucket into a corner.

'I want to see him.'

'My mother always used to say, "I want doesn't get".'

'Very funny.'

'As you see, he's not here and I can't conjure him from nowhere.'

'Can't conjure who from nowhere?' Brian dropped his front door key on to the kitchen table.

'You! Damned poaching bastard!' Drawing his fist

back, Sam punched with all his strength, sending Brian reeling into the passage.

Helen shivered when she walked into her house. If anything, it was even colder indoors than out. She loved sitting in the living room in the evening in front of a real fire, but she hated cleaning the grate and re-laying it and a coal fire was proving impractical when she was out at work all day. Even if she made it up before she left the house in the morning, and this time she hadn't, it took three to four hours of steady burning for the fire to bring the room to a comfortable enough temperature to sit in.

Judy had tried to persuade her to buy a gas fire when she had lived with her, but reluctant to block her fireplaces with permanent fittings, she had compromised and settled for electric. Unlike gas, the electric fires could be lifted in and out of the grates and although they were more expensive to run, she had been able to cling to the notion that the time would come when she would have a coal fire burning in every room.

That mythical, perfect time that she had planned, lived and waited for. *When Jack comes home. When the house is finished. When everything is exactly the way I want it. When I have time to light a fire in every room and live the way I always intended . . .*

Still in her coat, she switched on the electric fire in the kitchen and carried the fire from the dining room into the living room. Setting it on the ash-strewn hearth she plugged it in. Jack was home, the house was finished, everything was exactly as she dreamed it would be – except for Jack's absence and the signs of domestic neglect – and she still hadn't the time, or the inclination to light a fire in every room.

Sinking into the easy chair next to the fireplace, she looked around the room. Dust lay thick and grey, dulling the surfaces of the coffee table and cupboards. She traced a line along the table with her forefinger and looked at the coal-smudged hearthrug. She hadn't done any housework since Jack had left. No cleaning, washing or cooking. She had used the house like a hotel, going from bed to work and back, buying underclothes and stockings in the warehouse rather than start on the pile of washing stacked in the scullery. Whatever had happened between her and Jack, or would or wouldn't happen between them in the future, one thing was certain, she couldn't carry on living like this.

She glanced at the clock. It was after nine. The washing could wait, she could even cheat and take it to the laundrette on her way to work in the morning, but there was no way she could continue to sit in a room that looked this way. She went into the hall, opened the cupboard under the stairs and took out the vacuum cleaner, dustpan and brush, a duster and a tin of wax polish.

Jack pinned Sam's arm high behind his back and slammed him, face forward, into the kitchen wall. He looked over his shoulder at Brian. 'I've got him. You all right?'

'I'll tell you in five minutes.' Brian staggered to the sink and ran the cold tap. 'Is it too much to ask what that was for, Sam?' He wrung out a tea towel and held it against the side of his head.

'As if you didn't know!' Sam bellowed, fighting to shake Jack off.

'Stay still or I'll hurt you,' Jack threatened.

Brian lifted the tea towel away from his cheekbone. It was bright red with blood.

'You're going to have one hell of a shiner,' Jack predicted, 'and that cut will need stitching.'

Brian looked in the mirror above the sink and examined the damage to his face. 'This is a clear case of grievous bodily harm, Sam.'

'And what would you call what you did to me?' Sam countered antagonistically.

'I've done bugger all to you.'

'Only taken my bloody fiancée.'

'Judy.' Brian stared at Sam's reflection in the mirror.

'Don't come all wide-eyed innocence with me. She broke off our engagement today.'

'Judy finished with you?' Brian whirled around.

'As if you hadn't bloody put her up it!'

'I haven't seen Judy since the last time she was here.' Brian blinked hard as blood seeped down his face and dripped on to his pullover. As he clamped the tea towel back over his cheek, he realised his right eye was already closing up.

'You expect me to believe that?' Sam challenged.

'Believe what you damned well want.' Brian lurched unsteadily, leaned over the sink again and retched.

'You need to get to hospital,' Jack advised, twisting Sam's arm even higher in an effort to stop him from struggling. 'If I release you, Sam, will you go downstairs and stay there?'

'I'll kill the bastard . . .'

'That's what I was afraid of.' As Brian ran the cold tap again, Jack frogmarched Sam into the hall and yelled, 'Mike,' at the top of his voice through the open door that led to the basement.

'He's on duty,' Sam crowed.

'Then I'll call the station.'

Jack's threat to telephone the police brought Sam to his senses. 'I had every right to be angry . . .'

'You had no right whatsoever to attack Brian,' Jack lectured coldly. Freeing one hand, while keeping the other firmly clamped on Sam's arm, he held open the basement door. 'Go downstairs and stay there, or I will call the police.' As Sam stepped on to the stairs, he slammed the door behind him and slid the bolt home. 'Next time you want to come up here, try ringing the front door bell. Although if Martin and Lily have any sense, they'll give you notice to quit the minute they come back.'

*

'I'm all right,' Brian protested irritably when Jack prised the tea towel from his hand after he had finished telling him the news about Lily and Martin.

'I'm taking you to hospital.'

'No, you're not. Where're the spare keys to Martin's car?'

'He keeps them in the drawer in the hall table. Now where do you think you're going?' Jack shouted, as Brian struggled to his feet and left the kitchen.

'Out,' Brian called back, taking the keys and slamming the front door behind him.

Although the pub Martin had booked into was closed, as all the pubs in that area of West Wales were every Sunday, he spent most of the evening in the bar, sitting as close as he could physically get to the telephone. The landlady made him a pot of tea and a round of fatty ham sandwiches as a special favour after informing him that she didn't usually cater on a Sunday. But he discovered her generosity came with a hefty price tag when she presented him with a bill for one pound ten shillings that included the tea she had made for him, Brian and Helen earlier. He had thought the room was expensive at twenty-five shillings a night and, as he emptied his pockets to pay for the food and drink, he reflected that it was just as well Brian had insisted on paying for the room by cheque, in case he needed his cash for something later. If Lily had to remain in the hostel for more than a few days, he'd be making a serious dent in their savings just to remain near her.

The telephone rang twice during the course of the evening and, heart pounding, he jumped to his feet both times, not knowing whether to wish it was the hostel or not. From what the doctor had told him, there was no chance that he'd be able to take Lily home for a couple of days even if she did make a remarkable recovery, and the alternative reason for the matron to contact him was too horrible to contemplate.

Yet he couldn't stop thinking about it, or blaming himself for being pig-headed about the overdraft facility Lily had organised. What if she died? Or survived and lost the baby? A baby that now he knew existed, he wanted to be born healthy and perfect almost as much as he wanted Lily to be well again.

For the first time he understood what she had been trying to tell him, that it was the people in life that mattered, not the material possessions. Even if the garage failed – and if the first week of business was an indicator, it wasn't going to do anything of the sort – he would find another job. And with the rents coming in, they could manage without Lily's salary from the bank. If he hadn't been so stubborn and prickly, she might have confided in him and told him about the baby from the very beginning. Then they could have made plans and looked forward to the birth from the outset of her pregnancy, as his sister and John Griffiths had. Instead, he had behaved so badly that Lily had been afraid to tell him that he was about to become a father. His own wife, afraid of him!

The thought seared into his mind. He might not have hit Lily as his father had beaten his mother, but he had made her fear him. What kind of useless, pathetic husband did that make him?

At half past ten, the landlord and his wife went to bed, after telling him to answer the telephone, as any call in the early hours was unlikely to be for them. They had already informed him that if he needed to leave the pub, the back door was never locked, even at night.

At midnight he climbed the stairs to the room he had rented. It was clean, but that was about all that could be said for it. The furniture was old but graceless, rough and ready, heavy pine pieces that had probably been made for a farmhouse. The floor was planked with boards that looked as though they'd splinter into any bare feet that touched them, and the double bed was covered with a purple and green candlewick bedspread that clashed with the pale blue washed walls.

He had never thought a great deal about décor. His childhood home had been furnished with cast-offs, and the few essentials his mother hadn't been able to scavenge had been acquired as cheaply as possible. For the first time he realised just what an eye for colour and detail Lily had, incorporating the best of the furniture that she had inherited from her aunt with well-chosen new pieces to create a comfortable home for them, which, he was ashamed to realise, he had begun to take for granted.

Sinking down on to the bed, he shivered. The room was not only cold but smelled musty and damp as if no one had slept in it for decades. Kicking off his shoes, he lifted his legs on to the bed, pulled the candlewick bedspread over himself and strained his ears. Alert for a call that he hoped wouldn't come.

Judy checked the list of people to whom she had sent wedding invitations against the pile of envelopes she had stacked on the table. It had taken her most of the evening to address the envelopes. She had composed only ten letters and retreating into cowardice, she had begun with the people she knew were most likely to sympathise with her, like Lily and Martin, John and Katie. As she ran her finger down the seemingly endless list Sam's mother had provided her with, she wondered if it was etiquette to unload the responsibility for contacting Sam's friends and relatives on to him.

Unable to face writing another 'I regret to inform you', she closed her writing case and screwed the top back on to her fountain pen. Stretching her hands above her head, she realised that the hot bath she had soaked in for an indulgent three quarters of an hour earlier, had relaxed her to the point where she could barely keep her eyes open. A cup of cocoa and bed would be wonderful, a glass of sherry and bed absolute luxury. Opting for luxury, she opened the sideboard and took out a bottle of sherry and a glass. She was screwing the top back on to the bottle when the doorbell rang. She pushed aside the curtains and saw Martin's car parked in the street. Furious at the thought that Sam had borrowed it, she dropped the curtains, determined to ignore him. When it rang for the fourth time she ran down the stairs and shouted, 'Go away,' through the closed door.

'I would but I'm dripping blood all over your nice clean doorstep and I think I should mop it up while it's still fresh.'

The voice was familiar but it wasn't Sam's. 'Brian?' she ventured hesitantly.

'Get me a bucket and a scrubbing brush, Judy.'

Acutely aware that she was wearing a thin, artificial silk negligee and nothing beneath it she replied, 'It's late and you're being ridiculous.'

'And bleeding.'

'Is something wrong?' she asked urgently.

'Lily's ill, but—'

'Lily! What's wrong with her?' Her hand flew to her mouth as she wrenched open the door. 'Oh my God, you are bleeding!'

'I told you I was.' He looked down as she switched on the light. 'But I lied about your doorstep.' He pulled deprecatingly at his sweater. 'This has soaked up most of it.'

'You're an idiot.'

'Probably,' he granted mildly. 'I'd like to say you should see the other fellow but as he took me by surprise, he hasn't a scratch on him.'

'You said Lily's ill?'

He told her about Lily collapsing in the unmarried mothers' home, which led to details about Helen's trip to see the woman who was having Jack's baby, but before he could answer all the questions she hurled at him, much less explain everything to her satisfaction, he had to lean against the door post for support. Seeing him sway, she stepped back into the tiny hall.

'You'd better come up,' she conceded, allowing him to walk ahead of her. After she'd fastened the bolt and chain, she turned just in time to prop him up as he stumbled. 'You should never have driven here and in Martin's car too,' she scolded. 'What happened to yours? You haven't had an accident?'

'My car's fine, Martin has it. This,' he pulled Lily's bloodstained tea towel from his pocket and pressed it against the side of his head to staunch the blood he felt trickling down his face, 'is the result of a collision with Sam's fist.' He pulled a chair out from under her table and sat down.

'Sam did that to you! What did you do to him?' She ran into her bathroom to fetch antiseptic and her first aid kit.

'Nothing.'

'He wouldn't hit you without a reason, he's a policeman, for God's sake.' As there wasn't a bowl in the bathroom she dived into the kitchen to get one.

'He told me that you'd broken off your engagement.'

'That is nothing to do with you.' She filled an enamel bowl with cold water. 'I told him it was nothing to do with you,' she repeated angrily, as she returned to the living room and stood transfixed in front of him, clutching the bowl to her chest.

'Is there a clean cloth in there?' He pulled Lily's bloodstained tea towel away from his face and studied it.

'Yes.' Springing into action, she set the bowl on the table and took the ruined tea towel from his hand. 'This is bad . . .'

'Not that bad. Pull the edges together and stick a plaster over it.'

'It should be stitched. If it isn't, you could have a scar . . .'

'We'll tell our grandchildren it was honourably won.'

She met his gaze as she pressed the clean cloth over his cut. 'What did you say?'

'You heard.'

'Brian . . .'

'You love me,' he said simply. 'Almost as much as I

love you and I could kick myself for not seeing it before Sam did. But then Sam did the kicking for me. And he did us a favour. Left to our own devices I'm not sure that either of us would have said anything to the other. In fact I was hoping for an invite to your wedding.'

Still holding the cloth against his head, she dropped abruptly on to the chair next to his.

He closed his hand over hers and took the cloth from her. 'The plaster,' he reminded. 'Otherwise I'm likely to bleed all over your carpet.'

'It's not a very good carpet.'

'I agree, but it will look even worse with my blood all over it.'

She could feel colour flooding into her cheeks as she opened her first aid kit. Taking out a roll of plaster and a pair of scissors she murmured, 'How big shall I cut it?'

'How about as big as the cut?'

'Brian . . .'

'Yes,' he prompted eagerly when she fell silent.

'I wish you'd let me drive you to hospital.'

'You'd create a sensation dressed like that. They'd even walk out of the morgue to take a look.' He circled her waist with his hands as she stood in front of him and cleaned the cut.

'Are you never serious?'

'I am serious.' He winced, as she wrung the cloth out in fresh antiseptic and water and reapplied it. 'You would create a riot if you went out in that. Want to try it and see?' he dared.

'No, and I would put on decent clothes before I drove you to the hospital.'

'That would be a shame, I prefer you in indecent outfits. Ow!' he cried, as she dabbed at the cut to dry it. 'You're no Florence Nightingale.'

'No one ever spoke to Florence Nightingale the way you've just spoken to me.'

'How do you know some of her patients didn't fancy her?'

'I read the history books. She never married and was too busy ministering to the sick to have a boyfriend.' After judging the length of his wound, she cut a piece of plaster and covered it.

'That anyone knew about. She could have been a secretive lady.'

'I doubt it.'

He slid his hands upwards from her waist. She could feel his fingers warm, burning her skin through the wafer thin silk as he caressed her back. 'I like you in white silk and,' he grinned at the colour in her cheeks, 'beetroot complexion.' He grabbed her and pulled her on to his lap before she could protest. Jamming her between him and the table, he covered her mouth with his and kissed her long and thoroughly. 'Now tell me that you don't love me.'

'Why did you walk away from me that day on Swansea station?' she asked soberly.

'I told you at Helen's party. Because I was angry, young and stupid at the time. Angry because you wouldn't come back to London with me, too stupid to take what you were offering, because I'd got it into my head that you didn't love me and only saw me as a way out of a job you hated . . .'

'You got that bit right. Not about me not loving you, but about me seeing you as a way out of a job I hated.'

'Really?' Lifting her in his arms, he dropped her on to the sofa and sank down beside her.

'I was envious of Jack and Helen. Not just being married but having their own home and a baby to look forward to. And staying at home looking after a baby seemed an easier option than having to get out of bed every morning in a city I hated and fighting my way on to the tube to work in a studio full of people who despised me for being young, inexperienced and having the wrong accent.'

'I knew you were having a rough time . . .'

'I never told you the half of it. I was too embarrassed.'

'And look at you now.' He stretched out and pulled her back against him. 'Business tycoon . . .'

'Hardly. My mother and I only have eleven salons.'

'Only?' he said in amusement. 'You want more?'

'Yes,' she said determinedly.

'Good for you.'

'You mean that?' she asked in surprise.

'If the garage is successful, I can't see me being happy with one.'

'Then you do understand.'

'I understand this.' He slid his hand inside her gown and cupped her naked breast. 'And that's where my third fault comes in. I've explained angry and stupid but not young. I hadn't lived long enough when I walked away from you on Swansea station to appreciate that what we had was precious, and doesn't come more than once in a lifetime.'

'I hoped you would write but, much as I wanted to hear from you, I wouldn't make the first move,' she confessed huskily, disturbed by the effect his caresses were having on her.

'I've been wanting to apologise properly since the first moment I set eyes on you after I returned to Swansea.'

'Brian, this is . . .'

'Insane? Too quick? Too sudden?' He pulled at her tie belt with one hand while stroking her nipple with the other.

'All of that.' She clamped her hand over his. 'This morning I was engaged . . .'

'To the wrong man.'

'I had no business going out with Sam, much less accepting an engagement ring from him. Not when . . .' She faltered.

'It wouldn't hurt you to say it. Just once, Judy.' He turned her around and looked into her eyes.

'Not when I loved you.'

'Love me,' he corrected, as he finally succeeded in untying her belt. Opening her negligee, he kissed each of her breasts in turn before slipping the robe over her shoulders.

'Brian, I can't do this, there's Sam . . .'

'You broke off with him, remember.'

'Only this morning.'

'From what he did to me, I think he understands the situation between you.'

She tried to grab her robe, but he whisked it over his head and threw it behind him. Seconds later his pullover, shirt and vest joined it on the floor. 'I love you, Brian, I've never stopped loving you, but . . .'

'You're not engaged any more, Judy. And I've been dreaming about this since the last time you undressed for me. I can't believe that I was actually idiotic enough to walk out on you when you offered to make love with me. Please, my love,' pulling her close, he kissed her gently on the lips, 'don't allow happiness to slip away from us a second time.'

She lay between the sheets and watched while he unbuckled his trousers and stripped off the last of his clothes, and trembled when he slid into the bed beside her.

'You cold?' He pulled her naked body along the full length of his.

'No.'

'Then what?' he questioned anxiously. 'You still want to wait?'

'It's a bit late for that.' She wrapped her hands around his back.

'I'm glad you think so.'

'But . . .'

'Judy, you're not eighteen any more and I'm not twenty-one. You've been engaged for eighteen months, I've . . .'

'What?' she prompted. He nuzzled her neck.

'Philandered.'

She drew in her breath sharply as his hands moved lower. 'Brian . . .' Her voice rose in alarm.

'What's wrong, my love?'

'Nothing.' As he touched her again, she realised that nothing was.

Chapter Twenty

Brian waited while the telephone rang – and rang – and rang. When a sleepy voice he barely recognised, finally mumbled an incomprehensible grunt on the other end of the line, he said, 'Is that you, Jack?'

'Brian, have you any idea of the time?'

'Half past one, why do you ask? Aren't the clocks working in Carlton Terrace?' Brian replied with an exuberance that irritated Jack to the point where, if he had been in the room with him, he could have quite cheerfully emulated Sam's example, and punched him.

'I was asleep, the hall is bloody freezing, I haven't even got my slippers on . . .'

'My oh my, we are a joyless Jack.'

'You phoned,' Jack growled.

'Yes, have you heard from Marty?'

'No.'

'Could you nip round to Katie and John's, and Roy and Joy's tomorrow morning and tell them what's happened to Lily and Martin?'

'Already done.'

'Good, then if Martin doesn't phone and want me up there, I'll see you in the house about seven. I'm staying overnight with a friend.'

'He must be a bloody, long-suffering friend to put up with you prancing around, yelling into the telephone at this time in the morning.'

'A very long-suffering friend.' Brian raised his voice for Judy's benefit.

'Anything else?' Jack demanded irritably.

'No, that's about it, unless you hear from Martin. If there's anything I can do . . .'

'I'll phone you. Goodnight, Brian.'

'How can you phone me if you don't know my number?' Brian stared at the receiver but the line was dead.

'Is there any news of Lily?' Judy asked, as Brian padded back into the bedroom naked.

'No.' He turned back the bedclothes.

'I hope she's all right.'

'So do I,' he concurred fervently, sliding into bed beside her. Wrapping his arm around her shoulders, he pulled her head down on to his chest. 'We have some talking to do.'

'Yes, we do,' she agreed softly.

'Do we visit the vicar and the Mackworth tomorrow and tell them that you want the wedding and reception to go ahead as planned, apart from a change of bridegroom?'

'They'll think I'm insane.'

'Probably.' He kissed her forehead. 'But it seems a shame to let all that planning go to waste. I bet you've even bought the dress.'

'And sent out the invitations, ordered the cake, the flowers, the cars . . .'

'I feel I should warn you that if we do go for the change of bridegroom option, I'd rather Sam's relatives didn't come.'

'I have a lot of sorting out to do with Sam,' she mused soberly.

'I thought you did all the sorting that needs doing today.' He lifted his hand and checked that the plaster was still covering his cheekbone.

'Not really.'

'But you did break off your engagement as Sam said?' he enquired urgently.

'And returned Sam's ring. But there are so many other things to do, like tell everyone we sent invitations to, that the wedding has been cancelled. That's what I was doing when you turned up tonight. We invited a hundred and twelve people.'

'You know a hundred and twelve people well enough to invite them to your wedding?'

'I don't. Something like ninety odd are Sam's relations, and so far I've only written ten letters. And those were the easy ones.'

'Go to the printer's tomorrow and get him to knock up something that you can stuff into an envelope,' he suggested practically. 'I'll even lick the envelopes and the stamps for you, if you like.'

'Brian the martyr – it doesn't suit you.' Because she was still thinking of the pain she'd inflicted on Sam, her smile was tempered.

'I can be a martyr if the rewards are great enough.' He stroked the flat of her stomach with the back of his finger.

'We are supposed to be talking,' she reprimanded, clamping her hand over his.

'Yes, ma'am.'

'And don't come all humble, that doesn't suit you either.'

'No, ma'am.'

'Sam should have as much say about the wording of the letter that goes out as I do,' she continued, trying to keep both his hands imprisoned in hers. 'And we should draft something for the *Evening Post*, as we announced our engagement in it. Then there are all the cancellations to be made—'

'I accept that you have to talk to Sam about the letters and the announcement, but I can help you with the cancellations.'

'There's no need, my mother and I can do them between us.'

'So, what are you saying, love? That you have to see Sam again?'

'Yes,' she asserted reluctantly. 'I didn't mean to hurt

him but I have and I want to tell him that we are together before he hears it from someone else.'

'He knew about us even before we did,' Brian pointed out.

'I was angry when I drove away from him this afternoon. I have to make him understand that I didn't break off our engagement in the heat of the moment and I meant what I said, when I told him that it was over between us.'

'I rather think he got that part of your message,' he said ruefully, freeing his hands from hers and gingerly stroking his right eye, which was now completely swollen shut. 'If you think you should meet him, then go ahead, arrange it. But make it somewhere public and I'll go with you.'

'So, he can black your other eye?' she interrupted indignantly. 'Absolutely not.'

'Now that I've finally got you back after all these years, I'd like to keep you in one piece.'

'Sam won't hurt me.' She traced a line from his navel to the base of his throat.

'That tickles, and if I'm not allowed to tease you, you are not allowed to tease me.' He closed his hand over hers. 'And I'll guarantee he won't hurt you if I go along with you when you meet him.'

'I don't need a chaperone or a bodyguard.'

'Just a husband.'

Turning on to her stomach, she looked up at him. 'I don't remember you asking me to marry you?'

'I don't need to,' he grinned.

'You're taking an awful lot for granted, Brian Powell.'

'That's an odd thing for a woman in your state of undress to say to a man she's sharing a bed with. A man who incidentally forgot about everything when he was dragged in here.'

'Everything!' She looked at him in alarm.

'How do you feel about children?'

'That depends on who they belong to.'

'Us. I'd like a dozen. You?'

'Not quite a dozen, but I won't give up work when they come along.'

'I wouldn't expect you to.' He looked intently into her eyes and moved his hands down the length of her body. 'How about you cancel the wedding you planned with Sam and visit the register office with me tomorrow to see how quickly we can organise a wedding of our very own. I'll get Jack to cover for me in the garage at two o'clock and meet you there then, just in case they close from one to two for lunch.'

'You want a small affair where I wear a costume and you wear an old suit?'

'Not too old,' he qualified. 'I think I have one hidden away somewhere without holes in the knees. Do you have any problems with that?'

'No.' She recalled the conversation she'd had with her mother when she'd told her that she was more of a costume girl like Katie and Helen, than a white wedding dress sort of bride. 'In fact it sounds just about perfect.'

'Good, then we'll do that.' He glanced at the alarm clock on the bedside table. 'If we turn out the light, we might manage a couple of hours' sleep.'

'You tired?'

'No.' He lifted his undamaged eyebrow. 'You?'

'Not very.'

'I can think of just the thing to keep an insomniac girlfriend happy.'

'I never knew it could be like this,' she whispered, as he slid down in the bed beside her.

'Neither did I, my love.'

Jack returned to bed after Brian's call, but after an hour spent restlessly tossing and turning on his mattress, he finally went downstairs. The empty house closed around him like a mausoleum, silent and bereft of life. He was acutely and painfully aware of Lily and Martin's absence, and couldn't stop thinking about them – and Helen.

He knew exactly what his brother was going through and he felt for him, wishing there was something that he could do to help him and Lily. Brian had insisted that Martin hadn't known Lily was pregnant, but he couldn't think of a reason why she would keep news of that magnitude from Martin. Surely it couldn't be just because he was worried about the overdraft she'd taken out?

Unable to bear the thought of Martin and Lily losing their child before it was born, just as he and Helen had lost theirs, he sat in the living room, lit a cigarette and mulled over the wreckage of his marriage.

He knew just how much he had hurt Helen when he had told her that Maggie was carrying his child, because the thought of Helen making love with another man was sheer torture. And that was why he couldn't understand why she had visited Maggie. It had to be more than simple curiosity . . . but what? He had no shortage of ideas but rather than speculate, he felt he had to see her face to face and ask her why she had opted for a meeting that must have been as humiliating for her as it was painful.

It was high time he faced up to his responsibilities. What he had done to Helen, as well as the mess he had made of Maggie and their baby's lives. If Helen wanted to divorce him, the onus was on him to make all the arrangements, but just the thought of walking into a solicitor's office and taking the first step to end their marriage made his blood run cold. However, he couldn't continue to ignore the situation. If Helen wanted her freedom, he owed her at least that much.

He walked into the kitchen, opened a drawer in the cabinet and took out envelopes, a notepad and Lily's fountain pen. Sitting at the kitchen table, he began to compose a letter.

Dear Helen

If you'd like to divorce me . . .

Looking at what he'd written, it seemed tantamount to an invitation for Helen to do just that. Tearing the paper from the pad, he screwed it into a ball, flicked open the pedal bin, and tossed it in, before beginning again.

Dear Helen,
We need to talk . . .

That looked so trite, it joined his first effort.

Dear Helen,
I love you and I'm so sorry . . .

As he screwed up the third piece of paper, he reflected that at the rate he was going he would work his way through Lily's entire stock of Basildon Bond by morning. He lit another cigarette and moved to one of the easy chairs. What was the worst that could happen if he telephoned the warehouse in the morning and asked to speak to Helen? She refused to talk to him? Or she wasn't there and he would take that as a refusal to speak to him? Or she did speak to him – and then what?

They had been married for nearly three years and although they had spent only five weeks of that time together, if anything he loved her more now than he had on their wedding day. He had made a mistake – a horrendous one – he had hurt her deeply and that was why he had to allow her to decide the next step they should take. He only hoped that if she did choose to end their marriage, he would be man enough to accept the consequences of his actions and resign himself to spending the rest of his life without her.

'Brian, it's six o'clock,' Judy remonstrated, as he tried to kiss her goodbye – for the third time since she'd insisted it was time he went. 'The milkman and postman will be here in half an hour and if they see you leaving, or Martin's car parked outside this flat, they will put two and two together and do their adding up all over Mumbles and Swansea. My reputation will be mud.'

'I can live with a woman with a besmirched reputation. It's the beatings from rival suitors that I find hard to take.'

She looked guiltily at his closed eye and bruised face. 'That is not remotely funny.'

He threw up his hands and backed away from her, jamming the last of the toast and marmalade she had made for him into his mouth. 'I'm going even as I speak.'

'Thank you.' She handed him the keys to Martin's car.

'See you tonight as well as at the register office this afternoon?'

'Please,' she smiled.

'I like the sound of that "please" and the look of that smile.'

'Do me a favour?'

'What?' he asked warily.

She handed him an envelope. 'Push that through Sam's door.'

He eyed the envelope suspiciously. 'You want me to risk my head and other more vital parts of my body after the night of bliss we've just shared, by walking up to Sam's door?'

'He's on mornings this week, so he will have left the house at five-thirty.'

'You know his every move?'

'That is hardly surprising considering that I was engaged to the man until yesterday morning. And we agreed last night that I have to see him one more time.'

'When and where?'

'I suggested a café at four o'clock this afternoon. I said if he couldn't make it today I'd be there every afternoon at four this week until he could.'

'What café?' he enquired disarmingly.

'That would be telling.'

'If you tell me and stay there until six, I'll pick you up after I close the garage.'

'You will not.'

'I will.'

'You will not,' she repeated crossly, her temper rising.

'At the risk of sounding as if I'm in a pantomime, I will. I refuse to allow you to put yourself in danger.'

'You are not "allowing me" to do anything,' she erupted. 'I am in control of my life, not you. And I won't be taking any risk in meeting Sam. He's not an ogre.'

'Do you mind repeating that?' He touched the plaster she'd stuck over his cheekbone.

'For pity's sake, Brian, I was engaged to the man for eighteen months, and he never lifted his hand to me once in all that time.'

'Or shouted at you.'

'Of course he shouted at me.'

'Then he was halfway to hitting you.'

'If you believe that, then most of the couples I know are heading for the boxing ring. And for your information, every time Sam shouted at me, I probably shouted at him – and longer and louder.'

'So you were both driven to the point of violence.'

Seeing a glint in his eye that had nothing to do with anger, she pulled her dressing gown high around her throat. 'Neither of us was violent until you appeared on the scene.'

'So now it's my fault that Sam hit me?'

'You were the one who said Sam sensed the way we felt about one another, even when neither of us would admit it.'

'And you think that gave him the right to hit me?'

'Of course not, but look at the situation from Sam's point of view. Yesterday morning I was engaged to him and last night . . .' Colour flooded into her cheeks.

'Was perfect.' He pulled her close and kissed her throat below her ear. 'Wasn't it?'

'You know it was,' she murmured, her resolve to ask him to leave melting beneath his touch.

'Then what's the problem?'

'If we're to have any more nights . . .'

'If?' he broke in, alarmed by the thought that there might not be.

'*Before* there can be any more nights, I have to see Sam and finish what little is left between us, hopefully in a way that will leave Sam with his dignity intact and both of us with some self-respect. Although that is doubtful; however you go about cancelling a wedding, it's bound to look as if one of us didn't know our own mind.'

'As long as you know your own mind now.' He kissed her again.

'Enough to allow Sam to paint me as the wicked siren who abandoned him for another man.'

'As opposed to the faithful fiancée, seduced by an evil, conniving bastard, who only wanted to have his lecherous way with her.'

Summoning every ounce of strength and determination, she pushed him away from her. 'I love you, Brian Powell, but you really do have to go.'

'I love you too, snookems.'

'Snookems!'

'It's what my father used to call my mother. She never objected.'

'That doesn't mean I won't. Do you want me to cook for us tonight?'

'Yes, but we'll discuss what when I meet you at two.'

'Frogs and snails.'

'Perhaps.' He smiled, took the letter and finally left.

'And how are we feeling this morning?' The matron set a blood pressure gauge on the bed that the staff had carried into the treatment room and lifted Lily into the previous evening.

'Tired, a bit fuzzy. As if the world is not quite in focus,' Lily answered.

'That will be the drugs we gave you to try to stop you miscarrying. From the report I received after you were washed this morning, the treatment seems to have worked. There's been no more bleeding since last night?'

'No.'

'Are you glad?' The matron cleared a clutter of papers and instruments from a small table jammed between the bed and the filing cabinet and set the gauge on to it.

Lily looked the matron in the eye. 'I am very glad. I want this baby.'

'I was surprised to discover that your husband didn't know you were pregnant. Most married women inform their other halves as soon as they suspect a baby's on the way. You are nearly four months pregnant. You must have known your condition for at least two months.'

'I was waiting for the right time to tell him,' Lily said defensively.

'And there hasn't been a right time in the last two months?' The matron lifted Lily's hand and checked her pulse.

'Martin worries about money. He's gone into the garage business with a friend. They've only just opened.'

'And you need your salary to make ends meet until he starts earning enough to pay the bills?' The matron scribbled on a chart then reached for the gauge.

'Not really. I inherited a house and some investments so we don't have to worry about paying a mortgage or rent and if worst comes to worst we can cash in the investments to see us through until the garage starts making money.'

'So what's the problem?' The matron rolled back the sleeve of Lily's borrowed nightgown in readiness to take her blood pressure.

'Martin – he hates using what he sees as my money, although I keep telling him that it's ours now.'

'So, you pandered to his male ego and allowed him to think that he could go into business without dipping into the funds you inherited.'

'I had a hard time persuading him to use the money. I knew he was worried about paying it back. I didn't want to burden him with any more problems.'

'Like he was about to become a father.'

'I was going to tell him soon.'

'But not before it became obvious.'

'It wouldn't have been long, he'd already noticed that I was putting on weight.'

'And he didn't guess the reason.' The matron shook her head disparagingly. 'Men! Sometimes I think they are born without brains but more often than not I am convinced of it. How have you been feeling since you became pregnant?' She narrowed her eyes, giving Lily the impression that she already knew the answer to her question.

'A bit tired,' Lily admitted guardedly.

'I am not surprised if you have been working full-time as well as running a house and looking after your husband.'

'Martin does his share of the housework,' Lily remonstrated.

'But he would have done a lot more if he had known that you were pregnant.'

Lily was loath to concede the point. 'I suppose so.'

'So, you risked your own health and that of your baby in an attempt to preserve your husband's pride.'

'It wasn't like that!'

'Are you afraid of your husband?' The matron removed the gauge and reached for the chart.

'Of course not,' Lily countered indignantly.

'It sounds like it to me, if you wouldn't even tell him you were pregnant.'

'You don't understand. Marty is loving, kind, caring – too caring. He had a terrible upbringing and he worries about everything . . .'

'And you thought he'd worry less about you and the baby if he didn't know you were pregnant?'

'Yes.'

'Roll back the sheet. I'm going to check the baby's heartbeat.' The matron reached for a stethoscope and sat on the chair next to the bed. 'I wasn't always Matron of this place. I had twenty years of happy, fulfilling marriage before I came here and if there's one thing I learned during those years, it's that in order for a marriage to grow, you have to share everything. That means the bad as well as the good. No matter how dreadful your husband's childhood, I'm sure he wouldn't want you to try to protect him at the expense of your own or your child's health.'

Lily thought about what the matron had said while she examined her. 'The baby . . .'

'The heartbeat is still strong.'

'You're right. I should never have kept this pregnancy from Martin.'

'I know I'm right because I never saw a man as distraught as your husband was last night when he came here. It was difficult enough for him to accept that you were ill without discovering that you were pregnant and hadn't told him.'

'It must have been a shock.'

'That, young lady, is something of an understatement.' The matron gave her a small, rare smile. 'You get somewhat cynical about men, working in a place like this. But you have a good husband. He deserves your full trust. Remember that in future.'

'I will.' Lily smiled back at her. 'And thank you for looking after me.'

'My pleasure. It makes a change to have someone like you to care for, but as I told the doctor yesterday, we can't allow you to stay with us too long. The residents have enough problems, without coping with a happily married pregnant woman on the premises.' She rose to her feet as one of the kitchen staff came in with a tray. 'Set it down here, Evans, before you lift it on to the bed,' she ordered brusquely, picking up the gauge from the table.

'Yes, Matron.' The girl did as she asked.

The matron studied the plate of bacon, scrambled eggs and toast with a critical eye. 'Eat it while it's hot,' she advised Lily. 'If you need anything, ring the bell.'

'I will and thank you.'

'Right old battleaxe that one,' the girl muttered, spreading a napkin over the sheet before lifting the tray on to the bed. 'You comfortable, Miss . . . sorry, Mrs Clay?'

'I'm fine, thank you, and the matron really isn't so bad when you get to know her.'

'I'll take your word for it, but if it's all the same to you, Mrs Clay, I'd rather not get to know her any better than I do now.'

Martin woke with a start. Opening his eyes, he stared at the unfamiliar surroundings before the events of the previous day came flooding back. Cold, shivering, he threw back the bedspread and sat up. He felt frozen stiff, uncomfortable and grubby after sleeping in his clothes. He glanced at his watch. It was half past seven and it would only take him ten minutes to drive to the hostel. Taking a threadbare towel from a rail in his bedroom, he went in search of a bathroom.

'Breakfast, Mr Clay?' the landlady asked when he walked downstairs.

Wary of the bill he had been presented with the night before, he muttered, 'No thank you.'

'It's in the price.'

He glanced at his watch again.

'Full English breakfast,' she coaxed, as though she wanted to make amends for the extortionate amount she'd charged him for his sandwiches.

'I'd appreciate a cup of tea and some toast,' he said gratefully.

'And a couple of rashers of bacon. They are already cooked if you are in a hurry to see your wife.'

'In that case, yes please.'

'I'll bring it through to the lounge for you in a few minutes.'

The odour of stale beer and even staler cigarette smoke wafted towards him when he opened the door of the lounge bar. Before he could sit at a table, the telephone rang. Without waiting to be given permission, he picked up the receiver.

'Could I speak to Mr Clay?' barked an officious voice he recognised as the matron's.

'Speaking.'

'I thought you'd like to know that your wife had a restful night, Mr Clay.'

'She is better?' he asked tentatively.

'Much, and the baby's heartbeat is still strong. If you meet the doctor here at nine o'clock, he will be able to tell you more.'

'Lily is awake?'

'Yes.'

'Tell her I love her and I'm on my way to see her.'

'I will do that, Mr Clay.' As he replaced the receiver, he wondered if he'd imagined the sympathetic note in her voice.

'Have you heard from Martin?' Brian asked, walking into the kitchen where Jack was breakfasting.

'He phoned a few minutes ago. Apparently Lily had a good night and the baby has a strong heartbeat.'

'That's good news.' Brian picked up the teapot and reached for a cup.

'That is one hell of an ugly shiner.'

'I feel sorry for you having to look at it,' Brian said dryly.

'Did you get that cut stitched?'

'No. I had more important things to do.'

'Who is this mysterious friend you spent the night with?'

'Ask no questions and I'll tell you no lies.' Brian had eaten half a dozen slices of toast at Judy's but he was still hungry. He foraged in the bread bin and pulled out a packet of crumpets. 'Want one?'

'No thanks. If I don't get a move on, the boss might fire me.'

'The boss says you've time for a crumpet.'

'Still, no thanks.' Jack carried his cup, saucer, knife and plate to the sink.

Brian pushed a couple of crumpets into the toaster. 'I'm getting married.'

'Anyone I know?' Expecting one of Brian's jokes, Jack ran hot water into the sink.

'Judy.'

Jack's eyes widened. 'Christ! No wonder Sam punched you yesterday.'

'He didn't have anything to punch me for – yesterday.' The toaster popped and Brian extracted the crumpets. Reaching for the butter, he spread it lavishly over the holes allowing it to sink through to the base.

'Have you set a date, or are you happy with the one Judy fixed with Sam?'

'You cheeky bugger!'

'Might save yourself a few bob if you go for it,' Jack grinned.

'It's going to happen as soon as we can organise it.' Brian demolished a crumpet in three bites. 'And if you're good, you'll be invited. Now get your coat. I want that garage open by ten to eight.'

'All the signs are good,' the doctor told Martin. They sat facing one another across the desk in the matron's office.

'How soon can I take her back to Swansea?'

'Now there, I do urge caution. If your wife doesn't develop any other symptoms and if she remains quiet and rested until Friday and you can arrange transport—'

'That's no problem,' Martin broke in eagerly.

'The journey to Swansea will have to be slow and steady.'

'It will, I promise you.'

'And as soon as she gets there she will have to see her own doctor and at the first sign of a recurrence of anything like this she will have to be admitted to hospital.'

'Of course.' Martin was prepared to agree to almost anything as long as it meant that he could have Lily home.

'Your wife tells me she works in a bank.'

'As a secretary, yes,' Martin confirmed.

'She will have to give up her position immediately. You will want to discuss this with your own doctor but in a case of threatened miscarriage I recommend total bed rest until the birth. You have someone who can care for your wife?'

'I will.'

'And when you're at work?'

'I'll sort something out. My sister lives next door to us and Lily's uncle and his wife are up the road.'

'It's good to know families still rally around in an emergency.' The doctor left his seat. 'You'll want to see her.'

Jack waited until Brian was busy with their first customer of the day before asking if he could use the telephone in the office. After sending the receptionist out to make tea, he dialled the number of the warehouse. The minute it took for the switchboard to connect him to the buyer's desk dragged and he was resigning himself to failure when her heard Helen recite, 'Helen Clay, Buyer,' in a businesslike voice.

He steeled himself for rejection. 'It's Jack.'

There was a momentary silence before she asked, 'Have you heard how Lily is?'

'Martin telephoned this morning. She had a restful night and the baby's heartbeat is strong.'

'That's wonderful news.' Even on the telephone her relief was palpable.

He debated whether or not to mention that he knew she had been at the home but eventually settled for, 'I'd like to see you.'

'Why?'

'We are still married, Helen.'

'You want a divorce?'

'Do you?' When she didn't reply, he asked, 'Can I come to the house?'

'No.' The refusal was brittle but final.

'I'll meet you anywhere you like.'

'The beach in front of the house next Sunday morning at eight o'clock, there's generally no one about at that time.'

'Not sooner?'

'No.'

'And if it's tipping down with rain?'

'We'll wear raincoats.'

'Tea, Mr Clay.' The receptionist set a cup down at his elbow.

'As one of your women obviously wants you . . .'

'That was the receptionist Brian's taken on in the garage.'

'If you change your mind about next Sunday, Jack, don't bother to call again. I generally go for a walk around that time in the morning anyway.'

'Helen . . .' He realised he was talking down a dead line.

'Is everything all right, Mr Clay?'

'The tea's fine, thank you,' he replied abruptly.

Martin gingerly opened the door to the treatment room. Some time during the previous evening, the examination couch and desk had been carried out and replaced with a single iron bedstead. Lily lay flat in the bed, her head resting on a thin pillow. She looked at him warily as he stepped closer. Then he saw there were tears in her eyes.

'I'm sorry, Marty. I should have told you . . .'

'It's me who should be sorry, love,' he whispered. 'How are you feeling?'

'A bit groggy, but the matron said that's because of the morphine I was given to stop me from losing the baby.' She looked intently at him. 'I know you were here yesterday because the matron told me, but I'm not sure if

I remember seeing you or I dreamed it. Did you really say that you don't mind about the baby?'

'I only wish you hadn't felt that you had to keep it from me.'

'You were so worried about the money we borrowed and the garage . . . the garage.' She looked at the clock on the wall opposite the bed. 'You should be in work . . .'

'The boss gave me the morning off.'

'Marty, you have to go in.'

'I will,' he assured her, 'just as soon as I can be sure that you will be all right.'

'The doctor says I have to stay here for at least a week.'

'Which is why you have to tell me what you want from home so I can bring it up tonight.'

'You can't come and see me here every day.'

'Watch me.' He took her hand into his as he sat beside her. 'Promise me something.' He looked deep into her eyes. 'Don't keep any secrets from me, ever again.'

'I'll try.'

'Your wife should rest now, Mr Clay.' The doctor stood in the doorway, Matron behind him.

Martin nodded. 'I can come to see her tonight and bring some clothes?'

The doctor looked to the matron.

'As long as you realise that the visit will be short and supervised. Yes, Mr Clay, you can visit.'

As Martin left the house he felt as if he had climbed Everest – and was standing alongside Hillary.

Chapter Twenty-One

Elvis Presley's 'Heartbreak Hotel' was playing on the jukebox in the Italian café as Judy opened the door. Wishing that someone had chosen a more innocuous song, she looked around and saw Sam sitting in a booth, an empty cup and saucer and an overflowing ashtray in front of him. They stared at one another for a moment. When she realised that he wasn't going to acknowledge her, she went to the counter and ordered a coffee just as 'Heartbreak Hotel' was lifted from the turntable and replaced by 'Secret Love'.

Feeling as though fate was conspiring against her, she walked over to his booth. 'Can I get you anything?'

He indicated the cup in front of him. 'That is my third.'

'I said I'd be here at four, it's five minutes to.' She made an effort to keep the irritation from her voice.

'My shift finished two hours ago. Normally I would have gone to bed so I could have enjoyed my evening but you put paid to any chance of my doing that.'

Wondering if she'd ruined his evening by breaking off their engagement or by suggesting that they meet at four o'clock in the afternoon, she managed a bland, 'Thank you for coming.' Taking off her coat, she folded it, set it beside her, and slid on to the bench seat opposite his.

'You said we have to talk.' He pushed a cigarette into his mouth and lit it without offering her one. 'I take it you've changed your mind about what you said yesterday and want to apologise to my mother.'

'No.'

'You don't want the ring back.'

'No.'

'Then I don't see that we've anything to say to one another.' Closing his cigarette packet, he blew smoke into her face and returned it to his shirt pocket.

'I haven't changed my mind about breaking off our engagement but I shouldn't have done it the way I did. I was angry . . .'

'I noticed,' he broke in caustically.

'I think I had a right to be angry after what your mother did, Sam,' she said quietly.

'If you've come here to complain about my mother . . .' He fell silent as the waitress set a cup of frothy milky coffee, which only the Italian cafés seemed to serve, in front of her.

'I haven't, but she shouldn't have interfered with my choice of bridesmaids' dresses.'

'The dresses were for my cousins. It was reasonable of them to expect to get some wear out of them afterwards.'

'If they had paid for the material and met the dressmaker's bill I might agree with you,' she protested. 'But I chose a pattern and material that complemented the dress I had chosen for myself. I paid for them and I think I was entitled to have what I paid for.'

'Even if it would have been a waste, if they had only been worn the once . . .'

As Judy listened to his catalogue of excuses, she could hear the voice of his mother breaking through and, just like the day before, she wondered why it had taken her so long to realise that she didn't love Sam. All the signs had been there, obvious for her to see. Their constant arguments, more often than not about trivialities; the differences of opinion they had on just about everything important – like where they should live; whether or not she should work; the lovemaking that had been so disastrous for her from the outset. She shivered and wrapped her arms around herself, recalling Brian's tender caresses of the night before.

Little wonder her mother had been unable to explain

what making love could be like when it was with the right person. Even after she had experienced it, she had a problem finding words to describe how Brian had made her feel – loved, cherished, special, so very special . . .

'. . . You're not listening to me.' Sam's complaint shattered her thoughts. She started guiltily.

'Sorry.' She set aside her memories of the night before and tried to concentrate. 'There is no point in us discussing the bridesmaids' dresses now that they are made.'

'That is exactly what my mother said,' he crowed triumphantly.

'Please, Sam, we have more important things to talk about than the bridesmaids' dresses, like cancelling our wedding and deciding the most appropriate way to return our engagement presents.'

'Then you are still determined to cancel the wedding?'

'Surely you don't think that we can go ahead after everything that's happened!' she exclaimed incredulously.

'Provided you make a suitable apology to my mother, yes.'

'What about what you did to Brian?'

'You've seen him.' After a momentary pause, he added, 'You must have, Judy, to know what I did.'

'Yes, I have,' she conceded flatly, reaching for her handbag. 'I wrote ten letters to people we sent invitations to last night. I haven't posted them yet.' She removed one of the envelopes.

'Then you are having second thoughts.'

'No!' She only realised she'd raised her voice when half the heads in the café turned in their direction. Colouring in embarrassment, she pulled the letter from the envelope and handed it to him. 'I read it again this morning and it seems all right to me. If you agree with the wording I thought I would ask the printer to run off enough copies beginning "Dear" with a blank to be filled in, to send to everyone we invited.'

He smoothed the paper on to the table and read:

Dear Lily and Martin,

I regret to inform you that my wedding to Sam Davies has been cancelled. Sam and I both agree that we are not suited to one another. I am very sorry for any inconvenience this has caused you.

Yours sincerely,

Judy

'Since when have we agreed "that we are not suited to one another", he demanded acidly, 'and what inconvenience could we possibly have put Lily and Martin to, or anyone outside of our immediate families?'

'They could have already gone to some expense to buy us a wedding present and new outfits for the occasion.'

'Like my mother.'

'Please, Sam, we are talking about cancelling our wedding, not your mother.' She lowered her voice as the opening bars of 'Heartbreak Hotel' filled the café – yet again. 'Doesn't anyone in Swansea want to hear any other damned record?'

'Guilty conscience troubling you, Judy?'

For the first time she noticed a pile of shillings next to his cup.

'Sixpence a play or three for a shilling. You know me, I always go for a bargain.'

'You—'

'I had to do something to pass the time while I waited.'

She made a supreme effort to control herself and swallowed the word she'd been about to fling at him. 'Agreeing that we are not suited to one another sounds better than we had an almighty row,' she said, steering the conversation resolutely back on track.

'Or the truth, that you threw a childish temper tantrum and created the most appalling scene in front of my mother's friend Mrs Richards and—'

'Mrs Richards?' She looked at him blankly.

'The dressmaker,' he explained tersely, 'not to mention all my cousins who were far too young to have been subjected to the sight of you calling their aunt a lot of ugly names. As your future mother-in-law, my mother should have been accorded your respect—'

'Sam,' she interceded wearily, 'I quarrelled with your mother and made a mess of our engagement, but I'm trying to break it off in a way that will leave both of us a little dignity.'

'Don't bother. Everyone will soon know exactly what you are when you start going out with Brian Powell.'

'Whom you thumped.'

'He had it coming to him. And don't try feeding me that old story about there being nothing between you. When I challenged him, he didn't even bother to deny it.'

'There wasn't anything between us before you hit Brian, Sam, but there is now, and for that, I thank you.'

Brian slipped his arm around Judy's shoulders as he sat alongside her in the booth. 'I would have been here half an hour ago, snookems, if you'd told me where you two were meeting. You have no idea how many cafés there are in Swansea. I thought I knew the town and I was amazed.' He waved to the waitress and called her over to their table. 'Two coffees here, please, love.' He noticed Sam's empty cup. 'Would you like one as well, Sam? My shout of course.'

'Want some company on the drive?' Jack enquired, as Martin, freshly bathed and shaved, ran down the stairs carrying a small suitcase.

'So you can see this woman who is having your baby?' Martin questioned suspiciously.

'They wouldn't let me see her. Visiting is only allowed on Sundays and the last time I spoke to her, she warned me that she was going to tell the matron that she didn't want to see me again.'

'So, what will you do when I go into the house to see Lily?' Martin shrugged on his jacket and picked up his keys.

'Sit in the car and read a book.' Jack held up an Agatha Christie he'd borrowed from the library. 'I'm at a loose end and I thought, seeing as Brian is out, we could stop off for fish and chips on the way home to save us the bother of cooking.'

'As long as it is just company you want.' Martin picked up a bulging carrier bag topped by an enormous bunch of flowers that stood next to the front door.

'If you'd rather be alone . . .'

'As it happens, I wouldn't.' Martin checked the front door was securely locked after Jack had followed him out.

'Sure you have enough flowers?' Jack teased.

Martin stowed the case and bag in the boot of his car. 'The flowers are from Katie, Joy, Judy and Helen. They packed a whole lot of other things they said Lily would need in the bag as well. Books, chocolates, magazines and fruit, and Katie assured me she only packed the absolute essentials in the case.'

'I know women and their absolute essentials. You should have seen what they made me cart into Swansea hospital for Helen . . .' Jack's voice trailed into silence. He climbed into the front passenger seat of Martin's car.

'This must bring back a lot of memories you'd rather forget.' Martin started the car and drove around the corner on to the main road.

'It's bloody rotten luck this happening to both our wives.' Jack swore savagely.

'It hasn't happened to Lily yet,' Martin bit back.

'I'm sorry, Marty. I hope everything works out for you and Lily, and you have a beautiful bouncing boy like Katie's in – how many months?'

'Another five, give or take a couple of weeks, and I'm not sure how I'm going to get through them. The doctor warned me that Lily will have to take things easy and stay in bed for most of the time.'

'It will be worth it if you have a baby.'

'It will, if Lily and the baby are both healthy at the end of it.' Martin ran his hand through his hair. 'I've been such a bloody fool, Jack. Going around like a bear with two sore heads, growling at everyone because I wanted to take Brian up on his offer of a partnership but didn't think it right to use Lily's money to do it. And all the time too blind to see that she was pregnant and too afraid to tell me.'

'I wouldn't say afraid. Knowing Lily she probably didn't want to worry you.'

'If you can't confide in your husband or wife, who can you talk to?'

'Your brother?' Jack suggested.

'That's fine for me.' Martin looked gratefully across at Jack. 'But Lily doesn't have one.'

'She talks to the girls,' Jack consoled. 'There isn't much that Judy, Katie, Helen and Lily don't tell one another.'

'Lily didn't tell any of them that she was pregnant.'

'Probably because she wanted to tell you first.'

'Only I wasn't in a mood to listen.'

'But you will be from now on,' Jack countered staunchly. 'You can't go round for the rest of your life feeling guilty because you made one mistake in over two years of happy marriage.'

'Like you don't feel guilty.'

Jack lit two cigarettes and passed Martin one. 'It's the Clay curse. The men in the family are destined to learn their lessons the hard way. I didn't tell Helen about Maggie until she wrote to say that she was having my baby. If I had, maybe things would be different between Helen and me now.'

'And maybe they wouldn't,' Martin counselled. 'Can you imagine turning up after two and half years National Service and telling Helen that you'd slept with another woman? She'd have thrown you out of the house before you had time to drop your suitcase on the doormat.'

'So, she did it two weeks later.'

'You said they were good weeks,' Martin reminded.

'Which makes me all the more miserable now, because I know what I'm missing.' Jack opened the ashtray set in the dashboard and flicked the ash from his cigarette into it. 'Would you tell Lily if you slept with another woman?'

'I haven't slept with any other women.'

'I don't mean just since you married.'

'Neither do I.'

Jack whistled in amazement. 'But you were in the army, you were abroad . . .'

'The first thing I learned in the army is there is a lot of talk and very little action between conscripted military personnel and people of the female persuasion.'

'But say you slipped up now,' Jack persisted. 'Would you tell her?'

'I hope I'd have more sense than to "slip up" as you put it. But in answer to your question, no, I don't think I would, because I know it would hurt her.'

'I'm seeing Helen on Sunday morning,' Jack divulged suddenly.

'She got in touch with you?'

'I telephoned her in the warehouse yesterday.'

'And she was prepared to talk to you?'

'Just about.'

'Then there is a chance of you two getting back together,' Martin said eagerly.

'I don't think so.'

'There won't be if you insist on trying to adopt Maggie's baby. Or have you come to your senses and given up on that idea?'

'I haven't given up on it, but without a house and wife, and a divorce in the offing, I don't think I stand much chance of succeeding.'

'I'd say you stand no chance.' Martin predicted bluntly, squashing his cigarette butt into the ashtray.

'It just seems so bloody unfair, not for me, for the kid. I mess up and he or she gets strangers for parents.'

'That's not necessarily a bad thing. They could be perfect strangers and perfect parents and, for the moment at least, you still have a wife.'

'Meaning?'

'That if I were you, I'd turn up on Sunday dressed in a hair shirt, prepared to eat humble pie or anything else Helen's prepared to dish out to you. You and Helen are good together, kid.'

'Were good together,' Jack muttered gloomily. Turning his back on Martin, he stared out of the car window.

Sam sat back on the bench seat and glared, pale-faced from Brian to Judy. 'So you two are together.'

'Judy decided that you should hear it from her first and, after what you did to me last night, I thought I should be around when she told you.' Brian moved closer to Judy. The waitress brought their coffee. Sensing the fraught atmosphere, she set the cups on the table and retreated behind the counter.

'You—'

'Careful, Sam,' Brian murmured. 'It looks bad for the force if an officer is heard swearing in public, even when he's off duty and out of uniform.'

'How long has this been going on?' Sam demanded of Judy.

'As Brian said, only since you hit him last night.'

'You went to her flat after I hit you?' Sam turned to Brian.

'Yes.'

'And you let him in!' Sam challenged Judy.

'Yes.'

'And you agreed to go out with him . . .' Sam's face contorted in disgust. 'You went to bed with him, didn't you?'

'Sam . . .'

'Didn't you?' he reiterated, drowning her out. 'You climbed into bed with him,' he snapped.

'You've said more than enough,' Brian advised.

'She has been to bed with me, you know,' Sam taunted. 'Allowed me to do whatever I wanted.'

'Given the way you're shouting it to the world, I can understand why she gave you back your ring!'

Judy gripped Brian's arm. Outwardly he was in control, but his hands had clenched into fists and his knuckles were white with strain. 'What I have or haven't done with Brian is nothing whatsoever to do with what happened between us, Sam.' Judy deliberately pitched her voice low in the hope of lessening the tension.

'But you're not denying you slept with him.' Sam's mouth curled in contempt. 'There aren't many men who will take on damaged goods. But then perhaps you only want a common tart to play around with for a couple of weeks until something better comes along, Brian. But you'll need patience. Judy's frigid, but then perhaps you've already found that out . . .'

'Please sit at another table, Brian,' Judy begged. Fists still clenched, Brian rose to his feet. 'Please,' she reiterated when he hesitated. 'This is between Sam and me.'

Brian glared at Sam. 'Out of respect for Judy, I won't be listening but I will be watching every move you make, Sam. Raise your hand to her like you did me yesterday, and you won't know what hit you.'

'You think I'd hit a woman?'

'Wouldn't you?' As Judy gave him another imploring look, Brian moved to a booth from which he could watch Sam.

'Don't you think it would be best for both of us if we admit we made a mistake and go our separate ways, rather than trade insults?' Judy suggested when Brian was out of earshot.

'You'd like us to be friends, is that it? All sweetness and light, no blame, no recriminations.'

'I'll take the blame, but yes, I would like us to remain friends, if that's possible.'

'After what you've done?'

'I'm sorry if I hurt you, Sam. I didn't mean to.'

'If . . .' He dropped his voice as he caught sight of Brian sliding to the edge of his bench seat.

'I had no right to accept an engagement ring from you

and my only excuse for doing so is that I thought I loved you at the time.'

'So, are you saying you never did?'

'I cared for you,' Judy said slowly, 'but not enough. I should have realised how unsuited we were from the beginning. We were always quarrelling, even over what type of wedding we wanted and where we were going to live.'

'Is that surprising when he,' Sam sent a disdainful look in Brian's direction, 'was sniffing after you the whole time we were making plans.'

'Brian didn't visit me until after you told him that I'd returned your ring.'

'So, the same day you finish with me, you get engaged to him.'

'We are not getting engaged.' Judy took a deep breath and braced herself.

'Just as well,' Sam sneered, 'given the time you need to make decisions, Brian will be drawing his old age pension before you get around to marrying him.'

'Brian and I went to the register office this afternoon. We're getting married three weeks today.'

Sam jerked back against his seat as if he'd been punched in the stomach. 'That's before we would have been married . . .'

'It will be a quiet wedding, Sam,' Judy interposed. 'Nothing like the one we had planned.'

'My mother always said a hole in the corner register office affair was more your style.'

'She was right,' Judy answered evenly, drawing courage from Brian's presence behind her.

'I have nothing else to say to you.' Sam left the table.

'The letter?'

'Do what you want, you always do anyway.'

'And the announcement in the *Evening Post*?'

'You can leave that to me.'

'They won't print it unless we both sign it,' she warned, not trusting him in his present vindictive mood.

'Then to hell with putting it in the *Evening Post*.' He shrugged on his coat. 'I could sue you for breach of promise.'

'Why make one another miserable? It's not as if you've incurred many costs. Most of the expense of the cancelled wedding is going to fall on my mother and me.'

'There's the ring and my suit.'

'For pity's sake, Sam,' she pleaded, 'I've given you back your ring and I'm sorry about your suit, but it didn't cost anywhere near as much as my dress or the material for those damned bridesmaids' dresses, which your cousins are welcome to keep, and that's without the lost deposits and I'm not expecting you to foot the bill for those.'

'I should think not, when you were the one to call off the wedding.'

Tired of argument, confrontation, but most of all Sam's bitterness, Judy said, 'Goodbye, Sam. I'm sorry for hurting you. If there was anything I could do to make it right for you, I would, but I can't. I realise that you hate me now, but perhaps some time in the future we can be friends.'

'Friends!' He hurled the word back at her as if it were an insult. 'No, Judy, we can never be friends.'

'I'll drop your family's engagement presents off at Lily's house. You can pick them up from there.'

'Mind you don't forget any.' Turning on his heel, he strode out of the café.

'I hate leaving you here like this,' Martin whispered, as he glanced back through the open door of the treatment room.

'They are taking good care of me,' Lily assured him. 'The staff are brilliant and they won't let me do a thing.'

'But you must be lonely.'

'No, not lonely. I miss you, of course,' she smiled, 'but the staff call in every quarter of an hour or so, and the matron said that Emily can sit with me for half an hour of her free time tonight, if I feel up to it.'

'Who is Emily?'

'She was Judy's flatmate. She's here.'

'I didn't know.'

She linked her fingers into his. 'I'm lucky to have you. Emily's boyfriend broke off their engagement as soon as she told him she was pregnant.'

'You're not that lucky.' He squeezed her hand lightly.

'I should have told you I was having a baby.'

'Yes, you should, but we'll do all our talking and saucepan throwing when you come home.'

'On Friday.'

'Mr Clay, you are going to tire your wife out.' The matron entered the room, the blood pressure gauge tucked under her arm.

'Can I visit her tomorrow evening?'

'No, Marty,' Lily declared, 'it's too far for you to drive every night after working all day.'

'It's barely an hour.'

'That's two here and back to Swansea.'

'May I suggest that you telephone here night and morning, for a progress report on your wife, Mr Clay. If there should be a change in Mrs Clay's condition outside of those hours, I will get in touch with you right away, on either the home or work telephone numbers you have given me, and, as you just said, you can be here in an hour.'

'It's much more sensible, Marty,' Lily insisted, 'and that way I'll get all the rest I need, and you'll have time to get everything ready in the house for when I come home.'

'And what happens if you need anything in the meantime?'

'You've left me money, I can ask one of the staff to buy whatever it is for me.'

'We are looking after your wife, Mr Clay.' The matron set the blood pressure gauge on the table and picked up Lily's chart.

Martin looked from Lily to the matron. He knew he was beaten. 'What time can I pick Lily up on Friday?'

'If everything goes well, after you finish work for the day seems like a good idea, wouldn't you say?' the matron answered.

'Thank you for everything you brought and thank the girls for the flowers, chocolates and magazines.' Lily stretched out her arms expectantly, waiting for his kiss.

'I will.' Knowing he'd been dismissed, he bent over the bed and kissed her goodbye. 'See you on Friday, darling.'

'This is ridiculously sudden, Judy.' Joy set a tray of tea of tea and biscuits on the coffee table in her living room. Brian and Judy were sitting side by side on the sofa, Billy ensconced happily on Brian's lap with a Farley's Rusk and a picture book.

'Not really.' Judy poured the tea and handed her stepfather a cup. 'Brian and I have known one another for years.'

'At the risk of sounding tactless, most of which time you spent more than two hundred and fifty miles apart and I don't recall you mentioning any letters.' Joy took the tea Judy handed her.

'I think I'll get more hot water.' Judy picked up the teapot and went into the kitchen.

Roy looked to Brian, as Joy followed her daughter out of the room. 'You're remarkably quiet,' he observed.

'Judy and I know our own minds and we're both of age.'

'So you're going ahead with this wedding in three weeks no matter what Joy or I say?'

'Nothing and no one can stop me from marrying Judy, Constable Williams, but that's not to say that I'll risk souring relations between myself and my future mother-in-law by arguing with her before she's even accepted the idea of me as Judy's husband.' Brian gently took hold of Billy's arm as he smeared his pullover with soggy rusk. 'It does make a pretty picture, Billy, but it's better eaten than used as a crayon.' Billy promptly giggled and smeared another line to join the ones he'd already drawn.

'But you'll let Judy do your arguing for you,' Roy suggested.

'I know better than to stand in the firing line between mother and daughter. Besides I remember just how close those two are.'

'They're different sides of the same coin.' Roy produced a bottle of whisky from the cupboard next to his chair. 'Shall we turn the tea into a toast, or is it a bit premature?'

'Not premature at all.' Brian snaffled the last of Billy's rusk and diverted his attention by turning the page of the picture book. 'Do you mind if I skip the tea and just have the whisky?'

'At this time of day?'

'I'd hate to risk scalding Billy,' Brian replied artfully.

'How can you possibly be sure that you're not marrying Brian just to spite Sam?'

'Because I love Brian,' Judy interrupted, facing her mother head on.

'And yesterday morning you thought you loved Sam.'

'That's just it, I thought I loved Sam, but if I'd been honest with myself I would have realised I didn't and probably never had. When I told you yesterday that I was breaking my engagement, you agreed that I was doing it for the right reasons. I could never have been happy with him.'

'And you think you can be happy with Brian?' Joy questioned.

'I know I can be, in every and all possible ways.' Judy didn't even try to suppress her smile.

'You . . .' Joy's jaw dropped as she sank down on a chair.

'It happened last night. It was absolutely perfect and I

finally understood why you couldn't explain what love-making is like. What was it you said about you and Roy?'

'I can't remember,' Joy prevaricated. 'But whatever happened between us, didn't happen on the day I broke my engagement to another man.'

'It's not just the lovemaking, wonderful as that is. Brian and I have the same opinions on everything important. He doesn't care what happened between Sam and me, he doesn't expect me to give up work, he actually understands that I want to open more salons, and he doesn't mind where we live, as long as we're together. He's happy with us getting married in a register office with me in a costume . . .'

'All this after only one night.'

'I feel as if I've known him forever.' Judy sat at the table opposite her mother. 'Be happy for me.'

'It looks like you're not giving me any other choice. The kettle is boiling. Perhaps we should join the men and make some plans.'

'This time Brian and I have made all the plans that need to be made,' Judy countered, 'and when it comes to our wedding, the one thing we've decided on is no fuss.'

'That will please Roy.'

'And you?' Judy asked, topping up the teapot.

'A little bit of me still hankers to see my daughter walk up the aisle in a white wedding dress, but as long as you are happy . . .'

'If I was any happier I'd burst.' Judy picked up the teapot and opened the door. 'I have your blessing?'

Joy hesitated for the barest fraction of a second. 'Of course, darling.'

'And you promise not to worry about me?'

'That I can't do. Perhaps you'll understand why, when you have children of your own.'

'The sooner the better.'

As Judy walked down the passage and opened the door

to the living room, Joy wondered if she'd heard her correctly.

Lily was lying in bed desperately striving to think calm thoughts. The doctor had warned her that the more upset she became and the more tears she shed, the greater the likelihood of miscarriage. Taking a deep breath she tried to imagine a quiet, green, sunlit woodland scene. But even as she visualised the clearing between the trees and set Martin and herself beneath a canopy of leaves next to a tranquilly flowing stream, she placed a pram close by. With a baby . . .

Maggie knocked the door and pushed it open. 'The matron said that provided you're up to it, Emily and I can come and annoy you.'

'I'm up to it,' Lily answered, grateful for the interruption, 'but I have no idea where the two of you are going to sit. It's crowded enough with just me in here.'

'I'll take the chair until Emily comes. She's on washing-up duty after supper and rumour has it the supervisor trained under Napoleon. No one will be allowed to leave the kitchen until every single little thing is gleaming, but I managed to cadge a cup of cocoa for you before they embarked on the blitz.' Maggie set it on the table, before pulling the chair closer to the bed.

'Thank you.'

'Are you feeling any better?'

'Tired, but the matron said that's down to the drugs they are giving me.'

'But you still have your baby.'

'Yes.' Lily flushed uncomfortably before reminding herself, yet again, that she had to stay calm for her baby's sake. But she was intensely aware that Maggie was going to have to relinquish her child six weeks after she had given birth, no matter what.

'There is nothing quite like holding your first child,' Maggie advised sympathetically.

'If it is born all right,' Lily qualified.

'The doctor thinks there'll be problems?'

'He said it's impossible to be one hundred per cent certain at this stage but all the signs indicate that at the moment, my baby is healthy.'

'Then I'm sure he will be.' Maggie produced a bundle of knitting from a bag she'd carried in. 'Do you mind if I knit while we talk?'

'You're knitting for your baby?' Lily asked in surprise, looking at the shape of a tiny bootee dangling from the needle.

'We have to make layettes – for the adoptive parents.'

'That must be hard.'

'It is,' Maggie concurred. 'At the moment I try to live day to day and not think about having to give up my baby when the time comes, but sometimes I can't help myself. Some of the girls say they can't wait to walk away from this place, and their baby and the birth and adoption can't come quick enough for them. I understand why they say it, but I'm not sure that any of them really believe it. And the girls who want to keep their babies but can't, think it will be easier for me to give mine up than it will be for them because I have other children to go back to. If anything, that makes it all the harder. I can't stop remembering what it was like to hold them after they were born. To feed and care for them, watch them grow stronger every day, to enjoy the excitement of their first word, their first step . . . I'm sorry . . .' She apologised. 'I have no idea why I'm talking to you like this. I hardly know you, and you should be resting quietly, not listening to my problems.' She pretended to study the half-finished bootee. 'I've tried to keep my emotions under control since I came here but as you see, I don't always succeed.'

'I only stopped myself from crying at the thought of losing my baby now, because the doctor warned me that the more upset I became the greater the chance I had of losing him,' Lily confessed. 'I would hate to imagine what I'd be like if I knew that I had to give him up after he was born.'

Maggie dropped her knitting on to her lap and locked her fingers together. 'I've only myself to blame for getting into this mess.'

'You do know that I'm married to Jack's brother.'

'Helen said you were her sister-in-law and I did wonder if you were related through her brother, or Jack's.'

'Martin's not at all like Jack.' Lily looked to the photograph of them taken on their wedding day that Katie had packed, and the matron had set on the table where she could see it. 'He's three years older and when they were children he was always the more sensible of the two. But then you probably know that Jack had a reputation for being wild.'

'No, I didn't, because although it sounds peculiar considering the condition I'm in, I hardly know Jack. You surprise me. My husband, Gordon,' Maggie's eyes glowed as she mentioned his name, 'used to say that Jack was one of the most mature and level-headed National Servicemen he'd ever had under his command.'

'Jack married just before he was called up and it changed him. Made him more thoughtful and responsible . . .' Lily faltered, realising how ridiculous it was to tell the woman who was having Jack's child that he was thoughtful and responsible.

'I told his wife that I wish I'd never written to him.' She looked up at Lily. 'I wouldn't have if I'd known that they couldn't have children.'

'Helen told you?'

Maggie nodded. 'Did Jack tell you that he wanted to adopt the baby?'

'He told my husband he wanted to try.'

'It's impossible of course.'

'Helen and Jack were thinking of adopting a baby before this happened.'

'And I ruined his marriage,' Maggie added miserably.

'I think Jack has to take equal share of that blame.'

'The old witch finally let me go.' Emily breezed into the room, as much as anyone in the third stage of pregnancy could breeze. 'You wouldn't believe what she had us doing. I'll be smelling of washing soda, disinfectant and bleach for a month.'

'Chocolate as a consolation prize.' Lily offered Emily the box.

'Thank you.' Emily perched on the end of Lily's bed. 'So what have you two been gossiping about?'

'A bit of this, a bit of that,' Lily prevaricated, glancing at Maggie. 'Nothing important.'

Chapter Twenty-Two

Judy leaned in the doorway of her living room watching Brian. He was sitting in one of the armchairs next to the fireplace, his head on his hand, his eyes unfocused.

'Penny for them.' She took possession of the chair opposite his.

'That's a lot of money for one man's thoughts.' He smiled and she felt as though her heart was turning somersaults.

'The casserole won't be ready for another half an hour.'

'I can wait.'

The preoccupied look on his face troubled her. 'If you're thinking about what Sam said in the café . . .'

'I'm not thinking about anything that idiot said.'

'I'd rather we discussed it, than pretended I was never engaged to him.'

'I wasn't thinking about Sam, I was thinking about life. How my entire future hung on one incident that I cursed as sheer bad luck at the time.'

'When you were wounded in London?' she guessed.

'If I hadn't been invalided out of the Met, I might never have considered returning to Wales, much less Swansea, but when Ronnie and Will asked me if I'd like to manage a garage here for them, the first person I thought of was you.'

'You say the nicest things.'

'I told you, I was carrying a whole bundle of regrets over the stupid way we parted.'

'Why didn't you write to me?'

'The same reason you didn't write to me.' He turned up the gas fire. 'It would have cost me my pride. Besides, whenever I pictured you, there was always a man close by, faceless, nameless, but definitely there. I knew a girl like you wouldn't be alone for long. And although I kept writing to Martin, he never mentioned you in any of his letters, so I presumed you'd found someone else and he was too tactful to mention it.'

'Martin never told you I was engaged?'

'Not a word,' he confirmed. 'For all I knew, you could have been married with half a dozen children.'

'In two and half years?'

'Two sets of triplets.' She laughed and he settled back in his chair, looking at her. 'So, I headed back here thinking about you, when I should have been thinking about the garage, all the while hoping to see you and refusing to admit it, even to myself. Then, when you walked in on Jack's homecoming party I took one look at you and knew that I had to get you back.'

'Funny way you went about it. Teasing me . . .'

'The first thing I found out about you was that you were managing eleven salons, the second that you were engaged to Sam. I thought I'd lost you for good.'

'Sam was rather possessive that night. I was angry with him. I even had a row with him about it when he took me home,' she confessed.

'And that left me trying to pretend that I didn't care about your engagement. Then, just as I'm wondering if I can bear to live in the same town as Mr and Mrs Sam Davies, he tells me you broke it off with him.'

'And you came running.'

'Literally.' He opened his arms. 'Here, woman.'

She crossed the hearthrug, curled at his feet and rested her head on his knee. 'I love you, Brian Powell.'

'And I love you, soon-to-be Mrs Judy Powell, but only because of a string of coincidences that could have broken anywhere along the line and that terrifies me.' He stroked her hair, loosening it from the French pleat she'd clipped it into. 'I could so easily have lost you. Possibly for ever and that doesn't bear thinking about.'

'I had no idea what love was until I met you.'

'The first or second time?'

'The first, I was an idiot . . .'

'Last night we agreed we both were.'

'I still think we should talk about Sam.'

'How would you like me to tell you in detail about my relationship with . . .' He paused for a moment.

'With?' she prompted.

'I'm looking for the right words.'

'Words? You had a harem?'

'I refuse to discuss numbers on the grounds that you may discover something you can use against me at a later date. Let's just say, those I have philandered with.'

She burst out laughing again. 'You make it sound like you went out with three-quarters of the girls in London.'

'Probably more.' He sounded serious, but she glimpsed a mischievous glint in his eye.

She considered his initial question. 'I don't think I want to know the details of you and those you have philandered with.'

'Then you should understand why I don't want to talk about you and Sam.'

'Your ex-girlfriends aren't likely to turn up and say anything quite as horrible about you as Sam said about me this afternoon, are they?'

'Hopefully not.' He caressed her neck. 'Forget Sam, Judy. I have.'

'Truthfully?' She linked her fingers into his.

'I won, I have the girl.' He slid down the chair and sat on the rug beside her.

'It's important to me you know that I didn't make love to Sam until after we set the date for the wedding on the night of Jack's homecoming party and only a couple of times after that,' she blurted breathlessly.

'After an eighteen-month engagement?'

'It was disastrous,' she added, before she lost her

courage. 'I couldn't bear Sam touching me and he knew it. I think that's why he said the things he did.'

'I'm glad you didn't tell me that before last night.'

'Why?'

'It might have cramped my style. I would have been too afraid to,' his smile broadened, 'kiss you – and more.'

'Now you know the truth, we'll never mention it again.'

'We have better things to talk about – and do.' He wrapped his arm around her shoulders, pulled her close and kissed her. 'Poor you and,' his smile turned from mischievous to wicked, 'poor Sam. No wonder he loses his temper so easily.'

'He was mad at us this afternoon.'

'Yes, he was,' he mused. 'And that's why I don't like the idea of you living here alone.'

'That's ridiculous. I've lived alone for years.'

'You lived with Helen until Jack came home and you had a flatmate when you moved in here. Can't you get someone to come and stay with you?'

'For three weeks?'

'I can move in . . .'

'There's no way that I'll allow you to move in here before we're married. I'd lose what little I have left of my reputation. And that won't be much after Sam spreads his version of how I broke our engagement around the town.'

'You could move into Lily's,' he suggested. 'Martin would jump at the chance of you being on hand to help look after her when she comes home.'

'In the same house as you and Sam!' she exclaimed in disbelief. 'Are you mad?'

'Why not?' he cajoled. 'Jack bolted the internal door on the basement after Sam hit me, and I have a feeling that it will remain bolted. And there are two spare bedrooms on the first floor. All I'd have to do is creep down the stairs from my attic in the early hours and even if we're caught, Lily, Martin and Jack will never tell.'

'No,' she said determinedly.

'Then move into your mother's house for three weeks.'

'Absolutely not.'

'I'll worry about you every night and every minute we're apart.'

'I know Sam,' she dismissed. 'He's always been more of a talker than a doer. Besides, he's a policeman. He'd never risk his job by trying to get back at me. He's harmless.' She ran her fingers through Brian's hair and looked into his deep brown eyes. 'In the meantime I can turn the oven down. The casserole will take longer to cook, but the room is warm, this rug comfortable and I can dim the lights . . .'

As he returned her caresses, she accidentally brushed her hand over the cut on his cheekbone. As it throbbed painfully to life, he only wished that he, like her, could believe that Sam was harmless.

'Bedtime, ladies.' The matron opened the door to Lily's room.

'Can we visit Lily tomorrow, Matron?' Emily heaved herself from the edge of Lily's bed, but not before the matron had seen her.

The matron appraised Lily with a professional and critical eye. She appeared tired, but there was a smile on her face. 'For half an hour in your free time, but not if you sit on her bed again, Davies.'

'Thank you, Matron.' Emily smiled victoriously at Lily and Maggie.

'Lights out in ten minutes.' As the matron walked away, Lily looked to Maggie. 'The suitcase my husband brought is behind the door. Could you open it please, and hand me the writing case in it? You can't miss it, it's red leather.'

'I can, but you heard Matron, lights out in ten minutes.'

'If I start a letter now, I can finish it in the morning. You can post letters from here?' Lily asked anxiously.

'The post is collected every morning from the hall table.' Maggie found the case and handed it to her. 'Matron can sell you a stamp.'

'I have stamps.'

'Then just give the letter to whoever brings your breakfast and ask them to put it on the table.'

'I will. Thank you for keeping me company.'

'I never thought I'd envy anyone bed rest,' Emily sighed. 'You have no idea how much of a luxury it would be for me to have a room to myself after weeks of sleeping in the same room as seven other women.'

'Only a couple more months to go.' Maggie joined Emily at the door. 'Goodnight, Lily.'

'Goodnight.' As Maggie closed the door behind her, Lily opened the stud on her writing case. Resting it on her knees, she took her fountain pen from its holder in the spine and an envelope from the pocket stitched inside the case. Unscrewing the top from her pen, she laid the envelope on the blotter and began to write Helen's name and address.

'With that eye and those bruises, you have absolutely no right to smile as if you've swallowed a banana sideways, but given the circumstances, I suppose I can understand it.' Martin slapped Brian soundly on the back as he joined him and Jack in the kitchen. 'Jack told me the news about you and Judy. Congratulations.'

'Thank you.' Brian glanced at the clock as he sat at the table. 'You two are up late. Lily isn't . . .'

'She's not out of the woods but the doctor is reasonably pleased with her and they've given me orders to stay away until Friday when I hope I'll be able to pick her up.'

'That is good.'

'Want some beer?' Jack held his bottle to the light to check the amount left in it.

'I wouldn't say no to a half.' Brian lifted a glass down from the cupboard.

'Sam's moved out,' Martin divulged.

'I'm sorry, you and Lily are going to be out of pocket.'

'No, we're not. He swapped digs with another officer.'

'So the bad news is we still have two coppers living in the basement,' Jack joked. 'The good news is that one of them isn't Sam.'

'You can start advertising the attic as well. I'll be moving into Judy's in three weeks. And you can both wipe that look off your faces. It will be legal. We went to the Guildhall this afternoon and booked the ceremony for three weeks today.'

'Good God!' Martin exclaimed.

'Neither of us see any point in wasting time waiting when we've decided to go ahead. Frankly I would have married her today if they'd let me. It will be a quiet do, nothing like the one she had planned with Sam. I'd like both of you to be there but I won't close the garage on a Monday.'

'And afterwards?'

'Afterwards?' Brian frowned quizzically at Martin.

'The honeymoon.'

'We'll take that later when we can both get time off,' Brian replied carelessly. 'The important thing for us now is that we get married and live together.'

'That has to be the most unromantic statement I've ever heard,' Jack said flatly.

'You're wrong, Jack,' Martin countered. 'That has to be one of the most romantic things a man's ever said.'

'Romantic or not, we have a garage to run in the morning.' Brian finished his beer.

Seeing Brian's frown deepen as he left the table, Jack asked, 'Is your face troubling you?'

'No, I'm not happy about Judy living alone. Sam said some pretty vicious things to both of us this afternoon. If he were still living here, at least I'd be able to keep half an eye on him.'

'Literally,' Jack joked, looking at Brian's eye, which was still swollen shut. 'You're worrying about nothing. Sam wouldn't dare do anything to Judy.'

'Judy would agree with you. I only wish I could.'

'He's a policeman,' Martin reminded them.

'I know.' For all their reassurances, Brian still couldn't quell the uneasy feeling in his stomach.

'Important letter, love?' John asked, as he saw Helen pull an envelope from her bag for the third time that morning.

'From Lily,' she explained.

'I saw Martin this morning. He said it's still on course for him to bring her home tonight.'

'That's what Lily said. She's looking forward to it.'

'Are you going to visit her?'

'Yes. Yes, I am,' she said decisively. 'Judy told me that she's arranged to meet Katie in Lily's at four to give the house a good going over so everything will be clean and perfect when Martin brings Lily home. I think I'll give them a hand.'

'Martin told me that he, Jack and Brian have been keeping the housework under control. They might not appreciate your interference.'

'Men's idea of "under control" and women's are two different things. Whether they appreciate our interference or not, we are going to clean Lily's house.'

'That's exactly what Katie said, which is why she asked me to come home early so I can look after Glyn while she goes to help them.'

Helen lifted the last letter from her in-tray and slipped it into the filing tray. 'I've finished the summer orders, and sorted the initial ones for the autumn stock, so do you mind if I leave for the day?'

'Not at all.' John glanced at the clock. 'In fact, given the hours you've been putting in lately, I'll be glad to think of you relaxing for once. Go and have fun. Call Katie and Judy and arrange a lunch.'

'I have a few errands to run and I thought I'd do some shopping.'

'Even better.'

'I'll see you tomorrow morning.'

‘Helen . . .’ He began anxiously.

‘I’m fine, Dad,’ she interrupted. ‘Really, I’m fine,’ she repeated, aware that she hadn’t convinced him. She waited until her father went into his office before picking up the telephone on her desk and dialling a number she had asked Directory Enquiries to get her that morning.

‘Good morning, Powell and Ronconi garage.’

Helen pressed her pen down so hard on her notepad she splayed the nib. ‘Could I speak to Jack Clay, please?’

‘I’ll see if he’s free.’ There was a thud as the receptionist dropped the receiver and the sound of a door opening followed by a shout. ‘Jack, telephone.’

She imagined Jack dropping whatever he was doing and running towards the office. The image was very real and agonisingly painful. She could trace every line of his body, knew every nuance of expression on his face . . .

‘Jack Clay.’

‘It’s Helen.’

He hesitated for a few interminable seconds, then said, ‘You’re calling off Sunday.’

‘No, I want to help the girls clean Lily and Martin’s house this afternoon ready for when she comes home.’

‘I’m driving down to fetch her with Martin.’

‘I’d like to stay in the house until she arrives.’

‘And you don’t want me there,’ he speculated.

‘I won’t find it easy to be in the same room as you,’ she admitted.

‘With your father married to my sister, it may not be possible for us to avoid one another for the rest of our lives, Helen.’

‘I know.’

‘We need to talk.’

‘That’s why I telephoned.’

He dropped his voice to a whisper. ‘If you want a divorce . . .’

‘We need to discuss it.’

‘Not on the telephone,’ he declared. ‘You really want me out of the house tonight?’

'I know it's a lot to ask when you are living there.'

'I can be polite, if you can.'

'I suppose I could try.'

'And Sunday is still on?' he questioned urgently.

'We need to talk before then.'

'Name the time and the place and I'll be there.' When she remained silent he murmured, 'Sweetheart, I love you . . .'

Unable to bear the sound of his whispered endearments, she snapped, 'Do you get a lunch break?'

'I can get an hour off whenever suits you.'

She glanced at the clock. 'Half an hour, that way we can avoid the lunch time rush.'

'Half past eleven it is. Shall we meet in Castle Gardens?'

'Too public.'

'Then where?'

She thought rapidly. 'Brynmill Park. I don't know anyone who goes there at lunchtime. I'll meet you by the animal cages.'

'I'll be there.'

'You'll keep in touch,' Lily pressed. Maggie was packing Lily's case. She coloured in embarrassment when Maggie looked across at her. 'I suppose that wouldn't be appropriate.'

'We could exchange Christmas cards,' Maggie suggested, 'and add a line or two about what we're doing.'

'I'd like that.' Lily moved her legs over as Maggie set a pile of magazines on the bed. 'You can keep those if you like.'

'Are you sure?'

'I've read them.'

'The other girls would be grateful.' Maggie stacked them on the chair and looked around the tiny room. 'That seems to be about it.'

'You and Emily have both been wonderful. I was so miserable at the beginning of the week, it felt as if I'd have to stay here for ever and now I'm going home . . .'

Lily winced as a scream echoed along the corridor. High-pitched, panic stricken, it sounded like the cry of a terrified animal.

'Shouldn't they send for the doctor?' Lily turned to Maggie in alarm.

'If there were any complications the matron would have sent for him last night.'

'But that girl, whoever she is, has been in labour since yesterday.'

'Long labours are common with first babies.'

'That's normal?' Lily's eyes rounded in fear as another scream rent the air.

'No,' Maggie replied, 'but Marilyn's scared. She's been dreading the birth and by the sound of it, she's too frightened to help herself.'

'But she must be in pain.'

'Not as much as it sounds.' Maggie made an effort to sound reassuring. 'I've had four so I should know. Please, I know it's difficult, but try to ignore her. She and her baby will both be fine and,' she glanced at her watch, 'it can't be much longer now.'

Helen saw Martin's car parked close to the top gates to Brynmill Park in Glanbrydan Avenue. Pulling up behind it, she opened her car door and stepped out. It was a perfect summer's day. Wisps of clouds hung motionless in the sky, tingeing the deep blue with the merest hints of white. Two little girls dressed in pink shorts and blouses hurtled past, hand in hand. They ran through the gates chattering excitedly and all of a sudden she felt old and overdressed. The square-necked, slim-line, beige linen dress and small straw hat that had pleased her so much when she had dressed that morning seemed too elaborate for a walk in the park, and she found herself wishing that she was one of those two little girls running wild, carefree, with no problems that a grown-up couldn't solve for her.

But she wasn't a child any more. She was an adult with adult problems. She took a moment to slip on her black cotton gloves and hang her black patent handbag over her arm. She checked her hat was straight in the wing mirror of her car, set her head high and walked through the gates.

Jack had been watching for her and, as always, his breath caught in his throat when he saw her. She looked cool, beautiful and elegant. A wife any man would be proud of and he'd been stupid enough to hurt.

'Martin and I used to spend hours here when we were kids,' he said, as she drew close to him. 'We used to pretend the animals were ours. We gave all of them our own special names, the monkey, the rabbits, the guinea pigs, the birds.'

'I'm surprised you didn't run out. There are so many of them, especially birds.'

'There we cheated. All the blue ones were Bluey, followed by a number.'

'You could tell them apart?' She looked into his eyes, dark, tender and loving. It took all her powers of concentration to remember what he had done.

'No, but we pretended we could.' He held up a couple of paper bags. 'I bought a couple of cheese rolls and pasties in Eynon's. We could sit on that bench and eat them.'

'Snap.' She opened her handbag and extracted a bag containing two rolls that she'd bought in a baker's in the Uplands. 'I saw Martin's car parked by the gates, I'm surprised he lent it to you.'

'He offered when I told him I was seeing you.' He wiped the bench over with his handkerchief although it appeared to be perfectly clean. 'Would you like to sit down?'

'Why not.' She averted her eyes from his. Although she was dreading the conversation moving from general to more personal topics, she was finding it remarkably easy to talk to him, but once he sat beside her she felt suffocated by his proximity. Unable to look him in the eye, she unwrapped the roll she'd bought and laid it on the paper bag on her lap.

'If this can be taken as an example, I think it's safe to say that we can be civil to one another in Martin and Lily's house tonight,' he said quietly.

'I wanted to see you, because I think Martin and Lily will have enough to worry about when she comes home, without you staying with them as well.'

'I moved in as a temporary measure, but between work and what happened to Lily, there hasn't been much time for me to look for anywhere else. And Martin needed the company.'

'If he needs company, he has Brian and the boys downstairs.'

'Brian's moving out two weeks Monday. He's marrying Judy.'

'Judy told me.'

'Did you ask me here to tell me that you want a divorce, Helen?' Jack questioned suddenly.

'Would you blame me if I did?'

'No.' He looked her in the eye. 'If that's what you want, you should have it. There's no doubt that you deserve to be shot of me after what I did, but as I said on the telephone, I love you and if there is a chance – no matter how small – that you'll take me back, I'll do whatever it takes.'

'You know I went to visit Maggie.'

'Brian told me you were at the house when you telephoned to tell Martin that Lily had collapsed.' He followed her example and unwrapped a roll, but like her, he made no attempt to eat it. 'Why did you go there?'

'Because I wanted to see her for myself. She wasn't at all what I expected.'

'What did you expect?'

'A beautiful young girl,' she said simply. 'I'd imagined you cavorting on the beach with her, swimming, picnicking, you in trunks, her in a revealing two-piece . . .'

'I told you what Maggie was like and how it happened between us. Didn't you believe me?'

'I can't explain it, I just had to see her for myself.' She opened her roll and peered at the slice of cheese it contained. 'She told me that you wanted to adopt her baby.'

'I did.'

'You really think that you can bring it up on your own?'

'I hoped to, but everyone has quashed any ideas I had in that direction. A separated man without a home or money, whose wife has solid grounds for divorcing him, has absolutely no chance of adopting a child, even when it's his. I saw a solicitor earlier this week and he confirmed what everyone had been telling me.' He broke a piece of bread from his roll and tossed it to a pigeon scavenging beneath a litterbin.

'The baby is that important to you.'

'Yes.'

'More important than me.'

He glanced across and saw that she was watching him intently. 'No.'

'Then if I took you back . . . and that is an "if",' she warned, as his eyes lit up, 'you'd give up any idea you had of adopting the baby.'

'I'd like to say yes, but there wouldn't be any element of sacrifice on my part,' he confessed candidly. 'The solicitor told me that I had no chance of adopting the child and Maggie didn't want me to have the baby either. She's hoping that he will go to a settled home with a mother and a father who can give him all the love and attention he deserves, not a single man without a home, who'd have to rely on babysitters and outside help.'

'Sensible woman, Maggie.'

'Yes, she is.' He fell silent and she sensed that he was bracing himself to tell her something. 'If there is any chance that you will take me back, Helen, I meant what I said. I'd do anything to make you happy. And I swear I'll never as much as look at another woman again . . .'

'No, don't swear,' she cut in. 'None of us know what lies in the future.'

'Do you think there'll ever come a time when you would consider taking me back?' he asked.

'Not as my husband – not yet anyway,' she qualified. 'At the moment I don't even know how I feel about you and what you've done, much less make a decision as to how I can deal with it. But if you want, you can come back home.'

'Home – you mean to your house?'

'I'm not doing this for you, Jack, but for Marty and Lily. With everything that's going on in their lives at the moment, I think it's a bit much to expect them to cope with you and our problems as well.'

'Thank you,' he murmured humbly.

'You can have whichever one of the three spare bedrooms you want. And with both of us back under one roof it will be easier for us to make a decision about our future without involving your brother and sister, my father and half our friends.'

'As I said, I'll do anything.'

'You can start by not overwhelming me,' she warned. 'You hurt me – and badly. I feel as though I'm only just coming back to life and it's a slow and painful process. Day-to-day living is difficult enough without trying to analyse my feelings towards you, so let's just take it as it comes, one day at a time. Agreed?' She looked at him.

'Yes.'

'And if I think it's not working out between us and ask you to leave again, the next time it will be for good.'

'I understand.'

'You can come back with me tonight after I leave Lily and Martin's.'

'I'll ride my bike over. I'll need transport,' he explained, 'for work.'

She nodded. Breaking her roll into smaller pieces, she

threw the crumbs among the pigeons that had gathered at their feet. She crumpled the paper bag, put it in a litterbin and rose to her feet. 'I'll see you later.'

'Yes.' As she walked away, Jack felt something he hadn't experienced since she'd ordered him out of the house. A tiny spark of hope.

'You will remember – the slightest sign of any pain or any problem and you drive your wife straight to the nearest hospital,' the doctor warned Martin sombrely.

'I will.' Martin shook the doctor's hand.

'And you have arranged for your own doctor to visit Lily first thing tomorrow morning as I asked you to?'

'He said he'd be over straight after morning surgery,' Martin confirmed.

'By rights I should send her to the nearest hospital, but . . .' The doctor shrugged his shoulders. 'I can see that your wife will be much happier once she is closer to her home, and the more stress and anxiety we can avoid, the better it will be for mother and baby. It is less than an hour's drive,' he added, as though he were still trying to convince himself that he had made the right decision in allowing Martin to take Lily back to Swansea.

'Thank you for everything,' Martin said gratefully. They both turned as the matron approached, walking alongside Lily who was being wheeled in a chair by one of the staff.

'You look miles better, darling.' Martin smiled in relief.

'I feel miles better.' Lily grasped his hand. 'Better enough to walk to the car.'

'Oh no, you don't, young lady,' the doctor directed forcefully. 'I haven't kept you on a week's bed rest for you to go gallivanting now. You will take it easy, if not for your own sake, then for the sake of that baby you're carrying.'

'I promise.' Lily looked up at him. 'Thank you for everything you've done for me and the baby.'

'Just look after him until he can be safely delivered.'

'I will.'

'Now, we have to carry this chair out of the house and down the steps,' the matron interposed, steering the conversation back to the practical. 'I'll call another member of staff to help.'

'I've parked the car as close to the front door as I could get it.' Martin couldn't stop smiling at Lily. 'I could lift Lily out of the chair and carry her down the steps, there are only a couple of them.'

'As long as you don't drop her, young man,' the doctor warned gruffly.

'I'll tell my brother to open the car door.' Martin went to the front door and shouted to Jack.

Lily offered the matron her hand. 'Thank you.'

'Take care of yourself and your baby and let us know when he or she is born.'

'I will.'

The doctor stood beside the matron in the porch, as Jack drove Martin's car out of the courtyard and down the road.

'You think there are going to be serious complications, don't you?' The matron accompanied him to his car.

'If I'm right and the placenta is below the baby, yes. She'll be extremely lucky to hold on to it until it is viable.'

'She'll need a Caesarean.'

'Without a doubt, but I've seen worse cases end happily. Let's hope hers does.'

'If it does, it will be because you broke all the rules and kept her in here for a week.'

'Sometimes I wonder who the doctor is in this place, you or me. Keep a close eye on Mrs Jones,' he warned as he climbed into the driver's seat. 'If her blood pressure rises again, call me, or if I'm not around, telephone for an ambulance.'

'I don't need you to tell me how to do my job.'

'I know. See you in the morning.'

Matron watched the doctor drive away before turning back to the house. It was a cold, clear spring evening. She would have liked to walk around to the garden to admire the camellias that had just come into full pink flower. They looked splendid from her office window. And it was the time of year when she liked to examine the embryonic hostas and perennials pushing their way up through the brittle, dried remains of last year's debris. Buds were about to burst into life on the shrubs – but she had a hostel to run, girls and babies to look after.

Marilyn hadn't stopped crying since her baby had been delivered that morning and she dare not risk giving her any more sedation lest it contaminate her milk. A careful eye had to be kept on Maggie Jones. Pregnancies could so often be difficult in women of her age.

As she climbed the steps she reflected that duty was time-consuming but she couldn't understand just why it seemed so much harder to shoulder her responsibilities after seeing Lily off. Perhaps it was the way that her husband had looked at her when he'd arrived. Tall, dark, with brown eyes, Martin Clay didn't bear any resemblance to her late husband that she could recall, but there had been a look in his eye that had seemed familiar. A look that quite unexpectedly tugged at emotions she'd assumed she no longer possessed.

Chapter Twenty-Three

'Are you really all right?' Martin turned around in the front passenger seat and rearranged the rug he'd covered Lily with when he had set her down in the back of the car.

'I'm fine, Marty. Please stop worrying about me.' She clasped her hands around her knees and lay back on the cushions he had thoughtfully brought from home. 'After a week of being cooped up in one room, the world seems huge and full of colour. I can't wait to hear all the news. What has everyone been doing?'

'Slow down, Jack,' Martin shouted, as his brother negotiated a humpbacked bridge.

'Any slower and the hedgehogs will be overtaking us.' Despite the quip, Jack glanced anxiously at Lily in the mirror. 'That didn't jar you, did it?'

'No, you are driving beautifully,' she reassured. 'Now relax, the pair of you, or you'll both be nervous wrecks before we reach Swansea.'

'I'll relax,' Martin promised, 'but not until we get you home and you are safe and sound in bed.'

'Where do you want it?' Brian asked Judy, carrying Lily and Martin's television set into their bedroom.

'I'm not sure.' Judy looked at Helen and Katie. 'Where do you think it should go?'

'If you don't decide in the next two minutes, my arms will drop off,' Brian warned.

'Set it on the windowsill for the moment,' Helen advised. 'We'll need a table for it anyway.'

'Are you sure the aerial will stretch up here?' Judy pulled the sheet off the bed and straightened the under-blanket.

'John and Roy are seeing to it now.' Brian looked around the room. 'I thought you girls were supposed to be helping. The house was tidier before you started.'

'For your information, we're changing the bed,' Helen retorted cuttingly.

'Make yourself useful, darling, and see if you can find a table for the television.' Judy tied the bedclothes they'd taken off the bed into a neat bundle and set it outside the door.

'I'll see what I can do.'

Katie looked at her watch as she shook the bolster into a case. 'They should be here in half an hour. Do you think we will have finished by then?'

'There's only the television to sort out and the bed to be made,' Judy said briskly. 'My mother has the meal in hand and everything else in the house is spotless.'

'Judy, there's a mountain of furniture in here,' Brian shouted from the box room. 'I'm not sure which table will go best in Lily's bedroom.'

'Don't take too long deciding.' Helen gave Judy a sly grin. 'Or we'll never have it set up before Lily gets here.'

'Alone at last.' Brian shut the door of the box room as Judy joined him.

'We have work to do.' She pushed him away but not before she kissed him. 'Now where are these tables . . .' She laughed as he picked her up and swung her off her feet. 'Let me go, you brute.'

'If I thought you meant it, I might,' he murmured, kissing her again.

'Judy was never like that with Sam,' Katie commented, as the sound of Brian and Judy's smothered laughter echoed from the box room.

'She seems to be happier than she has been for a while,'

Helen agreed, shaking the eiderdown on top of the bedspread.

'To be honest, I was a bit worried about her and Sam. They always seemed to be arguing about something or other, but I hope they managed to break it off amicably. They're both such nice people, I'd hate for them to fall out.'

'Katie, Katie, Katie.' Helen shook her head. 'You're the sweetest person I know, but it's simply not possible for the entire world to live happily ever after.'

'It's just that I'm so lucky and happy with John and Glyn . . .'

'You want everyone else to be,' Helen suggested.

'Is that so bad of me?'

'No, it's wonderful of you, but what you have to realise is that you're an angel and the rest of us – well, let's say we're somewhat less than angelic and as such we don't deserve your happiness.'

'That's nonsense.'

'You know what they say. People get the lives they deserve.'

'Not always.' Katie hesitated nervously. 'I haven't liked to ask before, but you're here and Jack will be here soon, so is there any chance that you'll be able to forgive him?' she finished bravely.

'Could you forgive John if he had an affair with another woman?'

'If he asked me to, yes.'

'See what I mean about being an angel?' Helen picked up the polish and duster she'd used to clean the dressing table. 'But you don't have to be afraid that I'll thump Jack as soon as I see him. I met him earlier today and we managed to talk to one another in a civilised manner, which is why I'm here now.'

'Then there is hope?' Katie's thin face broke into a radiant smile.

'I wouldn't go that far. I'll just take these downstairs.' Helen picked up the bundle of bedclothes and made her way down to the kitchen. The hall clock chimed the half hour. Jack would soon be in the house. She shivered at the thought. She had managed to meet and talk with him in the park but then they hadn't an audience of their closest friends to cope with. And tonight – would it really be possible for both of them to live under the same roof and discuss building any kind of a future together?

She found herself wishing a year of her life away, because no matter what choices she made in the next few days or weeks, a year from now, for better or worse, she would have made them. It remained to be seen whether she would find herself in a situation she could live with.

Martin sat sideways in the passenger seat of his car, regaling Lily with the story of Judy breaking her engagement to Sam and arranging a marriage to Brian, but even as she made anxious enquiries about Brian's fight with Sam, she grew visibly paler.

'Don't tell me you're all right.' Martin's voice was rough with concern. 'You're as white as a sheet. If you're in pain . . .'

'I just feel a little cold and faint,' Lily whispered. 'But it's nothing, darling. Just the movement of the car and the smell of petrol.'

'I can't smell petrol, can you, Jack?'

'It's just having a baby.' Lily tried to smile, but her mouth seemed numb, her face muscles oddly stiff. 'All your senses are heightened; every time the staff opened my window in the hostel I could smell wild garlic and they said it was fields away . . .' Her voice faded as she lay back on the seat and closed her eyes.

'Do you want us to stop the car?' Martin reached out and took her hand into his. It was ice cold. 'Lily!' When she didn't respond, he gripped Jack's arm. 'Stop!'

As Jack checked the rear-view mirror before screeching to a halt, Martin leaped out and opened the back door. When he gathered Lily into his arms and moved the rug covering her legs he saw that her skirt was soaked with blood.

Jack fought a rising tide of panic as he looked from Lily to Martin. Desperately trying to keep a grip on his emotions, he studied their surroundings. The street was familiar; terrace houses stretched in unbroken lines either side of them . . . 'Get into the car, Marty, we can be in Swansea Hospital in ten minutes.'

'They should have been here half an hour ago. I hope everything is all right.' Katie walked from the living room where Judy, Roy, Brian and Helen were sitting with the two children, into the kitchen where Joy was transferring the vegetables and joint of beef she had cooked into Pyrex dishes that could be reheated in the oven.

'Perhaps the doctor wanted to check Lily over one last time,' Joy suggested, in an attempt to hide her own concern.

Katie checked the clock. It was twenty-five minutes to nine, exactly five minutes since she had last looked at the time. Brian had told them that Jack and Martin had left the garage at five. It was about an hour's drive to the hostel and an hour back, so even allowing for the vagaries of traffic and time for Lily to pack, which she was sure Lily would have done before Martin arrived, they were long overdue. 'Do you think we should telephone the hostel?'

'It might be an idea,' Joy concurred, stowing the last of the casserole dishes into the oven. 'On the other hand, if they had been delayed in the hostel, you'd think they would have telephoned.'

'I bet that's them now,' Katie said in relief as the telephone rang. Roy picked up the receiver and she stood watching, waiting expectantly in the doorway, but when he looked up and she saw the dark expression in his eyes, she froze.

Jack left the telephone kiosk and stood in the corridor

fighting nausea, as the potent mix of odours that he would forever associate with hospitals assailed his nostrils; antiseptic vied with disinfectant, boiled cabbage, urine and human sweat.

He'd left Martin in a small waiting room, set off the entrance to the gynaecological ward, a room so small he sensed it was used exclusively for the relatives of critically ill patients, and they'd had an enormous fight with an officious ward sister to be granted even that dubious privilege. She had informed them in no uncertain terms that husbands should wait at home and telephone their enquiries at two-hourly intervals. If it hadn't been for the intervention of a sympathetic doctor, he doubted that Martin would have been tolerated on the premises, let alone him.

He had promised Martin that he would return as soon as he had telephoned the house, but the thought of returning to sit next to his brother in that bleak, soulless, institution room, waiting for news that he suspected would be unbearable when it came, was more than he could endure. All his problems with Helen paled into insignificance when he compared them to what Martin was facing. The loss of his wife as well as his child.

How would Martin and all of them cope if the unthinkable happened? He suppressed the thought even as it formed. If he didn't think about it, nothing bad would happen. It couldn't. Not to Lily.

He continued to stand in the corridor, too numb to do anything other than absorb the sights and sounds around him. A nurse hurried down the corridor, her rubber-soled shoes squeaking against the linoleum. A subdued murmur of voices hummed from a sluice room on the ward ahead. A porter wheeled a trolley loaded with used cups past him. He stared at the radiator on the wall and mentally ticked off the thick metal bars. Lily would be all right. She wouldn't, would, wouldn't, would, wouldn't . . .

'Are you lost?' a staff nurse enquired briskly.

'No.' He resented her intrusion because she had stopped him on 'wouldn't.' Didn't she realise how important it was that he be allowed peace and quiet to run to the end of the radiator?

'Visitors aren't allowed to linger in the corridor, especially outside of official visiting hours,' she informed him sharply.

'I was using the telephone.'

'There is a public telephone outside the main gates.'

'I'm with my brother. His wife is seriously ill.'

'He should go home and telephone later.'

'They said we could wait.'

'What ward is she on?'

'The gynaecological ward.'

'I'm going that way. I'll walk with you.' The nurse escorted him as if she were transferring a prisoner.

Martin was still sitting in the same position. Slumped forward on a hard, upright, wooden chair, his head in his hands, as inert as a waxwork figure.

Jack sat alongside him. There was no point in asking Martin if he had heard any news of Lily. It was patently obvious that he hadn't.

'Come on, love.' John lifted Glyn from Katie's lap and leaned him against his shoulder. 'There's nothing we can do here. We'll go home and put the baby to bed.'

'I can't leave,' she protested, 'not until we hear how Lily is.'

'The minute we hear anything, I'll come round and tell you,' Brian promised, eyeing Roy who was pacing restlessly between the living room and the hall.

'I want to be here,' Katie insisted obstinately. 'If Martin or Jack come back, they'll need me.'

'From what Jack told Roy, there might not be any news for hours,' Brian reminded. 'You could be here all night.'

'I don't care.' Katie glared at Brian and he realised that she was in no state to listen to reason.

'I checked on Billy a few minutes ago, he's sleeping fast in the spare room,' Judy informed Joy when her mother returned from the kitchen where she'd been transferring the food no one wanted to eat from the stove to the fridge.

'Thank you.' Joy took Roy's arm. 'Come and sit down, Roy.'

'The phone . . .'

'Is not going to ring any sooner for you pacing around it.'

Roy allowed her to lead him to the sofa but, as he sank trembling and wild-eyed beside Judy, it was obvious he was in shock.

Unable to sit still a moment longer, Helen rose to her feet. 'Would anyone like a cup of tea?'

'That's a good idea,' Joy agreed, recognising Helen's need to do something useful. 'Judy, why don't you give her a hand?' As they left the room, she turned to Katie. 'John's right, Katie, you should put Glyn to bed.'

'Please,' Katie begged, 'let me stay, if only for a little while longer. Just until Jack telephones again.'

'In that case, I'll go next door and get a clean nappy, Glyn's pyjamas and the pram. He can sleep in the hall.' John went to the door.

'Give Glyn to me.' Brian held out his arms. 'There's no point in taking him outside until you have to.'

'I'll see if I can do anything in the kitchen.' Katie left the room.

'Katie is very close to her brothers,' Joy murmured.

'I discovered that before I married her.' John looked at Roy, and Joy knew they were both thinking the same thing. It wasn't only Martin who was going to be devastated if anything happened to Lily. She might only be Roy's foster daughter, but Joy knew her husband was as devoted to Lily as he was to his son.

'Mr Clay.'

Martin and Jack both jumped to their feet as a doctor dressed in a surgical gown approached them.

'Lily,' Martin stammered thickly, staggering and hitting the back of his knee against a chair.

'Sit down, Mr Clay, before you fall down.' The doctor, who was twice Martin's age and half his size, took him by the elbow and pushed him back on to his chair. Jack remained standing, hovering at Martin's side.

'Your wife has lost a lot of blood, she is very ill.'

'But she will recover?' Martin looked up, willing him to say yes.

'We'll know more in the next twenty-four hours. All that we can do for her, has been done,' the doctor assured him.

'Can I see her?'

'She is very ill. She needs absolute peace and quiet.'

'Just for a few moments,' Martin pleaded.

'The baby is still viable, Mr Clay.'

'Viable?' Martin repeated the word vacantly.

'Your wife is still pregnant.'

As comprehension dawned, Martin blurted, 'You're not trying to save the baby at the cost of Lily's . . . ?'

'It's not like that, Mr Clay,' the doctor explained patiently. 'Your wife's haemorrhage was caused by complications in her pregnancy, but we have stopped the bleeding. It would be more dangerous for us to operate and remove the baby than it would be to leave things as they are. She is stable for the moment. If she remains stable, she may continue to carry the baby, but it is far too early to make any prognosis concerning the pregnancy or her future condition. We simply have to wait and see how things will develop.'

'There is hope,' Jack pressed. 'I mean, there has to be hope – for both of them?'

'Yes,' the doctor confirmed cautiously, 'but as I said, the next twenty-four hours will be crucial for Mrs Clay and her baby. Why don't you both go home and get some rest?'

'Not before I see Lily,' Martin broke in insistently.

'That is quite out of the question.'

'I am not leaving here until I see Lily.' Martin reiterated. He spoke softly but the doctor recognised his resolve.

'You can look through the door, but only for a few seconds and we'll have to watch out for the ward sister. She'll skin me alive if she sees me bringing a relative into her ward at this time of night. And your brother has to stay here.'

Lily was lying in a small room at the end of the ward, a bewildering array of tubes going in and out of her body beneath the bedclothes, a bottle of blood on a stand next to her.

'We're trying to replace the blood she has lost,' the doctor explained.

'Can I hold her hand?'

'I'm afraid not, Mr Clay.' The doctor led him back to the room where Jack was waiting. 'You can telephone first thing in the morning.'

'I can't leave . . .'

'We're not anticipating any change one way or the other in your wife's condition before then.'

'Does Lily know she's still pregnant?'

'We'll tell her as soon as she regains consciousness.' The doctor nodded to Jack. 'Take your brother home, Mr Clay. And don't telephone before eight in the morning or the night sister will bite your head off.'

'Come on, Marty.' Jack tried to pull his brother away, but Martin continued to stand and stare. He couldn't help feeling that Lily would have had a smooth and uneventful pregnancy, like his sister Katie, if only he'd been sensible and accepting from the outset, instead of so stupidly and viciously proud.

Jack turned to look at Martin's house and switched off the car engine. The curtains hadn't been closed over the living-room window and he could see Joy, Roy, Brian and John sitting around the coffee table.

'Looks like everyone's waiting for us to come back.'

'I can't face anyone. You'll talk to them for me.'

Jack nodded, locked the car and followed Martin to the door. Before Martin had time to slip his key into the lock, Katie opened the door and fell sobbing into his arms. As Jack tried to prise her away, Martin shook his head.

'Give us a moment.' He sank down on to the stairs taking Katie with him. 'You go and tell everyone.'

'Lily?' Katie drew her head back from Martin's shoulder.

'They're doing all they can.'

'The baby?'

'Is viable – for the moment.' As Martin repeated the doctor's words, he looked up and saw Jack watching him with an expression almost as bleak as the one he had worn when he had told him that Helen had lost their baby.

'Stay here for the night, or if you don't want to do that, stay in your mother's house,' Brian tried to persuade Judy, as he walked her to the door.

She shook her head. 'I have to work tomorrow and if I start with the Mumbles salon I can come into town early and see if there's any change with Lily.'

'I wish you wouldn't go. It's one o'clock.'

'And the streets will be empty and quiet. Ten minutes drive and I'll be home. Besides,' she opened her car door, 'we should all try to get some sleep.'

'Fat chance of that tonight. If only there was something I could do!' he exclaimed vehemently, closing one hand into a fist and punching his palm.

'I think we all feel that way. But wearing ourselves out and getting angry isn't going to help Lily or Martin or their baby.' She kissed him. ''Night, darling, see you tomorrow.'

'If you come past the garage at lunchtime, I'll have sandwiches waiting.'

'Thank you.'

He stood breathing in the night air and watching while she drove away. The door opened again and Jack stepped out. He turned and gave Helen a hand to lift Glyn's pram over the doorstep.

'You're leaving?' Brian asked in surprise.

'Katie's insisted on staying with Martin,' Helen explained, 'and my father won't leave her so I volunteered to spend the night with Glyn next door.'

'Katie and Joy are making up beds in the spare rooms and John and Roy are sitting with Marty. I'll be back as soon as I've given Helen a hand to get the pram inside.' Jack took the keys Helen handed him and jumped over the wall while she wheeled the pram down the short path and around to her father's door.

'As someone has to open the garage tomorrow, I'm going to bed, but if there is any news . . .'

'You'll probably reach the telephone before us.'

'Not from the attic floor, I won't,' Brian demurred.

'I'll take my bike into the garage tomorrow, in case I'm needed back here in a hurry,' Jack said shortly.

'You don't have to go into work.'

'Yes, I do,' Jack answered. 'Whatever happens here, I've a feeling I'll need to be kept busy.'

'And Martin?' Brian asked.

Jack looked through the window. 'He has Roy.'

Judy parked her car outside her flat, picked up her handbag from the passenger seat and opened the door. She jumped back as a dark figure loomed over her.

'I'm sorry, I didn't mean to scare you.'

'You almost gave me a heart attack,' she accused Sam, getting out. 'What are you doing here?'

'As you see, I'm in uniform and on duty.'

'You're more likely to find criminals on Mumbles Road than the side streets.'

'The side streets are where most burglaries take place and there's been a spate of them around here lately.'

'I haven't heard anything.'

'You obviously didn't read tonight's *Evening Post*.'

'I haven't had time to read anything this evening.'

'Which is surprising, considering how late it is. Been somewhere special with Brian?' he sneered.

'No.' She turned to face him. 'I'm tired, Sam.'

'And you have a busy day in the salons tomorrow,' he taunted.

'Yes. Goodnight, Sam.' She couldn't help remembering Brian's concern, as she opened her front door, and shut it quickly behind her.

'No, don't come in, Jack.' Helen blocked his path, as he tried to follow her into John and Katie's house. 'I'm going to try and settle Glyn in his cot.'

'You might be better off leaving him in his pram until morning.'

'I'll think about it.'

'We'll talk tomorrow.'

She nodded. 'If there's any news . . .'

'I'll let you know.' He stepped outside and she closed the door softly behind him.

Katie had fed and changed Glyn before Helen had taken him from Martin's house, and although Katie, Jack and John had warned her that it might be best to leave Glyn in his pram, she felt he would sleep better in his own cot in his own room. Lifting him carefully out of the pram, she set him against her shoulder and carried him up the stairs, marvelling at how heavy he had become since the last time she had held him.

He rubbed his eyes sleepily and she laid him gently on his side in his cot, covering him with his blanket. She hovered expectantly. At his first whimper she lifted him out and sat in Katie's wooden rocking chair. Tucking a shawl, Welsh fashion, around both of them, she rocked gently, cradling the sleeping child and trying not to think about Lily, or how she was fighting to keep her baby. But no matter how hard she tried to concentrate on other things, she couldn't stop herself from picturing Lily lying in the same hospital bed, in the same ward she had been in after she had lost her baby.

Resting her cheek against Glyn's, she absorbed the scent of baby talcum powder, felt his velvet skin brush against her own, rested her hand lightly on his back as he breathed softly in and out, and was overwhelmed with a desire to protect and care for this tiny brother cum nephew of hers. He was small, helpless and vulnerable, yet capable of generating so much love.

Did that apply to all babies, or just to Glyn because she loved her father and Katie and knew how precious he was to them? Could she ever feel what she felt for Glyn for another baby? Could she love, care, protect and bring up a child that she knew was Jack's – and another woman's?

Mixed thoughts and emotions crowded in on her, most of them generated by the letter Lily had written to her from Cartref. As Lily had said – a baby in need of a home and loving parents was simply that, an innocent baby. Did it matter who its parents were? And despite everything, she couldn't help liking Maggie and feeling sorry for her . . .

Couldn't Lily see that her solution was too neat, too easy? It didn't allow for her feelings. Jack had betrayed her by making love to another woman. How could she ever forgive or forget that betrayal if she tried to bring up the child that had resulted from his unfaithfulness, as her own?

It was simply too much to ask of any woman. She looked at Glyn again and, as she smiled instinctively at the sweet, scrunched expression on his face, all the misery and anger that welled inside her subsided. It was too much to ask – wasn't it?

*

'I have to open the garage.' Brian handed Martin a cup of tea, which he set on the coffee table next to the two untouched cups of coffee that Roy had made for him in the night.

Martin nodded.

'Jack said he'll stay with you until you telephone.'

Martin glanced at the clock and rose to his feet.

'It's only half past six, Marty,' Jack warned. 'They told you to leave it until eight o'clock at the earliest.'

'What's the worst they can do to me?' Martin didn't expect Jack to answer him. 'I can't wait, not any longer.' Walking into the hall, he picked up the receiver and dialled the telephone number he had spent most of the night staring at.

Jack, Brian and Roy hovered awkwardly behind him. His voice was low but there were tears in his eyes when he replaced the receiver and turned around. 'She woke two hours ago. They say she's stable, and she still has the baby,' he breathed.

'She is going to be all right.' Jack wanted more assurance than Martin was able to give them.

'She is stable,' Martin repeated, 'and I can see her tomorrow.'

Brian slapped Martin's shoulder. 'It's going to take time but she's going to be all right, Marty, and so is the nipper. I can feel it, but just to make sure I'll light a candle for both of them.'

'I didn't know you were Catholic,' Jack said.

'I'm not,' Brian answered. 'But there's nothing wrong with hedging your bets, is there?'

Chapter Twenty-Four

'I couldn't leave Martin to face the last two weeks by himself,' Jack whispered down the telephone after glancing over his shoulder to check that no one else was in the garage office. 'But he had a call from the hospital this morning and Lily's doctor told him that she won't be able to leave the hospital until after the baby's born.'

'But that's months away!' Helen exclaimed.

'It could be as long as five months,' he confirmed.

'Poor Lily,' Helen commiserated, with all the sympathy engendered by her month's incarceration on the gynaecological ward.

'Martin's trying to put a brave face on it. He's telling everyone that she is in the best place, and they are allowing him to visit her four evenings a week for half an hour and an hour on Sunday afternoon, which is better than the twice weekly visits they allowed me when you were in hospital.'

'They won't get much privacy in a crowded ward.'

'She's in a cubicle because she needs to rest.'

'That's something, I suppose.' Helen fell silent for a moment. 'If you want to stay with Martin . . .'

'We discussed it after the doctor telephoned this morning. Martin insists there's no point in my staying with him. He's working long hours in the garage, as much to keep busy and take his mind off Lily as to build up the business, so we've scarcely seen anything of him the last couple of days, and as Katie insists on both of us eating our meals at her house I can't really do very much to help.'

'As long as you know that nothing's changed from the last time we spoke. You'll still be in the spare room.'

'I know, but as you also said, at least we'll be under the same roof, so we'll be able to talk – and it will be one less worry for Martin and Katie.'

'I saw Katie yesterday. Although she's putting a brave face on it, she's really upset about Lily – and Martin.'

'We all are. Is there anything you'd like me to pick up on the way . . .' He searched for a word that he could use instead of home.

'No, I told the grocer and the greengrocer to deliver my usual weekend order.'

'I thought they did it automatically.'

'Not since you left. I haven't been eating at home.'

He suspected from the way she looked that she hadn't been eating anywhere, but he refrained from telling her. 'I'll see you tonight then, Helen.'

'Yes, see you then.'

Jack replaced the receiver.

'I had to come in for this.' Martin wiped his hands on an oily rag that he stuffed back into his overalls pocket before picking up a box from Brian's desk. 'But I couldn't help overhearing. Helen's agreed that you can move back in with her tonight?'

'Of sorts. Do you mind?'

'As I said to you earlier, most definitely not, and once you're through her door, may I suggest that you pull out all the stops.'

'You can take that as given.' Jack sat on the edge of the desk and looked at his brother. 'But if you need me for anything . . .'

'How about to drive the getaway car when I break Lily out of hospital.' It was a poor attempt at a joke, but it was the first light-hearted comment Jack had heard Martin make since Lily had been taken ill.

'You want to break her out?'

'Of course. The last three weeks without her have been hell. I also have to admit that she's in the best place, and with you eating and doing your washing and ironing in Limeslade, Katie's extra workload will be halved.'

'I suppose so.'

'Frightened of messing up with Helen?' Martin asked intuitively.

'She warned me that the next time she asks me to leave, it will be for good.'

'All the more reason to give this opportunity everything you've got.'

'That doesn't make me any less terrified.' Jack followed Martin out through the door. 'Do you mind if I hang on to your spare front door key for a while?'

'I don't mind, but you won't need it,' Martin replied confidently.

'I only wish I could be as sure as you,' Jack muttered, forcing a smile as a potential customer walked in.

The first thing Helen did when she reached home was to open the back door and carry the two boxes of groceries that had been left in the shed into the house. She had almost finished stacking the last of the tins in the cupboard when there was a knock at the front door.

Determined to return the keys Jack had left when he had walked out, the moment he returned, she picked them up and ran to open it. To her amazement, Sam was standing on the step.

'I hope you don't mind me calling,' he stammered, clearly unsure of the reception he'd receive.

'No.' She remembered her manners as she recovered her composure. 'Not at all. Come in.' She opened the door wider and showed him into her living room. 'Sit down. Can I get you a coffee or anything?'

'No, thank you. I only came to give you this.' He set a small parcel he'd marked 'Fragile' in red ink on her coffee table. 'It's a christening present for Glyn. It's not much, just one of those two-handled china bunny mugs and a bowl. The kind where you have to eat all the porridge to see the picture at the bottom.'

'I'm sure Glyn will love it. But won't you give it to Katie and John yourself? They invited you to the christening.'

'Judy and I were invited to Glyn's christening when we were engaged.'

'I'm sorry. I heard what happened.'

'I didn't doubt you had,' he said caustically. 'No doubt she'll be going to the christening with Brian.'

'They are getting married on Monday,' Helen informed him calmly.

'They told me they'd set the big day.'

'I wouldn't call it a big day, it's a really small affair.'

'Yes, well, whatever. I'm sorry to drop in on you like this, but after what happened between Brian and me, I could hardly take the present over to Martin and Lily's house, or Katie and John's in case I saw him. So if you don't mind . . .'

'No, Sam, of course I don't mind.'

'Thank you.' He left his chair. 'I have to go. I'm on duty in a couple of hours.'

As she turned to see him out, she looked through the window and saw Jack striding up the path. Suddenly, all the anger, resentment and bitterness she'd fought so hard to control erupted in a single blinding flash of rage. She had an overwhelming urge to hurt Jack as he had hurt her. To torment him with nightmare visions of her with another man, just as she had been tortured by the idea of him with another woman.

Stepping in front of Sam, she locked her arms around his neck, stood on tiptoe and kissed him.

Jack was almost at the front door when he glanced through the window and saw Helen with Sam. He turned aside almost immediately, but the image had already seared itself on his mind. All he could see was his wife in Sam's arms, her blonde head thrown back as Sam pressed his lips to hers, her arms locked around Sam's neck, his hands closed familiarly around her waist as they meshed their bodies sensuously together.

He wanted to walk away but, mesmerised by the unbearably painful scene, he simply couldn't stop himself from looking through the window again. As he stared, Helen opened her eyes. She held his look until he found the strength to finally turn and retrace his steps.

'I can't say I expected this,' Sam smiled, 'but I can say I'm glad I came.' As he closed his hand over her breast, the noise of a motorbike engine revving furiously shattered the atmosphere.

Helen pushed him away. 'This is a mistake.'

'The hell it is.'

'You're hurting me,' she protested, as he gripped her upper arms to prevent her from moving.

'Then come here.'

'No. This is stupid. You don't care for me any more than I care for you. If we go any further, I'll be thinking of Jack and you'll be thinking of Judy . . .'

'The last thing I'll be thinking about is that stupid bitch,' he cursed savagely.

'She's all you'll be thinking about. You're still angry with her . . .'

'Of course I'm bloody angry with her, but at the moment I'm a damned sight angrier with you. Bloody teasing bitch, you're no better than Judy. Winding me up . . .'

'I'm sorry, Sam, I truly am. I didn't mean for this to happen. I don't know what came over me,' she lied, hoping that he hadn't seen Jack or connected the sound of the motorbike with him.

'I know what came over you. The same bloody thing that came over me. Sheer frustration. You want it. You know you do . . .' As she succeeded in pulling away from him, he snatched at the collar of her blouse and a hail of pearl buttons rained down on to the coffee table. His face darkened. She clutched the edges of her blouse together and screamed more in anger than terror.

'Get out!'

'Not until I've taken what you offered.' He stepped towards her.

'Get out!'

When he hesitated, she lowered her voice. 'You'll hate yourself afterwards if you don't, Sam. We've both been hurt and as a result we're a little crazy.' She fell back on to a chair. 'Please, Sam, just go. If you do, we can try to forget this ever happened.'

She was conscious of him standing, staring at her, but when she summoned the courage to look up, he was no longer in the room and the front door banged shut.

Trembling, she grabbed a cushion and, clutching it tightly, sank back in the chair. Thoughts whirled senselessly through her mind.

How could she have so weak as to succumb to such a stupid impulse? The only thing she had proved was that she was low enough to sink to Jack's level, only she didn't even have the excuses of drink, shock and a brush with death. Just plain jealousy and resentment.

'What do you mean there's been a change of plan?' Martin shouted, as Jack charged up the stairs with his suitcase.

'Just that,' Jack called back. 'I'm staying here.'

'What's all the noise about?' Brian wandered into the living room, a teacup in one hand, a comb in the other.

'It appears Jack's changed his mind about moving in with Helen. Either that, or she's changed her mind about allowing him to.'

'I take it he didn't tell you why?' Brian set his tea on the mantelpiece and checked his reflection in the mirror over the fireplace.

'He doesn't seem to be in a talking mood. Damn it, I really hoped that those two would settle their differences.'

'An affair that's resulted in a baby? Perhaps too many differences for Helen to accept.'

'I know,' Martin frowned.

'You're playing the big brother again,' Brian warned. 'Take some advice from Uncle Brian, other people's marriages are best left well alone.'

'You're looking smarter than usual but then that's easy for you,' Martin commented, deliberately changing the subject as Brian put the finishing touches to his Tony Curtis-style quiff.

'That's an odd sense of humour you're developing.'

'It comes of working and living with you.'

'Make the most of the last two days of living with me, not that I'll be here that much. I am taking Judy out to dinner in the Mermaid tonight. So don't expect me home early.'

'You have your own flat, key and life, so I'm not expecting anything. All set for a bachelor party here, tomorrow night after the christening?'

'I suppose I could get some beer in,' Brian said casually, 'but I don't want to make a big deal out of it.'

'I've never seen anyone quite so laid back about getting married.'

Brian lifted his undamaged eyebrow and stowed his comb into the inside pocket of his jacket. His damaged eye was almost back to normal, but there was still an ugly bruise and angry looking scar on his cheekbone. 'I've got the girl, the last thing I need to do is get too drunk to know what to do with her.'

'Saturday night in Mumbles. The dog end of policing in Swansea,' Sam grumbled, as he paced along the Mumbles Road with Mike. 'Nothing but underage drinkers, kids who want to be teddy boys and think the best way to go about it is to look for a fight with the hardest nut they can find.'

'And girls who are asking for trouble.' Mike eyed three girls who didn't look a day older than fourteen, dressed in skin-tight sweaters and straight skirts they could barely walk in. 'What's the betting one of those will wind up some poor idiot to the point of indecent assault tonight?'

Mike's comment brought a flush of embarrassment and guilt to Sam's face. 'I'm offering no odds. Not with tarts like those,' he added venomously. 'Some girls just ask to be raped.'

Taken aback by the bitterness in Sam's voice, Mike deliberately kept his reply low-key. 'Never mind, only another,' he glanced at his watch, 'two hours to go until midnight and then we can go home – me to my bed, you to drown your sorrows.'

'Bloody bitch,' Sam cursed.

'You're better off without her.' Mike spoke with a sincerity born of tedious hours spent listening to Sam's endless complaints about Judy.

'I know I am, but—'

'Think of all the tarts – and nice girls waiting to make your acquaintance that you would never have known if you had married Judy.'

Sam looked in the direction of the sea – and Judy's flat. 'Do you want to stay on the main road or check the beach for underage drinkers?'

'I'll stay on the main drag.'

'Meet you at the junction of Promenade Terrace.' Sam crossed the road and turned left. He stood and stared at the salon and the flat above it. All the windows were in darkness, but that didn't mean much. Judy had preferred to make love in the dark and if Brian was with her . . .

Angrily trying to put the thought from his mind, he paced around the block. When he was sure that Judy's car was nowhere to be seen, he slipped around the side of the salon.

'Is that smoke?' Mike asked when Sam rejoined him.

Sam turned back and squinted at the skyline. 'It looks like it.'

'You didn't see anything suspicious?'

'Not a thing.' Sam kept his face turned towards the smoke. 'You telephone the fire brigade; I'll go and see what's going on.'

Sam only ran until he was out of sight of Mike, then he stopped, hands on knees, ostensibly getting his breath back. When he straightened up a minute later, he heard a fire engine, bells clanging, hurtling towards him and realised that one of the neighbours must have telephoned the emergency services at the first sight of smoke. He continued to run towards the end of the street, then he saw it – a grey Morris Minor parked higher up and on the opposite side of the street to the spot Judy usually used.

Quickening his step, Sam reached the pavement outside the salon the same time as the fire crew. Thick, grey smoke poured from the roof of the building. Broad bands of fire snaked up the curtains of her living room, streaks of livid, brilliant life in a dense, smouldering, smut-filled atmosphere.

'Leave it to us, son.' A middle-aged fireman pushed him back, as he charged towards the building.

'You don't understand, that's my girlfriend's flat,' he cried, forgetting Brian.

'Is she in the house?' the fireman asked urgently.

'I have to see . . .' Breaking free, Sam rushed towards the side door. Before he reached it, a deafening, ear-splitting crash rent the air as the glass burst outwards from Judy's living-room window, sending a fireball roaring into the street. In the silence that followed, all that could be heard was the musical rattle of glass shards falling to the pavement.

Sam ran to the side door, hammering on it, just as another rush of flames burst through the glass panel.

'Was that a good meal, or was that a good meal?' Brian offered Judy his arm, as they left the Mermaid.

'It was good, although I'm surprised you noticed.'

'And what is that supposed to mean?'

'You stared at me the entire time.' She sniffed the air. 'Can you smell burning?'

'Yes.'

They looked at the smoke billowing above the roofline and realised it was coming from the direction of her salon. Quickening their step, they turned the corner, and Judy stared, transfixed in horror at the sight of her salon and the flat above it engulfed in flames.

'You can't go any further, sir, miss.' A policeman held Brian back, as he tried to push his way forward.

'That is my house,' Judy shouted.

'Why didn't you say so, miss?' He looked up and bellowed to a fireman down the line. 'This is the lady's house!'

As Brian pushed forward still holding Judy's hand, Roy appeared at their side.

'Thank God you're both safe.' Roy gripped Judy's shoulders and held her firmly. 'No further, love, not unless you want to be burned to a crisp.' Even from across the road they could feel the heat of the flames, as they consumed the building. 'We're evacuating the street.'

Judy glanced down the road and saw groups of people huddled together, some in their dressing gowns, watching the fire.

'I am so sorry, darling,' Brian breathed, 'but there's no chance of rescuing anything from that.' He wrapped his arm around Judy's shoulders.

'It could have been much worse, you could have been in it when it went up,' Roy observed. 'From what the woman who alerted us said, it was burning out of control within a minute of her seeing the first plume of smoke.'

'Someone's hurt!' Judy exclaimed, as an ambulance clanged around the corner.

'Sam,' Roy revealed. 'He tried to get in but he was beaten back by the flames.'

'He must have been crazy . . .'

'Hysterical, or so the firemen said,' Roy interrupted Brian.

Judy ran up the pavement to where Sam was lying stretched out on his back on a blanket.

'Judy,' Sam croaked in a hoarse, cracked voice. 'I'm sorry. You parked your car on the wrong side of the road. You weren't meant to be there . . .'

'Meant to be where, Sam?' Roy questioned.

'In the flat. I just meant for the salon and the flat . . .'

'You bastard.'

'Leave him, Brian.' Judy helped her stepfather pull Brian away from Sam, as the ambulance driver and his mate walked towards them carrying a stretcher.

'You heard?'

'We all did.' Roy looked Brian in the eye. 'Leave it to me. I'll ask the sergeant to send a couple of the lads down to the hospital to interview him. Arson is a serious crime.'

Brian watched the ambulance leave, then looked at Judy. 'I'm sorry, love, you've lost everything.'

'Only things that don't matter.' She gripped his hand. 'I have you.'

'And I'll help you to replace the rest. Your clothes, books, records, jewellery . . .'

'Thank heavens the pieces my grandmother left me are with my mother.' She allowed him to lead her away from the building that was still smouldering despite the fire brigade's efforts.

'If it takes for ever, I'll make it up to you.'

'It won't take for ever because everything's insured. The salon, the contents of the flat, all except . . .' She stopped suddenly.

'What?'

'My photographs. They were in albums. Photographs of me when I was a baby, growing up, with the girls . . .'

'Won't your mother and the girls have copies?'

'Some, but there's one that can't be replaced.' She

twisted her mouth into a grimace. 'The one we had taken in London at that Policeman's Ball.'

'Judy,' Roy shouted, running to catch up with them. 'Are you going back to Carlton Terrace?'

She looked down ruefully at the brown sack dress she was wearing. 'Seeing as I'm homeless, with only the clothes I stand up in to my name, it looks as if I have no choice.'

'You still have your car. Pure luck that you parked it so far up the street.'

'Someone was moving in when I came home. Their lorry was blocking my usual space.'

'You sure you are up to driving?' Roy asked.

'I'll drive her,' Brian volunteered. 'I doubt Martin will have gone to bed, he can run me back to pick up my car.'

'I am perfectly capable of driving myself . . .'

'Down, girl,' Brian commanded. 'It won't hurt you to take a little help now and again when it's offered.'

'No, it won't,' she muttered, looking back at the wreckage of what had been her home and salon.

Go and tell your mother that you are all right before she hears any different.' Roy hugged her.

'I will.' Judy opened her handbag and searched for her car keys. Finding them, she handed them to Brian.

'I guess I'd better ask Martin how he feels about letting his attic flat to an old married couple after Monday.'

'Think he'll mind?'

'Only if we try to keep greyhounds up there. Hey,' he opened his arms and held her as the first tears ran down her cheeks, 'it could have been worse.'

'Much worse,' she sobbed, as the shock finally sank in. 'You might not have listened to me and Roy and thumped Sam and ended up in prison . . .'

'And miss my wedding night, love? Never.'

As soon as the doors to the ward opened, Martin walked in and made a beeline for the nearest cubicle to the sister's office. When Lily glanced up from the book she was reading and smiled at him, he beamed.

'How are you feeling?' He set the bags he was carrying on to the floor and pulled a chair as close to her as he could get.

'To be truthful, a bit of a fraud. I wish I could get up, if only to go to the toilet and have a bath.'

'All this will be worth it if we have a baby.'

'That "if" is just the problem, when I've nothing to do except lie here, hour after hour, not daring to even hope too much in case the worst happens and I do lose our baby.'

'I've brought you something to help you pass the time.' He handed her one of the bags. 'It was Katie's idea, not mine, so if you don't like it, you can blame her.'

She opened it suspiciously. 'What is it supposed to be?' she asked, pulling out a handful of brightly coloured, pre-cut felt.

'The patterns, whatever they are, should be in there as well. They are a pile of glove puppets Katie cut out. They need stitching in something called . . .'

'Blanket stitch.' She opened the pattern book Katie had sent along with the felt cut outs. 'They are gorgeous,' she murmured, flicking through and studying the animal shapes. 'Have you seen them, Marty? That tiger is adorable and the panda, the cow – look at those horns. Glyn is going to love them.'

'Yes, he will.' Martin tried not to think of another child who would love them – if everything went well.

'Tell Katie thank you, and tell her I'm really sorry to be missing Glyn's christening and Brian and Judy's wedding. It is so unfair.'

'It is, but Katie's promised to send you a piece of the cake and, as Brian and Judy haven't even ordered one, Brian's promised to see the baker about a joint welcome home and wedding cake when you come out.'

'He would. I know he's only been living with us for a

couple of weeks but I'm going to miss him when I get home.'

'You're not actually.' As he told her the news about Judy's flat burning down and John having to open up the warehouse that morning just so Judy could replace the essentials in her wardrobe, he couldn't help thinking that Lily looked brighter and more animated than she had done since she'd collapsed in the hostel and he dared to hope that perhaps fate was going to smile down on them after all.

'Over here, Judy, smile and hold Glyn up, I'm taking one for the absent godmother,' Martin shouted, standing in prime position in front of the church with his camera. 'John, Katie, Jack, Helen, Roy, Joy, Brian, stand behind her.'

As they all dutifully lined up behind Judy, Helen self-consciously moved to the opposite end of the row to where Jack was standing, but during the quarter of an hour that it took for everyone to take photographs of Glyn's christening, she was aware of him watching her.

When Glyn started grizzling, John put an end to the proceedings by helping Katie and the baby into his car, after repeating his invitation that everyone go to his house. As Helen hung back, she saw Jack walking with Martin.

Bracing herself for rejection, she went up to him and asked, 'Can I give you a lift?'

Jack looked at his brother.

'We'll see you at the party.' Martin helped Joy and Billy into the back of his car.

'We'll be right behind you.' Helen unlocked her car, climbed into the driving seat and flicked open the lock on the passenger door. 'About the other day . . .' she began after Jack had climbed in beside her.

'I don't want to talk about it.'

'But—'

'After what I did to you, I have no right to ask you about it, and I really would prefer to forget it ever happened.'

'But I want you to know.'

'Please, Helen.' Resolutely staring through the windscreen, he watched Brian drive away.

'Are you still prepared to move in with me?'

'Are you still prepared to have me?'

'Yes.'

'Then I'll ride my bike over after the party.' He nodded to the road. 'If we don't join the others, they'll wonder where we are.'

'Lily loved the puppet idea,' Martin confided to Katie, as she carried a couple of plates of sandwiches into the kitchen where the men had congregated, as usual.

'I hoped she might. She loves sewing and she's much better at it than the rest of us. When she's finished those, I'll get her something to embroider. I wish it could be baby clothes but—'

'That would be tempting fate,' Martin interrupted. 'Are these ham?'

'They are, take two.' She looked at the rest of the men standing around the kitchen table. 'As you won't go to the food, I've brought it to you. We're cutting the christening cake in ten minutes.'

'We'll be there.' Brian glanced across to the corner where Jack was standing, brooding with an untouched beer glass. 'More beer Roy, Martin?' He opened a bottle and refilled their glasses before his own.

'It doesn't feel like you're getting married tomorrow,' Katie complained to Judy, as she and John saw the last of their guests to the door. 'You should be burning up in excitement . . . oh!' Katie clapped her hand over her mouth. 'What a stupid thing for me to say.'

'What a funny thing for you to say,' Judy laughed,

kissing Katie good night. 'As Brian said, we have each other and the insurance money – when it comes. What more could any young couple want to start married life?'

'A congratulations card and a cheque.' John slipped his arm around Katie's waist and handed Judy an envelope. 'We were thinking of getting you some silver, but in view of what's happened, that might prove more useful.'

'As we're not having a big do, we weren't expecting presents,' Brian said. 'But we are going to throw a party in a couple of months when we have somewhere to throw one.'

'We are?' Judy looked up at him.

'My mother's coming tomorrow but the rest of my family aren't going to be so easily done out of a wedding. The only way I could keep them away was to promise them a big do as soon as we're settled in our own place.'

'Thank you for telling me.' There was no malice in Judy's comment. She kissed his cheek. 'See you tomorrow, bridegroom.'

'Tie her to the bed, Joy, so she can't run away or be kidnapped. And get her to the Guildhall on time tomorrow, I'll take her from there,' Brian joked.

'I'll see what I can do,' Joy answered, as she walked up the street with Roy, Judy and Billy.

'So, who is going to this wedding tomorrow?' John asked Katie, when she'd closed the door on Martin and Brian.

'Joy, Roy, Brian's mother, his cousins who helped him open the garage, who are going to inspect it after the ceremony, and Judy and Brian.'

'Judy hasn't invited you or Helen?'

'She asked if we'd like to go, but to be honest we didn't want to without Lily and between her being in hospital and Martin being the way he is, and Helen and Jack . . .'

'No one feels much like celebrating,' John suggested.

'We all will when Lily comes home. With her baby,' Katie said firmly.

*

'You've picked up your keys?' Helen asked, as she left her chair and walked to the living-room door.

'Yes,' Jack replied.

'I'll make up a bed.'

'Please don't. I'll follow you up and make it while you have a bath. It won't take me long. Since Lily has been in hospital, Martin and I have become quite domesticated.'

'If you're sure . . .'

'I'm sure, Helen.'

'I'll say goodnight then.'

'Goodnight.' He sat and listened while she climbed the stairs. Shortly afterwards he heard the bolt slide home on the bathroom door and the taps being turned on. Leaving his chair, he checked all the doors in the house before following Helen up the stairs. The routine was so terrifyingly familiar, he tried not to think how he'd feel if she asked him to leave a second time.

He had just finished making up a bed in one of the spare rooms when he heard a sob. He walked to the door of the master bedroom and knocked. 'Are you all right?'

'Yes,' came a muffled reply.

'Can I get you anything?'

'No, go away.'

'Do you mean that?' he asked quietly.

'No.'

He opened the door. The room was in darkness; the only light came from the moonlight that streamed in through the unshuttered windows. Helen was sitting up in bed clutching a handkerchief.

'Is there anything I can do?' he questioned softly.

She shook her head

As he went to close the door, she called out, 'Stay with me, Jack.'

'You want me to sleep here, with you?'

She nodded.

'Helen, I couldn't promise to keep my hands off you if I did.'

'I wouldn't want you to.'

He went to her and pulled her head down on to his chest. 'I am so sorry for hurting you, sweetheart. Can we start again?'

'I don't know. I honestly don't.' She looked into his eyes, darkly glittering in the subdued light. 'But I do know that I want to try.'

'Mr and Mrs Brian Powell.' Brian handed Judy the glass of champagne he had poured for her before picking up his own. 'The wedding wasn't – how did Sam put it? – too "hole in the corner" for you, was it?'

'No, but talk about something borrowed and something new,' Judy smiled. 'If it hadn't been for John opening up the warehouse yesterday and Katie and Helen's help I would have had to get married in my brown sack dress.'

'And very beautiful you would have looked in it too, darling.' Brian sat on the sofa and patted the space beside him.

'Is that what my life is going to be like from now on, nothing but compliments?'

'You object?'

'Absolutely not and your mother is sweet. And after meeting William and Ronnie I can see where you get it from.'

'I am just breaking you in gently, a taster for when I take you up to Pontypridd.'

'Outings as well as all your worldly goods,' she beamed. 'You really do know how to spoil a wife.'

'Which reminds me.' Brian slipped his hand beneath the sofa and pulled out a parcel. 'My wedding present to you.'

'You've changed your mind about getting me a new car?'

'No, the wife of a garage owner has to drive around in a new car; it's an obligatory part of her duties to advertise her husband's business. This,' he dropped the parcel on to her lap, 'is an extra.'

'I have nothing for you.'

'I am devastated by your thoughtlessness and neglect, but seeing as you married me today, I'll overlook your miserliness and allow you to open your gift.'

'What is it?'

'You've lost your X-ray vision.'

Knowing she wasn't going to get any sense out of him while he remained in his present flippant mood, she tore off the ribbon and paper and uncovered a silver frame. Inside was the photograph of them that had been taken at the policeman's ball in London.

'Don't you like it?' he asked, as a tear fell from her eye.

'It's the best present I've ever had.'

'Thank you God for giving me an easily satisfied and cheap woman.' He rolled his eyes heavenwards.

'I didn't know you had a copy,' she whispered, when she could finally talk.

'That, I'll have you know, is a cherished memento of the best night of my life.'

'You said you gave me the only copy.'

'I didn't want you to think I was sentimental.'

'And now?' She smiled at him through her tears.

'And now you know I am. Come to bed, wife.'

Chapter Twenty-Five

. . . Jack loves and has only ever loved you just as I only ever loved my husband. Please, try to forgive him. It really wasn't his fault.
Yours sincerely,
Maggie Jones

Helen re-read the end of Maggie's letter twice before folding it and returning it to her handbag. She had looked at it hundreds of times since the day she had received it and now that she and Jack had been back together for more than three months it seemed strangely irrelevant – except when she thought of the baby Maggie was carrying, and the letter Lily had written to her during her week's stay in the hostel.

'Mrs Clay, Mrs Jones didn't tell me that she was expecting a visit from you today. You do know that we try to restrict family visits to Sunday afternoons,' the matron reprimanded, as she entered the anteroom.

Helen rose from the stone bench. 'Yes, I do, and I apologise for calling in unexpectedly like this. Mrs Jones didn't know that I was coming. In fact I didn't until half an hour ago. I had to visit a supplier in Carmarthen – I'm a buyer for a warehouse,' she explained, 'and I was driving close to here so I thought I'd drop in on the off chance that you would allow me to see her. How is she?'

'As well as a woman in her advanced stage of pregnancy can be in this heat. How is your sister-in-law?'

'You do know that Lily haemorrhaged again after she left here?'

'Yes, she wrote to me.'

'She's been kept on bed rest in Swansea hospital ever since.'

'She must be,' the matron did a quick calculation, 'almost seven months now.'

'Just over.'

'Please, tell her that I was asking about her the next time you see her.'

'I'll put it in my next letter to her and tell Martin,' Helen promised. 'He is the only one allowed to visit her.'

The matron glanced at her watch. 'If you'll excuse me, I have work to do. You'll find Mrs Jones in the garden at the back of the house.'

'Thank you.'

Helen left the anteroom, which, despite the heat, was the temperature of a fridge, walked down the short flight of steps into the courtyard and through the arch that led to the gardens. The heady scent of old-fashioned cabbage roses and pinks filled the still, hot air.

A group of pregnant girls were sitting on blankets spread on the lawn, but they were all far younger than Maggie. She held her hand above her eyes to block out the sun's glare and saw her, sitting on a bench set in the shade of a shrubbery with another girl she recognised as Emily Murton Davies.

'Mrs Clay, this is a surprise.' Maggie struggled to her feet and Helen was amazed by how much weight she had gained since she had last seen her.

'How are you?' Forcing herself to overcome her initial embarrassment, Helen shook Maggie's hand.

'As you see.' Maggie lowered herself back on to the seat. 'What brings you to this part of the world?'

'Business. I was passing the door, so I thought I'd call in.'

'I'll go and see what the other girls are doing.' When neither Maggie nor Helen tried to detain her, Emily headed down to the patio.

'Given this heat wave, I expect you'll be glad when the baby's born.' Helen sat beside Maggie on the bench.

'Not entirely,' Maggie rested her hands on her bump. 'These are the last weeks I'll be able to call him entirely mine, but I will be glad to see my children again.' Maggie folded a letter she had been reading and pushed it into an envelope. 'My mother collects everything the children write to me and sends it on once a week. Today I got a photograph as well. They have grown so much since I've been here.'

'May I see?' Helen pulled off her gloves and set her handbag on the ground at her feet.

Maggie handed her a snapshot of an elderly couple standing behind four formally posed children. The group looked stiff and awkward, but there was no mistaking the mischief in the two boys' eyes or the boredom in the pose of the two small and very pretty girls.

'They are lovely children,' Helen complimented, handing the photograph back, 'but the boys look a bit of a handful.'

'They are, but I have a feeling that you didn't come here to talk about me or my children.'

'No.' Helen looked Maggie in the eye. 'I came to talk to you because I think I'd like to adopt your baby.'

'"Think" seems an odd word to use in conjunction with adoption, Mrs Clay.'

'This isn't a spur of the moment thing. I am one hundred per cent certain that I want to adopt a baby. Jack and I are back together.'

'I am so glad.' Maggie smiled and Helen sensed that she was genuinely pleased for them.

'We talked about adoption before – before you wrote to Jack.' Helen averted her eyes and pushed her gloves into her handbag. 'And if it hadn't been for your letter we would have gone to our doctor months ago. He's a close friend of my father and he arranges private adoptions. Matches couples who can't have children with young girls who can't keep their babies.'

'But I'm not a young girl and your husband is the father of my baby.'

'And that is why I can't be sure how I'll feel when I see your baby for the first time. It won't be just any baby, it will be Jack's baby, and I honestly don't know whether I can bring it up.'

'Because you are afraid that the child will remind you that Jack was unfaithful.'

'Yes.'

Maggie shifted awkwardly on the bench. 'Has Jack asked you to consider adopting my baby?'

'No. We only started discussing adoption again two weeks ago because we both thought that our priority had to be rebuilding our relationship.'

'That was wise of you. Children can put an enormous strain on a couple.'

'If their marriage isn't strong enough.'

'And you are sure that yours and Jack's is now?'

'I am,' Helen smiled. 'It may sound odd, but if anything it's stronger than it was before he returned from Cyprus. We had been apart for so long I think we both had a slightly romanticised idea of the other, and since then – well, Jack hurt me and I – I don't want to go into it – tried to hurt him. But despite everything that's happened, we still love one another very much and the one thing that both of us want more than anything else is a family. I know Jack wants to bring up his child. We may not have discussed adopting it, but he has talked about you and how he'll feel when your baby is born and you have to give it up. He can't bear the thought of his son or daughter being brought up by strangers.'

'This child will need a mother as well as a father, Mrs Clay. The worst thing you could do is adopt it just because Jack wants to. You both have to be absolutely certain that you want to bring it up.'

'I know. That is why I'd like to see it before I make a commitment. Do you understand?'

'Are you also afraid that the child will look like me?'

'A little.'

'Thank you for being honest with me.'

'I've tried to imagine how I'd feel if I were you, and I had to give a baby away to be brought up by strangers. As it is, you've met Jack and me, and all the experts and the books insist that adoptions should be anonymous.'

'And you're not sure?'

'I will be, I know I will.' Helen said resolutely. 'Just as soon as I hold your baby, then I'll know right away whether or not I can bring him up. What I don't know is how you'd feel if Jack and I adopted him. Or even if it could be arranged.'

'I can ask the matron if she could arrange a private adoption.'

'Would you do that?'

'I'll think about it.'

There was a cry further down the garden and they both jumped up as Emily gripped a tree and doubled over.

Helen ran across the lawn and reached her before Maggie. Holding the girl, she looked around for a seat but the nearest one was the bench they had been sitting on.

'We need help. Now,' Maggie shouted to the girls sitting on the lawn.

'What's all this noise, ladies?' The matron sized up the situation as soon as she opened the side door. 'Bath and enema for you, Davies. You can have another few minutes with Mrs Clay if you like, Maggie.'

'Good luck, Emily,' one of the girls called, as the matron led her away.

'She looks terrified,' Helen said to Maggie.

'Probably because she is. I remember my first labour. I didn't have a clue what to expect and that made it ten times worse. My second, third and fourth births were much easier. But then, I was a respectable married woman and had a husband.' Maggie gave Helen a sad little smile. 'I promise to think about what you said and I will talk to Matron.'

'This is my telephone number at the office.' Helen handed Maggie a card. 'We're not on the telephone at home but my father is. I've written his number on the back. I've already spoken to him about this and he's agreed to see the doctor and do everything he can to help, should you allow us to have your baby.'

'If you want him or her.'

'You do understand . . .'

'That you have to see it first, yes.' Maggie walked towards the courtyard with Helen. 'I don't know how I'd feel about you and Jack adopting my baby because I haven't had any time to consider it. But I do know one thing, Mrs Clay, when the time comes, you and Jack will make wonderful parents.'

'Thank you.' Helen held out her hand as she reached her car. 'Goodbye, and good luck.' On impulse she kissed Maggie's cheek.

Martin glanced at his watch as he ran down the stairs. He was furious. Who in hell could be ringing him at six in the morning . . . then he thought of Lily and almost fell down the last half a dozen steps.

'Mr Clay, it's Swansea hospital.'

'Lily,' he muttered thickly.

'I'm sorry to ring you so early in the morning, Mr Clay.'

'Lily . . .'

'Your wife began to haemorrhage again last night. We had no option but to operate.'

Martin sank down on the bottom stair, unaware that Brian and Judy were standing on the landing behind him.

'We performed an emergency Caesarean. It's early days, but the doctor is confident that both your wife and your daughter will make a full recovery, Mr Clay.'

'A daughter . . .'

'She is small but considering the size of your wife and the fact that she's six weeks premature, at three-and-a-half pounds, she is not that small for her age and she's already proved herself a fighter. She's in an incubator and we are doing all we can for her.'

As comprehension dawned, Martin blurted, 'Lily and the baby are going to be all right?'

'It certainly looks that way, Mr Clay.'

'Can I see them?'

'It's against hospital regulations for fathers to visit outside of visiting hours but in view of the circumstances, the doctor thought that we might make an exception in your case. If you could call in this morning . . .'

'I'm on my way.'

'Mr Clay, it will be a short visit. Your wife is still recovering from the anaesthetic.'

'I'm coming,' Martin shouted.

'In that case, we'll expect you soon, Mr Clay.'

'You have a daughter.' Brian grinned, as Martin dropped the receiver next to the telephone.

'A three-and-a-half pound daughter . . .'

'Get dressed and I'll drive you to the hospital.' Brian ran down the stairs and replaced the receiver on its cradle.

'Congratulations, Marty.' Judy kissed his cheek, as he charged upstairs.

'I've a daughter . . .' Grabbing Judy, Martin pulled her on to the landing and jumped up and down. 'I've a daughter.'

'And the poor thing has an insane father.' Brian looked at Judy who was almost as excited as Martin. 'And a mad aunt.'

'If you'd both like to come with me, I'll take you to the nursery.' The sister led Martin and Brian out of the waiting area, pushed open a set of double doors and walked down a long corridor. They turned a corner, the sister opened yet another set of doors and stopped in front of a glass paned wall. Two nurses, both masked and gowned, were sitting, bottle-feeding babies in a large room containing rows of cots.

'The first incubator on the left, Mr Clay. That is your daughter.'

Martin stared at the tiny scrap of humanity lying in the glass box. To his amazement, the baby's eyes were open and her tiny arms and legs moving, waving in the air. It seemed incredible that something so small, so fragile, was capable of life.

'She may look a little strange now, premature babies generally do, but give her a couple of weeks and she'll soon catch up to where she should be.'

'Does Lily know that we have a daughter?' His voice sound odd, choked.

'We told her when she regained consciousness just before we telephoned you.'

'Has she seen her?'

'Not yet. As soon as she's strong enough, we'll wheel her down here.'

'Just look at those tight black curls. She's going to be a stunner, Marty.' Brian brushed his hand across his eyes.

'Can I see Lily?' Martin asked.

'For a few minutes.' The nurse looked at Brian. 'You'll have to stay in the waiting room.'

'Tell Lily she's a miracle worker and give her my love,' Brian called, as Martin and the nurse left him.

Lily turned her head and smiled sleepily when Martin tiptoed into her cubicle. 'Have you seen her?'

'Yes, and she's beautiful, just like her mother.' Martin pulled a chair close to the bed, picked up Lily's hand, and kissed it. 'But the best news is, if you lie there quietly and do as you're told, you are going to be fine.'

'And the baby?'

'Looks fighting fit. A real wriggler and squirmer. I can't wait to have you both home.'

'I can't wait to be home, Marty.'

'Mr Clay.'

'See you tonight, darling.' Martin kissed Lily and followed the sister out.

'Davies, you are not helping yourself and you are not

helping your baby,' the matron lectured. 'Now take a deep breath, pull yourself together, make an effort and push.'

'I am trying,' Emily gasped, thrashing around the bed.

'You are not.' The matron looked to a member of staff who was helping her. 'Is the cot ready?'

'Everything's been ready for hours, Matron.'

'Right, Davies, one enormous push should do it.' The matron glared with a steely eye, defying Emily to do otherwise as she laid her hand on her abdomen. 'I can feel a contraction coming. Now push!'

Emily concentrated and finally did as the matron asked.

'Good, we have the head, now another push when I tell you.'

Ten minutes later the matron held up a squalling, crying, red-faced baby. 'You have a fine baby boy. As soon as we have cleaned him up, you can hold him.'

The matron nodded to the woman who was helping her. Wrapping the baby in a towel she showed him to Emily who promptly burst into tears.

'I hope he doesn't remember the way his mother greeted him,' the woman said tartly.

'He looks just like his father,' Emily sobbed. 'Exactly like him.'

'You'll have to give him his first feed soon.' The matron tied off the umbilical cord and laid the baby next to Emily in the bed.

'Must I?' Emily begged.

'Someone has to look after him until he's old enough to go to his adoptive parents.'

Emily looked down at the baby in the towel. She felt tired, exhausted, and every part of her body ached. Then the baby fell silent and opened his eyes. They were blue, as she'd been told every baby's were, but they were an intensely rich blue that reminded her of Robin.

Turning away from the baby, she sank her head into the pillow and started sobbing.

'It's over. Another few weeks and you'll be able to go home,' the matron said in a softer voice.

'I don't have a home,' Emily burst out between sobs. 'No one wants me . . . or him.' She relinquished the baby to the matron.

'Try to get some rest. You need your strength. And remember,' the matron added, giving Emily the only words of comfort she could, 'the worst is over.'

'Annie Norah Clay.'

'Who has a nerve to lie there, looking as if butter wouldn't melt in her mouth after all the upset and worry she caused.' Brian drained his glass and set it on the table.

'Don't you dare criticise my baby, Brian Powell.' Lily jumped to her baby's defence.

'Given how protective her parents are, I won't try again. Is this what it's going to be like at our parties from now on, men in the kitchen, women and nursery in the living room?' he said, as Joy and Katie carried their babies from Lily's dining room into the living room and Jack and John headed for the kitchen.

'Wait until it's your turn.' Martin sat next to Lily and pushed his finger gently into his daughter's hand.

'Not me, my wife is a career woman.' Brian winked at Judy and followed John and Jack out of the room.

'Shall I get that?' Roy asked, as the telephone began to ring.

'Please, Uncle Roy,' Lily answered.

'Your Auntie Norah would have been proud as punch, love,' Roy smiled. 'Just you take it easy and take good care of yourself.'

'I'll see that she does,' Martin asserted.

'Helen,' Roy called, as he set the receiver down, 'it's for you. You left this number with someone.'

'I did.' Helen went into the hall and closed the door behind her.

'Sometimes, I think that girl never stops working. Or

our suppliers,' John grumbled. 'Who can be calling her this late on a Saturday afternoon?'

'I'm sorry, everyone,' Helen apologised as she returned. 'Jack and I have to leave.'

'We do?' Jack called from the kitchen. 'Oh, of course we do.' Abandoning his glass, he joined her.

'A baby?' Katie asked.

Helen glanced at Jack. 'Possibly, we're not sure.'

'Will you be bringing it home?'

Helen hesitated. 'We could be. The mother has already left the hostel.'

'You'll need baby clothes, a cot, nappies and a million and one other things,' Katie said practically.

'You have the keys to the warehouse,' John reminded. 'You could call in there and take what you want.'

'I'd rather not until we know we can have the baby for certain,' Helen prevaricated.

'If you are able to take the baby right away, you can always call back here. We can lend you whatever you need including formula and bottles until you have time to sort yourself out,' Katie suggested.

'Thank you.' Helen picked up her handbag.

'I'll keep my fingers crossed for you.' Katie kissed Jack's cheek then Helen's.

'Look after yourself.' Helen's eyes shone damply, as she kissed Lily and Annie goodbye.

'Good luck, see you soon and thank you for your present,' Lily gripped Helen's hand.

'Annie should be thanking me.'

'I'm going to have as much fun reading the books to her as she will listening to them.'

'See you all later.' Helen went into the hall to find Jack already waiting at the door.

'I take it that was the hostel,' Jack said, as he drove out of Carlton Terrace.

'Maggie had the baby late last night. The matron talked to her and they agreed to telephone us first thing on Monday morning to give her time to think about the private adoption. But when the matron went to see her an hour ago, she discovered that Maggie had packed her bags and left the hostel. There was a letter in the baby's cot asking her to telephone us and give us the baby.'

'Surely Maggie needs medical care.'

'The matron said the birth was straightforward and in her letter Maggie also said that she couldn't bear to nurse the baby for six weeks knowing she'd have to walk away from it.'

'Isn't this going to make your decision all the harder, sweetheart, knowing that the baby doesn't have any one special person to care for it while it's in the hostel?' he asked guardedly.

'I don't know, Jack. When we get there, do you mind if I see the baby alone?'

'If that's what you want.'

She sensed that he was wounded by her request. 'Please, I need a little time with the baby. I want to be sure that I can be its mother in every sense of the word, Jack.'

'I understand, I really do,' he added in response to her questioning look. 'Did the matron say whether the baby is a boy or a girl?'

Helen looked at Jack in surprise. 'Do you know, I didn't even think to ask.'

'As we're expecting a set of adoptive parents to arrive in the office at any moment, we left Mrs Jones's baby in here.' The matron opened one of the doors set off the upstairs corridor.

Helen walked in behind her to see Emily setting out a pile of baby clothes on a single bed, a small suitcase next to her.

'You should have taken your baby down to the office half an hour ago, Davies,' Matron admonished.

'I've almost finished packing his things, Matron.'

'Well, quick sharp.' The matron looked awkwardly from Helen to Emily.

'It's all right, we do know one another,' Helen explained.

'I know your case is slightly different, Mrs Clay, but it's totally against regulations for adoptive parents to meet any of our mothers.'

'You're adopting a baby?' Emily asked eagerly.

'We hope to,' Helen replied guardedly.

'But not your baby.'

Emily looked so crestfallen at the matron's pronouncement, Helen felt she had to say something. She looked in the cot closest to the bed. 'Is that your baby?'

'It's a boy,' Emily muttered.

Helen only just stopped herself from saying, 'Congratulations,' as she had done to Lily earlier. But this bleak little room with its twin beds, cots and two sets of drawers seemed a world away from Lily and Martin's comfortable house crowded with happy, smiling well-wishers.

'You know the rules, Davies. Finish packing and take the case and the baby downstairs. Then we'll call a taxi to drive you to the station,' the matron directed forcefully.

'I just need another moment.' Emily picked up two matinee jackets from the bed and laid them carefully in the case, smoothing the folds with the professional touch she had acquired in Lewis Lewis's.

'Mrs Clay.' The matron blocked Helen's view of the second cot. 'If you'd like to go downstairs and wait in the hall for a moment.'

Helen gave Emily a sympathetic look before walking down the stairs. A few seconds later Emily appeared with her baby in her arms, the matron following behind her with two small cases. Without looking at her, they both went into the office. Five minutes later the matron emerged.

'I am so sorry, Mrs Clay. Miss Davies should have

cleared that room half an hour ago. If you'd like to come upstairs with me now.'

Heart pounding, Helen walked slowly up the stairs. The matron opened the door and lifted Maggie's baby from the cot. 'Would you like a few moments alone?'

'Yes, please.'

'Why don't you sit in the chair?' Matron handed her the baby.

'Is it . . .'

'It's a boy.' The matron retreated and closed the door behind her.

Helen looked down at the bundle in her arms. The baby was small but not as small as Lily's Annie. But then he wasn't Lily's Annie, Katie's Glyn, or Joy's Billy. This was a baby who could be hers. Her and Jack's son – if she could only love him as a mother . . .

He stirred in her arms and crumpled his face, squinting up at her through barely open eyes. She pulled up his nightdress and cupped one of his tiny feet in her hand, studying his face. He stretched and lifted his hands, waving his minute fingers slowly in the air. They were perfect in every detail down to his tiny nails.

Steeling herself, she untied his knitted bonnet and slipped it off. His hair was as black as Maggie's had been fair. The thickest, blackest and curliest she had ever seen on a baby – just like his father.

She continued to stare down at the baby. His eyes widened and he looked up at her. 'You are very beautiful,' she murmured.

The baby creased his face as if he was about to cry.

'Sorry, little man, handsome is a better word than beautiful for a boy. But . . .' But? She lifted him on to her shoulder and paced to the window. Matron was seeing a tearful Emily into a taxi. She looked back at the empty cot in the room and thought of the baby waiting for his new parents in Matron's office. Emily was distraught, but was that any wonder when she was driving away from her son without even knowing what kind of people were going to adopt him or what sort of a life they could offer her son?

Then she thought of Maggie and how broken-hearted she must have been that morning, when she had packed her bags and fled the hostel and this beautiful baby . . .

But was Maggie's pain any worse or different from Jack's? This was as much his child as Maggie's. He had felt responsible for it and been prepared to love it from the very first moment he knew of its existence. So much so he had risked their marriage rather than try to conceal the child from her.

The baby nuzzled close to her and she wrapped her arms around him as he relaxed in sleep. So small, so trusting and deserving of the very best life had to offer. A knock at the door startled her.

'Come in,' she answered softly.

'I couldn't wait any longer, Helen. You don't mind, do you?' Jack hovered uneasily in the doorway, a strained, almost wild expression in his eyes.

'No,' she whispered. 'Have you seen the matron?'

He nodded. 'She told me it's a boy.'

She lifted the baby down from her shoulder and cradled him in her arms so he could see his son. 'Isn't he gorgeous?'

'Yes,' he croaked huskily.

'Just look at his hair. This is how you must have looked when you were born.' She bit her bottom lip as she saw tears start in his eyes. 'The next one we adopt is going to be a girl, and we'll get the doctor to arrange it.'

'You mean . . .'

'Go to Daddy.' She handed Jack the baby.

'Helen, I . . .'

She looked into his eyes. 'Maggie said we'd make good parents, Jack, and we will.'

Wordlessly, he sank down on the bed with the baby.

'We'll need a name for him. How about Gordon John Clay?'

'Gordon? Won't it remind you?'

'You don't think we should name him after a brave man who saved your life?'

'If that's what you want, Helen.'

'It's what I want.' She picked up a small case from the foot of the cot. 'Would you like to carry him downstairs?'

'Goodbye, and send my best wishes to the other Mrs Clay and her daughter.'

'We will.' Helen waved to the matron, who closed the door of the hostel before they even reached the car.

'She couldn't wait to see the back of us,' Jack said, opening the car door for Helen.

'It can't be easy looking after pregnant girls who know they have no option but to give up their babies.'

'Excuse me?' A man wound down the window of his car, as he stopped in the road outside the house. 'Is this Cartref?'

'Yes, it is.' Helen looked from the shining new car and the smartly dressed man to the nervous looking woman sitting in the passenger seat.

'Thank you. You see, darling, I told you it would be along this road.'

The couple drove into the courtyard and parked their car. Helen watched them climb out and walk up the steps as Jack took the baby from her.

'They look nice people, don't they?' she asked Jack. He handed her the baby when she was settled in the car.

'Yes.' He looked slightly mystified by her question.

'That's good.'

He climbed in beside her and looked down at his son. 'Straight home?'

'I warn you now, Gordon, that your father may take a bit of getting used to,' she addressed the baby solemnly. 'He doesn't always think about what he says. As if we can take you home when we don't have a cot, pram, bath, enough nappies, baby clothes, nappy pins, talcum powder bottles, formula . . .'

'I love you, Mrs Clay,' Jack interrupted, kissing her and starting the car engine.

'But will you still love me at three o'clock in the morning when I kick you out of bed to feed your son?'

'I'll love you all the more.'

'That's all right then.'

All Orion/Phoenix titles are available at your local bookshop or from the following address:

Mail Order Department
Littlehampton Book Services
FREEPOST BR535
Worthing, West Sussex, BN13 3BR
telephone 01903 828503, *facsimile* 01903 828802
e-mail MailOrders@lbsltd.co.uk
(Please ensure that you include full postal address details)

Payment can be made either by credit/debit card (Visa, Mastercard, Access and Switch accepted) or by sending a £ Sterling cheque or postal order made payable to *Littlehampton Book Services*.

DO NOT SEND CASH OR CURRENCY

Please add the following to cover postage and packing

UK and BFPO:
£1.50 for the first book, and 50p for each additional book to a maximum of £3.50

Overseas and Eire:
£2.50 for the first book plus £1.00 for the second book and 50p for each additional book ordered

---

BLOCK CAPITALS PLEASE

name of cardholder	*delivery address*
....	(*if different from cardholder*)
address of cardholder	....
....	....
....	....
....	....
postcode	*postcode* ....

☐ I enclose my remittance for £ ....

☐ please debit my Mastercard/Visa/Access/Switch (delete as appropriate)

card number ☐☐☐☐☐☐☐☐☐☐☐☐☐☐☐☐

expiry date ☐☐☐☐ Switch issue no. ☐☐

signature ....

prices and availability are subject to change without notice